a sweet celebrity romance

Thunderstruck

DANA LeCHEMINANT

ISBN: 978-1-965106-01-3
First Print Edition: October 2024
Bow and Arrow Press

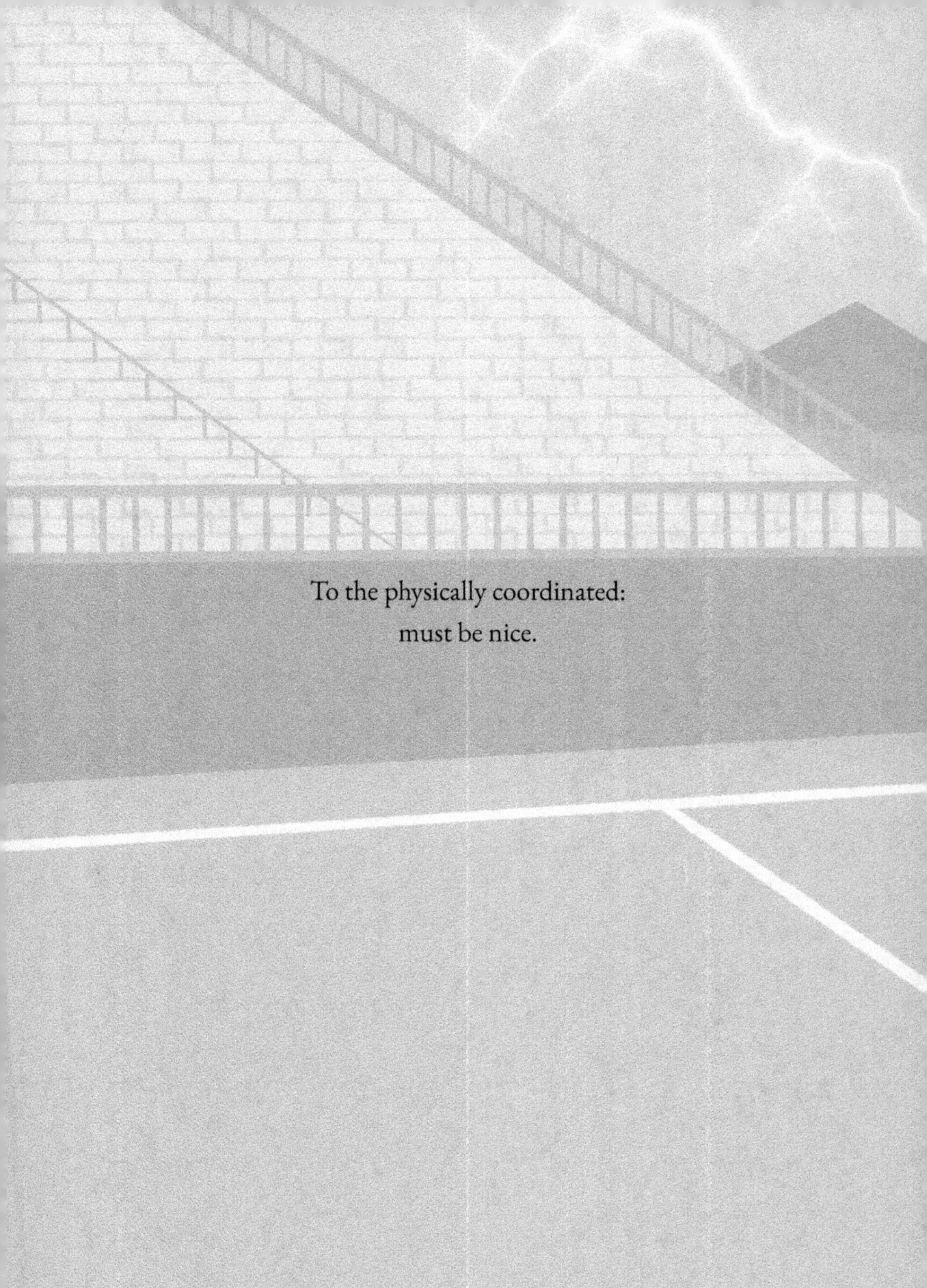

To the physically coordinated:

must be nice.

Thunderstruck:
stunned by great surprise or wonder

Hollywood Hot Scoop

Badgers' Bad-boy Buys Babe Bling

Happy Friday to all my Scoopers! As you know, we here at *Hollywood Hot Scoop* like to give you the latest and greatest when it comes to celebrity news, and you heard it here first! NFL legend and notorious ladies' man, Javier Gonzales, has popped the question and will soon be having the wedding of the century. The Portland Badgers' tight end is best known for his mad defense, quick feet, and, let's be real, his *tight end*. We all saw the full-page feature in *Sports Unveiled*. Wowee, but these players are built differently, am I right? Talk about muscles for days!

But I digress. You're here for news, and we've got you covered! (Unlike Javier's bod in that feature, wink wink!) If you didn't already know, Gonzales's soon-to-be bride is no stranger to *Hot Scoop*, and it's clear Sage Morrow has a type. Before Gonzales, she was the longtime lover of our favorite former quarterback, Cole Evanson, who has been taking the world of rugby by storm after his abrupt departure from football two years ago.

It's obvious that Sage, an avid Badgers fan, made the right choice last fall when she switched her affections from Cole to Javier, who just helped his team win the Super Bowl. This is a huge win for the Badgers, who had a record-low season last year after their Super Bowl loss with Cole at the helm, and it's clear the Oregon team is far better off without the football dropout.

We'll have more details about the wedding as they come. For now, we just have one question: Who is going to comfort Cole now that he is totally alone? I've seen the man's muscles, and with Sage moving on, he's going to need someone to keep him company and lift his spirits. I'll happily volunteer for the job!

Make sure you subscribe, and keep on sending in your own hot scoops! XO

CHAPTER ONE

COLE

Seven months ago

Of all the times for my girlfriend to call...

"Are you taking your turn or what, Evanson?" My teammate, who everyone calls Bean, narrows his eyes at me across the pool table.

I look down at my ringing phone again. This is the first time since I joined the Los Angeles Thunder rugby team a year and a half ago that any of the guys have even offered to let me join in on a game of pool, and I would be stupid to blow what could be my best chance to finally feel like one of them. But Sage rarely calls me out of the blue, and I worry something's wrong. "Give me a sec," I tell Bean and hurry outside the bar.

The call drops before I can answer it, but I call Sage right back, my heart pounding in my chest as it rings. And rings. When it hits her voicemail, I frown at my phone and leave a quick message. "Hey, sorry I didn't pick up in time. What's up?"

Then I send her a text.

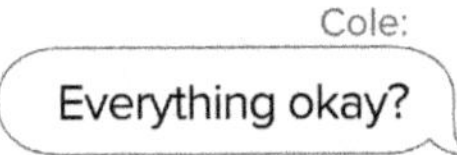

To my relief, she responds to the text, though I'm not sure why she wouldn't have answered my call.

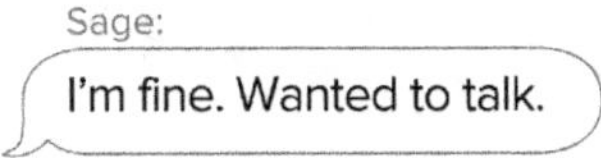

As I debate calling her again, I glance through the window and take in the annoyed expressions of the guys I'm supposed to be playing pool with. I don't blame them for being impatient, especially because they were just starting to warm up to me, the outsider.

I send another text, hoping Sage will give me a clear direction of how my night is going to go.

Truth be told, I'm surprised Sage wants to talk at all. For the last month or so, she's been extra busy. Every time I try to video chat or plan a weekend up in Oregon where she lives, she blows me off, which is why I've decided to head up that way next week to surprise her for her birthday.

Long distance isn't easy, I'll admit that, but I've been doing my best to make it work for the last year and a half. And I'm hoping this surprise makes up for me being so far from her. The books she likes to read all have these grand gestures from the guys, and my goal is to pull off something that comes close to her favorite love stories.

I even rented out one of the ice rinks in Portland because she loves reading hockey romances specifically. I'm not a hockey player, but I do play rugby. Which is almost as cool? Sage might not think so, but she loves me even if I refuse to strap knives to my feet. I'll do it this once because it will make her happy.

Though I should probably get back inside and stop making the guys wait, I try calling one more time, just in case Sage really needs to talk through something. Sage always comes before the team.

To my relief, she answers after a couple of rings. "Cole."

"Hey, are you sure you're okay? I know you've been stressed with—"

"Why do you never post about me online?"

I frown, looking down at my phone for a second. "What?"

"You never post about me. Are you ashamed to be with me?"

Swearing under my breath, I lean against the wall and settle in. So much for getting on the team's good side. They're not going to like me ditching the game, but this is more important. "Of course I'm not ashamed of you, Sage. I love you."

I have a ring sitting on my kitchen table that mirrors my words. I intend to give it to her next week as part of the big surprise. At least, I *want* to give it to her next week, but that all depends on if I can pull off the plans I'm putting into play. And if I can finally work up the courage.

"Sage, where is this coming from?"

"None of the other guys on the team are afraid to post pictures about their wives or girlfriends."

She means the Portland Badgers, the football team I haven't been a part of for a year and a half. I'm not sure how to feel about the fact that she's still paying attention to any of the guys from my old team, but that's not important right now.

"Javi says there must be something—"

"Javi?" As my eyebrows pull low, I try not to let my anger rise. I don't want to jump to any conclusions about my former friend. "Why were you talking to Javi?"

"We bumped into each other the other day, and he asked if you and I were still together because you haven't posted anything about me in *months*."

"Sage," I say, keeping my voice gentle. "You know that I have to be careful about things on the internet, especially with all the time I spend with Derek." As one of the most sought-after actors in Hollywood, Derek Riley is too high profile to be casual about privacy.

Sage scoffs. "Ah, right. *Derek*. With all the time you spend with him, you might as well be dating *him*!"

I hold back a groan. "He's my best friend."

"I thought *I* was your best friend."

Best friends talk more than once a week, but I won't say that out loud. Despite my best efforts, it's been so long since I regularly spent any time with Sage that sometimes it feels like we barely know each other. I'm *trying* to fix it. To get us back to where we were when I lived in Portland with her. I'm the one who moved away, but it feels like she's the one who keeps putting the distance in our relationship.

"Sage," I breathe, curling my free hand into a fist to try to keep myself from panicking. I don't like where this conversation is going. "I know it's been hard since I moved back to California, but—"

"Hard?" She laughs. "No, I don't think you know the meaning of the word hard, Cole Evanson. Not when you took the coward's way out. You could have been something great—*we* could have been something great—but you threw it all away. And for what? To pretend you weren't going to be a legend? So you could always come second to those fancy friends of yours? You can't tell me you're happy living in mediocrity, Cole."

I swallow the emotions that stick in my throat as her words settle over me, heavy and cloying. I feel like I can't breathe. "Of course I'm not happy," I say thickly. "Not when I'm so far away from you."

"So *come back*." Her words are pleading, and they feel like a knife in my chest. One that could be lethal as soon as I try to pull it out. But I have to. I'll never breathe if I don't.

"You know why I can't."

"I know why you *won't*," she counters. "Because you don't have any backbone. You're pathetic, and I feel like I've wasted the last eighteen months waiting for you to be someone you're not. I've been such an idiot."

"Sage," I croak. "I'm coming to Portland next week. Just wait a few days, and we can—"

"I'm done waiting for you, Cole. You're never going to grow a pair and be the man I need you to be."

"Sage, don't—"

The call drops. So does my phone, clattering on the sidewalk at my feet and landing face up so I can see the newly shattered screen.

I know the feeling.

Present day

This is not a hockey romance.

I don't know why that line keeps running through my head, but it's starting to get on my nerves. Maybe it's because I watched a hockey game last night even though I tend to avoid watching sports other than rugby. The game was playing on the TV over Sage's head in the restaurant, and watching it was easier than looking her in the eyes while she explained in detail why she broke up with me last fall.

I didn't ask her to do that. In fact, I would have preferred it if she didn't, but she said her conscience wouldn't rest easy if she didn't list out all the reasons she'd needed to tear my heart out of my chest seven months ago. She showed up at my house tonight without warning, dragged me to the restaurant, and dove right into her explanation like it was a completely normal thing to do on a Friday night.

This is not a hockey romance.

If it were, we probably would have ended the night making out in the bathroom instead of me left standing outside a Chili's in the rain with a wedding announcement held limply in my hand, watching the love of my life drive away to the airport because she thought it was a good idea to rub salt into the wounds she inflicted over the phone.

For some reason, I put the announcement on the fridge when I got home, as if I need the reminder that I'm not the guy who gets the girl.

You are cordially invited to celebrate...

Javi and Sage only started dating a couple of months ago, and their wedding is in less than a month. It's either a shotgun wedding, or... Or their relationship goes back further than our breakup. I don't know which one of those makes me feel better. They both suck.

"You with us, Rihanna?"

I blink, slammed back to reality by the irritated voice of my teammate, Gator. He's scowling at me as the noise of the crowd rises around us. It's nowhere near as frenetic as a hockey arena would be, given we're outside and the LA Thunder are one of three Major League Rugby teams in Southern California. Rugby is a growing sport in the US, but it doesn't get the same attention as a bunch of dudes with sticks and a puck.

Those guys get the crowds and the girls, apparently. That's what all of Sage's favorite books would indicate, something she never failed to tell me whenever she read a new one.

"Don't call me Rihanna," I growl, as angry with Gator as I am with myself for getting hung up on my ex. *Again.* I swallow my frustration and shake out my arms as we move back into play. We paused for an injury on the Jackals' side, which gave me too much time to think. Praise the heavens we're gathering up for a scrum to resume play and I can shift my focus back to the match against Dallas's MLR team. We're only down by five, and there's enough time on the clock for us to get a try if we keep possession of the ball. If one of my teammates can get the ball over the line, I can attempt to get a kick for two extra conversion points.

I could use a good kick to something.

This is not a hockey romance. If it was, I could get into a fight in the middle of this game and be praised for it rather than penalized. I'm not a violent person, but Sage's unexpected appearance at my door last night threw me.

I knew things were over between us the night she broke up with me over the phone.

Why would she come all the way to California just to remind me?

Gator tucks his arm around the hooker, Tink, as they get set up in the huddle. "You don't want me to call you Rihanna, then stop acting like a diva," he snaps and ducks down, disappearing into the scrum.

I roll the ball into the scrum as both sides fight for forward movement, and it ends up kicked back to me. I grab it, quickly assessing the Jackals' defense, and toss it behind me to the fly-half, Moxie, who immediately hands it off to one of the centers, who makes a break for it. He goes down halfway to the goal, thanks to two Dallas players, but I'm quick to grab the ball and toss it to the outside center, who throws it back to our fastest wing, Bean.

Bean barely avoids a tackle and dives for the try-zone, planting the ball on the grass with triumph.

Thank goodness. Though I feel the pressure building as I get set up to kick the conversion, my determination rises right along with it. After last night, I really need a win.

Though we're farther from the center of the field than I'd like, I settle the ball just how I'd like it. I take a breath, tuning out the sounds of the crowd, and then I kick, breathing a sigh of relief when the ball sails through the posts only moments before the clock runs out.

The rest of my team swarm the pitch in celebration, leaving me on the edge, and the small pleasure I feel for our win is only momentary. Seems like a lot of things are momentary lately, and the sinking pit in my gut as I join the rest of the Thunder in the locker room feels like a bad sign.

I'm blaming it all on Sage, but that excuse is only going to last for so long. This is a *me* problem. One I don't know how to fix. I haven't been the same since the phone call that ended our four-year relationship, and I feel like I'm slowly sinking deeper and deeper every time I try to pull myself out of the dark pit she threw me into.

"Drinks?" Moxie, our fly-half and team captain, sits himself down on the bench next to me once I'm showered and dressed. I was working up the courage to go back home to that stupid wedding announcement, but I waited too long if he thinks I might actually go out with the guys tonight.

I huff a laugh. "No thanks."

Moxie kicks his legs out, crossing one foot over the other as he reclines against the wall behind him. The rest of the team are goofing off as they slowly filter out of the locker room, all of them ignoring my corner like they always do. I may have earned the game-winning points, but that doesn't change their opinions of me. At this point, I don't think anything will.

"This is why none of them like you," Moxie says.

"I don't play to be liked." I wasn't the team's favorite person to begin with, coming from the NFL—football is an inferior sport in their opinion—but this whole thing with Sage has set me back when it comes to being accepted by the Thunder. I was starting to find my place back in October, but the last seven months have...sucked. *I've* sucked. I don't blame them for hating me. "As long as I play well," I mutter, "it shouldn't matter what they think of me."

I'm pretty sure my skills on the pitch are the only reason I'm still here. If Moxie ever gets better at distance kicks than me, I'm done for.

Chuckling, Moxie rolls his eyes and pats me on the shoulder. "I know this league is still new, but some of these guys are shooting for the national team. The Olympics. International contracts. They need wins to do that, and we play better when we're bonded as a team."

I raise an eyebrow at him. "Did they make you captain because you're so motivational, or does that part come with the gig?"

"Chicken and egg, my friend. Come out for a beer."

I shake my head. It's as much because I generally don't drink and because I know I won't be good company. My surly mood will only make the rapport worse; I don't have the energy to swallow my teammates' insults, and I'm likely to retaliate. "Next time."

Moxie scoffs but heads out, calling back, "You say that every time, Rihanna."

I really need to kill that nickname.

My phone rings when I finally head out to catch a ride, and the tightness in my chest eases when I see that it's Freya. If someone had told me half a decade ago that I would become close friends with a literal princess, I would have laughed. Or maybe not. At the time, I was pretty much on top of the world, so I might have thought a friendship like that was inevitable. But I'm glad we're friends, inevitable or not.

I could use her big sister energy right now.

I swipe the answer button as I start walking down the sidewalk. I'll walk off my remaining adrenaline from the match until the conversation is over and I can snag a ride through my app. "Hey, Peach, it's early." It's early morning in Candora, her island home.

Freya clucks her tongue. "For you it is late, Cole. I expected you to be home, but you are not."

My steps pause. While I'm glad to hear her voice, there's something strange in what she just said. "You're in California."

"And sitting on your couch. The match ended almost an hour ago."

I smile, which is a rare occurrence lately, and pick up my pace. I live too far from the stadium to actually walk the whole way, but I have a new pep in my step. "If I had known you were coming to the States, I would have headed out sooner."

"Are you making friends with your team?"

"I'm not seven." But I know she won't take my deflection, so I reluctantly add, "And no. I'm not."

"Why not?"

"I'm not having this conversation with you, Peach. I'm going to hang up so I can..." My words drop off when a sleek black car pulls up to the curb next to me. A door opens and closes, then the driver, dressed in a fitted suit and wearing a chauffeur's cap, moves to open the back door for me and fixes me with a steely-eyed stare. "I'm guessing this is you?" I say into the phone.

"If you refuse to use your vehicle," Freya replies, "the least I can do is offer mine."

I sigh, but I can't argue. I tend to get in trouble if I'm behind a wheel, so I avoid it whenever I can. "Thanks," I murmur, speaking both to Freya and to her driver. "See you in a bit."

By the time I reach my house, my excitement at seeing my friend has been dimmed by the exhaustion that always sets in after a match. When I made the switch from football to rugby, I figured the wear on my body would be similar outside of the fact that there's no padding in rugby. Quarterback to scrum-half is a relatively even trade role-wise, but it turns out rugby doesn't have the same ebb and flow as football. I'm on the field pretty much from the first second to the last with only a fifteen-minute break in between halves. It can be a brutal eighty minutes of gameplay, but I love it.

At this point, rugby is one of the few good things I have.

Nodding to Freya's latest bodyguard standing on my porch, a stony looking man with a bushy mustache, I step inside my front door only to be mauled by a blonde in heels. I grunt, but Freya weighs next to nothing so she's easy to hold as she embraces me, arms around my neck.

"Congratulations on your win," she says.

I didn't miss the wrinkled card she's holding before she hid it from my sight.

...celebrate the marriage of Sage Morrow to Javier Gonzales on Sunday, June Second...

Grimacing, I pry her off of me and keep working my way into the house so I can dump my bag in my room. "You know it's not nice to snoop, Peach."

"You put it on your refrigerator. I would hardly call that snooping." Freya sounds like she was born and raised in upper class London but spent her teenage years on the Scandinavian Peninsula, which makes sense given the location of her island country in the North Sea. But it makes it weirdly difficult to take her seriously when she says informal words like *snooping* in her royal way. "And besides," she continues, "your vulgar tabloid, *Hot Scoop*, shared about it half an hour ago."

I tend to ignore the stupid website, hoping they'll leave me alone, but I should have known better. Dropping my bag on the floor at the foot of my bed, I return to the front room and join Freya on the couch. "I'm glad you're here," I tell her, closing my eyes as I let my body settle.

"I told Derek about Sage's wedding."

"I'm less glad you're here," I grumble.

Laughing in her ridiculous, goose-like way—the only time she is not prim and proper—Freya rests her head against my shoulder and moves in close. I have no idea why she chose to look out for me after we first met, but I'm not complaining. No matter how busy she is, I can always count on her advice.

"Your friends should know that you are hurting, Cole," she says as she cradles my arm.

"I'm not hurting."

But my argument falls flat even before she murmurs, "Lies."

My friends are all famous in their own ways, and each of us has good reason to hide as much from the public eye as we can. But we don't like to hide from each other, even if it's difficult to open up sometimes. Freya knows I don't mean it when I say Sage didn't hurt me, and I'm sure the rest of my friends would agree.

I sigh and settle lower in my seat. I'm more tired than I thought. "When did you get here?"

"A few hours ago."

"You should have gone to Derek's and gotten some sleep." Derek Riley, the friend I've known the longest and the unofficial ringleader of our group, has a mansion in Malibu with space for all of us, though most of us like our own space when we can get it. Freya, however, usually stays there when she visits, and I doubt she slept on the plane ride over.

She mumbles something, half asleep already, then says, "You needed a friend."

As much as I don't want to admit it, she's right. Now that Sage is for sure moving on and leaving me in the dust, I feel more alone than ever, and that's not going to change.

The problem is the rest of my friends, just like Freya, are going to try to fix it all for me, which means by the time the sun is up in the morning, I'm going to have six people all thinking they know what's best for my life. I love them, but they can really be a pain in my rear end.

"That means you too," I murmur to Freya, who is sound asleep against my shoulder, and I slip into a dreamless sleep right along with her.

CHAPTER TWO

CARISSA

"It's not that I'm scared…" I bounce my leg up and down a few times, pretending my big sister isn't seeing right through my bravado while we sit in the back of a car and ride through the streets of Los Angeles. "I just… Rugby isn't my field, you know? I don't know anything about sports."

"But you *are* a licensed physical therapist." Darcy rolls her eyes. They're unnaturally blue today because she's dressed up as her fancy sports reporter persona, Tamlin Park. I found out about her alter-ego by accident when I showed up unannounced at her house in St. Louis last week and found her snacking in the kitchen looking like someone she isn't, and I'm still wrapping my head around it. Like, I've seen her on TV. A lot. And I had no idea it was her. Apparently she's been a well-known reporter for years, and this whole time I thought my sister was just a glorified intern.

"You're the one who said she wanted a change of scenery," Darcy reminds me and smiles down at her phone.

I try not to snoop, but I can't help it when my eyes are drawn to places they shouldn't be. Immediately I regret letting my gaze fall to the texts her husband is currently sending her. "Oh, I did *not* want to read that," I say, pretending to puke.

"Then you shouldn't have looked," Darcy says matter-of-factly. She types a text that has a lot of questionable emojis, hits send, and flips to the camera so she can check her makeup. Of which there is a lot.

I guess there would need to be to make her look like someone completely different. She's wearing a wig too, and I miss seeing the blonde curls we share. She was never meant to be a brunette, but the media site she works for makes all their reporters wear disguises for their safety.

"Is Houston still attracted to you when you look like this?" I ask, though I'm not sure I want to know the answer. The two of them have been married for two months, and they're definitely still in the sickening honeymoon phase. I should have considered the fact that they would be all over each other when I made the decision to visit her on a whim.

Fixing her lipstick, Darcy glances at me and smirks. "I don't think you want me to answer that question," she guesses.

I grimace. "No. I don't."

As she goes back to her absolutely not PG-13 texting, I turn my gaze to the window and take in the sights. I've never been to California before now, and it always felt like some magical land far away. I've spent my entire life in Pennsylvania, and up until two weeks ago I figured I would die there too. Now, I'm not so sure.

I'm also not sure if I can live in a state severely lacking in trees, but we'll see how it goes.

"I still don't know why you couldn't have found me a job in St. Louis," I mumble.

Darcy grabs my hand. "I would have if I could have. But honestly, I think it might be better for you to totally get away. Stretch your wings.

And the owners of the Thunder owed me a favor, which is how I was able to get you this job."

"I didn't even know we had rugby teams in the US." When Darcy told me she'd gotten me a job on the sports medicine team for the Los Angeles Thunder, I had to look up what type of sport rugby is. From the looks of things, it's a cross between football and soccer and a breeding ground for injuries. At least I'll have plenty to do?

"I think rugby is an underrated sport here," Darcy replies, "but it's really popular in the rest of the world."

My leg starts bouncing again. "I don't know why I agreed to this."

"Because you trust your big sister."

"Do you really think it's a good idea for me to move clear across the country and take up a job that is more specialized than what I'm used to? I know it's similar, but... I don't even know where I'm going to be living, let alone how to do a job that's so different from what I'm used to."

Squeezing my hand, Darcy gives me a warm smile that instantly calms me. She may not look like herself right now, but that smile is so familiar. "Rizzo, you'll be fine. I'm not about to drop you off in a strange state without making sure you have everything you need. We'll stop by the training field so I can do some interviews and introduce you to your new boss, and then—"

"Wait, you're taking me to the training field? I am so not prepared for that! Why didn't you tell me?"

She frowns. "Why do you think I'm dressed up like this? It's not for fun. Besides, I thought I told you. Hmm, maybe it slipped my mind because the team doesn't know we're coming either."

I gape at her. "What do you mean they don't know we're coming?"

"I get way better information when I show up unannounced. Anyway, I'll take you to the apartment Houston rented for you after we're done.

He said it's in a good area, and you know he won't have skimped on all the features."

There's no point in trying to fight her on her plans. I love my sister, but she has always been excellent at channeling her older sibling energy. "I both love and hate that your new husband is insanely rich," I grumble. I mostly love it, though, because it's not like I can afford anything on my own. At least my living situation is handled, even if the job thing is questionable.

Darcy snickers. "That's what happens when you're a world-class athlete."

"So what you're saying is these rugby players I'm going to be working with will all be rich snobs like Houston?"

Darcy laughs. "First of all, Houston is hardly a snob, and you know it. Second of all, no." Her laughter turns into a frustrated frown. "Rugby in the US isn't like baseball or football. Most of the players have second jobs because there's not enough money going around for them to make livable wages. *Yet*." Something tells me she's going to try to change that. If anyone can, Darcy can.

Still, I breathe easier knowing I won't be surrounded by people who think they automatically deserve anything they want. Or don't want. As I recently learned, men of privilege are dangerous, and I want nothing to do with them. Houston gets the only pass because he's my brother-in-law and actually pretty great.

"We're here," Darcy says as the car pulls to a stop. "You can still change your mind and come back to Missouri with me when I'm done here, but I think this will be a good move for you after everything that happened."

She means after I fell in love with one of my patients, risking my whole career as a physical therapist because I thought he loved me back. Spoiler: he didn't.

Maybe she's right. Maybe I do need a complete overhaul of my life, and I can't get any farther from my mistakes than sunny Los Angeles.

Who would have thought I'd have a mid-life crisis at twenty-five? Not me. I thought for sure I would last in my career of choice longer than two years.

"Well?" Darcy pushes her door open and turns to look at me with her perfectly sculpted eyebrows raised high.

I let out a deep and dramatic sigh, which is my way of trying to rid myself of all the fears holding me back. I make—er, *made*—my patients do that all the time, and it usually helped push them to work harder to overcome their obstacles. I'm hoping it works for me too. "I can do this," I say under my breath. "I can do anything I put my mind to."

"Yes, you can," Darcy agrees and steps out onto the sidewalk, telling the driver to wait for us.

It's easy for her to be confident. She's wearing gaucho pants and wedge heels and somehow making it look classy, and I'm over here in sweatpants and a hoodie I put on because the plane was freezing. I certainly don't need it now, but all I have on underneath is a hot pink tank top with a cartoon unicorn on it.

Darcy is already heading for the stadium, so I scramble out of the car and hurry after her while a voice in the back of my mind says I should change into something a little more professional. But if I turn back now, there's no way I'm making it into the stadium of my own free will.

I'm not Darcy.

My sister has always been confident—probably because she was the only girl on her high school baseball team—but it's still fascinating to watch her walk into a pro team practice with her head held high. She looks like she belongs here, and she completely ignores the heads that swivel in her direction when the players start to notice her.

I can't help but notice the *players*. My education was centered around the function of the human body, and I know the importance of muscle in protecting the other elements like bones and tendons. Plus, I had an athlete or two come into our clinic in Philly. But as I follow Darcy along the edge of the field, I am in complete *awe*.

I've never seen more beautiful legs in my life. Some of these guys have thighs bigger than my waist, their quads and hamstrings bulging in ways I've never seen before. I can't even admire their upper body strength because all I can see are calves and adductor muscles. It's a beautiful symphony of anatomical function. A demonstration of the majesty of the human body in a way I've never seen before.

I might be in heaven.

"Rizzo, will you hold on to this for me?" Darcy interrupts my gawking, stuffing something small into my hand.

I look down, surprised to see her wedding ring on my palm. "Why?" Should I be worried that she's already looking to stray from her perfect husband? But no, she would never do that, even if other people would. Not everyone is Peter.

Chuckling, she pats my cheek. "Will you relax? Tamlin isn't married, and some of these guys will be more open to talking to me if I flirt a bit. Houston knows the drill."

I slip the ring onto my finger. "I hope you're right." Goodness, it's getting warm, and I tug on the collar of my sweatshirt, trying to get some air flow. "I still can't believe you lied to me about all this," I say, gesturing to her getup.

She laughs as her eyes catch on one of the players as he approaches us. "I literally couldn't tell anyone. Not even Houston. That's why you had to sign that NDA."

Honestly, I have no idea what I signed. I trusted Darcy and Houston when they said it was perfectly safe, and all I know is I can't tell anyone that Darcy is Tamlin. Not even our parents, though that should be easy because I've been avoiding them. They don't know why I left my clinic in Philly either, which is a miracle unto itself. Thank goodness they recently stopped watching the local news.

"Tamlin Park," the player says, finally reaching us on the edge of the field. He's monstrous compared to the average human, but he honestly looks like one of the smaller guys on the team.

I don't think there's a single person on that field who is anything but a pure beast.

Darcy smiles wide and holds out her hand. "Malcolm Auxier. I've wanted to meet you for a long time."

Malcolm, whose last name sounded more like 'Oaks-yay' than how it's spelled on his uniform, folds his large arms, ignoring Darcy's outstretched hand. "This is a closed practice, Park."

This guy is so gruff and tough that he's incredibly intimidating, but Darcy doesn't waver. "Whatever you think I'm here to do," she says, "you're wrong. I don't do that anymore. I just want to talk about the game."

A few more players decide to join us, all of them big, burly, and beautiful. Though, one of them looks like he's been hit in the head a few too many times, one of his ears lumpy and misshapen. It doesn't matter because his shoulders are the stuff of legends, and he looks like he's seven feet tall.

"Oo, what did you do, Moxie?" one of the guys taunts as he wraps an arm around his teammate's shoulders.

Malcolm narrows his eyes. "Nothing. She claims she's here in peace," he says without taking his gaze off Darcy.

Darcy snickers and looks at the gathered guys, lingering on one who looks more nervous than the others. Most of them are smiling and actually look pretty friendly, but one guy in the back simply looks angry.

He's also insanely handsome, but his glower is enough to dampen any attraction in that direction. Besides, I shouldn't be looking at any of these guys with attraction because they are, hopefully, going to be my patients in a few days. Colleagues? Regardless, I will *not* fall into the same problem that got me here in the first place.

"You know," Darcy says to the group, "you only have to be worried about me if you have something to hide. But like I said, I don't do that anymore." She says that last bit to Malcolm, her smile growing. "I was hoping to talk to Coach Galvin."

"He's not here." It's the grumpy one who says that, his gaze growing harder.

"The coach isn't at practice?" I ask in surprise. I immediately regret it when half a dozen pairs of manly eyes turn to me, all of them assessing my sweats and messy bun. A couple of them, I notice with a spike of pleasure, seem to like what they see.

That doesn't matter! I remind myself. I am keeping a strict professional boundary between me and these ruggedly handsome men because I can't afford a repeat of Philadelphia. How many times am I going to have to tell myself that?

Based on how beautiful all these men are, I'm guessing it'll take a lot.

"Galvin had something to take care of today," Malcolm says, as much to me as to Darcy. "But if you're insistent on talking to someone, you can talk to me. I don't want you wandering around where you shouldn't. Your..." He eyes me, his eyebrows dipping low.

Darcy cups her hand around my shoulder. "This is your new rehab specialist, Carissa Paxton," she says.

A murmur ripples over the team, and their smiles of interest spark a dangerous fire in my belly. *No, Carissa. Bad Carissa!*

Malcolm, unlike his teammates, frowns at me. "Mel had a family emergency, so she isn't here to show you around."

"Mel's the athletic trainer," Darcy explains to me.

"Is *anyone* here?" I ask.

Several of the guys laugh. Malcolm's expression is more of a grimace. "You picked a bad day. I'll have one of the guys show you around while I talk to Park." He glances behind him as the guys all raise their hands eagerly to offer their services.

All but one. The grumpy one looks like he's regretting coming over here.

"Evanson," Malcolm says to him, much to the dismay of the other guys. "Mind showing Miss Paxton the facility?"

The grump's scowl deepens, and he looks like he very much minds. I wonder if Malcolm picked him because he was the only one who didn't look excited by the prospect of talking to me, though I can't imagine that's actually Malcolm's reasoning.

"I'm sure Bean would be a better fit," Evanson says, his voice a deep rumble.

The guy I assume is Bean, one in front with a goofy grin and the least amount of muscle mass, nods eagerly. "I got you, Cap," he says and steps forward.

Malcolm holds up a hand. "You still owe me sprints, Bean." Bean's smile drops into a disgruntled disappointment. "Cole, it won't take long, and you need a breather."

Evanson grumbles something but steps forward. "Fine." He holds his hand out to me. "Cole Evanson."

Though I still think I would rather walk around with Bean, I take hold of Cole's hand and try not to make a comment about how it dwarfs mine. He knows how big he is. "Carissa. But you can call me Rizzo." I say that to the guys in general, hoping it helps them see me as a friend. With muscles like theirs, I have a feeling I'm going to be spending a lot of time up close and personal with these men, and muscles are easier to loosen when they're relaxed.

A chorus of hellos follows my comment as the men wave at me and tell me their own names all at the same time. I didn't catch most of them, but I've got time to learn.

"So," Darcy says, holding her phone out to record Malcolm. "How are you feeling about your season so far?"

"We'll go this way," Cole grunts and starts walking without waiting to see if I'll follow.

I should probably keep up with him, but I can't help but turn to Bean and ask, "Is he always that grumpy?"

Bean snickers as his teammates laugh. "Always. Rihanna is our biggest diva."

Moxie, Bean, Rihanna... Apparently this is a team full of nicknames, and I'm extra glad I introduced myself as Rizzo. Maybe this new gig will work out better than I thought.

CHAPTER THREE

COLE

I KNOW WHAT MOXIE's doing. With Coach who knows where, the captain asked me to run drills with the forwards in an attempt to get me to bond with them, but it has turned into a morning of tense arguments and my teammates resisting anything I say. The guys don't like me being in charge of anything, muttering things about my questionable knowledge of the game because my head's too full of "princess play" from my years of playing football.

I know how to lead a team, and my last year as a quarterback got the Badgers to the Super Bowl, but I can't do anything for a team who still sees me as an outsider.

My frustration must have been clear on my face, and Moxie seems to think playing tour guide will help me cool off.

I've nearly reached the try-zone before I look back to see if Little Miss Paxton followed me, though I wouldn't be surprised if she decided to stay back and flirt with the guys instead. She was giving them all sorts of eyes, and I don't want to even think about the trouble she's going to cause. A distraction like her is the last thing we need, especially with Coach getting flakier every day.

As far as I know, he didn't even give an excuse this time.

To my surprise, Carissa is hurrying after me, her face red from the exertion needed to keep up with my long strides. I'm guessing she's not from around here if she's wearing a hoodie in May, though I can't decide if she's cold or stupid.

She answers my question by tugging the sweatshirt off as soon as she reaches me. "It's so much warmer than I expected!" she breathes. "Is it always like this in LA?"

I can't answer because I'm too busy staring at the technicolor unicorn printed on her body-hugging tank top. Little Miss, indeed. She looks like she's barely out of college, if that, and she's nothing but skin and bone.

Turning an even deeper red, she tucks her arms around her middle after tying her sweatshirt around her waist. "I didn't realize I would be coming to the practice grounds today," she mumbles.

"I didn't realize we were getting another trainer," I mumble back. Does she have a clue how to do her job? My money's on no.

Carissa shrugs. "From what Da—Tamlin told me, I'm more like an intern. Here to help Mel out for the next little bit."

I didn't miss her slip, and though I don't know of any Paxtons connected to the team, things are starting to make sense if Daddy pulled some strings to get her a job. Whoever her father is, he probably gives his little girl anything she wants.

And she is *little*. I'd put her at five foot four at most, and she looks like she might snap in a light breeze. Hardly the kind of person who could handle some of the things Mel does as our athletic trainer.

I grunt, not sure what to say to her. She shifts her stance, and light catches on an impressive diamond sitting pretty on her finger. Ah, so maybe Paxton isn't her daddy's name after all. And if she's married, her flirty eyes with the guys are even more annoying than they already were.

"We're a fairly new team," I say sharply, making her jump with my sudden words. "Just a few years old. So our facility isn't anything special." I point to the building behind us. "Locker room and weight room are in there, and Mel's got her training room inside and to the left, next to Coach's office." Not that that last bit matters, since Coach has been picking and choosing when he wants to show up this season.

I'm pretty sure he has decided we're not going to make any waves this year, so he's not going to waste his time on a losing team.

"What's the schedule?" Carissa asks. "Is Mel here for every practice?"

"If she can be." She just had another nanny quit on her, which is why she isn't here today and might explain why the team hired another person to fill the gaps she leaves. Though, it's hard to believe Carissa could actually be useful when she looks like she can barely lift five pounds, assuming she would even want to try. If she has any knowledge about sports medicine, I'll be flabbergasted, which means she's just another person sucking limited funds out of the team budget.

I swallow my negative thoughts. I don't own the team, so it's not my decision on who gets hired and why. I should keep talking.

"We practice every afternoon, but not all the guys make it to every one because of day jobs." I can't keep the bitterness out of my words with that one. When I was in the NFL, the worst player in the league was still making over seven hundred grand to sit on a bench all year. Most of my Thunder teammates are lucky if they make over twenty. Even Moxie, arguably one of the best players in MLR, only makes forty thousand, and that's in part because I refused to be paid more than the bare minimum despite getting signed at a higher salary. With a limited amount of funds allocated to the team, my lower salary meant more could go to his.

If this were a hockey romance, most of these guys would be millionaires.

I growl at the thought. Apparently my brain is still on that kick even though Freya spent all of Sunday trying to distract me by making me go through foreign policy documents with her. It was interesting but not as diverting as she hoped because I didn't understand a lot of it. I have some business knowledge, but politics are beyond me.

"I think Tamlin shares your opinion on rugby salaries," Carissa says, smiling as she studies me.

I glance down the field to where Moxie is laughing at something Tamlin must have said. He has relaxed in the last few minutes, which hopefully is a sign that the devious reporter wasn't lying when she said she wasn't here to cause trouble. I already get enough of that from the tabloid site *Hollywood Hot Scoop*, and I don't need it on the sports side too. Tamlin Park made her career by taking down players across a variety of sports, including rugby. She's dangerous.

"That's surprising," I say. "Especially considering she ran a story about overpaid athletes just a couple of years ago."

Carissa's smile grows, and I glance up at the sky in confusion because it feels like the world gets brighter. It's sunny. As always. Not a cloud in the sky. "My brother-in-law is Houston Briggs," she says. "And he was one of the highest paid athletes in the country before he retired. He hated it and thinks the money could and should be used elsewhere. Like education or healthcare. Or maybe rugby." She winks.

"Huh." I met Houston once, back when he was dating my actor friend, Bonnie, but I wouldn't have pegged the pitcher for a philanthropist. I glance at Carissa's ring again, trying to fit all the pieces together. Houston only has one brother that I know of, who is also a Briggs. Not a Paxton. "How did you say you're related to Houston?"

Somehow, she brightens even more. Her tank top is already blindingly pink, and soon she'll be impossible to look at. "He married my sister back in March."

Oh. I'll admit I wasn't in the best of moods when that wedding happened—that was when I found out Sage was dating her soon-to-be husband and my never-to-be-again friend, Javi—but I vaguely remember Bonnie mentioning Houston's bride's name as Something Paxton.

Bonnie was at the wedding and had plenty to say about it when she came home afterward.

Again, I wasn't paying much attention and didn't care to know about someone else's happy ending, but she might have mentioned someone named Carissa at one point. It doesn't explain the ring or her last name, though. Maybe it's just an engagement ring?

I grunt again, though it makes me feel cavemanish, and fold my arms. I don't know where to put my misplaced annoyance when I was expecting Carissa to respond differently to the money thing. "You met my friend, Bonnie, at the wedding?"

Carissa perks up, almost bouncing on her toes. "You're friends with Bonnie Aiken? Oh, I love her! And Hank too. Aren't they just the cutest?"

"The cutest," I repeat dumbly. Though, it's kind of true. Hank was practically made for Bonnie, and Bonnie's happier than I've ever seen her. Especially now that Hank is moving to Los Angeles so they can stop commuting back and forth from Colorado and California to see each other.

They made long distance work. Why couldn't Sage and I do the same? I know two months and two years are very different time frames, but Hank is giving up his whole life to come here. Sage never once considered the idea, not even when she told me how much she missed me. My necessary change in career didn't give her any reasons to come with me.

She might have if you were playing hockey instead of rugby.

I clear my throat, forcing away that ridiculous thought. Why do I keep going back to hockey when football is just as popular and a sport that I *actually* played? Maybe because Sage didn't read many football romances despite football players clearly being her type. There was something about hockey—and the sort of guy often portrayed in those books—that really did it for her...

"Anyway," I say roughly, "that's about all there is to show you. We play games most weekends. Half here, half on the road. You'll probably end up traveling with the team." Another cost we can't afford.

"What position do you play?"

Oh good, she wants to make conversation now. The guys have gotten back into running drills, and I should probably be out on the field with them. But I have a feeling Moxie wants me to keep Carissa occupied until I can hand her off to Tamlin again, and he looks like he's thoroughly enjoying his conversation. I narrow my eyes as I watch him. He's not just talking. He's very clearly flirting, and Tamlin is flirting right back.

I grit my teeth. "Scrum-half."

"That's a position?"

Turning my eyes back to Carissa, I raise an eyebrow and take her in again. She looks like she would be more at home in a shopping mall than on a pitch, and I have to wonder how she became connected with someone like Tamlin Park, who not only knows her sports inside and out but also probably played something, based on her build.

Holding back a sigh, I try to channel my inner Bonnie and pretend I can make friends with anyone. Liam is even friendlier, but I don't think anyone can match my musician friend's level of amicability. He's a golden retriever in human form. Bonnie is simply kind.

Kind has not come easily for me lately, but I need to try. If I don't, somehow Freya will find out I was rude to a woman, and I'll never hear the end of it. Freya of Candora may look like a gentle princess, but she can be terrifying.

I force a smile. "Yeah, it's a position. I'm guessing you're new to rugby?"

Carissa shrugs. "The only sport I've watched is baseball, and that's because my sister played."

"Do you mean softball?"

"That too, but she liked baseball better, which was fine by me because guys are more fun to look at."

I hate almost everything she just said. "Well," I say slowly, "there are fifteen players in the type of rugby we play. Eight forwards, seven backs."

"Is that kind of like soccer?"

Oh, I do not have the patience for this. If Moxie is flirting instead of talking shop, I can probably drop off my charge and get back to practice. "Not really," I mutter and start walking, praying she follows so I don't have to force her to come with me.

She keeps up fairly well, though she's in a light jog instead of walking. "That's what it looked like, anyway. When I looked it up online. It's like a mix of soccer and football."

"It's like rugby," I grumble. "Look, I should get back to practice, but I'm sure one of the other guys would be happy to explain it to you." A little too happy, but that's not my problem. None of these guys would do anything bad to her, but she'll have to learn how to deal with them on her own unless she wants them drooling over her all day, every day.

If she's anything like Sage, she probably does want that.

When we reach Moxie and Tamlin, I clap Moxie on the back and shoot him a look that says he needs to be done. "We're playing the Warriors on Saturday," I remind him. "And we have work to do."

"Right." His voice is full of disappointment, but he's smart enough to know he's our best chance at another win with Coach off in the wind. "Tamlin, it was nice to talk to you." I wonder if he means that, though I don't plan on sticking around to find out. I don't talk to reporters, so it'll be better if I head back to—

"Hey, Evanson." Tamlin's voice pulls me to a sudden halt, though I wish it didn't. "Any chance of a chat?"

I look back at her and study her amused expression. This is only my second season of pro rugby, and so far I've managed to avoid any interviews since joining the Thunder. But Tamlin has been the most persistent, reaching out every couple of months in the hopes of getting an exclusive. I talked to her once when I was playing for the Badgers, and though we lost the Super Bowl that night, she chose to talk to me after the game rather than to the quarterback from the winning team. She seems to think there's a story to tell now as well.

There's not, but I would still rather not talk to her. "There's nothing to chat about," I say, trying to keep my frustration out of my voice.

Tamlin's smile shifts, turning dangerous. "You and I both know that isn't true, Cole. A prime athlete like you doesn't leave a game at the height of his career to play a sport that doesn't have nearly the same popularity just for kicks. Everyone wants to know why you made the switch."

Everyone can shove it. That's what I want to say, but I keep my mouth shut until the anger eases. Maybe Moxie was on to something when he suggested cooling off. "Everyone thinks I was angry that the Badgers lost," I say with a shrug.

Tamlin tilts her head to one side, her blue eyes piercing in the sunlight. "Anyone who saw the way you played knows better. You gave it everything you had, but the other team was simply better."

I hate that her response almost brings a smile out of me. My sudden departure from football has been a hot topic for the last two years, and I kind of love how the mystery of my decision drives everyone nuts. Folding my arms, I take a step closer and tilt my head to match her. "You seem to figure out everyone's secrets, Park. Are you telling me you haven't discovered mine?"

She laughs. "Not yet, though I have my theories."

"Which are?"

"Your friendships, for one. Though, you could have tried to get traded to one of the NFL teams here and gotten the same result, so I don't think that's it."

"Are you sure?" I ask, taking another step. "Because everyone knows how close I am to my friends."

Tamlin purses her lips. "It's a strange grouping you have, Evanson. How did you even find each other? An actor, a rockstar, a princess, and Derek Riley?"

A gasp pulls my attention to the side, where Carissa has been standing, though I'd blocked her from my notice. Impressive, given the way she stands out like a highlighter. "You're friends with *Derek Riley*?"

Moxie laughs. "Have fun with that," he mutters and jogs out onto the pitch, leaving me on my own with two vastly different women with equal talents at getting on my nerves.

I turn to Tamlin first. "You can theorize all you want, Park, but my reasons are my own. Unless you're here to talk about the game and not me, I'm done talking to you." I look at Carissa now, who has stars in her eyes. She's already met Bonnie; Derek is also an actor and shouldn't be any more exciting. "You may be working with the Thunder, Paxton, but you and I are not friends. So don't bother asking. I won't introduce you to Derek. Or Liam Connolly. Or Bonnie, for that matter. If she wants to talk to you again, she can make that happen." My voice has gotten rougher as I've gone along, which means I'm probably getting ruder by the second, so I need to end this conversation and get back to my life. "Welcome to the Thunder," I grumble and turn, heading onto the field without looking back.

That's a lie. I do look back, but I wait long enough that I'm sure Tamlin and Carissa are on their way out. Tamlin leaves as confidently as she came in, but Carissa looks smaller than she already is, her shoulders hunched and her head down.

I curse under my breath. I just know that is going to bite me in the butt.

chapter four

CARISSA

It was strange enough when my sister started dating someone who once had an interview on my favorite late night talk show. Then I found out she's one of the most hated and respected sports journalists in the nation, admired by her peers and despised by the athletes she ruined by exposing their seedier sides. Now I'm sitting in a literal mansion, gripping a glass of iced tea that tastes like liquid gold, and I'm staring at an actual. Freaking. *Princess*. Because Darcy has somehow become *friends* with Bonnie Aiken and managed to get us invited over for brunch with *her* friends the day after we get to California. And one of those friends is the Princess of Candora.

The craziest part? It's Derek Riley's patio I'm sitting on right now. *Derek Riley*. Like, the hottest man in Hollywood and quite possibly one of the most famous people in the world right now. He hasn't made an appearance yet, but I am *in his backyard*. I have pinched myself multiple times because I'm not sure this is real, but every time it has hurt like crazy.

I don't belong here. Yet here I am. What is happening?

Darcy, who has been deep in conversation with Bonnie—holding her hands, no less, because they're apparently besties even though they both dated the same man—looks over at me for the first time in fifteen minutes and laughs. She says something to Bonnie, who smiles at me and nods, and then my big sister crosses the patio to sit in the chair next to me.

"You okay, Rizzo?"

I nod, the movement making me dizzy. "When you said we were going to brunch with one of your friends, I thought it was going to be, like, a college roommate or something."

She laughs and lowers her voice. "Honestly, I probably wouldn't have reached out to Bonnie, but Cole made me mad on your behalf."

I frown. "We're here because of Cole Evanson?" Granted, I didn't like what he said to me either, but it's not like I can blame him. I didn't exactly make a great first impression. "Is he going to be here?"

"No idea. I hope so, though you have to remember that he doesn't know I'm Tamlin, so I have to pretend I've never met him."

"Right." My frown grows deeper, though I'm so glad she looks like herself right now because she's something familiar to keep me grounded. Blonde curls, brown eyes, easy smile. Just like me. "Your life is a lot more complicated than I realized, Darce."

Laughing, she tucks her arm around me and squeezes. "You have no idea. You should have seen me when I first met Houston. I'm still not sure if I kept everything straight between me and Tamlin, and my poor husband thought he was being a world-class jerk by falling for both sides of me."

"Your husband is a world-class saint for putting up with your crazy."

"He really is." She gets a dreamy look in her eyes, her smile turning so warm that I can practically feel it. I'm so lucky she's here with me for another day or two, before I start my job and have to face real life again. Once she goes back to St. Louis and her perfect husband, I'll be on my own. And I certainly won't be drinking iced tea on Derek Riley's patio once I am.

Her Royal Highness, who introduced herself as simply Freya before answering her phone in a language I couldn't understand, glides across the patio and settles in the chair on my other side. I immediately sit up straighter, nearly dumping my glass into my lap in my panic because I have no idea how to act around royalty. I'm way too likely to say something stupid for me to be comfortable right now.

"Carissa," the princess says, "I am sorry for not properly greeting you when you arrived. I always have someone who needs my attention, but I wanted to tell you that I am so happy to meet you!"

I squeak something that I *think* is supposed to be words but definitely isn't. I clear my throat and try again. "No apologies necessary! I'm sure you're super busy all the time. I once dreamed about being a princess, but then I grew up and realized that's like politics and stuff and I really don't like politics because..." I clamp my mouth shut. I ramble when I'm nervous, but I don't need to start rambling about the politician I knew in Pennsylvania.

He's already the reason I moved across the country. I don't need him helping me make a fool of myself. Again.

Freya smiles and tucks her thin fingers around my wrist. She looks so delicate. And gorgeous. But there's an intelligence in her eyes that tells me she's probably a force to be reckoned with in that whole political arena I dislike. "I happen to adore politics, but they are not for everyone."

"Your accent is so beautiful."

She laughs, and the sound is...less beautiful. It's a real, hearty laugh that instantly sets me at ease because it makes her feel more human. "So I am told, though I am partial to your American sound," she says with a wink. "Now, Darcy tells me you have just moved to California. What brought you here?"

I look at my sister, who raises her eyebrows as if to say I'm on my own from here on out. She made the introductions, and now I have to look out for myself. I swallow. "I just got a job with the Los Angeles Thunder. Sports medicine."

"Oh!" Freya's grip turns stronger, her excitement clear in her eyes. "With Cole!"

With the ultimate grumpy man who, for some reason, seems to think very little of me. I'm blaming the unicorn tank top, though it could have been any number of things. It's terrible of me, but if I had known I might see Cole today, I probably would have worn the tank top again. Just to spite him. Instead, I'm in a yellow sundress that is adorable but looks extra frumpy next to a princess. "Yep," I squeak. "With Cole."

"They met yesterday," Darcy throws in. "Though I think Tamlin Park might have put him on edge because she was there too."

Freya clucks her tongue. "Oh, I do hope he was not short with you." I can't stop my grimace, and the princess droops. "Oh dear, he was. I will make him apologize."

My eyes go wide. "No!" I wince when the word comes out louder and sharper than I would have liked. "No, you really don't have to do that, Your Highness."

Laughing, Bonnie pulls up a chair to join our group and holds out a tray of veggies. "You can call her Freya," she says to me.

"Yes," Freya agrees. "Please do. I come here to get away from the importance."

"You're still more important than anyone I know," a male voice says right as I'm reaching for a stalk of celery.

I flinch, nearly knocking the veggie tray out of Bonnie's hand, though she manages to hold on to it and save the food. I turn to see who just arrived, my pulse spiking in anticipation.

It's not Derek Riley, like I feared, but that doesn't mean the sight of rockstar Liam Connolly isn't just as discombobulating as my introductions to everyone else this far.

"Oh my gosh," I whisper as blood rushes to my head, making me dizzy. "You're..."

Liam grins as he bends to give Freya a hug from behind. "Glad to see you one more time before you head home, Peach. I see we've made some new friends."

All I can do is squeak.

"This is Houston's wife, Darcy," Bonnie says cheerfully. "And her sister, Carissa. Darcy, Carissa, this is—"

"Liam Connolly," I finish for her. Like an idiot.

Thankfully, he laughs and holds out his hand for a handshake, which I manage with a bit of fumbling and only because I stare at the tattoo of a whale on his inner wrist. It's really him. And he's just as beautiful as he was on stage when I went to his concert a couple of years ago. His blond hair is longer than it was then, and his eyes are bluer in the Malibu sunlight than they were when he was on stage in Philly.

I feel like giggling, which is seriously dumb because the guy isn't even single. Everyone knows he's madly in love with a girl who once delivered his lunch to his house. His initial romance with Kasey was straight out of fanfiction, and I ate the whole story up. According to the tabloids, they never leave each other's sides.

"Where is Kasey?" Freya asks, as if reading my thoughts.

Liam shrugs and snags a handful of carrots before dragging a chair next to Bonnie and widening our circle. "Deep in conversation with your new tank," he says to the princess. "Where'd you dig this one up?"

I have no idea what he's talking about, but Freya groans and shakes her head. "He is abominably dull, but at least he is keen to keep me safe. Perhaps too keen."

Oh, they must be talking about the bodyguard who frisked Darcy and me when we arrived, though Bonnie tried to stop him.

"Better that than someone who would rather let you get into trouble." Chuckling, Liam turns his attention to Darcy and me. His gaze fills my belly with butterflies, but from what I've heard, he's one of the nicest guys on the planet. That's assuming everything the internet says is true, which I know is not. "Houston's wife, huh?"

Darcy nods, and I have no idea how she looks so relaxed right now. "You met him when he was dating Bonnie, didn't you?"

"Yeah. Nice guy. Congrats on getting married." Liam's eyes flit back to me, and suddenly they're a little less friendly. "What brings you two to California?"

When Darcy doesn't reply, I force myself to answer. She's only here because of me, after all. "I, um, I'm going to be working with the Thunder for a while. Alongside the athletic trainer."

A muttered curse pulls all our attention to the back door, and my stomach drops when I recognize Cole in the doorway. His eyes are locked on me, and his jaw is so tight that I have to assume he's angry. But the rest of his expression is fairly neutral, so other than the word that slipped from his tongue—which is pretty telling, let's be honest—I have no idea what he might be thinking about seeing me here.

I also don't have a clue why my heart rate has skyrocketed over the few seconds we've been staring at each other, so I am extra glad when someone else comes through the door beside him and thoroughly distracts me.

Derek Riley.

I probably shouldn't be even more starstruck by the actor than I was by the literal princess sitting next to me, but Derek Riley is the stuff of teenage fantasy. He's been a huge name in Hollywood for more than a decade and is one of those actors who somehow does it all, from stunts to languages to even singing in one of his movies. And he's *beautiful*. It's not just his face, which has that ruggedly handsome quality to it that is perfect for the movies, but he is remarkably fit and healthy. The paragon of the human form.

Then again, seeing him in direct juxtaposition with Cole next to him is making me realize Cole is just as well-formed. Maybe even more so. And while Cole doesn't necessarily have a big screen presence, he rivals Derek's looks as well. Cole's eyes are a dark brown, while Derek's are deep blue, but Cole has a strong jaw and a straight nose and an intelligence behind his gaze that—

Someone clears their throat, and I flinch. Just how long was I staring?

"Derek," Liam says, and there's laughter in his voice. "Have you met Houston's wife and sister-in-law?"

Derek smiles, and I swoon a little. "Not yet, but I've heard a lot about you, Darcy." He steps forward and grasps her hand, and my sister finally seems overwhelmed as she gapes at the man. He turns to me next, and his handshake is warm and firm. "It's nice to meet you..."

"Rizzo," I squeak out and then mentally kick myself for saying my silly nickname. "I mean Carissa. I'm Carissa."

Cole poorly covers a scoff. He's still standing by the door, his arms folded and a scowl now darkening his features. He may be handsome, but his personality isn't doing him any favors. When he notices me looking at him again, he nods his head slightly. "Paxton." Oh, he's not happy at all to see me here, and I can't decide if I love or hate his reaction.

On the one hand, I'm glad Darcy came up with this counterattack for his rudeness. On the other, I don't want to have to deal with his antagonism while I work with his teammates. Right now, I'm fully planning to let Mel deal with him whenever he needs help because I don't want to be any closer to him than I am right now.

Then again, I still haven't met my new boss, so there's no telling what choice I'll have, if any.

"Did you meet Carissa's sister as well?" Bonnie asks Cole. She's frowning as she glances between me and him.

Cole shakes his head, his eyes on Darcy. "Pleasure," he grunts.

Darcy looks like she might laugh, and I have to wonder what she makes of this rugby player. She didn't like how he talked to me, but she also couldn't stop talking about how he's an incredible athlete. She's desperate to figure out why he left football, and though she didn't say it, I know she wants me to try to find out. Based on his cool welcome today, I don't think that's going to happen.

Not unless I get the truth from one of his teammates, which feels way more likely.

"What brings you to California?" Derek asks. His eyes shift between me and Cole, though I have no idea what he might be thinking. The man is a blank slate beneath a mask of pleasant civility.

"Carissa just got a job with Cole's team," Bonnie answers.

"Ah."

A woman appears behind Cole, almost as recognizable as Derek because she was all over the internet when she started dating Liam a few months ago. Kasey pats Cole on the arm in greeting and heads straight for Liam, plopping herself onto his lap as she says, "Freya, your latest bodyguard is intense."

The princess sighs. "I am aware. I do not think he will last much longer than the others."

"I'm telling you," Derek says. He moves to the table stocked with brunch delicacies that I've been eyeing since we arrived but haven't been brave enough to approach. "I know a guy."

"You know far too many 'guys,' Derek Riley."

"Not true. But clearly you're not finding anyone suitable from within Candora, so maybe you need to look outside your country."

"Paxton." Cole's voice, though soft, pulls my attention back to the doorway, where he is still standing apart from his friends as they jump into a discussion about soldiers and bodyguards. He clenches his jaw and then jerks his head toward the far end of the patio, away from the others.

Does he want me to follow? I'm a little too fascinated by Derek's suggestion that Freya hire an American soldier to protect her, and I'm not sure I like the idea of being alone with Cole any more than I was yesterday.

But he narrows his eyes, and the silent challenge pulls me out of my chair like some double-dog dare.

When he reaches the edge of the patio, Cole folds his big arms and leans a hip against the wall that lines the stone-floored space. His eyes are on the glittering ocean below, but I feel his focus entirely on me.

"What's up?" I ask when he stands silent for too long.

"What are you doing here?"

Ah, so he's going to play it that way? I fold my arms to match him, though I know I don't look nearly as impressive as he does. "My sister wanted to see Bonnie again and called her up. Bonnie invited us to brunch, and I didn't know this was Derek's house until we got here."

He grunts, eyes darting over to Bonnie as if he's hoping to get confirmation of my story. "Regardless of how you ended up here, I'm very protective of my friends."

"Okay."

He doesn't like that response, his eyebrows pulling low. "And if I hear a single word out of Tamlin Park's mouth about me or any of them, I'll—"

"She's not like that," I argue.

He lets out a single laugh. "If you think that, you clearly don't know her."

Looking over at Darcy, who is watching us with interest, I have to fight to keep my laughter in. "I know her better than you think."

Cole's eyes jump to Darcy as well, and I realize my mistake.

"I mean, my sister lives in St. Louis like Tamlin," I say quickly, trying to backtrack. "And Houston has done some interviews with her, so they've kind of become friends."

"No sane athlete would be friends with a woman like that."

"Houston isn't an athlete anymore. He retired a year and a half ago." Ugh, I feel like I'm still digging a hole for myself, so I fight for a different topic. Really, I should just go back to my seat next to Darcy and soak in the reality that my sister can claim *Derek Riley* as a friend, but the look in Cole's eyes has me worried for Darcy's secret. "I'm excited to learn more about rugby. Do you like playing?"

The question seems to catch Cole off guard as he turns his attention back to me, his eyebrows even lower than before. "Do I like playing?"

"Yeah. I mean, I guess you probably don't do it for the money, huh?"

He laughs, but it sounds forced. "No. And yes, I like playing."

"Why?"

"You're not secretly a sports reporter working for Tamlin, are you?"

It's my turn to laugh. Mine, at least, is real humor, and it helps me relax. "Oh, I know next to nothing about sports. Give me back pain or a knee replacement, and I'm your gal, but I have the coordination of a toddler, so I never followed in my sister's footsteps." I cringe. "Like playing baseball, I mean. Anyway, was there something else you needed, or did you just want to threaten me?"

Oof, that's not what I wanted to say, and I almost clap a hand to my face.

The only thing that stops me is Cole's smile, which is so unexpected that it literally takes my breath away. It's only there for half a second, but boy, does the man have a *smile*. "Threatening was the main goal," he says and stalks across the patio to sit next to Freya, leaving me entirely off balance. I definitely don't have a clue how to interact with this man, and I don't anticipate that changing.

That's going to make things interesting.

CHAPTER FIVE

COLE

"I'm going to regret asking this," Derek says.

When he doesn't continue, I look up from the book I've been pretending to read. "What?"

He smirks and shakes his head, sinking deeper into his chair until he looks like he might slide out of it. It's unusual for him to slouch, and he only ever does it when the two of us are alone. I've never figured out why he doesn't relax with anyone else. "What has you in such a bad mood?"

I knew I shouldn't have stayed as long as I have, but for some reason I didn't want Carissa to think she scared me off. She and her sister were here for hours, both of them charming the pants off my friends, and now I'm missing practice because the Paxton sisters only left an hour ago. I could have left much sooner, but Freya is flying back to Candora tonight so I wanted to soak up as much of her time as I could.

The sun is still high, bathing the two of us on the back patio with more heat than I'd like, but Derek's view can't be beat. And it's kind of nice to take a moment to breathe.

"I'm not in a bad mood," I say.

"Sure you're not."

"I just don't think you should be okay with Bonnie inviting randos to your house."

Yawning, he stretches his arms overhead and clasps his hands behind his head. "They weren't randos."

Of all people, I thought Derek would agree with me. He's too famous to be careless, and the more movies he's in, the worse it gets. He can't leave his house without being recognized, even in the most innocuous places. "She's your ex-girlfriend's ex-boyfriend's wife's sister," I point out. "That feels pretty random."

Derek laughs. "She's a friend of a friend. And part of your team now. Besides, Carissa was nice. I don't see why you were so cold to her."

I could argue that I wasn't cold, but it would be a lie. Groaning, I rub my hands down my face and wrap them around the back of my neck. It's only Tuesday, which means I have four days before the next game. With Freya on her way back home, I don't have anything good to distract me from the fact that in a few weeks Sage is marrying a guy I once called a friend. I should be at practice, but today exhausted me.

I barely spoke to Carissa, and she was *exhausting*. With the way she chatted so easily with my friends, it was clear she is everything I'm not when it comes to social skills lately, and I can't stop dreading how much time she's going to waste if she starts distracting the guys at practice.

"Freya asked me to give you some homework." Derek says it so casually that I don't register what he says at first, but then he looks over at me, mischief in his eyes.

I gape at him. "Homework," I repeat.

He shrugs. "It's not the first time I've made you do homework."

"No, but the first time, I was twenty years old and failing half of my classes."

Snickering, he lifts an eyebrow at me. "You wouldn't have passed if not for me."

I hate that he's not wrong, but I'm not about to take this sitting down. Metaphorically. "Big talk from a guy who didn't know how college even functioned."

"Which is why I was wandering around USC."

"You looked ridiculously out of place."

He laughs, shaking his head as if I said the funniest thing he'd heard all week. "Well, I'm sorry I got into acting in high school and never got the chance for a college experience, otherwise I might have fit in better. Why do you think I sat down and started talking to you?"

I lift my shoulders in an exaggerated shrug. "Beats me." And it's true. Of all the people on the campus, I'm still not sure why he went for the jock a few years younger than him and who was too cool to have friends outside the football team.

I was on suspension because of my grades and had no idea what to do while my buddies were all in Michigan for that week's game, and out of nowhere this vaguely familiar guy sat down and started asking me about college life. I didn't recognize him at first, but the other students on the quad did, and we only managed a short conversation before he got swarmed by giggling co-eds.

He asked if he could come by my apartment that night to talk more, and then he started signing autographs.

I'd figured out who he was by the time he knocked on my door that night, and though I thought it was strange to discuss with a Hollywood actor what it was like to be a student athlete, Derek was easy to talk to. Easy to trust. He seemed to pick up on things no one else did, and that was probably why I listened when he said I should spend more time on my classes so the football thing could work out for me because it clearly made me happy.

I got drafted the next year, so I never graduated, but some of the business and finance classes I ended up taking are a big part of why I can afford to play rugby for pennies. Investments have ensured I'm set for life, though I'll never live like Derek does. Some of his lavish lifestyle is out of necessity, like bodyguards and a mansion on its own street, but a lot of what he has is because he can.

The rest of us might be famous in our spheres, but we don't come close to Derek.

"Anyway," he says, still grinning, "I'm supposed to make sure you make friends with guys on your team. So this is going to be as much work on my end as it is on yours."

"Ha." I roll my eyes. "When did you and Freya become my parents?"

"Come on, you know it's not like that."

"Sure feels like it. I'm not doing homework."

"There are consequences if you don't." Derek hops to his feet and comes to stand in front of me, backed by the sun and looking like some sort of avenging angel with the way it makes his hair glow. He hasn't played one of those in a movie yet, but clearly he should. I'm mighty tempted to remind him that he's human by kicking him in the gut. Lightly. Those abs of his are valuable, and he's in the middle of shooting a movie. "Maybe don't refuse until you know what's in store if you do," he says.

That feels mildly threatening, so I stand to match him. "What sort of consequences?" I've known this guy for eight years, and I've seen plenty of his flaws to know he's not nearly as perfect as the world thinks. He's generally untouchable, but I know his pressure points if I need them. "I'm not afraid of you."

"Are you afraid of Freya?"

"Terrified."

"As you should be. And if you don't try to make friends with your teammates, she's going to force you to go to Sage's wedding."

Instead of me kicking Derek, I feel like I'm the one who just got a heel in his gut. I drop back into my chair, dizzy and nauseous, because a threat from Freya Alverra is not something to take lightly. Sage's wedding? Is she serious?

"Yeah, that's what I thought," Derek says, folding his arms as he looks down at me. "It sounds extreme, and it is, but frankly I'm in agreement with her. You've got to get over this funk Sage has put you in. She's controlling your life as much as she did when you first met her."

My eyes jump up as anger flashes through me. "What is that supposed to mean?"

"It means you're letting what she did to you affect every aspect of your life. You're always stressed. You complain about practice all the time. You're angry. You rarely hang out with us, and when you do, you're not really here." He sighs and shakes his head. "I've been trying to give you time and help you through gentle nudges, but my way clearly isn't working. And I miss my friend, Cole. Don't let Sage destroy the man you were."

I clench my jaw, hating the way emotion rises in my throat, choking me. "She isn't—"

"I liked Sage because you loved her," Derek says, narrowing his eyes so his expression turns hard. "But you and I both know she wasn't good for you. Why can't you admit that?"

Thoughts that have been on repeat for the last seven months flicker across my mind, but I try to ignore them. It's not easy, given the uncertainty building in my chest. *You're pathetic. I've wasted the last eighteen months waiting for you. You're not the man I wanted you to be and never will be.*

Swallowing, I push myself to my feet, desperate to get away from this conversation and the feelings of inadequacy that have been following me for I don't know how long. Since before Sage dumped me. "All that, and you want me to go to her wedding?" I growl. "To the man who used to be one of my best friends?"

Derek's expression doesn't shift. "I want you to take back your life, Cole. I want you to stop letting her ruin another relationship with your team just like she did in Oregon."

It's a solid blow and leaves me feeling hollow as my mind drifts back to my time with the Badgers. The friends I left behind along with a life I loved. "Leaving Oregon had nothing to do with Sage," I mutter, knowing I shouldn't say anything at all.

Derek puts his hand on my shoulder, clear pain in his eyes. He doesn't often show that kind of vulnerability, and it's the only reason I don't shift away from his touch. "Then *why* did you leave? Why won't you tell me?"

"It's not that I don't want to tell you," I say, my voice thin. I *desperately* want to tell him why I left football. He's my best friend, and keeping this from him for the last two years has been killing me.

Derek's expression hardens once more, turning into the mask he wears more often than not lately. "I know," he says gruffly. "You can't."

I really can't, and I can't even explain why because it's not like I'm under oath or contract or anything except my desire to be a decent human. There are so many things I wish I could say right now. *My team was corrupted. Players were being paid to rig games. I almost agreed to do it too.* But I can't say any of that.

"Right now," Derek says carefully, "I don't think going to that wedding is a good idea, but like I said, I'm with Freya on this one. So you'd better start trying harder with your team, or this is going to get ugly."

I want to tell him that nothing has to turn ugly if he and Freya back off, but I know better. They are looking after me, and they're both too stubborn to back down without a good reason. I don't think *I don't want to go* is going to cut it. So I slip from his hold and mutter, "I'll try to make friends," because I have no other choice. Freya can and will force me to go to Sage and Javi's wedding, though I have no idea how. She wouldn't make an edict like this if she didn't have some sort of leverage over me.

And going to that wedding would be disastrous in so many ways, so it looks like I have to play nice with my team.

It would be a whole lot easier if they would play nice in return.

CHAPTER SIX

CARISSA

I LOVE MEL. MY new boss is no-nonsense but unerringly sweet and encouraging, and as she leads me around on an in-depth tour of the Thunder's facility and explains the job, she makes me feel like I might actually have a place here.

Most of the things she tells me are pretty straightforward, but I definitely have some homework before I can really be of use to the team. I don't mind. Learning new things about the human body always puts a skip in my step, and Mel clearly needs the support. She got divorced last year and has been struggling to find consistent daycare for her son, Raiden, so having a second staff member will give her some much-needed flexibility.

After what went down in Philly, I'm desperate to be helpful.

"And it sounds like practice is ending," Mel says right as a cacophony of voices fills the tunnel. We've ended the tour in the small training room that serves as Mel's office, where I'm probably going to spend a lot of time. "Which players did you meet when you were here before?"

I laugh nervously, bracing myself as if all thirty guys might try barging into the tiny room. "Honestly, that day was kind of a blur. I remember Moxie. And..." And Cole, who clearly doesn't like me. "Bean? I think."

Mel chuckles and gestures for me to move to the back wall as the voices get louder. "Bean is a fun one, and he's a major flirt. Even with me. If he ever crosses a line, let me know."

Nerves fill my belly, and it suddenly feels like I just drank a whole liter of soda in one go. But I don't have time to worry about crossing lines because half a dozen bodies spill through the doorway.

"Hey, Mel!" they all greet, their voices bright and happy. Not at all what I expected from rough and gruff men like them.

Then they see me.

The man at the front comes to a standstill so quickly that it looks like he just saw Medusa and was turned to stone. The two behind him collide right into him, knocking him over so all three tumble to the ground. One more man trips onto the dog pile, but the other three manage to stop in time, their eyes locked on me with unveiled interest.

"Boys," Mel says, "this is my new assistant, Carissa."

"Rizzo, right?"

I recognize Bean at the back of the group—he's the one who spoke—and one of the ones on the floor looks mildly familiar. The other five haven't met me yet and have no qualms about staring at me.

I wave, ignoring the bubble of nerves in my belly. "Yeah, Rizzo is great, if you want. That's what my sister calls me."

"From that Travolta musical or the rat?" a burly bald man asks.

At the mention of the Muppet character, a snicker cracks through my nerves, and I manage a smile that doesn't go unnoticed. Those on the floor scramble to their feet, wrapping arms around each other and squeezing in close so they all fit in the small space. "The rat. Don't we look alike?" I bite my lip, curious to see how they react.

Their smiles and laughter fill me with energy and push away the last of my anxiety.

"You're way more attractive than the Muppet," Bean says, and the other guys are quick to agree. Just like before, he looks a lot smaller than the other guys, who all look like they have the sheer power of oxen. That's not to say Bean is in any way small. These rugby men are built differently from anyone I've ever seen, but I have my guesses about his nickname. Compared to the guy whose shoulders he's holding, Bean looks like a beanstalk, tall and thin.

He also looks the friendliest, though none of these guys look threatening. Even with their size. I can't imagine they'll pose any actual threats in a professional setting like this, but it's nice to see the kindness in their gazes, which haven't shifted from me for a second.

Mel clears her throat, and the guys snap out of their stupors and shuffle closer to us. The first man holds out his hand, complete with loose and dirtied athletic tape around a couple of his fingers. "I'm Sharkie. It's nice to meet you, Miss Carissa." He sounds British. Or thereabouts.

The next man's hand is sweaty and entirely engulfs mine. "Scratch." His voice comes out almost hoarse.

The next pushes his way to the front. "French Roast. Welcome to the Thunder." His accent is decidedly *not* French, though I have no idea where he's from. New Zealand, maybe?

"Gator," the next guy says.

"Ruffles."

"I'm known as Gary," the last man says in a thick Australian accent.

That one catches me off guard. "Do you not have a nickname?"

The room bursts into laughter, and he rolls his eyes. "My name is Jeff."

As soon as Jeff—or should I call him Gary?—lets go of my hand, Mel steps up and puts her arm around my shoulders. "Alright, boys, if you need my help, you can stay. If you're just here to gawk at our new friend, go hit the showers. You smell terrible." The men all start talking at once and pushing forward, but she holds up a hand and silences them. "*Real help.*"

To my surprise, five of the men turn around and leave, grumbling as they go, leaving just Bean and Gator.

Mel sighs. "Shoulder again?"

Gator ducks his head, dark hair bouncing. "It's Bandit's fault. Bad tackle." Now that I'm hearing more out of him than just his name, I'm pretty sure he's from one of the Polynesian islands. I have no idea which one.

"It was an *awesome* tackle," Bean says.

Mel raises an eyebrow at him. "And what's wrong with you?"

Using Gator's shoulder—hopefully the uninjured one—for balance, Bean holds out his leg. "It's tighter than a..." He glances at me. "It's tight."

"Sit," Mel instructs him and holds out a hand to Gator. "Let's see if it's the subscap tendon again."

I'm not sure what I should do. I figure watching Mel at work is the best way to get a sense of what she does day-to-day, but my eyes catch on Bean's stiff movements as he lowers himself into a chair. Frowning, I take a wary step closer to him. "Your hamstring?" I guess.

He nods.

"May I?"

As his eyebrows shoot up, he clearly has no idea what I'm asking but nods anyway, probably too curious not to.

I've dealt with plenty of tight muscles, and I have a bit of massage training to go with my PT degree. So I'm hoping I can help him. Crouching down, I tuck my fingers around his massive thigh and dig my fingers into the muscle underneath.

Bean yelps and nearly kicks me in the gut. "Ah, sorry."

Though I know I'm half his size and far from intimidating, I narrow my eyes at him. "What kind of stretching did you do before practice?"

He shrugs. "The usual kind?"

"I'll believe that when I see it," Mel says from the other side of the room. She's wrapping ice around Gator's shoulder but watching me at the same time.

Sounds like I need to get here early enough tomorrow to catch the team's warmup routine. With my hands still clamped around Bean's leg, I smile up at him and say, "I could rub it out for you, but you're not going to like it."

He snorts. "You? No offense, but you're tiny."

"So are you," I shoot back. Compared to the rest of the team, anyway. "Maybe you shouldn't judge me before giving me a chance to prove myself, *Bean*."

Something sparks to life in his eyes as he matches my stare. "You making fun of my name, Rizzo the Rat?"

"Do you want my help or not?"

"I'd like to see what you can do."

Twenty minutes later, Bean and I are *both* in tears, though mine are of laughter while his are from pain. I'd be worried about him if he wasn't giggling at the same time while he lies face down on the padded table and I dig my entire elbow into his hamstring to try to work out the most stubborn part of the knot in his muscle.

"For heaven's sake," I say with a grunt of exertion. "Do you *ever* stretch?"

Mel, who has since sent Gator to the locker room, sips from her water bottle and watches me with a satisfied smirk. "He pretends to," she says lightly.

Bean growls and grips the edge of the table. "Are you trying to crush my leg, woman?" Then he's back to laughing, which I'm guessing is a defense mechanism against the pain. When he can breathe again, he twists to look at me. "Or is this payback for underestimating you?"

"The second one," I tell him, still trying to get at the ridiculous knot in his muscle. Finally something comes loose, and I switch back to my hands and run my fingers down the length of his leg, from just below his glutes to his knee. There's still a lot of tension, but hopefully it won't bother him nearly as much.

"Is the torture over?" Bean asks.

I wipe a layer of sweat from my forehead with my arm. That was a serious workout, but it feels good to be back at the job. Even if this looks a lot different from what I'm used to. Plenty of my patients cried back in Pennsylvania, but none of them ever threatened to punt me into the stands. I also learned a couple new words from Bean today, though I don't plan to use them.

"Tell you what," I say to Bean, digging my fingers into his thigh again so he knows I'm serious. "Promise me you'll start stretching before and after practice, and I'll let you get off the table."

Scoffing, he lifts up on his elbows as if to get up without making any promises.

I roll my knuckles over the most tender spot of his leg.

He collapses with another unmanly yelp and starts laughing again, sprinkling in some colorful curses to go along with it. But once I let up, he tilts his head and gives me a genuine smile. "You don't play, Carissa Paxton. I admire that in a woman."

"Ahem." Two men stand in the doorway with matching expressions of disappointment and concern. Cole is looking anywhere but at me, while the other studies me. Moxie, the captain.

Moxie looks at Mel, who smiles, and turns his attention back to me. "What's going on in here?"

"Torture," Bean grumbles.

"I'm still waiting on that promise," I say forcefully. To Moxie, I keep my voice soft. "I was helping him with a tight hamstring."

"Still?" Cole's eyebrows drop low as he looks at Bean, who rolls his eyes back at him. "You're supposed to be—"

"If I wanted your opinion," Bean snaps, "I would ask."

I take a step back in surprise. No matter how angry Bean was at me while I worked his leg, his threats never felt real. But his antagonism toward Cole puts a chill in the room.

Moxie sighs, but Cole doesn't seem surprised. Putting a hand on Moxie's shoulder, he mutters something into his ear and disappears. While I still feel the frigid tension between him and his teammate, Bean relaxes as soon as he's gone.

Moxie doesn't. "You know that's not helping anything," he says to Bean.

Ignoring the comment, Bean looks at me. "I promise to stretch. Can I get up now?"

I probably shouldn't love the way he seems afraid of me, but I figured out quickly that the best way to help people heal was to show them I meant business. And with this team being full of men who are so much bigger than me, I need to make sure they don't get the wrong idea about me. I may be small, but I'm not one to be pushed around.

"I'm going to hold you to that promise," I say and step back.

Bean scrambles off the table, probably to get as far from me and my elbow as he can, but he only makes it two steps before he stops and looks down at his leg. "Wow." He wiggles around as if testing the muscle and grins back at me. "Okay, Miss Magic Hands." With a clap on Moxie's shoulder, he heads for the locker room.

I can feel two pairs of eyes on me, but I grab a towel and start wiping down the table, suddenly self-conscious.

"How's Gator's shoulder?" Moxie asks. Thankfully, it's not a question I can answer, so I keep my head down.

"I'd rather he sit out this week's game," Mel says, "but it's up to you. I know he's your best prop."

Mel said the coach isn't as hands on as he could be, but I'm still surprised by the way she's talking to Moxie like he's the one in charge. He's team captain, so of course he has some say, but just how flaky is Coach Galvin?

Moxie lets out a deep sigh, and there's enough frustration in his tone to make me look up. "Coach won't like it if I take him out of the starting fifteen." He runs a hand through his hair, turning his gaze to me. He seemed nice enough when Darcy was talking to him, but the intensity in his eyes soaks through my skin, telling me that this guy won't bend to my will as easily as Bean did. "So, Paxton. You gonna be torturing my players a lot?"

Heat floods my face, which means I'm probably red as a tomato. It may take a lot to get under my skin, but I do not hide embarrassment well when it hits. "Oh. Well, it took a lot to work out the muscle, so I thought I should—"

"Don't apologize," Mel says. "He deserves it."

"Bean is not big on stretching," Moxie agrees with a nod. "It's a miracle he hasn't been injured."

"It's a miracle he can walk," I mumble back. "Will he actually keep his promise to me, do you think?"

Glancing at the doorway behind him, Moxie shrugs. "Hard to say."

Now that I only have him in front of me rather than an entire team of beautiful men, I can see why he's the team captain. There's a calmness about him, a steadiness that I haven't seen in any of the other guys thus far. He's probably close in age to me, somewhere in his mid-twenties, but his vibes are older.

He's also entirely gorgeous, hazel eyes and curly brown hair above sharp features, not to mention the sheer amount of muscle on the guy. He's more of a lean build than a bulky one, but he could probably squat with me on his shoulders without breaking a sweat. He almost gives Cole a run for his money when it comes to attractiveness.

Almost.

"Can I ask you something, Moxie?" I say, stepping forward so we're not talking across the room. I don't mind Mel listening in, but I'm glad when she busies herself with organizing the kinesiology tape and ice packs.

Moxie is wary, his eyes narrowing as I approach. "Sure."

"What was that between Bean and Cole?"

Tension fills his body, muscles straining as he folds his arms. "That was nothing."

"I don't think that was nothing." Bean may have hissed out a million threats against me while I was working out the muscle in his leg, but other than that I've only seen him good natured and friendly. He was anything but when it came to Cole. "Shouldn't your team be, I don't know, a team? They weren't exactly chummy."

Moxie kicks the door jamb out from under the door and doesn't say anything until the door swings shut behind him. "Here's the thing you need to understand," he says, an edge to his voice. "Cole is my best player, but the rest of the team will never admit it."

"Why not?"

"He's a newbie to rugby and got drafted early, which drives them nuts because it's not easy to make it on a team when the league is so small. Plus, Cole came from the NFL, and most of the guys see football as an inferior sport. "

I consider that with a frown. "That makes no sense. I've never watched a rugby game, but I've seen plenty of football. Those guys take a beating every game and are seriously athletic."

Moxie chuckles and shares a grin with Mel. "Don't let any of the guys hear you say that, Paxton. You'll be an outcast like Cole, and we need you."

We need you. Those words settle over me like a warm blanket in the middle of January, and I can't hold back my smile. "You need me?"

"You have no idea," Mel says, her voice thick with sincerity. "I nearly cried when I heard you were coming on. I'm trying to take care of these boys, but this single parenting thing is harder than I expected."

Moxie's lips press together, and he takes a step toward Mel, as if he wants to comfort her, but he stops himself and shakes his head. "We know you're doing your best," he tells her.

I don't want to interrupt whatever moment they're having, but my curiosity is burning too bright to ignore. "Why is Cole an outcast? Because he played football?"

"That," Moxie says, "and he hasn't been especially friendly ever since his girlfriend broke up with him back in October."

Mel *tsks*. "Can you blame him? That girl ripped his heart out."

Oh boy. And here I was thinking Cole was just a grump with a high opinion of himself.

"I know that," Moxie says, "but it's not like he's trying to get over her. He just keeps getting worse."

"You know how he felt about her!"

"Not really. He barely talks to me."

"He doesn't have to say the words. Sometimes you can just tell how a person feels about someone by looking at them."

I clear my throat. While tempted to let them keep talking about Cole so I can learn more about him, I don't think this is the kind of conversation he would want me to hear. I don't need a reason to get even more on his bad side. "Any other advice? Bean was easy to figure out, but this is a big team. I want to make sure I'm as helpful as possible. As quickly as possible."

Moxie opens his mouth, but Mel lets out a loud curse as she looks at her phone. Wincing, she offers me a quick apology, then says to Moxie, "Another daycare fell through. I need to go."

"Of course," Moxie says and steps aside so she can scurry out the door with her bag. As soon as she's gone, he sighs and shakes his head. "She needs help," he mutters.

I know nothing about kids—the curse of being the baby of the family—but I wish I had some way to help. "Could she bring her kid to practices?"

"If Coach is gone, probably, but there's no way to know if..." He stops himself and scrunches his nose as he looks at me. "You're friends with Tamlin Park," he says, as if reminding himself.

I laugh. "Trust me. I barely know Tamlin." It's true enough, considering Darcy is so different when she's playing the part of her reporter alter ego. "I don't have any intention of giving her anything she could use against the team. I need this job, so I'm on your side." I'm sure Darcy will ask if I learn anything interesting, but I mean it when I say I don't plan on sharing any secrets. My sister may have gotten me this job, but I intend to keep it on my own merits.

No way am I letting this one implode like the last one.

Humming, Moxie studies me carefully, then nods, as if deciding he can trust me. "What's your background, Paxton?"

"You can call me Rizzo. Or Carissa."

He smiles briefly. "Carissa."

"Up until a few weeks ago, I worked in a physical therapy office back East." I can see his question even before he opens his mouth, so I add, "I was one of the therapists." Too many people have assumed I was a receptionist or something because I don't look old enough—or strong enough—to be a PT.

He hums again. "Cole says I should keep an eye on you."

As my jaw drops, I can't help but find this whole thing hilarious. I barely talked to the man, but there's something about me he clearly doesn't like. "Cole is paranoid," I say with a grin. "My sister is friends with Bonnie Aiken. You know, the actress?"

Moxie chuckles. "I know."

"So I was hanging out with Cole's friends yesterday, and I think he's convinced I am up to no good."

"It does seem conveniently coincidental."

Shrugging, I grab my bag from where I left it behind Mel's desk, since there's no point in me hanging around if she's not here to show me the ropes. "Maybe, but it's still coincidental, no matter how convenient. I promise I'm just here to work."

But when I open the door and find half a dozen men waiting in the hall for me with bright and eager smiles, a blush steals across my face. "Oh. Um. Hi."

"Bean says you have magic hands," one of them says.

Cue an even hotter blush. "Does he now?"

"We were all hoping to get a taste."

Moxie comes up behind me and clears his throat as he rests one hand on the door frame above me, the other on my shoulder. It's a welcome show of support, whether or not that was his intention. "Careful what you say next, Tink," he mutters.

Tink, the one who spoke, turns beet red and shakes his head wildly. "I meant with muscle stuff! Like she did with Bean! Mel's always fixing the other problems and never has time to help with the minor stuff."

"That's not really in my job description," I say, which is true. But there are few things I hate more than disappointing people, and they're all looking at me so hopefully. I don't want to set a precedent of giving massages willy-nilly, but I could make sure they're doing proper stretches. "But I could try to help."

Their looks of relief and excitement send a jolt of pleasure through me. That's something I could get used to.

Chapter Seven

Cole

I should have left. That's starting to feel like a pattern with me, and yet I'm still sitting on the edge of the training pitch instead of on my dad's back porch, where I'm supposed to be, because Carissa Paxton has once again made herself a nuisance.

Rolling my eyes, I swallow a gulp of water and tell myself—again—that the only reason I'm here is because I chose to be. I could have left an hour ago, when practice ended, and Carissa probably would have been fine.

It's that 'probably' that has kept me here longer than I need to be.

I trust the guys on my team, but after the talk I heard in the locker room today, that trust is hanging by a thread. All of the single guys—and some of the taken ones—were quick to express their interest in Carissa, which is ridiculous because Bean's the only one who can say he's spoken to her for more than a few seconds. I can't decide if he's more interested than he was to begin with or if he's afraid of her. It might be both.

Besides, Carissa is engaged. She's not even available.

But now there's a bet on who will get a date first, and high stakes tend to turn people into idiots when they are otherwise rational. That's why I'm watching Carissa teach the guys some stretches on the field. Not because I want to win the bet but because I'm worried Carissa will be the one to lose. According to Bean, who is out there stretching with the dozen other guys who have stuck around, Carissa can take care of herself, but I'm not willing to leave her safety up to her.

I wonder if she knows how to say no.

Right now, she's hugging French Roast's extended leg while he lies on his back on the ground, and despite knowing she's helping him stretch his hamstring, the position they're both in looks...questionable. And isn't at all convincing me that it's a good idea to leave.

My phone buzzes where it's resting on my leg, and I look down at the text, unsurprised to see the message from my dad.

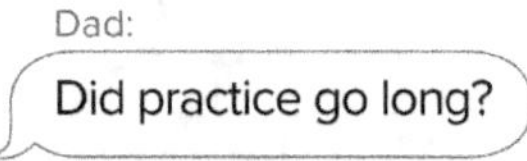

I could lie and say yes, but even through a text he would know it's not the truth. Sighing, I pick up my phone and type back a response.

Cole:
No, but something came up. I'll be there soon.

That all depends on how long Carissa plans on doing her little yoga routine.

I do feel bad that I've delayed our weekly barbecue, but Dad will understand. He and Gramps would kill me if they ever found out I left a girl like Carissa on her own with half a rugby team, even if these guys are all pretty decent. Sure, it would make more sense if I was actually over there stretching with them, but despite Freya's threats, I'm no more interested in the idea of befriending my teammates than they are in accepting me.

My phone buzzes again, and I grit my teeth when I realize it's not my dad this time but the princess herself. Seriously, does she have a camera trained on me at all times or something?

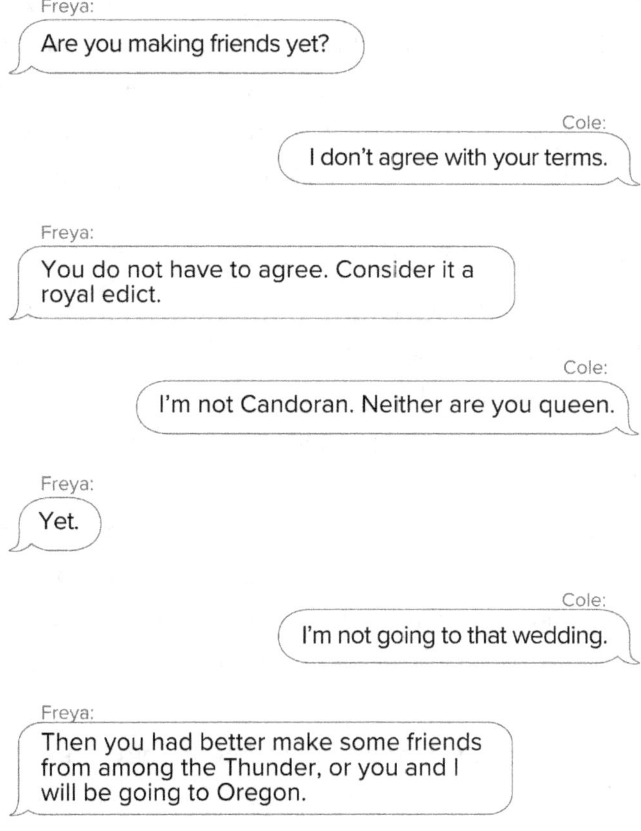

"You could have joined us, you know."

My head snaps up at the sound of Carissa's voice right in front of me. It hits the wall behind me, and I groan from the impact. "Have you never learned not to sneak up on people?"

She bites her lip, clearly trying not to laugh. "Well, you've been watching me for the last forty-five minutes, so I figured you saw me coming."

She noticed me? Great. Now I'm not only a grump but a creepy grump. Why do people use that word, anyway? It sounds ridiculous. *Grump.* It was one of Sage's favorite tropes in books, though I never understood the appeal of a surly romantic partner. As the team's resident grump, I'm not the kind of guy anyone would want to date, and I certainly wouldn't let any of my female friends date someone like me. I'm a walking red flag.

Maybe I should have gotten this way *before* Sage dumped me so she would have stuck around. Then again, Javi's not necessarily a grump either, so she must only like the grumpy type in books. Not real life. In real life, she likes pro football players. Super Bowl ring owners. Morally questionable guys.

I need to say something, but I have no good reasons for watching Carissa's stretch lessons. Not reasons she'll like. I grunt and shake my head. "I wasn't watching you." I was watching the *guys*. And okay, maybe I was watching her some of the time.

Folding her arms, she raises an eyebrow at me. "Why don't you like me, Cole Evanson?"

Under other circumstances, I might have appreciated her refreshing directness, but too much of my mind is caught up in Freya's edict and knowing I'll have to explain to Dad and Gramps why I was late for dinner. I don't have the bandwidth to deal with a metaphorical princess on top of a real one.

Grunting, I push myself to my feet and sling my bag over my shoulder. "I don't dislike you." It's a lie, and we both know it, so I start walking toward the exit before this conversation gets out of hand. Now that everyone's leaving, she'll be fine.

That thought only lasts long enough for me to catch the way French Roast is eyeing Carissa behind me, as well as a few other guys taking their sweet time to head to the parking lot.

I slow until Carissa catches up to me. "Sorry," I say, if only so we can keep talking until she reaches her car. If I'm with her, the guys are less likely to try to get her one-on-one. "I'm not great at conversation." That has always been true, but it's gotten worse since Sage left me.

Carissa laughs, the sound filling the air with sparkles. Metaphorical sparkles, of course, but it's enough to catch the attention of anyone within earshot. Not that any of these guys weren't already watching Carissa... "I kind of figured that one out on my own. You've pretty much done nothing but threaten me since we met."

Okay, when she puts it like that, I feel like a jerk. Which I am. But I don't like being called out on it.

"I didn't..." I huff and come to a stop at the edge of the parking lot. I don't know where her car is, or I would head straight for it. "I didn't threaten you."

Carissa lifts one delicate eyebrow.

"I *warned* you."

"The word 'threaten' literally came out of your mouth when we were at Derek's house."

I'm sticking my foot in my mouth, and that's straight up disgusting. My foot has been in locker rooms for most of my life, and who knows what nasty things grow in those. "Yes," I admit. "I did say that." And for some reason I keep this train wreck of a conversation going. "But I didn't mean it."

"So why did you say it?"

Running a hand through my hair, I search the parking lot for some sort of escape but come up empty. I need to catch the bus before I miss Gramps's ribs. If I show up too late, he and Dad will have eaten them all without remorse. "Because I say a lot of things I don't mean," I mumble. "Were..." How am I supposed to ask this without the guys hearing me? They're slowly inching closer, like lions hoping to pick off the easiest prey. I don't know if that prey is me or Carissa, but I don't want them coming closer regardless. "How did your stretching thing go?"

Carissa grins and wraps her fingers around the strap of her purse. She's not wearing the ring she had on the first day she was here, which probably explains why the guys are all drooling over her. "I think the team was hoping for something a little more hands-on, but I wore myself out with Bean."

My mind is going places it shouldn't, conjuring up some of the scenes that were in Sage's books. I believe the term she used was *spicy*. That does not refer to what Carissa is talking about, so I shouldn't be thinking it.

I cough. "He wasn't too rough, was he?" Well that didn't help steer me in the right direction. "I mean, he was nice to you, right?"

Another glittery laugh from Carissa pulls the team even closer, and I notice Bean among them. Hopefully he's too far away to hear anything, but based on the way he's glaring at me, he's probably thinking he needs to protect Carissa from *me*. I don't blame him.

"Bean was fine," she says with a shake of her head. "In all fairness, I was really digging into his leg, so he's not responsible for any of the words that came out of his mouth."

I swear under my breath, cursing his mouth in the presence of a woman. The hypocrisy of that thought is not lost on me. "If he ever gives you trouble..." I'll do what? Punch him? That would be a *great* way to make some friendships with my teammates. I don't generally like violence—one of the reasons I play a position with less tackling than others—but I doubt any of the Thunder players would be surprised if I decked one of them one of these days. I've gotten angry enough to set some precedents.

Derek's words flash through my mind. *You're angry.* I was never angry before Sage, and I hate that he's right. I hate more that I don't know how to fix it. I'm not hung up on my ex, but I can't move past her either, and I'm just...stuck. Sinking.

With her lips twisting in an amused smirk, Carissa looks to her left and meets Bean's gaze. "He won't be any trouble. We understand each other now."

Whatever that means, I don't like it, but her deliberate eye contact pulls Bean all the way over to us, a bounce in his step. "Need a ride, Magic Hands?"

"Dude," I breathe, shaking my head at the nickname.

He, of course, ignores me. "I know you don't have a car, and Rihanna here doesn't drive, so he's useless."

I curse again as Carissa's warm brown eyes fall back on me, her curiosity on full display. "Why don't you drive?" she asks.

Because every time I get behind the wheel I get too anxious and tense to drive smoothly and safely. But I will never in a million years admit as much to my teammates. I need them to respect me, to tolerate me, and that will never happen if they think I'm too wound up to do something most adults can do by muscle memory.

Shrugging, I keep my mouth shut, and I feel like a pathetic moron when Carissa hooks her arm through Bean's and follows him to his car. There was nothing nervous in her body language, so I think she'll be okay. She had better be. As far as I know, Bean is a decent guy, but if I hear he did anything she didn't like...

"You're wasting your time, Rihanna," Tink says, bumping his shoulder into mine like we're buds. We're not. "A girl like that won't look twice at a guy like you."

A few other guys chuckle, and then they all head to their cars and leave me standing on the sidewalk with my jaw clenched so hard it might never open again. I don't need these guys to like me, no matter what Freya wants for me. But I really don't want their opinions of me to be right.

Gramps is just taking the ribs off the grill when I step through the back door of Dad's house in Sherman Oaks, which means they waited for me. Guilt threads through me, but I ignore it and grab the plate out of Gramps's hands as soon as he loads the last of the meat.

"Smells good, Gramps!" I say, holding the plate high out of his reach when he swipes for it. "What are you two going to eat?"

Gramps's next swipe is more of a fist to the stomach, knocking the air out of me. He snatches the plate and snickers. "You're getting slow, Lemon."

"I am not," I complain breathlessly.

"Then what took you so long?" Dad asks, coming through the back door with a bowl of his famous potato salad. "You should have been here over an hour ago."

"I told you." Massaging my abdomen, I settle myself at the patio table and start dishing up coleslaw onto the three plates already set out for our dinner. "Something came up. Geez, Gramps, have you taken up boxing? That was quite the uppercut."

"The senior center has a kickboxing class every Tuesday and Thursday," Gramps says. He sets the ribs on the corner farthest from me, apparently convinced I'll still try to steal all of them.

I laugh. "Kickboxing, huh?"

Dad rolls his eyes as he sits across from me. "He already bought a bag and installed it in the basement."

Oh, they're not kidding? "I'm going to have to see that in action," I say with a chuckle.

I've been here less than three minutes, and already I'm feeling the weight of the day melt away. I shouldn't have stuck around after practice. Carissa can take care of herself, and she doesn't need me messing up her life. What was I even trying to protect her from?

There must be something in my expression because both Dad and Gramps grow still and fix their eyes on me.

I become suddenly engrossed by the cabbage on my plate. That lasts maybe two seconds before I can't help but look up at them again because they're never this quiet.

It's moments like these, when they give me matching looks of bemused curiosity, that father and son's similarities are the most obvious. Gramps still has his hair, though it has gone mostly gray, and he also has a pep in his step, enough for him to keep up with Dad. And take up kickboxing, apparently. Dad has Gramps's round chin, a trait I also inherited, and though his eyes are a lighter shade of green, they have the same piercing power that Gramps's do.

I don't have their eyes. I got mine from my mom, who I've been told was everything warm and dark and sensual.

No kid wants to hear his mom described like that, but seeing as I never knew her, I'm happy my dad talks about her at all.

"What?" I finally say when the staring continues beyond what I'm comfortable with.

Dad blinks and dishes himself some potato salad.

Gramps is not so easily deterred. "Something is different about you, Coleman."

"Ha!" I roll my eyes. "Nothing is different." That's part of my problem.

"No, I think Gramps is right," Dad says.

Maybe it's because something in my gut is agreeing with them, or maybe it's because I'm starving. Or maybe I'm desperate to change the subject. But I do the only thing I can think of and shove an entire rib in my mouth, bone and all.

Dad chuckles. "That's one way to avoid a conversation."

And maybe a good way to choke. There's no dignified way to get out of my self-imposed predicament, so I spend the next several seconds with my fingers in my mouth, prying the bone loose while tearing the meat free and chewing.

Gramps clucks his tongue as he watches me with furrowed brow. "And you wonder why you're single."

That blow hits harder than his fist in my gut. I don't think he meant his comment as an attack, but I feel it deep in my chest, sharp and burning.

Free of my makeshift gag, I wipe my hands and face clean with a napkin, taking my time before I speak. "You know why I'm single." The words are small but so, so heavy.

"You were too good for her anyway," Gramps says, waving away the gloom that has settled back over me.

Dad, on the other hand, reaches across the table and puts his hand over my fist. We're not an especially affectionate family, the three of us, but when Dad does something like this, it feels like he can see straight into my soul. He knows the things I refuse to acknowledge, even to myself.

I need a change of subject, and I need it fast.

"Freya was in town," I say, stabbing my fork into a potato.

Dad still looks like he wants to chat about my breakup with Sage, but Gramps gets a twinkle in his eyes at the mention of my royal friend. "Ah, Her Highness. Did she ask about me?"

I chuckle. "Of course she did. She would have stopped by if she'd had the time."

While all of my friends here in Los Angeles have met my dad and grandpa, only Freya regularly visits. She says that because she never got to know her own grandparents, who all passed when she was little, she wants to borrow mine. No one else has living grandparents, so I'm happy to let her borrow Gramps whenever she wants.

Especially because Gramps fancies himself in love with her.

"I still don't understand why you haven't married that angel of a woman," Gramps says.

I don't know whether to laugh or roll my eyes. "And become king of a small country? That's a disaster waiting to happen." For more reasons than one. "Besides, Freya is like a sister to me." We get along great, but there has never been any attraction between us.

She acts like my big sister too, which brings me full circle to today's annoyance. I *really* don't want to make friends with my teammates right now. But I want to go to Sage's wedding even less.

As always, Dad seems to read my thoughts, though he's focused on his food as he talks. "I came across an article the other day. About Sage and Javi."

I groan. "Are you reading tabloids now?"

"When they have your name in them, yes."

"You know those are total bull."

"Are they?" He looks up, meeting my eyes with that look he gets when he thinks I'm doing something wrong. I got that look a lot as a kid, but lately it feels like I've been getting it more and more as an adult. I may be twenty-eight, but he's still my father. "Because every time your name comes up," he continues, "there is always a nugget of truth."

I hate that I can't argue. I've been lucky when it comes to *Hollywood Hot Scoop*, the most prolific tabloid site in the area, in that my name is usually only mentioned in passing connected to one of my friends. Liam got himself into a decent amount of trouble last fall, and Bonnie's relationship with Hank was all over that thing. Derek is pretty much constantly on their radar, no matter what he does.

But with Sage and Javi getting married, I have a feeling I'll be brought back to the forefront.

"I'm lying low," I say, even if that's not exactly a response to Dad's comment. "Once the wedding happens, there won't be any reason for me to be in any stories."

"Except you've met someone," Gramps says.

I drop my fork. It clatters on the patio floor, the sound condemning the trajectory of this conversation. I'll never be able to deny it now, but how in the world does he know?

I clear my throat, my skin turning itchy under their stares. "Not like that," I say in defense. "We have a new rehab specialist."

"A woman," Dad guesses.

"A pretty one?" Gramps asks.

If I answer that honestly, it'll only make things worse, so I gloss over that question and explain to the best of my ability. "She's young and inexperienced, and I'm worried the guys are going to cause problems for her."

"Hmm." Gramps rests his head in his hand and studies me the same way he studied game tape back when I played football. He tries to do the same with rugby, but he doesn't fully understand my new sport yet. He does understand me, though. He practically raised me alongside Dad and has seen me through my highs and lows. "I thought your teammates were decent fellas."

"They are," I agree. "But even the best of men turn into idiots when around a beautiful woman."

"Aha!" Dad says. "She *is* pretty!"

I curse under my breath, then flinch when Gramps smacks me in the side of the head and warns me to watch my language. "Sorry," I grumble, glad they stopped using a swear jar a couple of years ago. I'm pretty sure I fully funded the cruise they went on a couple of years ago thanks to that jar. "No matter how pretty Carissa is, I have no desire to see her as anything but a colleague."

"Why not?" Gramps leans in close, dropping his voice to just above a whisper. "Is she crazy?"

Dad whacks his arm. "Don't call people crazy, old man. But tell me, why have you already discounted this Carissa as an option?"

Why am I sitting here having this conversation with two men who haven't dated in nearly thirty years at minimum? That's a better question, but I answer Dad anyway. "Even if she and I were both single—which she isn't—it wouldn't mean we're a good match. And I'm not interested in dating anyone."

"For now," Dad prompts.

I shake my head. "It's a bad idea to let myself get attached to someone, and you know it." And this conversation is going to go in circles if I'm not careful. "Can we get back to the fact that Gramps has taken up kickboxing?"

I can see in both their eyes that they don't want to change subjects, but they also know that if they push me too hard, I'll drop the conversation and leave. I love them both, but sometimes I'm convinced they're invested in my love life only because they don't have their own. Like me, I don't think they have plans to change their single statuses. Doing so would be...dangerous.

Evanson men and happily ever afters don't mix.

"I think I'm getting the hang of the roundhouse kick," Gramps says, catching hold of my evasion. But he shares a look with Dad, and I know deep down I'm only going to be able to avoid the dating conversation for so long.

Hollywood Hot Scoop

Gowns, Grumps, and Gorgeous!

TALK ABOUT BEAUTIFUL! SAGE Morrow, fiancée of the Portland Badgers' star tight end, was seen trying on an absolutely stunning wedding gown this morning. No word yet on if this is the one, but I'm sure we all can agree that Javier Gonzales will be blown away no matter what she wears at the altar. She's a catch, no doubt about that!

I know what you're all wondering, and yes, we have updates on her jilted ex, rugby's favorite scrum-half, Cole Evanson. One of our sources caught him looking surly after yesterday's practice. While that's nothing new, check out the mystery woman who has come onto the Thunder scene. Is this a new love interest for our brokenhearted hero? If it is, Cole's going to have to put on a smile now and then or she'll realize she can do way better than a surly scrum-half.

If I were her, I'd hold out for an introduction to someone like Derek Riley, who was seen surfing the waves on Huntington Beach last week. If you missed the slideshow, check it out here!

We'll keep you updated on Cole's broody day-to-day, as well as give you all the scoops on the wedding of the century as it draws closer! Hit

that subscribe button, and we'll see you for the next *Hollywood Hot Scoop*!
XO

CHAPTER EIGHT

CARISSA

A CAR WOULD BE really nice right about now. Or, you know, all the time.

While I thought I had the bus schedule all figured out—I got to work yesterday just fine—I've been standing here at the bus stop for more than half an hour. Not only am I stuck in the blistering California sun, but I've been hit on by no less than three skeevy men, one of whom might have tried to grab hold of my arm if a kind old man hadn't been walking past at just the right time. He stayed at my side until the creep left, then continued on his merry way.

Right now, I'm blissfully alone, but I don't know how long that'll last. I'm two minutes away from calling a rideshare even if it'll cost an arm and a leg to get me to the practice fields from here. Yes, Houston got me an apartment in a decent neighborhood, but it's so far from the Thunder stadium that I'm starting to think it might be a good idea to look for somewhere closer.

Sighing, I look down at my phone. I'm running out of time if I don't want to be late, but I'm also realizing I'm going to run out of money far sooner than I'd like if I miss the bus like this too many times.

Right as I'm opening the app store to download a rideshare app, a silver Prius pulls up to the curb right in front of me. Alarm bells start ringing in my head—stranger danger at its finest—but then the back window rolls down to reveal none other than Cole Evanson.

"Need a ride?" he asks.

I shield my eyes with my hand to see him better. "Um. No. I'm sure the bus will be here any second." It's a lie, and I'm pretty sure he knows it. I also don't know why I'm bothering, since the car he's in is exactly what I was about to order for myself anyway, and we're going to the same place. I think it's because he doesn't like me, which is not something I'm used to.

Glancing to his left, he lifts a single eyebrow and pushes the door open, scooting to the other end of the seat.

I'd be stupid to argue, so I scurry inside the air conditioned car before my stubbornness gets in my way.

"Uh." The driver, a young man in his early twenties, looks back at me. "I don't think I should—"

"I'll pay you extra," Cole says at the same time I say, "It's okay. I know him."

We look at each other, and though I can't say I know what Cole's thinking, I've got my guesses. He's probably wondering, like I am, which of our assumptions is right. Is the driver wary because technically I should be paying for my ride? Or does he think Cole is picking up some girl on the side of the road? Maybe it's both, but when Cole hands a hundred dollar bill up to him, the driver flips the car into gear and drives off.

I nearly choke as I watch that bill disappear into the guy's pocket. "Um, I thought rugby players had terrible paychecks."

Cole grunts, his eyes out the window now. "They do."

"That was like a month of groceries."

That gets a chuckle out of him, though there's no trace of a smile. I've only seen him smile once, but it's something I would love to see again. What does it take to get a grump like Cole Evanson to smile? "You must not eat much," he says.

I mean, I don't, but that doesn't change the fact that he's seriously overpaying for this ride. Leaning closer, I drop my voice in the hopes that the driver doesn't hear me. It's unlikely, given how small this car is. "You paid him way too much."

Sure enough, the driver's eyes meet mine in the rear view mirror for half a second, narrowing slightly as if warning me to keep my mouth shut. It's not like Cole could ask for the money back. I mean, he could try, but we're at the mercy of the driver here.

It's a strange concept, trusting strangers to get us to our destinations safely. What if they're high? What if they're escaped criminals who stole the car? What if—a gasp escapes me—what if this driver is actually an international spy and we've just been inadvertently pulled into his mission?

"You okay?" Cole asks, and I realize I'm still leaning toward him.

I shift back to my side of the seat and nod. "Yes. Fine."

"I paid him so he won't ask questions," he says, louder this time.

The driver gulps. Maybe he's thinking *Cole* is the international spy.

I could see it. Cole has the build and the glower and the cash, apparently. What kind of person carries hundred-dollar bills around like that? I think I've only seen one or two in my lifetime, and they always go straight to the bank because I cannot be trusted with that kind of cash.

"Are you sure you're okay?" Cole asks, still watching me.

I'm going to assume all of my thoughts are painted right across my face because, unlike my sister, I'm crap at hiding things. "Do you know how many candy bars that money could buy?" I resist the urge to clap a hand to my face. *That's* what I decide to go with? Candy bars? Maybe I got heat stroke standing in the sun.

Cole laughs again, this time with the smallest upturn of his lips. "Candy bars," he repeats, and his eyes do a slow head-to-toe of my body.

"I can't help it if I have a fast metabolism," I say, folding my arms as if that might hide my painfully thin frame.

"And a serious sweet tooth," he counters.

"That's more by choice."

"Did you get home safely last night?"

The question catches me so off guard that my response is snarkier than I usually allow myself. "No, I spent the night on the street."

The driver coughs, though I can't decide if he's laughing or genuinely concerned for my safety. I hope it's the second one. Cole, on the other hand, curls his hands into fists on his lap and clenches his jaw until it looks like a muscle might snap. It's another argument for him clearly despising me, and I still don't know why.

But then he takes a deep breath and softens. "I get that it's none of my business," he says, his voice low and rough. "But if any of the guys were to put you in any kind of danger like that, I'd..." He shakes his head. "Maybe don't joke about it? I'm stressed enough as it is."

Wait. *Wait.* Was he actually worried about me? Ignoring the bubble of warmth in my belly, I twist in my seat so I'm facing him, one leg curled up beneath me. "First of all, I'm pretty sure Bean is more afraid of me than anything after the way I manhandled him on that table."

The driver coughs again, but I ignore him. He can make whatever conjectures he wants about what I just said.

"Second of all," I continue, "he walked me all the way to my door and wouldn't leave until I'd locked it behind me."

Cole's eyebrows rise. "Oh. Good."

"And third of all, you're right. It's none of your business. You clearly don't like me, so there's no reason for you to worry about me." Even if a part of me yearns for his concern. I put up a confident front, but especially after my career-damning relationship with Peter, I have zero faith in my own abilities. I couldn't figure out a bus schedule more than one day in a row! I only have a part-time job, I'm not paying my own rent, and the homesickness hit me so hard last night that I almost called Darcy at three in the morning to ask if I could go back to St. Louis to stay with her. Newlywed stage and all.

It's only when Cole's expression softens that I realize tears are welling up in my eyes.

Sniffing, I turn to look out my window and will myself to calm down.

"I realize we're not friends," Cole says. "But if you need to talk? I'm a good listener." We're both quiet for nearly a minute before he adds, "And I don't know you, Carissa. I don't have the right to dislike you."

Huh. That's actually really...nice. "I'm extremely likable," I mutter, mostly to fill the silence. Not because I think that highly of myself, though history would agree with my statement. Honestly, my likability causes problems sometimes, like when a high profile client starts wanting to spend time with me away from the PT office because he tells me I "bring sunlight to his life" and he "doesn't want to give me up."

"I don't doubt it," Cole says, and we fall into silence again.

In general, I'm not a silence kind of person. Darcy and I are both talkers, so our childhood was filled with endless conversation that sometimes drove our parents mad. So I last maybe two minutes before I blurt out a new topic.

"Why don't you drive?"

Never would I have called Cole relaxed, but he must have been because he suddenly tenses up.

"You don't have to answer that," I say quickly. "It's none of *my* business."

But I do think the driver thinks it's *his* business because his head is tilted toward the backseat, like he's hanging on our every word.

Cole notices this too, his eyes narrowing into slits as he looks forward at our eavesdropper. Without saying anything, Cole unlocks his phone and opens up a text. He reads for a moment, and then he curses under his breath. "You can drop us off here," he says, though we're still several blocks from the stadium.

The driver's shoulders slump. "But—"

"*Pull over.*"

He does, and fear grips my heart as I reluctantly slip out of the car, followed closely by Cole. Cole grabs his bag from the trunk, and we stand there in the sun next to a cinder block wall until the Prius is out of sight.

"I'm sorry," I whisper. "I shouldn't have asked about—"

"I'm not angry about that." He holds his phone out to me.

I have no idea what I expected, but it certainly wasn't a tabloid article about a football player in Oregon. What does this have to do with...*oh*. There's a picture. Of *me*. Well, the back of my head, anyway, but I'd know those unruly curls anywhere. The focus is on Cole, but that's definitely my hair. Still confused, I read through the article quickly. It kind of feels like I'm suddenly outside of my own body, like this moment isn't real. I've heard of this tabloid. Houston was in it once, several months before he met my sister, but that makes sense because he's famous and he was dating a movie star. Bonnie.

And Cole is *friends* with famous people, but this article is insinuating he's just as famous as his friends.

"I'm sorry," Cole says when I hand his phone back. His lips are pursed as he reads through the article again. "I didn't think anyone would bother hanging around practices."

I think I'm going to have to do some Googling as soon as I'm away from this man. Just how famous is he? Famous enough that he doesn't bat an eye at handing a hundred bucks to a rideshare driver.

"Okay, so..." I don't even know what I should ask. "What does this mean?"

Cole shrugs and adjusts the strap of his bag. We are definitely both going to be late to today's practice, but he doesn't seem to mind. "That depends."

"On what?"

"On if *Hot Scoop* decides you're important."

"I'm not important." In fact, I cannot stress enough how much I *do not want to be important.* "And it's not like you and I would ever date."

"Obviously not."

Okay, well, that was a bit uncalled for. He didn't even hesitate. And while I've accepted the fact that he doesn't like me, I refuse to let him brush me off so easily. I told him I was likable, and I am determined to prove it. There's no *obviously* about it. "I'm a great girlfriend," I say as casually as I can manage.

Cole's eyes jump down over my body once more, leaving me feeling like I'm on display. "Girlfriend," he repeats, like he's seeing how the word tastes in his mouth. "Not a fiancée?"

I frown. "I don't think there would be much of a difference."

"I suppose it's a matter of commitment."

"That's usually how engagements work." And I have no idea what we're talking about now. I'm good at having inane conversations, but this is...different. This isn't a ninety-year-old man who just had a hip replacement and wants to talk about his days as a typist in the Army. This is a big and burly rugby player of undetermined fame who is talking in a way that makes me think I should know what he's trying to say underneath the words he's actually speaking.

I fold my arms. Might as well just ask. "What are you implying, Cole Evanson?"

His eyes slip downward again, but this time they rest on my hand. "Does your husband-to-be know you're not wearing your ring while you're at work?"

"I never wear rings at work. And I'm not getting married." But then I realize what he's really asking, and heat floods my face. "Oh. Oh, that ring the other day wasn't mine."

Cole scoffs. "The very expensive, very real diamond on your finger wasn't yours?"

"First of all, how do you know it was real?"

Rolling his eyes, he starts walking toward the stadium like this conversation is over.

It so isn't. "Second, it really wasn't mine. I was holding on to it for my sister."

"Why?"

"Because she didn't want any of the team to..." *Oh no.*

Cole stops dead in the middle of the sidewalk, and though he doesn't turn around to look at me, I see every bit of his tension in his massive shoulders. Is it too much to hope he's too dumb to make the connection?

That *question* is dumb. Of course he's smart enough to figure out what I just let slip.

As I slowly creep forward to get close to him again, Cole grips the strap of his bag, knuckles turning white. He turns when I reach him, and I swear his dark eyes shoot lasers straight through me. "Tamlin Park is your sister." It's not a question. "Darcy goes undercover as Tamlin, doesn't she?"

I nod, only because at this point I don't think I could get into more trouble than I'm already in. "Please don't tell anyone," I squeak. "I signed a whole contract thing that says I'm not allowed to talk about it."

He clenches his jaw as another realization hits him. "*Tamlin Park was in Derek Riley's house.*"

Oh, he's really angry. And I don't blame him. Still, I have to try to fix this before Darcy flies back here and strangles me for ruining her whole career. "She's not going to do anything. Derek doesn't have anything to do with sports."

"But I do!" He runs his hands through his hair and takes several steps away from me, like I might damage his career by simple proximity. "Are you her spy?"

"No!"

"Of course you'll deny it. Am I going to see something about Bean in today's news?"

"No," I say again, though I'm wilting. He's *so* mad. "I—"

"It's bad enough that you show up here with your little good girl act and distract the guys with your flirting. Now you're going to pretend you're more than just a pawn in your sister's game?"

His words feel like a slap to the face, knocking me back a step. Darcy may be better than me in pretty much every way, but she wouldn't use me like that. "I didn't flirt with the guys," I whisper, knowing he won't believe me. No one ever does.

Tears sprout in my eyes again, partly because I really don't like it when people are mad at me but mostly because this is probably the end of my time with the Thunder. Look at me go! I lasted one whole day before I messed everything up. Cole is going to warn his teammates, who will refuse to interact with me, so I'll be useless to Mel and lose my job and have to go back to Philly with my tail between my legs because what else can I do? Clearly I'm not cut out for...anything.

And after the guys welcomed me so warmly after practice yesterday, I was actually excited about working with them. I even stayed up late to learn a few things on the training side so I could do more than massage a hamstring and demonstrate some stretches. What if they thought I was flirting, just like Cole?

Why do men always take my friendliness for more? Why does it always get me into trouble?

"Are you just going to stand there and pout?" Cole asks sharply. "That might work on some guys, but I'm not—"

"You've made your point," I snap, but the tears are coming whether I want them to or not. I wrap my arms around myself, desperately wishing for someone familiar to tell me everything will be okay.

"Are you...?" Cole groans, running a hand through his hair again as his expression shifts from anger to something softer. "You're crying."

I sniffle. "I'm aware of that, thanks."

"Carissa..." He growls something under his breath, and just as he opens his mouth to say something else, a car pulls up beside us.

"Evanson?" It's Moxie, and he leans across the passenger seat to look at us. "Carissa, what's going on?"

I grab the passenger door handle and climb inside before either man can stop me. "Can I get a ride to the stadium?"

Moxie stares at me for a second before looking at Cole again, a clear question in his eyes.

Instead of offering an explanation or apology, Cole simply adjusts his bag and starts walking.

"Are..." Moxie clears his throat. "Are you okay?"

"Not really, but I'll be fine."

"What did he say to you?"

"Nothing."

"Look, I know he can be rough around the edges, but he's a good guy. If he said—"

"He didn't say anything." I sink into my seat, knowing Moxie won't believe me. Though I don't like the way he judged me, Cole has every reason to distrust me. I can't stop him from telling everyone else about Darcy, but I also can't tell Moxie why Cole definitely hates me now. I'm sure breaking my NDA more than once would make things worse, and that's the last thing I need.

There's nothing I can do now except wait.

One of these days, I could really use a win in life.

Chapter Nine

Cole

"Wanna tell me why you made our new specialist cry today?" Moxie graciously waits until the locker room clears out before he asks that one.

With the way the guys were even more obsessed with Carissa today than they were yesterday, my foot-in-mouth syndrome probably would have resulted in my execution before practice ended, so I've spent the bulk of practice in the weight room. I took my time in the shower, waiting until the locker room sounds died down, but I didn't change fast enough to avoid the captain.

I knew it was only a matter of time before Moxie confronted me.

If I told him the truth I learned today, that Carissa is Tamlin Park's sister, he would probably validate my anger. Then again, he was all chummy with Tamlin when she was here. But if he knew Tamlin wasn't Tamlin and that she's actually married to an extremely famous baseball player...

I'm still trying to wrap my head around the idea that the incredibly likable blonde woman with Carissa at Derek's house the other day is the same leggy brunette who for most of her career has ruined lives. If Darcy is so good at acting, what might her sister be like? Maybe Carissa isn't the peppy and innocent girl she's shown me so far.

"What was your take on Tamlin Park?" I ask instead of answering Moxie's question.

As he settles on the bench next to me, Moxie gives me a brow-furrowed look that clearly says he's not okay with my change in subject. "Park? She doesn't seem as predatory as I've heard, but it's not like I want to be BFFs."

I choke out a laugh as I pull on a fresh t-shirt. "You did not just say BFF."

"Stop changing the subject. What happened with Carissa?"

She's related to Tamlin. I could say that so easily. It's not like I signed an NDA, and I'm sure the world would be better off knowing the ruthless reporter is actually an alter ego. But something stops me. Darcy was...nice. Bonnie loves her, and I generally trust Bonnie's opinion. And Carissa is so convinced that Tamlin—Darcy—isn't a threat.

Maybe I should give Darcy the benefit of the doubt.

Maybe Carissa deserves that too.

She certainly doesn't deserve some of the things I said to her this afternoon. I haven't been able to stop thinking about what came out of my mouth in my anger and fear, especially because Moxie showed up before I could apologize.

"I was a jerk," I say after a long moment of silence.

Moxie snickers. "You? No!"

"I don't appreciate the sarcasm, Auxier. I know I've been...gruff lately."

That just gets another laugh out of him. "We're downplaying everything? Okay. Carissa seemed *upset* this morning."

He's in rare form today, and I wonder if it's because of my tension with Carissa or because practice didn't go well today. This is the third day in a row that Coach failed to show up, and at this point it's a gamble if he'll be at Saturday's game. What is he being paid for? Moxie is doing most of the coaching anyway, so we might as well use that money on the guy who deserves it.

Sighing, I stuff my sweat-soaked clothes into my bag and drop onto the bench. "I offered her a ride, but I'm not in a great mood as it is, and she…" Why can't I just call her out on her tie to Tamlin? "She triggered something. It wasn't her fault."

"The guys noticed she's upset, and they've spent more time making her laugh than they have fixing our lineout issue."

I grunt. "She's going to bring nothing but trouble."

Moxie doesn't say anything for a long time, making me wonder if he agrees with me or if he's trying to find a way to counter my comment. But what he ends up saying is nothing like what I expect. "She's the only reason Mel didn't quit this afternoon."

"Mel was going to quit?" Alarm pulses through me at the thought of our athletic trainer leaving us. Sure, we could hire a new one, but we're already treading water as it is, and Mel has been the best thing to ever happen to this team. She doesn't take any crap from the guys, and she has a talent for convincing stubborn men to take the small steps to avoid injuries. Without her, we probably would have lost half a dozen guys to injury before the season was halfway over.

Shrugging, Moxie gives me a grim smile that isn't at all comforting. "With all the stuff with her kid and finding childcare, she's barely managing everything. If I knew how to help her, I would."

I don't know a ton about Mel outside of her work with the team, but I do know she's had it rough since her divorce. I should probably make an effort to talk to her more, though it's not like I would be good company. "But she didn't quit?" I ask.

"Nope. Carissa talked her out of it. Honestly, I'm getting the sense that Carissa could talk *anyone* into doing or not doing something. She's weirdly persuasive."

I'm fully aware of that, which is part of the problem. She could have been lying through her teeth about her sister's intentions.

Have I always been this paranoid? Probably, though I'm going to blame some of it on being friends with Derek as long as I have. He has paranoid on lock down, no matter how much he pretends otherwise. It's not his fault, given the nature of his career, but I do think it makes it hard for him to grow close to people.

And maybe my paranoia is also... I swallow, not sure I want to let my thoughts go down this path. Sage often tiptoed around what she really thought and felt. I convinced myself that it was because she worried about how her feelings would affect others, but looking back, it's harder to justify the way she always did whatever it took to get what she wanted.

Not everyone is like Sage, but there's a part of me that will always wonder if a person is showing me how they really feel.

Moxie is watching me, waiting for a response, but I don't know what to say. I would have loved to avoid this conversation entirely. So when I say nothing, he rolls his eyes and gets to his feet so he's looking down on me. "I'm going to be your captain for a second, okay?"

"As opposed to...?"

He purses his lips. "Your friend, Cole."

Oh. "I didn't realize we were friends," I admit, though it hurts me to say it out loud. What does that say about me that I can't tell when someone considers me as more than a teammate or acquaintance?

"Annoyingly, that illustrates the point I'm about to make. You need to be better."

I already know what he means, but I ask anyway. "Better about what? I'm already the best scrum-half the Thunder has had."

"I'm only going to allow that response because you're right." He folds his arms, narrowing his eyes at me and reminding me why he's the team captain. He's an easygoing guy, but when he needs to, he can drive a point home. "I mean you need to be better with your relationships."

"I—"

"I'm not talking about your celebrity gang. The whole world knows you and Derek Riley are tight and have been for years. I'm talking about outside of that. I'm talking about the people who are supposed to rely on you but can't because they don't know you."

Why do I get the sense that I'm about to get homework from yet another person in my life? I'm lucky I didn't get some sort of direction from my dad and Gramps last night, though I'm sure one or both of them is gearing up for it.

Moxie takes a deep breath. Apparently this is going to be hard for me to hear, based on the worried look in his eyes. "Cole, if you're not careful, this breakup is going to ruin your life. You're already on thin ice."

I grit my teeth as the words 'thin ice' immediately spark life back into the line I thought I had gotten over. *This is not a hockey romance.* If it was... If it was, I wouldn't be the hero. I'd be the guy who scares the girl into the arms of the guy who deserves her.

"I don't..." A locker room isn't a great place for a heart to heart, but after the way I turned on Carissa this morning, I'm pretty sure I've hit my lowest of low. At this point, what do I have to lose? Moxie and Derek are both right about this breakup interfering with my life, and it's only gotten worse since Sage showed up here last week to give me the wedding invite.

I'm falling apart. Becoming someone I don't like.

I clear my throat. "I don't know how to get over this, Mox. It feels like she ripped my heart out of my chest and tore it to pieces, and I'm not alive anymore. I don't know how to keep going."

Whether he expected me to say something so raw, Moxie barely reacts outside of sitting next to me again, his eyes on his feet. Apparently we're friends, but I doubt he was prepared to be bombarded with honesty. I wasn't prepared to give it. I haven't even told Derek any of this stuff, so the fact that Moxie got it out of me so easily is telling.

What it tells remains to be seen.

"Okay," he says after a long spell of silence that leaves the locker room feeling spacious and cold. Two things it has never been. "I'm not going to pretend I'm an expert on matters of the heart, because I'm not."

But he's a decent guy, and I'll take any advice he might give me.

"You dated Sage for a while, yeah?"

I nod. "Almost four years."

"And you were thinking of marriage and all that, right?"

Another nod. I still have the ring. It's sitting in the back of my underwear drawer even though that's probably the least safe place I could put something so valuable. If anyone were to break into my house, that would be the first place they look. "I was waiting for a good time to propose."

"Waiting for how long?"

I turn to look at him, wondering why he wants to know something like that. "I don't know. I got the ring like a year before we broke up." Before she dumped me.

Moxie nods as if he'd expected an answer like that. "So you knew you wanted to be with her forever, but you spent a year trying to work up the courage to tell her as much. Why do you think that is?"

"Because I'm cursed." Oh. No. That's not what I wanted to say. That's not the kind of thing you say to someone and expect them to take you seriously, which is a problem because I am dead serious.

Clearing his throat, he matches my gaze with an unreadable expression and a whole lot of thoughts behind his eyes. "Cursed," he repeats.

I push to my feet and head for the door before this conversation gets any further away from me. "Forget I said anything."

But when I reach the hallway, I collide with a petite blonde who squeaks in alarm as my momentum sends her flying backward. I catch Carissa's arm—thankfully—and we stand motionless for a few seconds until I realize she's hanging at a forty-five-degree angle. Tugging her upright, I make sure she's steady before I take a step back.

"Sorry," I say, though it's more of a grunt.

Her eyebrows dip low. "What's cursed?"

I swear under my breath and fold my arms, but at least it seems like she only heard the tail end of our conversation. "Nothing. Uh." I should apologize about this morning. I know I should. But seeing her freckled nose and warm brown eyes is only reminding me that I have done nothing but distrust her since the moment she got here, and she'd be better off without me anywhere near her.

"Apparently Cole is cursed," Moxie says, coming up behind me. "Sorry, Carissa. I thought this conversation would be..." He glances at me. "...shorter. You ready?"

I'm assuming Moxie is Carissa's ride home today, which is way better than any of the other guys but still not something I like. Of anyone on the team, Malcolm Auxier is the one who would, without question, treat a woman right. Carissa might actually fall for him.

Though Carissa nods, her eyes are on me. "Why are you cursed?"

"I'm wondering that myself," Moxie adds.

There is no way on this good earth that I will explain with Carissa standing there and looking at me with so much wariness. It's one thing to confide in Moxie, a man I trust almost as much as I trust Derek. But expecting me to open up to a woman who has every reason—and resource—to make my life a living hell? That's a hard no.

I shake my head. "I'm not talking about this."

Moxie lets out a heavy sigh that speaks of nothing but disappointment, which settles over me, almost suffocating. He's my only friend on this team, and if he's ready to give up on me, it must mean I'm truly hopeless. "Need a ride, Evanson?"

I don't want to say yes, but after the way the driver this morning was eagerly listening in on my conversation, I'm getting the sense that more people are going to be paying attention to me than I'd like for the next few weeks at least. "It's out of your way."

He rolls his eyes. "So is Carissa. She lives just down the street from you."

Carissa meets my gaze, but only for a moment before she's back to looking at her scuffed sneakers. If I had to guess, she's worried I'm going to share her sister's secret and is waiting for me to drop that bomb in front of the most important person on the team. I don't know if it's her fear or my guilt that ultimately keeps my mouth shut on that subject.

"I'd love a ride," I tell Moxie. "I won't make a habit of it."

Taking hold of Carissa's bag and slinging it over his shoulder, Moxie leads the way to his car.

He doesn't say anything to me until we're halfway to my neighborhood and he says my name, pulling my attention away from my phone, which has only marginally distracted me from my thoughts. "You could, you know," he says.

I furrow my brow. "I could what?" He and Carissa have been silent up front, leaving me to read through comments on the *Hot Scoop* article that posted this morning to make sure no one has figured out who Carissa is. There is plenty of speculation, but no mention of her name.

Moxie chuckles. "Make a habit of getting a ride. Take advantage of our unusually charitable teammates who will be in proximity to your house every day." He winks at Carissa.

She blushes, and the embarrassment is endearing. Not that she needs to endear anyone to her, especially not me. It seems Moxie is well on his way to earning her affection as it is, and I'd rather not get in the middle of that if I can help it. "I really don't need everyone to go out of their way for me," she says, glancing between us. "I plan to take the bus as much as I can."

I match Moxie's wrinkled nose at the thought of someone like her taking a bus everywhere. "Those buses are disgusting."

"And you shouldn't wait at bus stops by yourself," he says.

"The area is decent," I add, "but not necessarily safe."

"Plus, the—"

"Easy, boys," Carissa says, holding up a hand and shutting us up. Her grin is wide and warm, and just like the first day I met her, that smile brightens the whole car around her. "I grew up in Philly. I may be small, but I'm a tough girl. I can handle myself."

Moxie meets my gaze in the rear view mirror, his concern obvious. She could be tough as nails, but that still wouldn't lessen either of our worries. Even if she *can* take care of herself, she shouldn't have to.

I groan as years of lectures from my dad and Gramps flash through my head. If they caught wind of me letting Carissa fend for herself, I'd never hear the end of it. I can fix this, but I don't know if she'll let me. I'll have to try.

"I have an idea. Drop us off at my place?" I say to Moxie, hoping he understands my implied meaning. He may not know my plan, but I want him to know my intentions are good.

Though he narrows his eyes for a moment, probably questioning my reasoning, he nods after a second and takes the turn into my neighborhood. When he pulls up in front of my house, Carissa doesn't move, which I expected, though I know she heard me say 'us' because she flinched.

Moxie must like me if he's willing to stick around once I'm out of the car. He could easily drive off and take Carissa to her house, but he doesn't.

I knock on the passenger window and press my lips together when Carissa only rolls it down a few inches. She has every reason to be short with me, and I don't know if she'll go for my idea, but I want to try to kill two birds with one stone. Make up for the gruffness I showed her this morning and give her a way to avoid the bus.

"You don't have to trust me," I tell her through the space in the open window. "But do you trust Moxie?"

She looks at him. I can't see her expression, but his smile is warm and friendly. Too friendly, maybe. When she turns back to me, there's enough curiosity in her eyes to know I've taken a step in the right direction.

"I want to help you," I tell her. "But to do that, I need you to get out of the car. I promise I'll get you home safely."

After one more glance at Moxie, who says something too soft for me to hear, Carissa pushes the door open so quickly that I have to jump out of the way. "I don't like this," she says as she tucks her purse over her shoulder. "Mostly because I can't decide if I should like *you*."

That gets a smile out of me, however brief. "It's probably better if you don't like me," I mumble. I salute Moxie, who gives me a warning look before driving off. Honestly, I half expected him to hang around, just in case, and his trust in me soothes a small part of my aching soul. If such an excellent judge of character can see good in me, maybe I'm not all bad.

"Come inside for a sec," I say, gesturing toward my front door.

Carissa scratches her chin as her eyes dart between me and the house. "Nothing weird or bad is going to happen to me, right?"

I roll my eyes. "I wouldn't tell you if it were. But no."

Apparently that's enough to get her to trust me, and she leads the way up the stepping stone pathway to the porch.

I hope I'm doing the right thing.

Chapter Ten

Carissa

I don't know why Cole wanted me to come with him, but I'm leaning into Moxie's insistence that he can only have good intentions. Then again, there's that saying about the road to Hell being paved with good intentions, and Darcy has always told me I am too trusting. Am I about to be murdered by a surly rugby player who may or may not be cursed?

What kind of curse are we talking about anyway? I've been desperate to ask more about that little bit of conversation I accidentally overheard, but Cole clearly didn't want to talk about it.

It feels like the kind of thing he *should* talk about, but so far Cole hasn't been much of a talker. He's certainly not talking now as he unlocks his front door and steps inside the house, sliding his shoes off onto a mat in the entryway. He moves to the side to give me space to follow him in, and I stop dead.

I don't know what I would have expected an ex-football player's house to look like, but it wouldn't have been this. Given his friendship with the likes of movie stars and an actual princess, I probably would have imagined a sterile, oversized mansion if I'd had the chance to imagine in the first place. But this is...

"Darling," I breathe, my eyes jumping around to take it all in. The front room is smaller than I expected and tells me that the house must have been built several decades ago, though everything looks updated and cared for. The floors are a polished dark wood, the walls a buttery yellow, and plants are everywhere. His hodgepodge furnishings all somehow match despite being various colors and styles, and there's a noticeable lack of a TV, which is not something I would have expected from a sports guy. And every wall is peppered with paintings, none of them matching in technique or subject.

I can feel Cole's eyes on me, but I'm pretty sure my face is the color of a tomato based on the heat blazing beneath my skin, so I keep my head turned away from him.

"I have to be honest with you," I tell him. "This is not what I expected."

He chuckles, the sound a deep rumble in his chest. "What did you expect?"

"Not this."

"You expected something like Derek's house."

I look at him now, if only because he sounds like he's trying not to laugh. His expression holds no humor, but I can almost see it in his eyes, hiding behind the armor he wears.

There's a chance I looked up more articles about him while Mel and I were watching the guys practice today, and if I can believe half of what the internet says about Cole Evanson, he has good reasons for being a little grumpy. He got dumped last fall, and the internet decided to air all his dirty laundry, consistently calling back to the fact that he lost the Super Bowl right before he quit football and took up rugby. Add in the fact that his girlfriend is engaged to one of his old teammates, and I'd be gruff too!

"I guess..." I tilt my head, still trying to see more of that amusement that I heard in his voice just now. "I guess I don't know you enough to know what to expect with you." Especially because I don't think he said anything about Darcy.

Throughout all of practice, I kept waiting for the guys to start confronting me about my relation to someone they have every reason to be wary of, but they were all just as friendly as they were yesterday. Maybe even more so. Cole was in the weight room for pretty much all of practice, like he was actively avoiding his teammates.

Cole purses his lips and glances into the kitchen behind him. "Thirsty?"

"No, I'm curious." But I scrunch up my face as I get a sudden awareness of my dry throat. "Actually, yeah, I am thirsty."

Nodding once, Cole slips into the kitchen, and I follow him as he pulls a glass pitcher from the fridge, which looks just as retro as the rest of his house with its avocado-green doors and rounded edges. He pours what looks like lemonade into two glasses and holds one out to me.

"I'm sorry," I say, taking the glass, "but did we go back in time at some point?"

Cole chuckles as he returns the pitcher to the fridge. "I'm well aware my tastes are far from modern."

That's putting it lightly, and the aesthetic is nowhere near what I expected with a guy like him. Taking a sip of the lemonade, I'm about to tell him how much I like his tastes when the sourness of real lemon hits my tongue. I choke as I inhale a drop of my drink in my surprise, but thankfully I cough it out quickly.

Cole grimaces. "Is it bad?"

"It's delicious!" To prove it, I chug half the glass, then regret my choice when I think about how much I could have savored the flavor. I don't even remember the last time I had real lemonade. "Did you make it?"

He shrugs.

"Cole, this might be the best lemonade I've ever had." Now I'm wondering if he can make anything else, or if this lemonade is a one hit wonder. Based on the appliances sitting on the kitchen counter—the KitchenAid mixer is *not* retro—I get the feeling he spends a decent amount of time in this kitchen.

A man who can cook? If he wasn't so gruff, I'd probably be falling hard and fast for this guy.

The lemonade suddenly tastes bitter as that thought rolls over me. It's a good thing Cole is as sour as the lemons he used because I can't afford to fall for any of my patients. Not even the cute ones like Cole.

Especially not the cute ones.

"So," I say, tracing the condensation that has already formed on the outside of my glass. "I'm assuming the reason you brought me here isn't to cater to my sweet tooth."

Though Cole isn't the most expressive of people, I can still see his expression fall. For a moment, we sort of bonded over the lemonade, but I just brought the tension back.

"Right," he says, rinsing his cup before putting it in the dishwasher. *Be still my soul.* He's clean too. He does the same with my cup and then grabs a keychain from a hook on the wall. He pulls open a door on the other end of the kitchen, reaching around in the darkness for something, and a second later a garage door opens and fills the space with the golden light of sunset.

Curious, I step closer and peer past him to find a shiny, deep blue car sitting prettily in the garage. "You have a car? Why don't you drive it?" But I wince as soon as the words are out of my mouth. There are plenty of reasons why a person does not or cannot drive, and I don't want to come across as judgy. "I didn't mean—"

"I get severe anxiety when I drive." Cole speaks so quietly that I almost don't hear him. "I *can* drive. And I do. Sometimes. But only when I have to." His lips press together as he meets my gaze. I can practically feel his discomfort as he adds, "I don't generally tell people that."

"So why did you tell me?" I'm whispering like he is. I don't know if it's because I don't want him to stop telling me things or because I'm standing with my back against the doorframe mirroring him, so we're standing just a few inches apart. Maybe it's because my heart is aching for him. There's enough emotion in his words that I would guess there's a reason he gets anxiety when he drives. One that will make me feel a connection to him I probably shouldn't feel.

This is my problem. As soon as people open up to me, I get attached. What is it about vulnerability that is so compelling?

Cole swallows, his eyes dropping to the keychain in his hand. "I don't know." He shakes his head. "You are dangerous, Carissa Paxton."

This moment feels safe, a strange thing when Cole Evanson is involved, which probably explains the question that shoots out of my mouth. "Why didn't you tell Moxie about Darcy?"

He looks up again, cocking his head to one side. "What makes you think I didn't?"

I cock my head to match him. "Why, Cole?"

"Because it's not my secret to tell."

That surprises me more than he would probably like, but after the way he reacted to finding out about Darcy's alter-ego, I was so sure he would tell as many people as he could. "Thank you."

"You have a license, right?"

The question catches me off guard. "To practice PT in California? Of course." When he lifts a dark eyebrow, my eyes drop to the keychain in his hand. "Oh wait, did you mean to drive?"

Cole snorts. "No, to kill," he drawls. "Obviously I mean to drive, though I'm glad to know you're licensed for your job."

Was he actually wondering if I'm allowed to work in this state? I might have made some mistakes with my last job, but I'm not stupid enough to risk liability. But I choose to ignore that and focus on his actual question. "Yeah, I have a driver's license. Why?"

He stuffs the keychain into my hand, and I look down to see the keys for the fancy car next to us. I don't recognize the brand, which probably means it's expensive.

"Cole?" I say the word breathlessly as I try to understand what's happening right now. "Are you giving me a car?"

He barks out a laugh and moves out of the doorway to open the driver's side door of the car. Instead of getting in, he holds it open and gestures inside. "Of course not. But I'm letting you borrow it for a while if you agree to take me to practice every day." He says it so matter-of-factly, like he's not letting a virtual stranger use his very nice, very expensive car.

"But you don't know if I'm a good driver."

He lifts that eyebrow again, and I can't help but study his face as he waits for me to move from the doorway. Something has changed between this morning and now, and I don't know what it is. But he looks different. "Are you a good driver?"

Part of me wants to tell him no, but I'm rather proud of my perfect record. "I'm a great driver."

"Then what's the issue?"

I step forward if only to not feel like I have to shout at him. The problem is this is a single-car garage, so there are not a lot of places for me to go without standing directly in front of him, with the open car right next to me. It smells like a new car, and I can't help but take a deep breath of the smell of leather. Moxie's car is nice but smells a bit like gym socks, and Bean's car was...a little terrifying. Coming closer was a bad idea because now that I have a clear view of the pristine interior, my resolve is crumbling by the second.

I badly want to say yes to his offer, no matter how ridiculous it is.

"Cole," I say, forcing my eyes to him. His house faces west, which means the sinking sun is glowing directly behind him and making it difficult to see his expression. "I can't take your car."

He folds his big arms, which feels a bit like a cheap trick, given the sheer amount of muscle on him. I'm a sucker for a strong and functional muscle group. "Why not?"

"Because you don't even know me. What if I steal it?"

"You won't."

"How do you know?"

"I don't."

"I can't take your car, Cole."

Instead of continuing what feels like would be a never ending argument between us, Cole leans closer. Closer. *Closer* until I shrink away from him and run into the car, losing my balance. His hand tucks behind my head to prevent me from hitting it against the frame, but he does nothing else to stop my fall onto the driver seat. "Great," he says, bending down and picking up my feet to stuff them inside. He shuts the door before I can react.

And at this point, I already know I'm not going to be able to say no. Not only does the car smell *so good*, but it's *so pretty* inside. And insanely comfortable. And it's one of the fancy ones that doesn't even need a key because I just push a button and it rumbles to life beneath my touch.

I'm stroking the steering wheel when Cole slides into the passenger seat and gives me a smirk. "You're taking the car," he says. Not a question.

I sigh. "Fine. But you'll tell me if you ever need it?"

"I won't need it."

"But in case you do, you should have my number." I hold out my hand for his phone, ignoring the thrill that runs through me when he places it in my palm without hesitation. The sun is on his face now, illuminating his dark eyes so I can see the flecks of caramel in the brown, and everything about him looks so much warmer than it has so far.

There's *definitely* something different about him, but I still can't quite place what it is.

Clearing my throat, I force my focus to the phone and add my contact info, complete with a selfie that I take because the lighting is fantastic right now. "I'll have you know," I say as I hand it back to him, "I told the rest of the guys on the team that they couldn't have my number."

Cole's eyebrows shoot up, though his gaze is on the phone in his hand. On my picture. "Why?"

"Because I believe in boundaries. And I don't date people at work." *Never again*, I silently add.

"Why?" he asks again, this time while looking at me.

I don't want to admit the truth, but he told me something so personal when he explained why he doesn't drive. I owe him something personal in return. My heart kicks up into an uneven rhythm as I curl my fingers around the steering wheel and speak to my lap, my throat growing tight. "Because the last time I did that," I say, my voice strained, "it didn't end well for me."

Dang it, I wasn't supposed to start crying!

I sniff and reach for the gear shift, as if I can drive away from the wounds that are still raw and ragged.

But Cole wraps his hand over mine, and with his other hand he pushes the start button and turns the car off again. "I've already told you I'm a good listener," he says, his voice impossibly gentle, "but you should also know that I wasn't raised to let a woman cry if I can do something about it. Can I make you dinner?"

Is he serious? Based on the concerned look in his eyes, I think he is. I nod slowly. "I was planning on popping in a TV dinner and watching *Bridgerton* on my phone until I fell asleep in the hopes of keeping my mind off the fact that I'm three thousand miles away from home and don't know anyone in this city. But your idea sounds better."

He wrinkles his nose. "*Bridgerton*?"

"Don't knock it until you've tried it."

"I *have* tried it." He slips out of the car and opens my door before I can figure out where the handle is. "My ex was a fan. Me, not so much."

I nearly say 'Your ex sounds like my kind of gal' but stop myself at the last minute because that's probably not the sort of thing he wants to hear. "Too much lovey dovey nonsense?" I guess, taking his hand and letting him help me up.

Cole looks like he's chewing on his words as we stand there for a moment, still hand in hand. He seems to be debating the merits of answering my question. "I don't mind romance," he says after a moment, and his words come out gruff. "Aspects of it, anyway. Sage, my ex, loved reading those hockey books that are popular, but I've always thought they were..." He coughs and drops my hand. "Problematic is the nicest way to put it."

Snickering, I bite my lip and try to imagine someone like Cole reading a hockey romance. "Did she like the spicy ones or the strictly kissing ones?" Huh. Apparently big burly guys can blush, and that answers my question. "The spicy ones? While I can't say I generally read those ones, I hear they're fun."

"They're something," Cole agrees and leads the way back into the kitchen. "Are you sure you want to stay for dinner? I don't want to pressure you into—"

"I was serious when I said I was going to use questionably histori-cal television to soothe my loneliness," I say, settling myself down on one of the kitchen chairs. I'm immensely grateful for the distraction this conversation is offering. "And I haven't had a chance to do much grocery shopping. Plus, you've already caught my interest in your cooking skills with your lemonade, so I was probably going to beg you to cook for me at some point anyway."

He grunts and starts rummaging around in the pantry next to the fridge. "Lemonade isn't cooking, so you might be putting too much faith in my skills. I'm not Derek."

It takes me a second to process that, but when I do, my jaw drops. "Wait, are you saying Derek Riley can *cook*? I thought he would have people for that."

"He does have people for that, but he only uses them when he has to. Did you ever see the movie *Food for Thoughtless*?"

I shrug. "Hasn't everyone seen that movie? But just because Derek played a chef, it doesn't mean he *is* a chef."

Cole is nearly smiling when he emerges from the pantry with a box of pasta in his hand, and the sight of him is breathtaking. Which is a problem. I've already broken my rule about not giving out my phone number, which is dangerous enough. I don't need to start making plans to get another smile out of the man. There's no way I wouldn't get attached.

"Not many people know this about Derek," he says casually, like we're not talking about one of the most famous people in the country, "but he never does something on screen that he can't do in real life. He worked undercover in a restaurant for three months before he started filming *Thoughtless*."

I may have spent an afternoon with Derek and found him to be as stunningly handsome in real life as he is in the movies, but I refuse to think he can actually play the piano or shoot a bow and arrow with perfect accuracy. "There's no way. He probably told you he can do all those things to make himself look better."

The laughter that comes out of Cole makes me jump, not because it's loud or sudden but because I honestly wasn't sure if he knew how to laugh. In the time I've known him, he's been so stoic and has only given me a single real smile. Granted, I haven't spent all that much time around him, but his teammates have had plenty to say about their total grump of a scrum-half. They've said he rarely showed emotion, even before he got dumped. Then again, maybe I shouldn't listen to guys who are unafraid of expressing how much they don't like their rookie teammate.

"I've known Derek Riley for eight years," Cole says as he fills a pot with water, "which means I knew him before he knew how to cook. I'm the one who taught him to surf. He took guitar lessons from Liam, who more than once declared Derek a hopeless cause because he was so bad at it starting out." Pausing, he frowns and cocks his head. "Maybe don't tell your sister any of that."

I grin. "I promise Darcy has no reason to besmirch any names. She prefers telling uplifting stories anyway, and the main reason she came to the field as Tamlin was because she helped me get the job with the Thunder."

Though he moves to the fridge, he stops with his hand on the handle and looks back at me. "Can I ask you something?"

Shrugging, I brace myself for whatever it might be. If he has to ask about asking, that means I probably won't like it. "Sure."

"Why come all the way to Los Angeles when you don't know anyone here?"

Yep. I don't like it. But the man is making me dinner, so I force a smile and get to my feet. "Can I answer that later? I promise I'll tell you, but I'm going to have to work up to it."

He waits until I approach him and am only a foot away, and he studies me as if hoping to find the answer to his question on my face. "You don't have to tell me anything, Carissa."

There's no unspoken 'but' in his sentence, which I appreciate, but I can see it in his eyes. He's curious, and that curiosity probably isn't going to go away if we start carpooling. And since I don't especially want to take the bus again, that carpooling thing will for sure be happening.

I won't be able to avoid the question for very long, so I might as well get it over with. "I want to tell you," I say quietly. "But first, how can I help with dinner?"

CHAPTER ELEVEN

COLE

I DON'T KNOW WHAT happened. I started the day angry with Carissa and distrusting everything about her, and by the time we finish the simple meal we made—grilled chicken, fettuccine, and steamed asparagus—she feels almost like a friend. A friend whose smiles hit me square in the chest with terrifying precision every time she unleashes them, which is often.

After the way I treated her, I don't deserve those smiles, but I have a feeling I'm going to treasure them because they won't last. I can't let them last.

Still, I can already tell they're an addiction I may not be able to shake.

We talked mostly about movies over the last hour and a half, particularly the ones Bonnie and Derek have been in, and that kept our conversation light and impersonal because the topic doesn't involve either of us. But she promised she would tell me why she came to Los Angeles, and while I don't want to push her into sharing, I'm desperate to know what happened to her. If it takes this long for her to work up the courage to talk about it, it must be big.

With cleanup done, we're standing in my kitchen, an awkward silence filling the air between us. Against the curiosity pulsing through me, I nod toward the car keys that she left on the table next to her purse. "I meant it when I said you can borrow the car."

Her lips twist up. "I know. And I'm grateful."

I hope that means she'll take me up on my offer. Not only will I feel better about her ability to get around safely, but it'll mean I don't have to get stared at by rideshare drivers who recognize me in their backseats. Some have even tried to pull me into conversation before, something that will be more of a problem now that *Hollywood Hot Scoop* has turned their attention to me again, and it gets annoyingly tedious to ignore people while trapped in a car with them. I'd much rather spend the drive with Carissa.

Which is a strange feeling. It's been a long time since I wanted to be around someone.

I clear my throat, desperately searching for a way to nudge our conversation back to where it was before I started cooking. "Would..." How am I so bad at this? There's an easy answer to that. I haven't been on a first date in literally years. But this isn't a date, so it shouldn't matter. I take a deep breath. "Would you like to sit on the back porch for a bit? My yard isn't all that big, but it's nice in the evenings."

It's nice in the evenings? I sound like an eighty-year-old woman.

Thankfully, Carissa smiles and nods. "I'd like that. It's too early for me to go to bed, and I don't especially want to cry tonight."

Does that mean she won't tell me what happened?

She must see my question on my face because she shrugs with a small laugh. "At least not by myself. I've never been away from home before, so this is..."

"Hard," I finish for her, and she nods. "I know the feeling. When I got drafted by the Badgers, it was the first time I wasn't within easy driving distance of my dad and Gramps. I hated it."

A sound comes out of Carissa's mouth that reminds me of the way women coo at puppies and kittens. I don't love it.

"I was going for solidarity," I grumble, "not pity."

That gets her laughing, which is just as endearing as her smiles and makes me wonder if inviting her to stay longer was a bad idea. I'm starting to like her company more than I should, and that can't end well. "Sorry," she says despite sounding anything but. "I just didn't think a big guy like you would get homesick."

"I happen to really like my dad and Gramps." Gesturing with my head for her to follow, I lead the way down the hallway and out the back door.

I meant it when I said my yard was small, and aside from a few trees and flower patches, it's nothing but the small porch that holds a couple of chairs and a glider bench. We sit on the bench, which squeaks when it rocks under our weight. I should probably fix that, but it's not like I spend much time back here. If I'm not at my dad's, I'm with Derek or Liam.

I forgot how peaceful it can be back here.

"It's darling out here," Carissa says once she's settled, a solid few inches of space between us. It's the same word she used when she first walked inside my house, and I can't decide if it's good or bad. She obviously likes my house, but that doesn't mean she likes *me* or thinks I fit my space. Sage always thought my house was too quaint for someone of my status, and it was an arguing point on the rare occasions she came down to California. She never understood how much I desperately needed something familiar when everything else in my life was changing. I didn't plan to settle here permanently, but she never believed me when I told her that.

Huh. It's funny how easy it is to see the red flags in a person when you're looking backward.

"Okay," Carissa says before I can respond to her opinion about my yard. "I said I would tell you about my rule and why I'm here." She twists and curls one leg up so she's facing me. "And I know this is going to sound hypocritical of me, but first I need you to promise that you won't tell anyone what I'm about to tell you."

Intrigued, I nod. But I also say, "Technically there's no hypocrisy. Just you sharing things you're not supposed to share."

As pink blossoms across her cheeks, she rolls her eyes at me. "The Darcy/Tamlin thing wasn't mine to share, but this thing is. I don't want you to tell anyone because it's mortifying."

The urge to reach out and take hold of her hand comes on so suddenly that my fingers lift off my lap before I stop myself. I hate the idea of someone as sweet and bubbly as Carissa being so embarrassed, but we're definitely not at a point in our friendship where I can try to offer comfort. I don't even know if we're friends.

I vaguely wonder if becoming friends with Carissa fulfills Freya's expectation because Carissa is technically part of the team, but I push that thought aside and smile. "I'm better at keeping secrets than you'd think. I won't tell anyone." I tilt my head, too curious not to ask. "Do you believe me?"

She tilts her own head to match, just like she did earlier, and I can't help but smile at the way she's so easy to like. I was an idiot before now. "Is it weird if I say yes?"

"Probably."

"Well, I do believe you."

"Stranger things have happened."

"Are we friends, Cole?"

The question settles warm in my chest, no matter how out of the blue it feels. The fact that she's wondering the same thing I was makes this all easier to stomach. I don't trust easily anymore, but I want to trust her. "Do you want to be my friend?" I ask.

She nods. "Even though you were mean to me."

"I was awful." Admitting as much hurts, but I think I've been doing okay tonight. I've been trying, anyway. "I'm sorry."

Carissa smiles. "So we're friends?"

"Yes."

"In that case." She heaves a deep sigh and then says everything all at once, in a single breath. "I fell in love with one of my patients and only found out he was married when our relationship became a scandal on local television because he was running for governor and someone took a picture of us on a date."

Well there's a sucker punch to the gut. I can't find words to say so I sit here and gape at her like a fish, which is not the kind of reaction I'm sure she was hoping for. Only one rough word makes it out of my throat. "Oh."

She ducks her head, letting her blonde curls fall around her face. "Yeah. It was kind of awful. He wanted our relationship to be a secret, and I thought it was because he was my patient, you know? That was bad enough. But then I found out about his wife and kids, and..." She presses her face into her hands. "I was such an idiot."

This time, I can't stop myself from reaching for her. I take a wrist in each hand, pulling her arms toward me until her face is free and she looks up with tear-filled eyes. "The only idiot in that situation was him." My voice comes out more growly than I would like, but I can't help it. Whoever this guy is, he needs a firm punch to the face. I hope his wife plans to leave him and find someone better.

Sniffling, Carissa looks down at my hands circling her tiny wrists. "I shouldn't have fallen for him in the first—"

"Hey. Don't do that to yourself. You didn't do anything wrong." But I frown as I think about everything else she's told me. "Is that why you're here? Why you left your physical therapist job?"

She nods. "They fired me because I was a liability and an embarrassment. And no one else in the state would hire me because Peter's campaign team pushed all the blame on me. I'm lucky it wasn't a big enough story to spread out of Pennsylvania."

A curse slips out of me when I remember the *Hot Scoop* article that dropped this morning. If anyone figures out who Carissa is, they're going to dig. And whoever runs that stupid website is good at doing their homework. If there was any news coverage about the scandal, *Hot Scoop* will find it.

I need to make sure they don't have a reason to dig.

"Forget what I said." The words are out of my mouth before I can stop them, and I drop her hands, rising to my feet and putting as much distance between us as I can without stepping off the deck into the bushes. "I don't need a ride."

"But—"

"Just use the car, and I'll get myself to practice."

"Cole, what—"

"I'm not going to argue with you!" I snap, then flinch when I catch sight of her tears. *Oops.*

She sniffles and swipes a finger across her cheek. "Okay."

I swear again, hating how easily I slipped back into the guy who makes her cry. I need to explain, but I don't know if I can do it well enough for her to understand. "I don't want my mess to become your mess and make everything worse for you," I say as gently as I can. "If anyone sees you with me like they did yesterday, your past is going to catch up to you really fast." *And the people who dig it up will be ruthless.* Grimacing, I shake my head at her. "You don't want to be associated with me, Carissa. You don't want to be my friend."

"What if I do?"

"You don't."

"Why not?"

"Because I'm cursed." I swear once more and clench my jaw. But I suppose, after that bombshell she dropped on me, it's only fair that I do the same. She was honest with me, so I'll be honest with her.

Even if I hate it.

I take a deep breath, holding it in my lungs and refusing to meet her teary gaze. "I'm cursed, Carissa. Anyone who gets close to the men in my family, they... It doesn't end well." That's not quite true, so I shake my head and stand up, hoping the distance makes it easier to explain. "I don't mean anyone. I mean...I mean anyone who gets *close* to me. Anyone I let into my heart. The people I love. The...the *women* I love."

Okay, wow, that sounds like I'm telling Carissa I love her so she should stay away from me, and that's the furthest thing from the truth. Yes, I feel a budding connection to her, but I don't know her. A few hours in each other's company, during most of which I was antagonistic, hardly counts as time to get to know someone.

She's still staring at me in silence, so I shake my head again. "I'm not explaining this well."

"No," she agrees.

"My great-great-grandma was trampled by a horse when my great-grandpa was ten." I wince at the horrified look in Carissa's eyes but keep talking. "Great-grandma died of smallpox only a few years into being married. My grandma got cancer only a year after my dad was born, and my mom..." I stumble over my words. "She died giving birth to me. My..." I clench my hands into fists, hating how hard it is to talk about this after so many years. "My high school girlfriend? Car accident when I was driving us back from Senior Prom. She was in a coma for two months before she finally woke up."

Carissa gasps, wiping tears from her cheek with her palm. "That's why you don't drive."

I nod, trying to swallow the lump that has lodged itself in my throat. "The crash wasn't my fault, but I still feel responsible. If she hadn't been with *me*... And then—" I stop talking before I mention Sage, who got stuck in an elevator not long after we started dating. One of the lines snapped and trapped her in between floors for a few hours. She laughed it off as coincidence and refused to break up with me, even though it had only been a few months since she first asked me out and I was adamant that she would be better off without me.

Her determination was endearing and the main reason I let myself think maybe she'd be okay if we stayed together.

I shrug. "Cursed."

Slowly getting to her feet, Carissa approaches me like she would a wounded animal. With caution. "That's not a real thing," she says, which is exactly what I expected her to say. "Besides, we can still be friends."

I shake my head. "We're friends *now*. But what if..." The fact that I'm even considering the possibility of something more than friendship should be sending me into a mental breakdown when only a few hours ago I told Moxie that my heart was irreparably broken. What has this woman done to me? She's like some goddess putting me under her spell and making me believe things might get better.

I stuff a hand into my hair. I need to change the subject before she reads too much into things. "I can't believe I just told you all of that."

Her laugh, though small, warms the space between us. "This is probably going to make me sound vain or conceited, but people tend to tell me things they wouldn't normally tell a stranger. Like, all the time. I must have one of those faces."

"It's more than that." Though, I have no idea what I mean. There's something about her that makes me want to get close to her, and I can't blame the team for tripping over each other to get to her. She's magnetic. A couple of hours of having her in my house, and I don't want her to leave. Folding my arms, I think back to today and how Moxie said the team paid more attention to Carissa than they did to their job.

Something tells me it's only going to get worse the more they get to know her.

Taking a small step back to give me some air to breathe that doesn't include her sweet scent—a lightly floral smell that reminds me of my dad's backyard in the early spring—I try to keep my voice calm and steady as I say, "So you want to avoid dating any of the people you work with, right?"

Her eyebrows dip down; I don't blame her for being confused about my choice of topic. "Yeah."

I twist my mouth to one side. "They're not going to make it easy on you."

"They never do."

Yeah, I can imagine most men fall in love with her as soon as they speak to her. I wasn't willing to admit it, but even I was drawn to her that first day we met. If I had been in a better mood, I might have acknowledged it then.

I'm man enough to admit it now. "I don't blame them. You're..." I grimace and take another step back.

She tilts her head. "I'm what?"

"Special. And I'm not willing to risk your safety, no matter how much I want to know you better."

"Cole, you're not cursed."

"It doesn't matter." Mostly because she's wrong. "I'd rather be up front with you now than risk something later." That probably makes me sound like a jerk again, but it's the truth. My high school girlfriend got lucky, and it's a miracle nothing worse ever happened to Sage during the time we were together. "I won't be asking you out, Carissa."

Thankfully, she smiles as her eyes trace my face. "I like your honesty, Cole. And even if you did ask me out, I would say no."

"Good."

"Good." With her smile still intact, she looks around my yard for a moment, then lets her breath out in a heavy exhale. "I should go."

I don't want her to go, but it's for the best. We can be friends, but that's all we'll be, so I don't want to let myself get too attached. "You'll take the car?" I ask.

The question prompts a giggle. "*Yes*, Cole. I'll take the car. You and Moxie can stop worrying about me."

"Not likely," I grumble and follow her back into the house and out to my Audi.

I stand in the open garage and watch her drive away until I can't see the taillights anymore. My idea to let her borrow the car that has sat idle for too long was desperate at best, a scramble to keep her safe, but I can't be mad that it gave me this chance to get to know her better. My first impression of Carissa was so wrong, and I've never been happier to be corrected.

But now that the red of the brake lights has faded, leaving the neighborhood in the soft darkness of twilight, I press a hand to my chest and note the way I feel less hollow than I did this morning.

I feel more alive.

And that's going to be a problem.

CHAPTER TWELVE

CARISSA

Coach Galvin is different from how I expected him to be. When Darcy first told me about the job, she said the coach was an even-keeled man with a knack for strategy, and he came to the Thunder after coaching the Irish national team for several years, which supposedly means he's good at what he does.

Today I've been mostly focused on Mel as she teaches me the most common way to tape players' limbs for stability or support, but I've also spent a decent amount of time watching the coach direct his team.

And by "direct" I mean "shout at." Profusely. I've learned some highly creative insults and curses over the last couple of hours.

"I've seen half-dead grannies run faster than you!" Coach yells when Bean gets hold of the ball and darts through the defense. Honestly, as far as I can tell, Bean is the fastest guy on the team and just now outran three different guys before he got stopped. "Have you been lying around all week, Henderson? Taking it easy when you think the boss isn't looking?"

It's the first time I've seen Bean look anything but confident. He tosses the ball aside to reset the play as the coach keeps tearing into him. I'm pretty sure he's trying not to let the insults get to him, but he's failing. Even from several yards down the field, I can see the pain on his face.

"Is the coach always this harsh?" I ask Mel.

She looks up from the new roll of tape she was unwrapping and wrinkles her nose. "He didn't used to be. He was a good coach at first."

"What changed?"

She shrugs. "We lost the last two seasons? I don't know. But he's in an especially bad mood today."

After the next play, Bean gets the ball again but is tackled almost immediately. It takes him a while to get up, and when he does, he's limping. Coach shouts at him again and points to us before turning his furious attention to the rest of the guys.

For someone who's injured, Bean reaches us surprisingly quickly and flops onto the grass in a heap.

"Are you good to take this one?" Mel asks. "I need to check on Raiden." When I nod, she hops to her feet and heads to her office to check her phone, leaving me alone with Bean.

I grab the tape, determined to do the best job I can so I can avoid any shouting directed at me. Mel introduced me to the coach before practice started, and he only spoke with me long enough to confirm I'm the person the owners hired. And that was enough interaction for me.

"Where's the pain?" I ask Bean.

"Hmm?" He was watching the drills the team started running, but he looks back at me and shrugs. "Oh. Uh. Here." He points vaguely at his shin.

I purse my lips. So much for proving myself. Did he really fake an injury to avoid getting yelled at some more? "He's wrong, you know."

Bean grits his teeth, eyes on his legs. "About what?"

"You're insanely fast."

Scoffing, he runs a hand through his sweaty hair and shakes his head. "Apparently I'm not."

"I'm pretty sure you can run circles around the rest of the team." I glance up and realize the coach is watching us. Face heating, I shift so I'm facing Bean and start wrapping his leg, not caring if he's not actually hurt. "Don't listen to him."

"Did you know he played on six different champion teams?" Bean watches me work, a deep furrow in his brow. "Everyone says he's brilliant, and maybe he is, but I wouldn't know because the only thing he's taught me is how pathetic I am."

"You're not pathetic, Bean." I pause, waiting for him to meet my gaze. I can't have a serious conversation with him while calling him Bean. "What's your actual name?"

That gets a smile out of him, which helps me relax a bit. Maybe he's not too downtrodden. "Wyatt."

Smiling, I return to my taping as I talk. "Wyatt, if your coach doesn't respect you and the effort you put in, nothing he says against you is worth your time. You know you're fast, and you know how much your team relies on you."

Wyatt grabs my hand, stopping my movement. "Thanks, Rizzo. You're right. Um..." He swallows. "I know I was a jerk for shouting at you the other day, but maybe you and I could—"

"How does that feel?" I tug my hand free, knowing my face is bright red right now. I stand up, hoping that conveys how much I don't want him to finish his sentence. I knew this would happen eventually, that one of the guys would finally work up the courage to ask me out, but I hoped it would take longer.

I'm terrible at saying no, and already the guilt of turning him down is building in my stomach and leaving me queasy. And he hasn't even asked me yet!

Wyatt stands as well and tries to wiggle his foot, with little success. He gives me a sheepish smile. "Uh, you probably need more practice. I'm happy to be your dummy. We could grab dinner and bring it to my place so you can—"

"Oh, um." Gah, this would be so much easier if he wasn't such a nice and friendly guy! "I don't think that's a good idea, Wyatt."

His expression falls. "Oh."

Sweet merciful heavens, he looks like a kicked puppy, and my resolve is slipping. "We work together, Wyatt, and that's a boundary I can't afford to cross." But maybe I could do it this once. It would be work. I can make sure he knows that, and there won't be any harm in getting to know him better, right? Especially after that verbal beating he got today, he probably needs a win. "Maybe—"

"Paxton!" The sharp call of my name makes me jump.

I peer around Wyatt's shoulder to see Cole jogging toward us. Most of his expression is neutral, but his eyebrows are pulled low. "Yes?" I squeak. I can't decide if I'm grateful for his interruption or annoyed. We didn't talk much this afternoon after I picked him up to come to practice, so it's hard to know what kind of mood he's in today.

Cole glances at Wyatt, who clenches his jaw, before turning his attention back to me. "What happened to Mel?"

"She went to check her phone."

"I was hoping she could help with my knee. It's feeling loose today."

"Oh." With the tape still in my hand, I hold it up and shrug. "I could help. Apparently I need the practice."

Cole glances down at Wyatt's obstructed ankle and suppresses a chuckle. "Clearly. Bean, you probably won't want to stay away from Coach for too long and give him more reasons to shout at you." He claps

Wyatt on the shoulder and gives him a raised eyebrow look that instantly sours Wyatt's mood.

Grumbling something under his breath, Wyatt tears a couple strips of tape from his skin and heads back into the fray, leaving me alone with Cole.

I narrow my eyes at him. "You didn't have to do that."

Chuckling, he folds his arms, which has the effect of making him look bigger than he already is. Yes, I trauma-dumped on him last night, but that doesn't give him the right to butt into my affairs. I've already used him more than a good friend should by borrowing his car, and I don't know how to feel about him stepping in to save me from attention.

"For your information," he says, "I was serious about wanting Mel's help. But I may have delayed coming over here until I noticed you were uncomfortable."

"I wasn't..." I stop when he raises an eyebrow at me. Apparently he's really expressive with those eyebrows when he chooses to be anything other than stoic. "Okay, so maybe I didn't know how to let him down easy."

"All you have to do is say no."

"That's easy for you to say!" Crouching down, I slap the end of the tape onto the side of Cole's thigh and pull it down to his shin on the opposite side, doing the same in the other direction to make an X below his knee. It takes a lot of concentration to avoid letting my fingers stray over his muscles. This man's legs are huge. "How's that? And I can't not worry about hurting someone's feelings, so rejecting him feels cruel."

Cole tests his step and nods. "That's great, actually. Not the cruelty part. My knee. Bean's feelings will be fine, and you have every right to say no when this is your job."

"His name is Wyatt." I don't know why I'm advocating for him, but whatever.

Cole smirks at me. "I know his name, Carissa."

"Then why don't you use it?"

"I'll call him Wyatt when he stops calling me Rihanna."

I almost forgot that's what they call Cole; they rarely talk to him anyway. "Where did your nickname come from?"

"Coal under pressure becomes a diamond."

I frown. "I get that, but what does that have to do with Rihanna?"

"It's one of her songs."

"Ah."

"And they think I'm a diva because I was used to wearing padding when I got tackled." There's a shout behind him, and he glances back, nodding at someone. "I should get back out there." He puts a hand on my shoulder. "Just say no. Unless you honestly want to say yes, that's all you need to do." With another smirk, he jogs back onto the field.

I don't know what it is, but there's something about him that feels...lighter? It's as much in his facial expressions, so much looser and less reserved, as it is in his body language. He was so stiff before, even last night, but today he's moving with more fluidity in his steps.

It's great for his flexibility and for preventing injuries, but as I watch him laugh at something Moxie says to him, I wonder if this change is benefiting him in other ways too.

And I wonder what made the change in the first place and if it has anything to do with me.

"Well that was interesting." Mel pops up at my side out of nowhere, making me jump.

Breathless, I press a hand over my heart and ask, "What?"

"Cole."

"What about him?"

She purses her lips, looking at me in the same way my mom used to look at me when she thought I was lying about something. I almost *never* lie, but I have the worst poker face in the history of ever, which means sometimes people think I'm lying when I'm not. "Did something happen between you two?"

Aside from him being raw and real and making me a simple but delicious dinner and giving me a space to feel safe enough to admit what happened with Peter and letting me borrow his car because I don't have one? "No, of course not," I say. "I barely know him."

And while that's true, I know more than I ever thought I would. I may not know his favorite foods or why he started playing rugby or how he became friends with a movie star, but I know he has a lot of trauma that he hides from people and thinks he can't let himself be happy and loved because of some crazy family history.

I pick him out of the mass of men on the field and watch the way he is so focused as the players gather to throw the ball into play from the sideline. One of these days I'm going to need to learn the rules of this game, but it's fun to watch regardless. Tink throws the ball at the same time several players lift French Roast straight into the air to catch it. French Roast tosses it to Cole before touching the ground, and Cole throws it immediately to Moxie behind him, who makes a run for it but tosses the ball to the side to another player—Sharkie—who bolts forward but is tackled only a few feet later.

Cole is right there in the mess of men, grabbing the ball and doing it all over again. Every time a player goes down, he's there to keep the ball moving.

Why don't any of his teammates like him? Even I know he's good at what he does, and I don't have a clue how the game works.

Mel clears her throat, pulling my attention back to her. "I'm just noticing a shift," she says.

I'm going to be spending a lot of time with this woman, so I sigh and lift my shoulders in an exaggerated shrug. "I guess we became friends last night. *Just* friends," I add when her eyebrows fly high. "He's letting me use his car so I can get to work every day."

"Interesting."

I want to ask what is so interesting about it, but at the same time I don't. I already know Cole's relationship with his teammates is strained, and he doesn't need me gossiping about him. The tabloids do that enough.

I Googled his name again last night after I drove to my apartment, both to revisit that article with me in it and to see more of what people say about Cole Evanson the rugby player. Honestly, they don't talk about his game much. Most of the stories are about his ex getting married soon or tedious blathering about his friendships. I came across a few older stories that speculated about Cole's reasons for leaving football, and I quickly moved away from those.

I know Darcy would love to get the scoop on why Cole switched to rugby, but I don't want to betray anyone's trust the way I accidentally did hers. Her secret is safe for now, but I won't do anything to risk that. Cole's secrets have to be safe too.

Especially when he looks over at me every once in a while and gives me a quick smile. Whatever has changed in him, I want to make sure it stays.

For the rest of practice, Mel walks me through what will happen at the game tomorrow, and I'm glad for the distraction. If I watch the beautiful men on the team for too long, my heart starts to get wild ideas. Mostly about a specific beautiful man. The game will involve a lot more potential for injury than practice does, so I force myself to pay attention to my job.

Difficult though it may be.

CHAPTER THIRTEEN

COLE

"Evanson! A word." Coach waves me forward as the rest of the guys shuffle toward the locker room at the end of practice.

I consider pretending I didn't hear him, but I know that's a bad idea. Still, I don't like the way the team starts grumbling about special treatment as they pass me. Internally groaning, I reluctantly follow Coach to the edge of the pitch, wincing when he puts an arm around my shoulders.

I felt like I was making some headway with the team today. We were meshing better than usual, and some of the guys even joked around with me in between drills. But Coach treating me like his best buddy isn't going to win me any favors. They already think I bought my way onto the team.

"You're looking great out there, Evanson." Coach speaks louder than he needs to, which garners some glances back from those still within hearing distance. Bean is one of those, glaring at me despite Moxie talking to him as they walk. "Better than ever, I'd say."

"Today was a good day," I mutter. And it was. For the first time in a long time, I didn't have a cloud hanging over me and making everything fuzzy and muted. It makes no sense, considering I lay awake for a long time last night while my thoughts battled for dominance. Half of me wants to keep building this friendship with Carissa, while the other half wants to stay as far from her as I can get. Neither half is taking the lead. I should be exhausted, but I'm not.

With his arm still around me, Coach leans in close. Too close for my comfort. "I've been thinking, son." I wish he wouldn't call me that, but at least we're alone on the pitch now. "What this team really needs is someone who can lay down the law. Someone who isn't afraid to make enemies."

I have no idea what he's talking about. "Sir?"

"This team needs a captain who won't coddle his wings when they're falling behind."

A curse slips off my tongue. Is he saying he wants to replace Moxie as captain? "Auxier is the best captain in the league."

"Maybe." He rubs his chin, squinting up at the sky. "But what if *you* could be better?"

Swearing again, this time far louder than I should, I slip out from under his arm, shaking my head with vehemence. He wants *me*? "Sir, with all due respect, I can't—"

"Don't be modest, son. I know how well you led the Badgers in your heyday. Any quarterback that can get his team to the Super Bowl can lead a bunch of idiots on a rugby pitch."

Does he have any idea how stupid he sounds? This is *his* team. And none of these players are idiots. We may not be top of the league right now, but we have more wins than we do losses and have been getting better all season. Thanks to *Moxie*. If he puts *anyone* in Moxie's place, this team will crumble.

Putting me in there will be a disaster.

"Sir, my objection isn't about my own skills." I choose my words carefully, knowing things could get worse if I get on Coach's bad side. "The team respects Auxier in a way they'll never respect me."

"That's because you haven't *taken* their respect, Evanson."

I clench my hands into fists. "I'm not—"

"Think about it. This could mean big things for you in the rugby world, and I know you're not the type to pass on an opportunity. Just say the word, and you'll have the power."

"I don't want—"

"I'm glad we understand each other." Clapping his hand to my back, he heads for his office without a glance back.

As soon as he's gone, I let out a yell and kick a ball someone left on the pitch. It flies toward the other end of the pitch in a smooth arc, almost better than any kick I've done intentionally. I can't be impressed with myself because my anger keeps building with nowhere for it to go.

There are so many things wrong with Coach's mindset. I meant it when I said Moxie is the best captain out there. He keeps a cool head, gets along with everyone, and isn't afraid to step in when his teammate is wallowing over a girl who dumped him months ago. And that says nothing about his playing. He could easily be playing for a national team anywhere in the world, but he likes to keep his life small.

But if Coach took him out as captain? I don't know what that would do to him. Moxie *loves* this team.

Growling, I wish I had another ball to kick because I can't go to the locker room and look Moxie in the eye. But I also can't stand here and hope my frustration wanes on its own.

Today was going so well. Carissa picked me up right on time and spent the drive singing along to one of Liam's songs on the radio. The whole team was looking sharp on drills, and our practice plays were the best we've ever done.

Why did Coach have to decide to show up and ruin everything?

Carissa finds me pacing the try zone near the tunnel, her bag slung over her shoulder and a wariness in her eyes that pulls me to a stop immediately. "Are you okay?" she asks.

I want to tell her what Coach told me. I need someone else to know why I'm so agitated. But I can't tell her. I can't let anyone know what might happen. "I'm fine."

"You can tell me—"

"This is something that needs to stay a secret." I wince as soon as the words leave my mouth. The hurt from my comment is clear as day in her eyes. "Carissa, I—"

"I get it. I talk too much, and I've already spilled one big secret, so there's no reason for you to trust me."

I swear under my breath, glancing toward the tunnel to make sure none of the guys are heading out yet. The last thing I need is them thinking I've hurt their new favorite person, even if it's true. "I trust you," I say, my voice strained.

Carissa purses her lips. "But not enough."

I need to get my phone. But doing that requires entering the locker room, and I'm sure Moxie will be waiting for me now that I've delayed hitting the showers. How can Coach think about replacing him? With *me*? Moxie actually cares about the guys on his team, beyond the pitch, and I...

I'm too good at putting distance between me and everyone I interact with. It's a defense mechanism, but not for me. For them. The closer people get to me, the more danger they're in.

"I don't need a ride today," I say, shifting so there's more space between Carissa and me. "You're welcome to head out."

She doesn't move. "Cole, you were fine twenty minutes ago. What happened? Did the coach say something to you?"

The fact that she was paying enough attention to me to know I was in a good mood, *and* to know Coach pulled me aside, does something to my insides. I'm so used to the team ignoring me that it feels strange to get positive attention from someone who isn't one of my close friends or my family. My resolve slips.

"I'll tell you," I say, clenching my hands into fists. My words mirror hers from last night. "But not here."

"Where?"

"Can you get my things for me?" I could probably leave my stuff, but it's my phone that I can't bring myself to leave behind. Something tells me I'm going to need Freya's pragmatism, and it gets harder and harder to find time to video chat with her the closer she gets to her election to become queen. I need to be able to text her.

Glancing back toward the tunnel, Carissa lifts her eyebrows. "From the locker room?"

I curse under my breath. That's a terrible idea. "Never mind." I'll send Freya an email.

"No, I don't mind." Carissa hands me her bag, but I grab her elbow.

"*I* mind." Some of the guys don't bother with things like towels half the time, and there's no way I'm letting someone like Carissa subject herself to sights no one should have to see.

Carissa giggles, her nose wrinkling adorably. "What if I close my eyes?"

"Let's just go."

"No, now I'm curious." And she slips free of my hold before I can stop her, jogging to the tunnel and disappearing.

"Curious?" I repeat in horror. If not for the overwhelming fear that I'll run into Moxie and let slip Coach's ridiculous idea, I'd chase after her and physically bar her from entering the locker room. Instead, I stand in the evening sun, silently praying that the guys have an ounce of modesty when in the presence of a lady.

By the time Carissa returns with my duffel weighing her down, I've run my hands through my hair so many times that it's probably sticking straight up, but I don't care. "You don't look traumatized," I say, maybe too hopefully. I grab my bag before it pulls her off balance. I don't remember what's in here, but she's far too small to have carried it all the way out here.

"You make it look like it weighs nothing!" she says, ignoring my comment.

I'm going to push the issue. "Please tell me everyone was fully dressed."

"Are all rugby players made of pure muscle like you?"

"Carissa."

She snickers, but crimson lights up her cheeks. "They covered up as soon as I walked in. But you also have to remember that I'm up close in people's business regularly, so I'm not really fazed by the human body."

"I'm not worried about the human body. I'm worried about *men's* bodies. Those ones, specifically." It shouldn't bother me this much. Carissa can look at whatever she wants, and if she says a naked man doesn't faze her, then... My stomach twists. It still bothers me.

This had better not be jealousy.

"We should go before one of them takes your nonchalance as an invitation," I grumble and start heading for my car.

Carissa laughs as she follows me, and I hate how much the sound improves my mood. Jealousy and enjoying her laugh are two things that are going to make a friendship difficult. "For the record," she says, "I didn't see anything because I wasn't looking. The only person I talked to was Moxie."

I stop so suddenly that she runs into me. "You didn't tell him anything, did you?" I ask, turning to face her.

"Like what?" She rubs her arm, probably where she collided with my bag.

If Moxie knows I'm in a bad mood after talking to the coach, he's going to ask why. I roll my shoulders as discomfort builds inside me. "I don't know. Anything."

"I just asked him which locker was yours. Does your bad mood have something to do with Mox—"

Without thinking, I press a hand over her mouth and pull her in close by the strap of her bag. "Not here," I repeat, only my words have no *oomph* because her eyes have gone wide. Looking at them up close, I marvel at the gold ring around them and the way the rich brown is broken up by threads of the same gold. Like little lightning strikes running through the irises.

They're kind of beautiful. More than kind of.

My hand slowly slips from her mouth, but instead of stepping away, I lean in closer, mesmerized by the soft pink of her parted lips. What if...

"Cole, is this your new girlfriend?"

Crap. Crap crap *crap*! I step back, but the damage is already done as the paparazzo who spoke snaps several photos from his car window. He shouts more questions, but I grab Carissa's hand and tug her forward, ignoring the way she stumbles behind me. We have to get out of here.

As soon as Carissa gets close enough to the car for it to unlock, I shove my bag into the backseat and slide into the driver's seat. Carissa's past is going to be dredged up, her privacy dropping to zero. The guy likely got a clear shot of her face. That, and the fact that she's here at the stadium and wearing a Los Angeles Thunder polo, is plenty for someone to figure out her name and her connection to the team.

With a stream of swears on my tongue, I impatiently wait for Carissa to get settled in the passenger seat, and when she fumbles with her seatbelt, I grab it and buckle it for her.

"Cole, maybe I should—"

I throw the car into reverse and back out of the spot too quickly, but I'm desperate to get out of the parking lot before the pap can follow. I have a good route planned out to my house in case I ever need to make a hasty retreat—a trick I learned from Derek—but I don't know if it will make a difference. The photographer is already on my heels.

Does he plan on following me home?

"I should never have become your friend." I grip the wheel tight as I speed from the lot. "I should have let you leave on your own. I shouldn't have touched you."

"Cole."

I hit the call button on the steering wheel and tell the Bluetooth to call Ethan.

"Who is Ethan?" Carissa asks as the speakers start ringing with the call.

"A publicist." I don't work with him personally, but Derek, Bonnie, and Liam all do. If anyone will have good advice, he will.

"Cole?" Ethan's voice is full of concern. Probably because I only call him when there's trouble. "What's going on?"

"I need to hire you." I take a turn too quickly and swear under my breath when Carissa grips the door handle. I force my foot to lift off the gas a fraction and check the rear view mirror to make sure no one is behind us. With enough turns, I should be able to lose the paparazzo entirely. But I won't relax until I know he's gone for sure.

Ethan's quiet for a minute. "Okay. What's up?"

"I did something I shouldn't have."

"That sounds ominous."

"It's not…" I growl as I reluctantly stop at a light. Now that we're not moving, the anxiety is starting to creep in, but I do my best to ignore it. "I just got photographed."

"Doing what?"

Technically nothing, but with how close Carissa and I were and the angle at which the pap was watching us, I'm sure it looked like I was doing a lot more than I was. I take a deep breath, and when the light turns green, I gun it. "We have a new rehab specialist on the team. Carissa." I glance at her, and she stares back at me, her face full of fear. I don't know if it's from the paparazzo or from my driving. Probably both. I force myself to slow a little more, my fingers tight on the wheel. "She's already been on *Hot Scoop* once."

"The blonde?"

Carissa squeaks.

"Uh, she's here with me by the way."

"Hi." Ethan waits a moment. "What did you do, Cole?"

"Nothing. But…"

"They think I'm his new girlfriend," Carissa says. "I'm not, by the way."

"Why do they think that?"

"Because it's *Hot Scoop*," I snap, taking another sharp turn. "And I might have been close to her."

"Close," Ethan repeats, and I glance at Carissa. "Cole, you're going to have to give me more than that if I'm going to know what needs to be done here. What happened?"

I came dangerously close to kissing her.

I see the stop sign too late and slam on the brakes. The car skids to a halt at an angle and partway into the intersection right as a huge pickup passes in the other direction and swerves around us.

I nearly drove right into it.

My heart rate skyrockets, flooding my body with panic and dizziness. My mouth goes dry, my vision hazy. Fumbling for the door, I stumble out just in time to vomit onto the road and sink to one knee as my chest constricts, painfully tight.

"Cole!" Carissa's voice is muffled. Like she's speaking from above while I'm at the bottom of a pool. "Cole, are you okay?" Hands press on my shoulders, hot and uncomfortable.

I shake my head, wishing I could shake away her touch too. "Give...give me a sec." I'm going to need more than a second. I could have killed her. I'm such an idiot. *I could have killed her.*

"Cole, you need to get out of the road." She tries to lift me.

I'm an immovable rock, frozen in place as my mind rushes back to prom night. The Jeep that ran a red light. The shards of glass and metal that flew from the passenger side. I still have the scars. My girlfriend ended up far worse.

Why am I not over this by now? I've had *years* of therapy. Bianca never blamed me. *It wasn't my fault.* And I know that.

Today would have been my fault. *My fault.* I'm too dangerous for anyone to get close to me. *Too dangerous to love.* I could have killed her.

"Cole." Carissa crouches in front of me and plants her palms on my cheeks, forcing me to look at her. "Please. Stand up. I'll take you anywhere you want to go. Please."

The heat of the asphalt burns into the skin of my knee, but I barely feel it. I'm too focused on the heat of Carissa's gaze. Her fear is gone. Now there's nothing but determination and strength in her lightning-studded eyes.

She's the most beautiful person I've ever seen.

Dangerous. And I could have killed her.

"Please," she says again.

The tension in my body crumbles. Exhaling weakly, I nod and struggle to my feet. I'm pretty sure she helps me stand, which is ridiculous because she's tiny. But as she guides me around to the passenger seat, holding some of my weight, I realize she's stronger than she looks.

I collapse into the seat and bury my face in my hands, willing myself to breathe. To calm down. My heart is still racing, trying to beat out of my chest.

Carissa doesn't say anything as she moves the car out of the intersection and drives a block or so, pulling onto a side street and parking along the sidewalk. By some miracle, we remain alone, but I know better than to think that will last. Someone will have noticed me in the street.

"I'm sorry." The words come out of me in a breath because that's all I have the strength for. My chest is too tight to let me breathe.

"It's okay, Cole."

"No." Though I'd love to keep hiding, I turn to look at her. She still has that strong look in her eyes, and now I can't look away. "It's not okay. I should never have... I put you in danger." *I* did that. Not a curse. *Me.* "This is why we can't...why I won't... I'm sorry. I'm so sorry."

Her fingers adjust their hold around the steering wheel, fair and slender. Everything about her build suggests she's delicate, but there's not even a tremor in her hands. Whatever fear she had while I was driving like a maniac, it faded quickly. "I told Ethan we would call him back. He sounded pretty worried about you."

"Later," I beg. It was bad enough that Carissa just saw me at my low, and I don't need Ethan mentioning anything to my friends. I know he would.

The display lights up with a call from Derek, and I curse under my breath. Ethan must have already said something to him. I can only imagine the kind of things Derek might say with the limited information Ethan could have given him. He'll infer the panic attack and make a bigger deal out of it than he needs to.

"Should I answer it?" Carissa asks, her hand hovering over the button. Her eyes are fixed on me.

I swallow, still fighting to take full breaths. I'm starting to notice the bitter taste in my mouth, but reaching for my water bottle in the backseat sounds too daunting. "I don't know." I love the guy, but I don't think I have the energy for Derek either.

The call ends, and only a few seconds later it lights up again with Freya's name.

I sigh, some of my lingering tension releasing with my exhale. "Sometimes I hate my friends," I grumble, then nod even though I'm not sure I can have a conversation right now.

Carissa hits the button, and the car fills with Freya's strong voice. "Coleman Evanson, what in the world is happening?"

"I'm fine."

Carissa meets my eyes again, and her lips twitch with a smile before she mouths, *Coleman?*

I narrow my eyes, managing a full breath. *Finally.* Now, if I could just get my heart to stop racing...

"You do not sound fine," Freya argues. "I heard—"

"Whatever Derek told you, he doesn't know anything." Stupid voice tremor. I sound awful, and I drop my head against the seat in exhaustion.

"Where are you? Derek will come so you are not alone."

I scoff, shaking my head, but this conversation is working well to get me to finally relax. Or maybe it's the way Carissa is biting her lip to keep from smiling, locking my attention on her. I wonder how soft that lip is. I swallow, forcing my focus away from Carissa's mouth. That's what got me into this mess in the first place. "I'm not alone, Peach." I sound stronger now.

"Oh?"

"Hi again, Your Highness," Carissa says, waving at the display even though there's nothing there but the radio.

I crack a weak smile, grateful for the distraction. "You don't have to call her that," I whisper.

"But she's a princess!" Carissa whispers back.

"Yeah, but—"

"What happened? Derek is worried." Freya's voice has dropped into a gentler tone, which I appreciate. When she gets worked up, she can get impressively loud. "And so am I. You have been struggling."

Carissa's smile slips.

I sigh. "I told you. I'm fine. Carissa and I had a run in with a pap."

"I do not like it when you call them that," Freya complains. "It sounds like my appointment with my women's physician."

Women's physician? Carissa mouths.

I laugh weakly and shake my head. "Peach, you really need to work on sounding more human."

"I am royalty, Evanson. I will speak how I speak."

"Okay."

"What did the photographer witness?"

I meet Carissa's gaze, for the first time wondering what her perspective on the moment is. Did she think I was going to kiss her? Because I'm not sure if I would have actually done it.

But I wanted to.

When she remains silent and mostly unreadable outside of a slight blush of color in her cheeks, I say, "I'm sure he thinks he came across an intimate moment."

Freya gasps. "*Did* he come across an intimate moment? Are the two of you—"

"Of course not." I wince, realizing how that sounds. "Carissa and I are friends."

"You did not think of her as a friend a few days ago. She was your enemy."

"That was a few days ago." And oh, how wrong I was. Carissa is my...well, *friend* doesn't feel like the right word. I don't know if any of my friends could have gotten me away from that panic attack so quickly.

Carissa skipped the friend stage and jumped right into seeing the deepest parts of me. It's like she has latched on to my soul, and her hold on me was strong enough to pull me out of the panic.

Dangerous.

"Hmm." Freya is quiet for a long time, and though I planned to text her, I can't wait for this conversation to end.

"Peach, I promise I'm okay," I say, surprised that it's actually true. I'm exhausted, but I'm...okay.

"And I won't leave him until I'm sure he'll continue to be okay," Carissa says.

I'm even more surprised by that, enough so that I gape at her. I've brought her nothing but trouble, and yet there's no sign of deception in her words. She really does want to make sure I'm okay. I can't help but smile at her as I reach back and grab a water bottle from my bag. She never does what I expect, in the best ways, and I'm starting to realize how much I like the way she surprises me.

When Freya speaks again, a hint of emotion softens her words. "Thank you, Carissa. Cole does not often trust people, but I am glad he has come to trust you. The man needs more women in his life."

I choke on my water, spewing it all over the dash and coughing uncontrollably as my lungs try to expel what I just inhaled. "Freya!" I gasp.

"What?" she replies. "You do."

"I really don't."

"Because you are cursed, yes?" Thank goodness I already told Carissa about the family curse, though I still don't like the way it sounds when someone else talks about it. "Cole, you are too intelligent to truly believe in something like fate. Loving a woman will not lead to her death. Carissa, has he told you his ridiculous notions?"

I'm not sure I want to hear what Carissa has to say.

Pressing her lips together, Carissa seems to debate how she wants to answer. "He told me about his family history," she says.

Huh. I don't mind that answer.

"Hmm." Freya pauses again, then lets out a deep sigh. "There is more I could say on the subject, but I should go. My bodyguard has realized I am awake and is concerned."

I swear when I realize what time it is. "Peach, it's four in the morning there!"

"I am aware."

"Why are you awake?"

"Because I was worried about you, Cole. And you should control your language, especially in the presence of a lady."

"I don't mind," Carissa says at the same time I grumble, "I know." We look at each other, smiles playing on both our lips.

"Thanks for calling, Freya," I say. "It means a lot."

"I need you to take better care of yourself, Cole. Please."

Though I roll my eyes, I appreciate how much she worries about me. "Promise."

As the call ends, silence fills the space around Carissa and me. I usually crave quiet moments like this, but not after all that's happened since practice ended.

It's been a lot.

I clear my throat. "So."

Carissa smiles. "So. Your friends really do look out for each other, don't they?"

I nod right before I catch a hint of wistfulness in her words. Jealousy. But I have no idea if she's jealous of my friends or something else. Just in case, I say, "Freya has been like a big sister to me ever since we met several years ago. She can be overprotective, but I love her."

To my delight—or maybe concern—Carissa's smile brightens. "You have a princess for a sister, huh?"

"Don't tell my Gramps. I think he's secretly in love with her and wants her to become my new grandma."

Carissa snorts and covers her mouth. "How old is your grandpa?"

"Forty-five years older than Freya, give or take, though you'd never guess it. He has the energy of a man half his age, which is probably what fuels his delusion."

"He sounds great."

"Do you…" I stop myself before the rest of the sentence comes out. I can't ask that! It would be doing exactly what I shouldn't do.

But Carissa tilts her head, a question in her eyes. "Do I what?"

I'm too tired to pretend I don't want her to come with me. At this point, I might as well let Carissa see the whole of my life now that she's seen the ugliest parts. If my curse or my anxiety haven't scared her off, maybe nothing will. It feels selfish to hope she'll want to be my friend even with the threat of tabloids looming over us—I should probably call Ethan before it gets too late—but it's been a while since I had to deal with anything too prying. It would be nice to have someone else going through it with me.

"Do you want to meet him? My Gramps?" I gesture to the street ahead of us. "He and my dad live just around the corner."

I'm already regretting this, but Carissa eagerly shifts the car into gear again and asks me where to go.

I guess I'm bringing a woman home to meet my family for the first time in…ever.

Chapter Fourteen

Carissa

This is a bad idea. I know it's a bad idea, but as I pull into the driveway of a house that's at least double the size of Cole's, I'm practically brimming with excitement. After everything I witnessed over the last twenty minutes, the chance to see where Cole came from is one I don't think I could pass up. There's so much more to this man than what I first saw, and everything I learn about him makes me like him that much more.

That's exactly why this is a bad idea, but I've never been good with self-control.

"So I should probably tell you some things," Cole says, shifting in his seat to face me.

I raise my eyebrows. "What things?"

He grimaces and glances at the house. "I've, uh, never brought anyone home. A woman, I mean. Outside of my friends."

A thrill runs through me at the thought that I'm special enough for him to invite me into this part of my life, but I tamp it down. "We are friends, Cole."

"They're not going to think so."

"What about your ex? You guys dated for like four years."

He cocks his head, a bit of a smile tugging at his mouth. "Have you been reading up on me?"

I shrug, trying for nonchalance, but I can't fight the grin that spreads across my face. "I might have. I was curious."

"Curious like you were when you walked into a locker room full of naked men?"

Heat flashes across my face. "Okay, when I said that, it was more in reference to what the guys would do. Not because I wanted to see anything." And thank goodness I didn't. While I'm no stranger to human anatomy—thank you, college classes—I have no desire to see more of the Thunder than I already do. I'm an admirer of the human form, but not to that extent.

Cole chuckles. "Whatever you say. And no, Sage never met my family. She rarely came to California, and when she did, she only ever wanted to spend time alone with me. Even my friends barely interacted with her."

I wrinkle my nose. "And you never saw any red flags there?"

"Ouch." Thankfully, he doesn't seem too offended. His expression is more curious than anything.

"I'm just saying." I hold my hands up in defense. "If you dated for that long and she never wanted to meet the man who raised you, maybe you should have questioned things." And maybe I'm being too harsh, considering I'm the woman who didn't question it when her boyfriend wanted to keep their relationship a secret from *everyone*.

"Huh." Cole scratches his chin. "Maybe you're right."

"I'm always right. That's definitely not true. But I'm right about this."

He laughs again, and I'm so glad that he has relaxed after his panic attack. I should never have let him get behind the wheel in the first place, but now I know he wasn't kidding when he said he gets severe anxiety while driving.

"Anyway," he says, "because you are a beautiful, single woman, my family are unequivocally going to think we're dating. And nothing I say will convince them otherwise."

Beautiful. Telling myself to ignore that, I purse my lips as we both look at the house. It's well maintained and surrounded by greenery, which feels out of place in LA but instantly makes me feel more at home than I have since coming to California. "What if I tell them there's no chance I'll ever be your girlfriend?" I ask, though the pit that forms in my stomach makes me wonder if I really mean that.

Cole shrugs. "They will try to talk you out of it. They don't know we're here, so if you don't want to deal with a couple of old men telling you how gallant and handsome I am, I'm more than happy to have you take me home."

"Not a chance. What else do I need to know?"

Cole's smile warms the whole car, and I feel like I might combust. Hot dang, that's a smile, and it might be the first full smile I've seen from him. It's even better than the one he gave me at Derek's house earlier this week.

That feels like ages ago.

"Gramps has apparently taken up kickboxing," he says, still grinning. "And Dad will at some point wax long and poetic about my mom."

"That's adorable," I say on a breath. "The mom part, not the kick-boxing part. Though I think your grandpa doing kickboxing might be adorable too."

"Nothing about Gramps is adorable." Cole takes a deep breath as if gearing himself up for the next item on his list. "Both of them believe in the family curse as much as I do, no matter how many times they deny it, so it's probably better if we avoid that topic tonight."

The curse. I agree with Freya when she said Cole is too smart to believe in something like that, but I saw the look in Cole's eyes after we nearly crashed today. Real or not, the curse has him terrified of emotional intimacy. He's so afraid that if he gets too close to someone, she's going to die, which is why he never lets himself truly love anyone.

I gasp as a realization forms in my head. "Is that why you and Sage never got engaged?"

Cole's thick eyebrows drop down. "What?"

Okay, yeah, I can't blame him for being confused because he wasn't following my thought process. I grab his hand as if the physical connection might let him see into my head. "Your curse. You were with Sage for so long but never got engaged. Because you didn't want her to die!"

He opens his mouth. Closes it. Opens it again. All the while staring at me with his dark eyes. They're such a dark brown that when the sun isn't shining on them, they look almost black. But they're not black because when they're in the sun they're the color of the chocolate caramel sauce I was obsessed with at the ice cream parlor near my house in Philly.

Man, I miss that sauce.

"I don't..." Cole frowns and looks down at our hands. "Maybe. Or maybe I saw all the red flags but refused to admit it to myself."

"Mel and Moxie think she broke your heart."

"She did." But he presses his lips together, like he's trying to understand something. His thumb brushes over the skin of my hand, rough but at the same time soft. His hand is so much bigger than mine, swallowing up my fingers. I'd bet if he pulled me into a hug, it would feel the same but on a full-body scale. That sounds incredibly nice. "But maybe it's not as broken as I thought," he murmurs.

What in the world is *that* supposed to mean?

A knock on Cole's window makes us both jump and pull apart. An older man stands in the driveway, a wide smile stretching across his handsome face. His hair is peppered with gray, his skin lined with wrinkles, but I can't decide if it's Cole's dad or grandpa because there's so much life to him. For sure he's one or the other because he looks so much like Cole.

Sighing, Cole pushes the door open. "Gramps."

Dang, Gramps looks good for a seventy-five-year-old.

"Who is this little miss?" Gramps bends down to look past Cole and get a good look at me.

I smile, suddenly nervous. "Um, hi. I'm Carissa."

"You're Carissa."

"Yes."

"This is Carissa." He says that to Cole.

Cole rolls his eyes. "Yes. Can I get out?"

"But—"

Shoving his shoulder into his grandpa, Cole knocks the man straight into the bushes to make room for himself. I nearly shout in protest, but Gramps bursts into laughter.

"Is that how you tackle on the rugby pitch, Lemon? You need to spend more time at practice, I think."

"You want to see a real tackle, old man?" Cole ducks down, arms out wide.

I scramble to get out of the car. "Cole, don't—"

But Gramps solidly punches Cole in the gut and crows in triumph as Cole goes down, crumpling into a ball on the cement. "I'm telling you, Lemon," Gramps says, looking down at him. "You're losing your touch in your old age."

I have so many questions, most of which must be on my face because Gramps starts laughing as he comes over to my side. "Please tell me you're not dating him for his muscle, Miss Carissa."

"She's not dating me at all," Cole groans from the ground. He struggles up to his feet, still hunched in on himself. But there's a smirk on his face as he narrows his eyes at his grandpa. "Was that all you've got?"

Gramps moves to hit him again, and Cole flinches away.

"If you two are going to fight," another voice says from the front door, "do it in the backyard before you take out my begonias." Cole's dad. Outside of his lighter coloring, he looks just like his son, and he's got the stern dad look dialed in as he peers down from the landing several steps above us. My dad had to use that look on Darcy and me all the time when we were growing up.

But I've never seen someone use it on their *parent* before.

"He started it," Gramps says, pointing at Cole.

"And I'll finish it," Cole replies and lunges forward, knocking Gramps into the closed garage door with a bang.

"That's enough of that!" I say, slipping between them before Gramps can retaliate. I put a hand on each of their chests and glare. "You're both big strong men. I get it."

Cole's dad whistles low. "And who are you?" he asks.

"This is Carissa," Gramps says.

"You're Carissa?" Cole's dad replies.

"I'm Carissa," I say, trying not to laugh.

"I think we've all established that this is Carissa," Cole says with exasperation. But then he smiles at me, and I feel every ounce of his happiness like I just got struck by lightning.

Wow.

"Are you going to bring Carissa inside?" his dad asks.

Cole coughs and glances down at my hand, still pressed to his firm chest. He hesitates for a moment before he grabs hold of it. "Right. Yes. Um, Carissa, this is my Gramps, Whit."

"Call me Gramps," Gramps says, shaking my other hand with vigor. "It is lovely to meet you, Carissa."

How many times can a person's name be said in one conversation before it starts to sound wrong? I think we're pushing the limit.

"And my dad," Cole says, nodding up the stairs. "August."

August nods. "Carissa." There's laughter in his voice, and it makes me want to laugh along with him even if I don't understand the joke.

"That's enough of that," Cole says and gently tugs me to the stairs. "Ignore them," he tells me as we climb. "No matter what they say."

I won't be doing anything of the sort. I'm about to get an insider look into Cole Evanson, and I will be soaking in as many details as I possibly can. He already looks lighter than he ever has before now, like this is the one place he can fully relax, and I'm desperate for more of that megawatt smile of his.

If the internet knew Cole had a smile like that, he would likely replace Derek as the sexiest man alive.

August's house is much like Cole's when it comes to aesthetics, though it feels more modern and less mismatched. I love all the warm woods and colors and the way it feels so much like a *home*. Derek's house was great and all, but I would never feel entirely comfortable there. As I take in the open layout of the Evanson abode, I'm instantly at ease.

"Like it?" August asks, folding his arms as I meet his gaze in the entryway. He has a very easy nature, as evidenced by the soft smile on his face, and though he doesn't have his son's bulk, I can tell he keeps himself fit and healthy, just like Gramps obviously does.

I match his smile with my own. "It's beautiful."

"It's Cole's."

"*Dad*," Cole grumbles.

August laughs as I turn to face the man at my side. "This is your house?" I ask Cole. "What about the one in my neighborhood?"

"That's mine," Gramps says behind us. "Built it myself in the eighties."

"Then why—"

"My son thought Gramps and I needed the space more than he did and practically forced us to move here," August says, shaking his head at Cole like he thinks he's an idiot.

Clearly uncomfortable, Cole rubs the back of his neck with his free hand; he's still holding mine with the other. "I didn't force you to do anything."

"Are you hungry?" Gramps asks me. "I've got some pulled pork sandwiches I could heat up. Unless you're one of those vegans."

I can't help but laugh at the way he's eyeing me like I might be extraterrestrial. "What's wrong with being vegan?"

"Absolutely nothing." His tone says otherwise.

"Well, I'm not, and that sounds delicious."

"You don't have to stay," Cole tells me with a squeeze of my hand. "You can go whenever you'd like, and I'll catch a ride later."

I study him for a moment, trying to figure out if he wants me to stay or if he'd be happier if I made my excuses and left. Though he isn't smiling right now, his dark, magnetic eyes seem to be saying a lot.

I hope I'm reading him right when I say, "I'll stay as long as you do."

Something sparks to life in his expression and fills me with warmth.

"Well," Gramps says, clapping his hands and heading into the kitchen. "Lemon, your girlfriend is delightful."

"Not my girlfriend," Cole says at the same time I ask, "Lemon?"

"Short for Coleman," August says with a shrug. "Sort of."

Cole slips his hand free from mine, filling me with disappointment that I shouldn't feel, but then he presses it to the small of my back as he leans in close and murmurs, "I should probably call Ethan. Will you be okay?"

August smacks his shoulder. "What are you insinuating, kid?"

Cole rolls his eyes. "That you and Gramps are menaces to society and should never be left alone with a pretty woman."

"Like that Julia Roberts movie?" Gramps asks from the kitchen.

I would laugh if I wasn't floating from Cole's compliment. He's already called me beautiful, but it feels different when he's saying it to someone else and not me alone. It feels more real.

"I can handle myself," I say when Cole looks at me, waiting for an answer to his question. His hand is still pressed to my back, which has me overheating.

Nodding, he pulls out his phone and disappears deeper into the house, the warmth of his touch lingering.

The instant Cole is gone, August shuffles me into the kitchen and directs me to a stool at the counter where Gramps is assembling sandwiches. "Tell us everything," he says as Gramps leans in.

I blink. "Everything about what?"

"You and Cole!" Gramps says, like it should be obvious. "When did you start dating?"

"Never," I reply. "We're not dating."

"But you've been to my house."

"Once."

"Did he make you dinner?" August asks.

I glance between the two men, trying to decide how much I should tell them. Cole didn't prepare me for a full on interrogation. "Yes, but—"

"Date," both men say together. Then Gramps says, "You were driving his car."

"Because he's letting me borrow it," I argue. "I..." I pause when my phone buzzes with a text. Though it's rude to check it in the middle of a conversation, I so rarely get texts that I'm too curious not to.

It's from a number I don't know.

Unknown number:

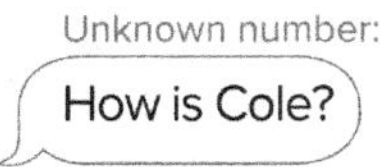

"Bad news?" August asks.

Looking up, I shake my head and smile at the way he looks so concerned on my behalf. "Just a text from a number I don't recognize. It must be someone who knows Cole."

"Is it a 310 or a 424?" Gramps asks.

I look down at the area code. "Um, a 310."

"516 or 891?"

"891."

"That'll be Bonnie," Gramps says with confidence.

Sure enough, another text comes in a second later.

> **Unknown number:**
> Oh, this is Bonnie, by the way! Bonnie Aiken.

"You have all of Cole's friends' numbers memorized?" I ask as I save Bonnie's number in my contacts. "I don't even have my own parents' numbers memorized."

Gramps scoffs. "Kids these days."

"Not all of us have a photographic memory," August says with the weariness of someone who has had this conversation many times.

They start arguing, and I turn my full focus to my phone.

> **Carissa:**
> Hi Bonnie!

> I think he's okay. We're with his dad and grandpa right now.

> **Bonnie:**
> Oh good. Gramps can always get him in a good mood.

> I hear you got a taste of the paparazzi. Are YOU okay?

> **Carissa:**
> I'm fine. But I also haven't gotten on the internet since it happened.

> **Bonnie:**
> We haven't seen anything show up yet, but we'll keep you posted.

"Bonnie says hi," I say immediately upon receiving the message; it sounded like their argument was getting heated, and I figured I should interrupt.

Gramps grins wide. "Bonnie is a lovely one. Not quite as lovely as Princess Freya, but close. I'm glad she found herself a man like Hank. Have you met her fella?"

"I met her fella a couple of months ago in Sun City," I say, giggling with the word 'fella.' "I didn't really get a chance to get to know him, but he seemed nice. I've hung out with everyone else, though. Including Freya."

"She fancies me, you know," Gramps says.

"In your dreams, old man," August replies with a roll of his eyes. "Cole doesn't normally introduce strangers to his friends."

I can hear the accusation as much as the curiosity, both of which bring a smile to my face. "Oh, he didn't have a choice. My sister married Houston Briggs and became friends with Bonnie, and Cole was furious when I showed up at Derek's house the other day."

"Houston Briggs? Now *there's* an athlete," Gramps says, almost wistfully. "I miss seeing him on the mound."

I raise an eyebrow. "Are you a Red-tails fan?"

"Nah, Dodgers, but you can't deny Briggs was good at what he did."

"He's also an incredible brother-in-law."

"So what brings you to LA?" August asks. "More importantly, how did you end up with the Thunder and getting together with Cole?"

I chuckle, shaking my head at the way both men watch me so intently. Cole wasn't kidding when he warned me they would be relentless. "We're not together," I say again. "And I was working as a physical therapist back East but had to find something new, and a connection of mine got me in with the team here, on the sports medicine team."

"With Mel?" August asks. "She's great, though she's had a tough break this year with the divorce."

I nod, wishing I could do more for Mel. She's trying so hard to make things work on her own, but it's easy to see she's slowly drowning. "Hopefully I can be helpful to her."

"I'm sure you will be." Gramps reaches across the counter and pats my hand when he says this. "Now, how about you start explaining how you and Cole came to be a couple."

"Friends," I correct.

"Agree to disagree."

Wrinkling my nose and grinning at him, I shake my head but start talking anyway. "He offered me a ride yesterday after I missed the bus."

"Cole was driving?" August asks, clearly surprised.

"No, it was a rideshare. But after that, he and Moxie decided it wasn't safe for me to take the bus, so he offered to let me borrow his car and give him rides to practices."

August and Gramps exchange glances, and I wish I could hear their silent conversation. Even if I'm mostly in the dark, it's clear they're surprised Cole would let me use his car. "Moxie is a good man," August says.

"And very handsome," Gramps adds.

"He's a catch, for sure."

"Not as good as Cole, of course."

"Obviously."

I bite my lip. "Maybe I should tell you both that I have strict rules against dating people I work with."

"Why?" they ask at the same time.

Shaking my head, I consider telling them about my sordid past but decide against it. I'm glad Cole knows, but I'd rather keep it as close to the vest as I can. "Reasons," I say.

"That's why you think you're not dating Cole?" Gramps asks.

"That's why I'm *not* dating Cole."

That gets them both laughing, and I can't help but join in because these men are delightful and warm and remind me of home. While I did sleep better last night after my evening with Cole, this is the first time since Darcy headed to the airport that I don't feel the pain of homesickness.

Can I just stay here always? The house is big enough that there's probably a guest room somewhere.

"So you're not interested in Moxie?" Gramps asks.

Before I can answer, a soft voice behind me says, "Moxie has bigger things to worry about than dating right now." Cole comes up beside me, arm brushing mine as he reaches forward to grab the plates Gramps has made up for us. "Sorry, boys, but I need to steal Carissa now. And no, you can't come with us."

Both of them grumble and groan, but Cole ignores them.

Giving August and Gramps a smile, I follow Cole out onto a beautiful deck that overlooks a luscious garden. The sun has sunk low enough that the whole yard is in shadow, nice and cool compared to the heat we get during the day, and with the trees dotting the property line, everything is calm and quiet back here, like the rest of the city has disappeared.

"This is amazing," I say.

Cole chuckles as he sets the plates on a gorgeous wood table and gestures for me to sit across from him. "Not darling?"

I grin. "It's that too. If this is your house, why don't you live here? I mean, don't get me wrong. The other house is great too. But this one is extra nice." And it has a pool, which looks terribly inviting.

"I spend plenty of time here too, but I like having my own space. Dad and Gramps put up with a lot, raising me, so I figured they deserve the nicer house for a while."

"So they both raised you?"

He shrugs, poking at his sandwich. "Single parenting is not for the faint of heart, and Gramps was alone for so long. Same with my dad. We all look out for each other."

Cole told me about his grandma and his mom, but I guess I never put two and two together. Gramps and August both lost their wives far too early. It's heartbreaking.

To keep myself from tearing up in sympathy, I put my focus into the sandwich and take a bite. The pork is sweet and spicy, and Gramps added a layer of cool coleslaw onto a bun that is way fancier than the ones I buy at the store. "Holy mama, this is good," I say with my mouth full.

Cole laughs. "Gramps is way better at cooking than I am."

"Yeah," I agree after I swallow. Then I wince. "I mean, dinner last night was delicious! But this is…"

Biting his lip in amusement, Cole watches as I take another bite. "Better," he repeats with a nod. "I'm only a little offended that you didn't hesitate with your agreement."

Heat floods my cheeks, though I honestly can't say if it's from embarrassment or because of the way he watches me as he digs in to his own sandwich.

We're both quiet until our sandwiches are gone, but that's about as long as I can wait before I start asking questions. "What did you mean when you said Moxie has bigger things to worry about?"

Tension fills Cole's shoulders, and I worry I asked something I shouldn't, but then he says, "Coach pulled me aside after practice today."

"I noticed that."

"He wants to replace Moxie as captain."

I gasp and get the sudden urge to drive straight over to the coach's house—wherever that might be—and give him a piece of my mind. "Are you kidding? That's the stupidest idea I've ever heard."

"That's what I told him."

"Why would he tell you something like that? Doesn't he know you and Moxie are friends?"

Cole tips his head to one side, like my question confuses him. "You think we're friends?"

Well now I don't. "Aren't you?"

"I guess so."

"That's not what friends say."

"As I'm sure you're starting to guess, I don't easily get close to people. Especially lately." He shakes his head, keeping his eyes on his empty plate. "Coach wants *me* to be captain, which is an even stupider idea than replacing Moxie in the first place."

I try to imagine Cole taking up Moxie's role, but no matter how much I'm starting to like this guy, I can't see it.

He snorts a laugh. "Yeah, see? It's stupid."

I wrinkle my nose. "I'm not good at hiding my thoughts. Clearly."

"I like that about you."

At the rate we're going, this man is going to make it so hard to keep thinking of him as just a friend. It was only yesterday that I worried he would ruin my unsteady life here in California because he hated me and my connection to Darcy's reporter life, and now he's calling me beautiful and telling me things he likes about me.

This is a dangerous game we're playing, but I'm no quitter.

"What'll you do if Coach decides to make the switch?" I ask, running my finger along the edge of my plate.

Cole watches the movement with an intensity that makes me shiver. "I don't know. It's not like the team respects me, but I don't know who else could do the job. It's always been Mox."

At least he knows that he's not a favorite among the other guys, but that doesn't make the situation better.

"Okay, what about this?" I say, pushing my plate to the side and resting my elbows on the table. "Say the coach makes a stupid decision and puts you in as captain instead of Moxie. What's to stop the two of you from working together? You technically hold the title, but you defer to Moxie."

A beautiful smile lifts his lips as he leans closer and rests one hand on the table, dangerously close to mine. "So basically keep everything the same?"

"Exactly."

"I don't think Coach would go for that."

"It's not like he comes to practices anyway."

Cole's eyes glitter with amusement in a way that sets my belly fluttering. "Good point."

I force myself to ignore the attraction building between us, even though it feels like something is pulling taut, threatening to snap at any moment. "So this is why you were in a bad mood?"

He nods. "Then the paparazzo took pictures of you, and... Well, you saw the rest. I'm sorry. I should never have let myself drive in that state."

Reaching across the small space between us, I take hold of his hand and try not to dwell on the way something sparks between our skin. It's just static electricity. Not a spark of connection. "Cole, you were trying to protect me from that guy. I can't be mad about that."

"But you can be mad that I nearly got you hurt. Or worse." His fingers flex around mine as he takes a slow, deliberate breath, his dark eyes on me. "Carissa..." Whatever he's about to say, I'm riveted to every word. "I..."

Piano music starts filling the air, like it's coming from the heavens. Am I hallucinating? Strings start up next, and a male voice begins singing about whether or not he's told someone he loves her.

Cole shuts his eyes with a groan. "Are you serious?"

"You hear that too?"

He turns to the house and shouts, "Turn it off!"

Two faces disappear from a dark window at the same time the blinds fall closed.

Cole leaps to his feet, but I tighten my hold on him so he doesn't go far. "I'm gonna kill them," he grumbles.

It is taking everything in me not to start laughing. "I think it's adorable."

"Van Morrison?" he shouts at the house. "Really?"

A slightly muffled voice replies, "It's a classic!" I have no idea which one of them speaks.

Cole sighs. "We should head out. It's your first game tomorrow."

I am so excited to see the Thunder in action, even if I feel wildly unprepared for my role on the sidelines. Hopefully no one gets injured and I can just be there to supply water and encouragement. I'm *great* at encouragement.

"We're sneaking out the side gate," Cole says, tugging me to the side of the house. "They don't deserve to say goodbye to you."

It's not until we're in the car and halfway to Cole's other house—Gramps's house, I guess—when I remember. "Oh, what did Ethan say?"

Cole's expression grows hard, which doesn't feel very promising. "He said we'll just have to wait."

I don't like that, but at the same time, I almost don't care. Tonight was another great night with Cole, and as long as I can keep learning more about who he is, does it really matter what people say about us?

Hollywood Hot Scoop

Is Cole Carousing with his Coworker?

In a shocking twist, it seems local rugby hero Cole Evanson is finally over his ex. Who's the lucky lady who won his affection? *Hollywood Hot Scoop* has the answer! Carissa Paxton, sister-in-law to the World Series-winning pitcher, Houston Briggs, has recently joined the LA Thunder staff as a rehabilitation specialist. It seems the locker room showers aren't the only thing steaming up at the rugby stadium. A Scooper caught Carissa getting cozy with our favorite player after yesterday's practice.

That's right! Cole has been caught in Carissa's snare and looks more than ready to put his heartbreaking ex behind him. Is this true love? Or is Cole finally on the rebound just in time for Sage Morrow and Badgers' Javier Gonzales to tie the knot? Carissa had better hope Cole doesn't drag his feet like he did before, or she'll be the next to run off with one of his teammates.

Vote below on which Thunderclap you think Carissa should choose when Cole eventually messes things up! The charismatic captain, Malcolm Auxier? Or maybe she's more into beastly brutes like tighthead prop Harvey Kavinski? Pick your poison and get a coupon code for a ticket to tonight's game against the Utah Warriors! And as always, make sure you hit that subscribe button, because I have a feeling we're in for a wild ride. XO

CHAPTER FIFTEEN

CARISSA

WOULD IT BE A bad idea to ask Cole to explain the rules of rugby to me tomorrow? Probably. But I still like the idea of spending a good chunk of my Sunday with him, up close and personal as he walks me through a game that is as thrilling as it is bewildering. I'm motivated as much by a desire to spend time with him as I am by a real interest in rugby.

I've made it almost halfway through the game against the Utah Warriors without needing to do much outside of taping a few ankles and shoulders because Mel is pretty on top of things, which means I've spent most of the evening watching these big, burly men ram into each other without padding or inhibition. It's fascinating the way nothing seems to stop the game like it does in other sports. Even when Moxie kicks the ball out of bounds—*into touch*, according to the Thunder's announcer—the players are always ready to lift each other into the air to catch the ball when it gets thrown back in. The ball gets passed over and over, sometimes too quickly to follow, and unless someone is running with it or kicking it forward, it always moves backwards. When someone gets tackled, Cole is there to grab the ball and keep it moving with a quick pass.

And the energy! The crowd is wild and loud and a lot more devoted to the team than I expected after such a quiet week, and there's one particularly rowdy group that has all sorts of chants that they start up, the words echoing through the stadium as the rest of the crowd joins in.

The Thunder is up by ten points as we near the end of the first half, and I'm feeling good about the future of this game.

Hefting my backpack of supplies—tape, wraps, water, etc.—higher on my shoulder, I wander along our sideline as both teams set up for what I think is called a scrum. Half a dozen men on each side lock arms and duck their heads, creating a sort of structure held up by the strength of their legs alone. Cole rolls the ball into the middle of the pack and both teams start pushing, trying to be the stronger side as the ball makes its way beneath the Thunder's legs. It reaches the back, and Cole grabs it again, tossing it straight to Moxie, who passes it sidelong to Sharkie. Sharkie makes it a few yards before he gets knocked down by a Warrior. Two other Thunder players join him and keep the Warriors at bay, getting the ball free for Cole to grab it and toss it to Moxie once more.

Moxie makes a break for it in between two of the Warriors, and the crowd goes wild. A defensive player moves to tackle him, but Moxie twists to the side to dodge, nearly running into another player. He pivots again, then crumples. Did he get tackled? I didn't see anyone close enough. The ball slips from his hands, and a Warrior picks it up and runs, but none of the Thunder seem to care because Moxie's still on the ground, hands fisting the turf and his teeth gritted in pain. The crowd stills.

My stomach twists into a knot.

I've spent the last forty minutes watching these guys collide into each other at breakneck speeds. Slam into the ground with every tackle. They all get up, bruised and battered but ready to keep playing. Seeing Moxie motionless on the ground has filled me with cold dread.

Thankfully, Mel isn't frozen like me and is already on the field, crouching at his side and talking rapidly as she touches his right knee.

"And play will stop for an injury on the Thunder side," the announcer says. His booming voice knocks some sense into me, and I dart forward to see if Mel needs my help.

Moxie is shaking his head when I reach him. "Not like this," he tells Mel through measured breaths.

Mel frowns. "You're either being a baby, or this is worse than I'd like. And you've never been a baby, Auxier."

Moxie clenches his jaw, sweat dripping down the sides of his face. "I'll be fine for the second half."

"Carissa, help me get him up."

We each grab an arm, and Moxie groans as we haul him to his feet. He's putting weight on his leg, which is a good sign, but that doesn't mean he avoided serious injury. Surrounded by sweaty Thunder players, we slowly move off the field to words of encouragement and concerned questions.

"Dean Oldman will sub in for Malcolm Auxier and finish out the first half," the announcer says, and the rest of the team reluctantly heads back onto the field to play the last few minutes.

By the time we get Moxie to a chair, he looks completely spent, and I have a bad feeling that he's downplaying the amount of pain he's in. I don't think anyone touched him during that play, but from what I saw, I can guess what might have happened.

I really hope I'm wrong.

"Talk to me, Malcolm," Mel says. Her voice wavers as she crouches in front of him. She seems to be trying to see inside his knee with how laser focused she is on it.

The knee is already swelling, and as we were walking, his leg kept wobbling, like he had no control over where the limb went. I've seen that before.

"Mel!" someone shouts.

She bites her lip, reluctant to leave.

"Go," Moxie breathes. "Carissa's got me."

I nod to agree, and Mel reluctantly jogs down the field to help another player. She passes Cole, who meets my gaze with a furrowed brow before he returns to the game.

"It's bad, isn't it?" Moxie says, pulling my eyes back to him. "I can see it in your eyes."

My stomach knots again. "I'm not the expert here. Mel should—"

"Tell me."

"You might have torn your ACL."

He moans, closing his eyes and dropping his head back. "Tell me something else."

I worked with plenty of knee injuries at the clinic, and while it'll take a physician to offer an actual diagnosis, I know what I saw. "Did you feel anything pop?"

He growls. "Am I going to regret it if I say yes?"

"Do you think lying to me will change the outcome?" I throw back.

The announcer says something about the first half coming to an end, and we're suddenly swarmed by the Thunder. They all want to know what happened and if Moxie will be okay, and he puts on a smile and forces out some jokes before telling the team to hit the locker room. There are only fifteen minutes in between halves, so he probably doesn't want them to waste any time.

As the Thunder filters into the tunnel, Mel joins me, looking frazzled. "I'm not very optimistic," she whispers to me.

"Me neither," I whisper back.

"I can hear you," Moxie whispers in turn. His eyes are closed again, his whole body tense. "Someone tell me I can still play. Please." Based on the desperation in his voice, he already knows that's not going to happen.

Tears fill my eyes, and I furiously try to blink them away as I turn my back to Moxie so he doesn't see. He'll recover. Eventually. But if I'm right about his ACL, there's no way he's playing the rest of this season. When my vision clears, I realize not all of the Thunder went to the locker room. Cole is standing just a few feet away, his expression anguished as he stares at Moxie.

I don't think. I just step forward and wrap my arms around Cole's torso even though he's hot and sweaty. He tucks his arms around me without hesitation, and I don't know if he's comforting me or the other way around. I was right about how it feels to be held by him, but this is far from the circumstances in which I would have liked to experience Cole's enveloping hold for the first time. Still, I bury my face in his chest and cling to his protective embrace, hoping he can make everything better.

Some first game this has been.

Chapter Sixteen

COLE

"That was a hard loss, boys," Coach says, "but we can learn from tonight's performance and do better in Portland in two weeks. We're going to spend this week focusing on..."

I tune him out. I don't think anyone is actually listening to him as he prattles on. We just want to hit the showers and check on Moxie. He refused to leave the pitch until the game was over, but as soon as it was—Warriors up by seven—Mel took him to the clinic. I don't know how long it'll be before we hear what the damage is, but Carissa seemed pretty sure it was a torn ACL.

If that's true, Moxie will be out the rest of the season, which means...

"And we need a new captain with Auxier injured," Coach says, echoing my fears.

The room grows silent as the guys finally turn their attention to the coach.

"He can still be captain even if he's injured," Tink says, not bothering to hide his outrage.

Coach scoffs. "We need a captain *on* the pitch."

"Moxie will be back to playing in a few weeks," Scratch argues.

"Not from what I hear," Coach says.

I swallow when his eyes meet mine. I'm in my usual corner, ignored by the team for now. But that won't last long. *Don't do it*, I silently beg, shaking my head at him.

But Coach smiles and points at me as he says, "Evanson will take Auxier's spot as captain for the rest of the season."

I've never heard the locker room this quiet. I swear the guys can hear my pounding heart and churning gut as their heads slowly swivel in my direction. "That's a bad idea," I say, flinching at the sound of my own voice in the eerie silence.

Coach narrows his eyes. "Are you questioning me, son?"

Why did he have to call me that in front of everyone? Rising stiffly to my feet, I shake my head. "Perlman is right. Auxier can still captain from the sidelines, and it's not like we're an international team, so it doesn't matter if—" I cut myself off when a buzz starts filtering through the room, accompanied by glares and glowers.

Got it. Don't minimize the value of our team. But I was trying to defend Moxie and keep myself out of this mess, so I thought they would be on my side.

"What about Henderson?" Sharkie says, pointing at Bean. "He could be captain."

Bean splutters in horror as Coach laughs. "Don't be ridiculous," Coach says.

"Or the Aussie," Tink says, pointing at Gary. "He's played pro for years!"

Coach snarls. "This isn't a debate! My decision is made. We need someone with a talent for leadership, and Evanson is the only one who can hack it."

Thirty pairs of eyes turn to me again, and I want to shrink into my locker and disappear. There were sixty guys on the Badgers' roster, and they never once intimidated me like this, so what's my problem? Stupid question. The Badgers actually liked me.

"Sir," I say weakly. "Can we talk about this?"

"We *already* talked about this," Coach argues. "You knew this was coming."

I curse as several players jump to their feet and start spouting off questions to both of us even though Coach starts inching his way to the door.

"What do you mean, he knew?"

"Did you purposefully get Moxie injured so you could take his place?"

"Were you planning to replace him before he got injured?"

"What makes you so special, Rihanna?"

"That's enough!" I shout, loud enough that the men nearest to me flinch. "Of course I didn't get him injured. He's our best player and my friend!" Coach slips out the door as I talk, which doesn't help my frustration. *Coward.* "And yes, I knew, but I hate the idea as much as you do. No, I'm not special, something you all have made very clear over the last two years." I run a hand through my sweat-soaked hair, desperate for a shower after that second half. It's a miracle we didn't lose by more because none of us were really in the game, too worried about Moxie.

"Look," I say, completely exhausted. "I don't deserve to be your captain. I don't *want* to be your captain. But there's going to be no changing his mind, and there will be hell to pay for all of us if we fight him on this."

If it were any other team in the league, it probably wouldn't be a big deal, but Coach is so rarely at practice, and his assistants are crap at keeping things organized. Someone has to lead this team.

"Mox will always be our captain," I continue, partially because I don't like the way the team is so quiet. I need to fill the space. "I'm not taking his or anyone's spot. But I'm going to do what Coach says. Got it?"

At least thirty seconds pass before someone speaks. "So," Bean says and folds his arms, commanding the attention of the others. "Did you buy your way to the top?"

Forget the shower. Grabbing my bag, I throw it over my shoulder and push my way to the door, cursing Coach as I go. This is never going to work. They'll hate me more than ever now, and without Moxie to be a buffer between me and them, their opinion of me is only going to get worse.

Moxie's injury had better be superficial, or I'll have an entire team out for my blood.

As I make my way down the corridor, I realize a light is on in Mel's space, and since I know she's out with Moxie, my steps slow. Is Carissa still here? After the game, she got a few players situated with ice bags and wraps, and then she disappeared. I figured she went home.

I shouldn't stop. I ordered a ride this afternoon to get here earlier than she did, and she would be well in her right to assume I'll book a ride home as well. My nerves are frazzled, so I can't guarantee I'll be as nice as she deserves. It would be better for both of us to get some distance for a bit.

My feet take me through the open training room door, though I stop just inside and take in the scene. Carissa's on her own, as I would expect, and sitting on the table with an arm around her shins and her chin on her knees. She looks extra small, balled up like that as she scrolls on her phone. She looks like she needs a friend.

"Hey." The word croaks out of me.

Her eyes jump toward me, but nothing about her position moves. How long has she been sitting like that? "Hi."

"Any word on Moxie?"

She shakes her head. "Mel said he won't be able to get an MRI until Monday, so she's going to stay with him until then and make sure he's okay."

"What about her kid?"

"I guess her parents live nearby, and they always take Raiden whenever Mel has a game. They offered to keep him for the weekend."

I'm glad Mel has a support system. I'm extra glad Moxie has someone to look out for him. I can't pretend I know much about his life outside of rugby, but I do know none of his family live nearby. And even if he does consider me a friend, I doubt he'll want to see me. I'm sure someone on the team has already texted him and told him about Coach's decision.

While I stand in silence, Carissa seems to see me for the first time, lifting her head as her eyes trail over me. I wonder what she sees. "Do you always forgo a shower after playing?" she asks.

I chuckle, though I'm hardly amused by my current situation. "Showers are overrated."

"Are they, though?"

It's a good thing I'm clear on the other side of the room from her so she doesn't have to be assaulted by my smell. That last half was brutal, both mentally and physically. "With Moxie out, Coach told the team I'm taking over as captain," I admit. "They didn't take it well."

"Oh." Unfolding herself, Carissa tucks her phone into the pocket of the leggings she's wearing and comes closer. Her nose wrinkles, probably when she gets a whiff of me. "What are you going to do?"

"No idea."

"Showering is a good first step."

This time my laugh feels more real, and I tug on one of her curls. Then I frown because that was a weird move and not something friends do. With her standing so close, I get sudden flashbacks to the moment before the second half when she slid into my arms. I don't know why she did it, but I do know it took everything in me to let go after she did. It's been a long time since someone hugged me like that outside of Bonnie and Freya, and their sisterly hugs don't exactly get my heart pounding.

With Carissa, I don't even have to touch her for my blood to heat beneath my skin. Every time I'm with her, it gets worse, and seeing her in my house last night, smiling and laughing and fitting in so easily with my family, I might have passed a point of no return.

My arms itch to wrap around her again, so I grab the strap of my bag with both hands and take a subtle step back. I can't tear my eyes from hers, however. Those gold-infused eyes have me transfixed. And the longer I look, the more I realize there's something else behind her subdued mood. "You okay?"

She bites her lip. "Um. There's an article about us."

Swearing, I dig into my bag for my phone. I tend to ignore it on game days to keep my head in the zone, but the several texts from my friends and a missed call from Ethan jumpstart my heart into an erratic rhythm as I pull up the *Hot Scoop* article Derek sent me in a text. I read it quickly, expecting the worst, but all in all it's not as bad as I expected.

Still, this is Carissa's first real foray into the tabloids. "How are you feeling about it?" I ask.

She shrugs, keeping her eyes on my chest rather than my face. "It's hard to say. I thought for sure they would say something about Peter—my ex—but..." Another shrug.

"Unfortunately, this could only be the start. You and I should probably keep our distance from each other so we don't give them reasons to look at you more closely." I'm not sure I've ever wanted anything less, which is only more reason to stay away from her. Not easily done. At some point in the last couple of minutes I moved close to her again without meaning to.

"But I'm your ride," Carissa argues, looking up. "How are you going to get to practice?"

I chuckle. She's something else, worrying about me when it's her being dragged into the media. Outside of my friends, I've never met anyone like her. "The same way I did before you showed up, Paxton. Believe it or not, I can generally take care of myself."

"Can you?" Her eyes go wide. "I didn't mean that how it sounded! I just mean you seem like you do better when you're around people, and your friends would probably agree."

I can't decide if I like how much she notices about me or if it scares the crap out of me. Derek often says something about being known. He says being known can be a good thing, but when you're famous, not many people truly want to know you. They decide which parts of you they want and despise the rest.

But she's right. Isolating myself doesn't do me any good, something I also learned from Derek back when we first met. He's a firm believer that no one should be alone. I can't imagine how difficult it's been for him to stay away the last few days, especially after I ignored his call yesterday.

Though my fingers itch to send him a text and assure him that I'm fine, I can't bring myself to look away from Carissa. I swallow the words that rise in my throat—*Would you take care of me?*—and instead say something far more innocent. "I guess, if you're offering a ride, I'd be stupid to refuse."

Carissa lifts a saucy eyebrow that pulls me right back into her orbit and the sweet floral scent that envelops her. "You guess?"

The curl I touched earlier is still hanging on its own by her cheek, and I can't stop my hand from rising. I run the curl between my fingers, loving the way it bounces back into place. There's a playfulness to her hair that matches her open personality. "I would love a ride," I amend.

She takes a breath, lips parting, and I'm pretty sure she leans closer. "Good," she whispers. "Because I'm starting to really like our drives together."

My phone buzzes in my hand. I jump back a full step, landing myself in the doorway, and shake my head as if the movement can knock some sense into me. Even if it weren't Derek calling me, I'd answer the call just to give myself a distraction before I get pulled back into Carissa's inviting eyes.

"Hey," I say, lifting the phone to my ear.

"Finally," Derek replies.

Resisting the urge to sigh, I lean my shoulder against the doorframe. "You do know I had a game tonight, right?"

"Yeah, and I also know it ended almost an hour ago."

Carissa makes her way to the back of the room, but her scent still lingers in the air around me. I watch her grab her bag and busy herself with organizing supplies like she's right at home here. She's been here less than a week, and it already feels like she's been a part of the Thunder since the beginning.

Or maybe I am simply getting used to having her around.

"Cole," Derek says.

I pull my gaze from Carissa so I can focus on my phone. "What?"

"You okay?"

"Fine."

"Lies."

I grit my teeth. My friends are good at calling out each other's moments of dishonesty, which is great until it happens to me, apparently. I don't like to lie, so it's not often anyone has to say anything. Taking a deep breath, I drop my voice even though Carissa already knows all my issues.

Most of my issues.

"Moxie got injured tonight," I say.

"I heard. Is he okay?"

I explain what Carissa thinks it is and that we won't know for sure until Monday. But Moxie's injury isn't all of what's bothering me, and

Derek seems to know as much with the way he's being pushier than usual. So I close my eyes and say, "Coach told the guys he's making me team captain."

However I expected Derek to react to that announcement, it wasn't for him to burst into laughter. "Seriously?"

I growl. "Why is that funny?"

"Don't get me wrong. It sucks for Moxie, and hopefully he can get back in the game quickly. But dude. If ever there was a time for you to make friends with your teammates..."

I switch my phone to the other ear and glance behind me to make sure no one has left the locker room. "If ever there was a time for them to hate me even more," I counter. "They love Moxie."

"And Moxie likes you."

"I don't know why."

"Cole, I know you're in a funk right now, but I wouldn't be friends with you if you weren't a good guy and worth knowing. So maybe cut the self-deprecation and focus on what you can do about this situation."

I should have known better than to talk down on myself when Derek Riley is on the phone with me. Considering how perfectly he presents himself, advice like this should come across as insincere, but Derek has spent too long in the limelight to be anything but genuine when it comes to self-image. He knows how hard it is to be in the public eye and the media's judgment.

He's said it often enough that I can hear it in his voice: The only opinion a person should worry about is the one they have of themself. The one they can control.

"I don't know how to make this work," I say as my eyes lift to find Carissa. She has her purse now and is leaning against a cabinet, watching me. I ask my question as much to her as I do to Derek. "How do I get them to trust me?"

"I think this might be one you're going to have to figure out on your own," Derek says.

Carissa tilts her head, a thoughtful look in her eyes. I'm more inclined to listen to her right now, whatever she might have to say.

"But you should start with being open with them," Derek continues. "Something tells me you haven't let them know you, especially over the last few months."

"I've been with this team for nearly two years, Derek. If they don't know me by now…"

He chuckles. "Do they know why you don't drive?"

"No, but—"

"Do they have any idea why you left football in the first place?" That question has some bitterness on the edges.

I wince, gripping the phone tighter. "No. And they never will."

"Why not?" I hear what he's really asking. He's asking why I haven't told *him* why I left the NFL when he knows how much I loved football. "Cole, I know you have your secrets—we all do—but if you carry everything on your own, eventually it's going to become too heavy for you and you'll crumble under the pressure. You need to trust your team so they can trust you in return."

I genuinely don't know if he's talking about the Thunder or our group of friends, and that worries me. Since Sage dumped me, I've been pushing my friends away in my pitiful attempts to lick my wounds and heal, and I have known from the beginning that that's a bad idea. But keeping everyone at a distance is the only way I know to cope with fears. My friends will never let me get far, which is more than I deserve after the way I've been acting the last few months.

I can't keep my teammates at a distance. Not if I'm going to have a chance to keep the Thunder from falling apart without Moxie on the pitch. But Derek's right. If I want those guys to trust me, I can't keep up so many walls that they can't even see me.

Voices echo in the corridor behind me. Panic shoots through me, and I scurry deeper into the room, shutting the door behind me and flipping off the light.

"Let me call you back," I whisper into the phone and hang up before Derek can protest, throwing the room into complete darkness.

Turns out I'm a coward.

chapter seventeen

CARISSA

I wish I had been nosier.

I was trying to be a good friend and give Cole some space so he could talk to Derek in private, but hearing Cole's side of the conversation made me desperately want to creep closer and try to overhear whatever Derek was saying. Cole didn't seem to like it, but I could practically see him lowering his shields at the end there.

And now I can't see anything at all.

If I had had worse self-control, I might have been next to Cole and not freaking out by myself in the dark.

"Cole?" I whisper, my voice trembling against my will. There are too many things in the room for me to trip over if I try to move closer to him.

He swears softly. "Sorry. I panicked."

That's great and all, but I don't like being in the dark, and there aren't any outside windows in this place. The corridor outside is too dimly lit to offer much light through the frosted glass in the door, so I feel like I'm in a giant, empty void, which might be one of my biggest nightmares coming to life.

"Cole," I say again, hating how pathetic I sound. I am a grown woman, for goodness' sake!

He swears again, and I can just barely see his body move in front of the window in the door. The sounds of voices and footsteps passing by offer a nice reprieve from the silence but aren't as comforting as I would like. "I'd turn the light back on," Cole says, his voice gentle, "but the guys will get the wrong idea about us. I don't want to put you in that situation."

"Fine. I get it. But..." I swallow and strangle the strap of my bag. "I really don't like the dark. At all."

Something touches me and I shriek, only to be tugged off balance and into a solid chest. "It's just me," Cole says softly. "Sorry."

I don't care how sweaty he is. I wrap my arms around his torso and grip the back of his jersey. Kit? I think it's called a kit. It's surprisingly tight on his body, but I hold on to it anyway.

"I'm sorry," Cole says again, and his arms wrap me up in a protective hold, just like he did on the field. His hands are warm on my back as he envelops me, and it feels so nice to be in his arms that I start to panic about how much I want this. How much I want *him*.

How did that happen?

"Cole?" I whisper into his firm chest.

"Hmm?"

"You smell terrible."

He laughs and tries to pull away, but I hold on tight. This could be my last chance to be held by him because I can't let myself fall for this man. I have to stay focused on my job and make a new career for myself. It's as much about avoiding Cole's very public life as it is building a rapport with the team so they trust me to look after them.

"I know," Cole says, and I realize with horror that I was speaking my thoughts out loud. "This can't happen."

"Because of your curse?" I ask.

His hold tightens. "Yes. But also...the guys are all hoping for a shot with you, and if they hate me now..."

I tilt my head back, trying to see his face in the darkness. I can't see much, but I can tell he's looking down at me. "Are you trying to say they'd be jealous of you if we started dating?" A chill runs through me at the thought, and it's probably a sign that I have a serious problem.

Cole's hand moves up my back to my neck, then around to my jaw. "You have no idea," he murmurs. "Which is why this is a very bad idea."

"What's a bad idea?" I murmur back because I can't tell if he's leaning in to kiss me and I would very much like him to do that.

"Everything when it comes to you."

His nose brushes mine at the same time my phone starts ringing in my bag. He's instantly gone, leaving me breathless as I dig into my bag to silence the stupid interruption before someone hears. But when I see that it's Darcy calling, I figure I should probably answer it.

"Hey."

"Don't you *hey* me, Carissa Lynn Paxton! What is this about you and Cole Evanson? Is any of this article true?" She's so loud that Cole snickers, probably hearing every word.

I heave a sigh, wishing I had saved this conversation for when I was alone. "Are you going to shout at me this whole time?" I ask calmly.

Darcy scoffs. "That depends on the answers to my questions. Tell me you're not hooking up with one of the players."

"I'm not hooking up with any of the players, Darce. Would you relax?"

Cole coughs.

I reach forward to smack him, but he catches my hand and presses it between both of his, pulling me close again. Even if he can't see my expression, I glare at him. "This is not a game we should play," I whisper, shivering when he chuckles.

"What?" Darcy says. "Are you with someone? Are you with *Cole*?"

"I'm not dating Cole!"

"You'd better not be."

I frown, momentarily distracted from the warmth of Cole's hands. I can almost see him now as my eyes adjust. "What does that mean? What do you have against Cole?"

Darcy scoffs again. "He's a professional athlete, Rizzo."

"And?"

"And...and professional athletes are egotistical hotheads."

"Hey!" a male voice says in the background. Houston, probably. "You *married* a pro athlete."

"Technically, I married a *retired* pro athlete," Darcy counters. "And you are a decent human."

"Cole is a decent human," I throw out there. "But I'm still not dating him."

"Are you sure?"

Of course, Cole chooses that moment to start massaging my hand, which is a ridiculous thing for a guy to do when he is just as adamant about our relationship staying in the friend zone as I am. Then again, he's the one who was about to kiss me. Never mind I was about to let him.

"Will you stop?" I hiss, tugging my hand free.

"I'm sorry," Darcy says, probably thinking I was talking to her. "I just know how much power the media can have, and I don't like that you've been dragged into the tabloids. The two of you look seriously cozy in this picture, Rizzo."

That photo is nothing compared to the way I feel each inch between us right now. Cole is, thankfully, keeping his hands to himself now, but I am all too aware of how intently his focus is on me, like I can feel his gaze more than I can see it in the darkness.

"You don't have to worry about me," I say, hoping I sound believable. "I don't want to be in the tabloids any more than you want me there, and Cole and I were just talking when that photo was taken."

"Well..." Cole says, the word guttural and low.

I go for a smack again, but he moved farther than I thought, so I lose my balance and tumble forward. Right into his arms.

"How are things going with the job, anyway?" Darcy asks. Thankfully I held on to my phone.

But I can't answer my sister because I'm currently in a dip, Cole's eyes sparkling in the dim light from the corridor as he looks down at me. I can almost make out his expression, and the sight of it sparks a fire inside me. "Can..." I swallow and try again. "Can I call you back tomorrow? It's been a long day." And I need to address Cole's apparent lack of control.

"Yeah, of course." Darcy sounds disappointed. "I want to hear all about your first game. I haven't had a chance to watch it yet."

She doesn't know about Moxie.

The thought sobers me. I make my goodbyes and struggle upright again, tucking my phone away as I find Cole's face in the darkness. The corridor is quiet now, so it's probably safe for us to leave without being caught by any of the Thunder.

"We should go," I tell Cole.

"Yeah," he agrees.

We move slowly, checking around corners and searching the parking lot for teammates or photographers, but we make it onto the road without incident. Thank the heavens for that. I wasn't kidding when I told Darcy it has been a long day, and I didn't need to risk accidentally admitting my growing feelings for this man while scrambling to explain to someone why we're still here so long after the game.

"Okay," I say when we're well on our way. "We probably need to make some rules."

"I'm not always a fan of rules," Cole replies.

I glare at him. "Work with me, Lemon."

He chuckles. "Okay. Rules. Like what?"

"I am way too tired to think about that right now."

"You could come over for lunch tomorrow and we can hash it out. I'm meeting my friends later in the day, but we could..." He stops when I look at him again, his eyes narrowing. "You want to hang out with them again, don't you?"

I bite my lip. "I didn't say that."

"Trust me. You did. You say a lot with your eyes."

The fact that he can already read my expressions has me squealing internally. This man is dangerous.

"In my defense," I say, "you are friends with literal movie stars and one of my favorite musicians. And they love me. You know they do."

"Unfortunately," he grumbles. "Fine. You can come to my place for lunch, and then you can join me at Derek's. As long as you promise to stop looking at me like that."

Though I'm doing my best to keep my focus on the road, I can't help but grin at him. "Like what?"

"Like you want me to do what I almost did in the dark." He may be grumbling, but everything about his expression is telling me he wants the same thing.

I turn up the AC and lock both hands around the steering wheel. "How did this happen?" I ask.

"What?"

I move my hand through the space between us, returning it to the steering wheel before it gets any ideas. "This. You and me. You hated me just a few days ago."

"I didn't hate you. I was wary. And we've had this conversation before."

"Not like this." Against my will, my hand moves to the console between us.

Cole looks at it for only a second before he reaches over and tucks his fingers between mine. "You're right," he murmurs. "This is different. And I don't know how it happened. I didn't think I could…"

He trails off, leaving a thick silence between us.

I focus on the way his thumb brushes along mine, how his hand feels so natural. I'm far too comfortable with our current situation, so I find the best way to break the building tension. "Did you love Sage?"

His eyes flit over to me for only a second before returning to the road ahead. "Yeah. I wanted to marry her."

"Why didn't you?"

"Because I didn't want her to get hurt." There's more to his answer—I can practically feel it—so I keep quiet until he adds, "And maybe we weren't as good together as I thought."

A lot of articles from a couple of years ago called them "The Perfect Pair," like they had been designed for each other. Was that the glamorization of the media because she was beautiful and mature and elegant? Every picture I saw of the two of them made them both look so majestic. Cole was always in some sort of suit or his football uniform, and Sage always wore a sparkling dress or a girlboss pantsuit. I doubt she ever wore sweats or a tank top with a unicorn on it.

It's weird, though. I can't picture Cole living in the spotlight like the articles all said he used to. Yeah, he was a celebrated quarterback who made bank because of his skills, but this man next to me is something different. He's understated and down to earth. Humble and caring.

We reach his house long before I'm ready to say goodnight to him, but it's for the best that we get at least a few hours apart. Something changed when I held him during the game, and I don't know if we can go backward.

"Tomorrow?" Cole asks, turning his head to give me a small smile.

My smile is much wider, but I doubt it does to him what his smile does to me. I doubt my smile feels like a bolt of lightning straight to the chest. "Tomorrow," I agree. "I'll be thinking about you all night." The blood drains from my face. "Wait! I mean I'll be thinking about rules because we very much need them and..." I drop my face into my hand. "Wow, that came out so wrong."

Cole's hand wraps around my wrist, pulling my hand free, and I turn to him just as he presses a warm kiss to my cheek. "I'll be thinking about you too," he says and slips out of the car to head inside.

Yeah, we're in trouble.

CHAPTER EIGHTEEN

COLE

I FEEL LIKE AN idiot. A teenage idiot full of hormones as he waits for his longtime crush to show up for a study session set up solely to get some time alone with her. Not that I'm speaking from experience...

Though I generally consider myself a neat person, I spend Sunday morning deep cleaning my house. I order a grocery delivery with way more food than I could eat in a week—and I can eat a lot. I spend nearly an hour in the shower, both to ensure I am fully clean and because I have a stern conversation with myself about setting boundaries and *sticking* to them, which has never been a problem for me before.

But when Carissa rings my doorbell and greets me while wearing a flowery pink sundress that accentuates the blush of her cheeks, I'm ready to throw those boundaries out the window.

"Hi," she says with a warm smile.

I think I smile back, but I'm not fully in control of my faculties at the moment. She doesn't look any different than she did the last time she was at Derek's, but something about Carissa in a dress has me stunned. Overcome.

She points a finger at me. "You'd better stop that, Coleman Evanson."

"Stop what?" I manage to say.

"Stop looking at me like you want to devour me. I came here to make rules, remember?"

Why? Why do we need to make rules? Because of my stupid curse? That's all it is. *Stupid*.

Easy, Cole. I can't risk her safety just because I'm attracted to her.

I step aside to let her in, and the way she smiles at the sight of my space feels like a tightening vise around my heart. It's a welcome change from the ache I've been stuck with for the last half a year, but so very dangerous. I both want to cling to this feeling and run away before it becomes permanent.

I clear my throat. "So."

Carissa's smile grows. "So."

"I thought you could help me make lunch." Did I decide to have her help because cooking together is a perfect way to flirt and be in each other's space and accidentally touch? Yes. Am I regretting that decision?

Nope.

Carissa narrows her eyes as she glances toward the kitchen. "You are trouble, you know that?"

"Is that a no?"

"I'd love to help. But that doesn't mean you're not trouble." As she passes me to head into the kitchen, her hand runs along my chest to my shoulder, turning me to jelly. "And two can play at that game, Evanson."

By the time I work up the nerve to join her, she has already found an apron and tied it around her waist. She picked my favorite one, USC cardinal and gold with a worn Trojans logo splashed across the front.

"Is this where you went to school?" she asks, looking down at it.

I nod. "Gramps bought the apron as soon as I got accepted. Wore it every time he cooked during away games, for luck." Whenever I had home games, he and Dad were always in the stands cheering me on. I still remember my first college game and seeing them with the best seats they could buy.

Grabbing another apron—this one a plain red-checkered one—Carissa leans up on her toes to tuck it over my head. "Did Gramps buy one with the Badgers' logo too? I didn't see it in the pantry."

That's because I threw it out when I came back from Oregon. "Yeah, he probably has it somewhere at the other house," I lie.

"Do you ever miss football?"

This conversation is creeping in a direction I'd rather not go, but I'm finding it difficult to do or say anything that might upset the woman in front of me. I want to tell her everything. "I miss the game," I say, hoping she leaves it at that.

I may *want* to tell her everything, but that would be a terrible idea. It wouldn't just endanger my heart, trusting her that much, but it could put *her* in actual danger. If she knew about how half of my teammates were being paid to rig the games for certain outcomes, she might tell her sister. And no matter how much Tamlin Park might be changing her tune, that's a story no reporter worth her salt could resist.

A story like that would completely destroy the Badgers, and there are still good men on that team. Not to mention any of the perpetrators—the coach, the owner, even one of the players—would likely be able to trace the source back to me, and what would happen then? There's a lot of money in that scheme, which means a lot of potential danger for me and anyone associated with me.

"Whoa," Carissa says, stepping closer and looking up into my eyes. "Are you okay? You just got...glowery."

I force my forehead to relax so I'm no longer glaring. "My football life was complicated," I say too sharply. "I don't like talking about it."

"Got it. What are we making for lunch?"

And that's that. I expected Carissa to push—Derek would have—but instead she let the subject drop. I exhale the breath I was holding in preparation to resist her persistence, and I feel almost dizzy. I'm overwhelmed by the sheer awe I feel when around this woman. "You..." I furrow my brow again, this time in confusion rather than frustration. "You don't want to know why it was complicated?"

She laughs, the sound filling my small kitchen with light. "Of course I want to know why. But you said you don't like to talk about it, and I respect that."

My reaction is instinctual and thoughtless and impulsive. Stepping forward, I bend down and press my lips to hers in an earnest kiss of gratitude. Then I freeze, my mouth still flush with hers.

"Oh," Carissa says against my lips.

Her open mouth and the taste of her breath are maddening, but I use every ounce of self-control I possess to keep from wrapping her in my arms and giving her a *real* kiss. That doesn't mean I move. We're both motionless, breaths mingling in the middle of my kitchen as if trapped in time.

Time's still moving with each tick of the clock in the living room, but I'm not so sure we're moving with it.

"I'm not sorry I just did that," I say, once I've found the will to speak.

My voice breaks the spell, and Carissa takes a step back. "I am," she says and brushes her tongue along her bottom lip.

Disappointment surges through me. "Oh."

But she smiles. "Only because now I want you to do it again." Though I step forward, she presses a hand to my chest to keep me at a distance. "This is why I said we should make rules, Cole. I'm starting to think my interest in you isn't going away anytime soon."

This might be the strangest situation I've ever been in. "You're interested in me?" I ask, feeling a smile creep onto my mouth.

Carissa laughs. "Has that not been clear before now?"

"Just curious." I fold my arms to keep myself from reaching out and pulling her closer. Her hand still rests against my chest, and I'll let it stay there as long as she wants it to. She can probably feel the rapid beat of my heart, and I don't care. "For the record, I am extremely interested in you too."

A beautiful blush splashes across her cheeks. "But we shouldn't act on our interest."

I nod and lean closer. Not a lot, but enough for her to notice. "No, we shouldn't."

Oh, that blush. The way she colors so easily might be the death of me. "You're giving me mixed signals here, Cole. I mean it!"

"So do I." I chuckle and bite the inside of my lips as she shakes her head at me in clear frustration. "But that doesn't mean I like it."

We both have good reasons for sticking to a strictly platonic relationship, but I don't know if I've ever encountered anything that will be harder. Not now that I've gotten a taste of her and know without a doubt that she mirrors my attraction. I can't call what I did a kiss—not one worth remembering—and everything in me wants to show her how I really kiss.

"Maybe we should make our rules *before* lunch," she says, biting her bottom lip.

"None of that," I say immediately, pointing to her mouth. I take a large step back and swallow hard. "And no licking your lips either."

She grins. "Like this?" Running her tongue in a full, exaggerated circle around her mouth, she laughs when she catches sight of the pained look on my face. "Okay, I will avoid anything lip related as long as you stop flexing."

I glance down at my still-folded arms. "I'm not flexing."

An agonizing moan ekes out of her. "Seriously?"

Well now I *want* to flex. And I do, if only to get that sound out of her again.

Carissa shuts her eyes as she groans. "This is going to be harder than I thought. You rugby men are something else."

"Are you telling me you're going to be drooling over the whole team every day?" I ask in a growl.

She sighs. "A little, but mostly just you."

"That's what I thought."

"Cole, this is ridiculous."

"I agree. Let's throw out the whole concept of rules."

When she looks at me again, something has shifted inside her. The amusement and attraction are gone, replaced by sadness and worry that instantly turn my blood to ice. "It's a bad idea, Cole. You and me. You know it is. I only just started with the team, and if we give that *Hollywood Hot Scoop* website a reason to poke around with a sharper stick, it's going to hurt us both."

I don't care what happens to me, but I hate the idea of anyone getting close enough to Carissa to hurt her. Stomach clenching, I drop my arms and nod. "Okay. You're right. You don't deserve to be dragged through the mud. And I need to figure out how I'm going to keep the team from falling apart while Moxie's in recovery, which is going to take all my concentration. Can't have you distracting me."

Carissa tucks her arms around herself, and I ache to hold her like I did last night. "Does this mean we're doomed to only ever be friends?"

"Ugh, I hope not." I shake my head, marveling at how quickly my whole life view has changed. A week ago, I was miserable because I thought I had lost the love of my life when Sage left me. Now...now I'm worried I'll never even get a chance with the woman who outshines Sage in every way. "I will treasure your friendship, Carissa. But I will always hope for more."

She smiles. "Me too."

"But you're right, and the timing is...not great."

That gets a laugh out of her. "It's terrible."

"I can wait."

"Me too."

"Friends?" I hold out my hand to her, desperately hoping she'll take it.

She does, tucking her fingers into mine. "Friends." Her eyes, so warm and electric, lock onto mine and pull me in, and I'm only inches away when we both tug our hands free and retreat to opposite ends of the kitchen. "We should probably avoid touching entirely."

"Good idea," I agree.

"And only spend time together while at work."

"I like that even less than the no touching rule," I grumble but agree to that one as well. "If anyone asks, we're friends."

She giggles. "We *are* friends."

"And *only* friends," I confirm. "No matter how much I wish otherwise."

Her playful scowl weakens my resolve to an alarming degree, but I have to stand strong on this. We both do.

I cough, folding my arms again and dropping them once more when Carissa's eyes trace my arms. "Should we get cooking?" I ask, finally tying the ties of my apron. It's a good thing Carissa didn't try tying them for me, or we never would have gotten to the rules. "If we're late to the get-together at Derek's, they'll wonder why, and it's better if we avoid any questions."

She nods firmly and puts her hands on her hips, sporting her cardinal and gold apron with pride. "Tell me what to do, Chef. I'm all yours."

A rush of desire runs through me, and I shake my head. This is going to be the worst friendship of my life.

CHAPTER NINETEEN

COLE

"I WAS WONDERING IF you were going to show up." Liam greets me with a smug smile that shifts as soon as Carissa steps onto the patio behind me. "Oo, and you brought our new friend!"

"Carissa!" The whole group says her name with the familiarity of old acquaintances, and I am quickly forgotten.

I can't help but roll my eyes as I sit next to Hank, Bonnie's boyfriend. I offer my hand to him. "Welcome home. How was the move?"

He chuckles as Bonnie returns to his other side after greeting Carissa with a hug. "Easier than you'd think. I didn't have much more than books."

"And he only brought half of those with him," Bonnie adds, taking his hand. Her broad smile speaks volumes as she and Hank lock eyes.

They've only known each other for a couple of months, but I've never seen Bonnie happier. I'm glad they found each other.

I make the mistake of looking over at Carissa, and heat courses through me when she returns my look with one of her own and darts her eyes toward the happy couple. I clench my jaw and force my eyes to Kasey and Liam, who are sharing the chair next to Carissa. "Any news on the movie?" I ask Kasey.

I'm usually better at keeping up with my friends, but the last couple of weeks have been rough.

"Movie?" Carissa asks, twisting in her chair to face Kasey.

Blushing, Kasey leans into Liam's embrace. I don't know why they always share a chair when there are plenty of seats, but she's almost always in his lap. The two of them need to get married already, but Liam keeps dragging his feet. "A screenplay I wrote recently got acquired by a film studio," she tells Carissa with a shrug. "It's no big deal."

"It's a huge deal," Liam argues. "And the story's about me, so you know it's going to be good."

Carissa laughs so freely that I can't look away. I'm glad she's comfortable with my friends, even if the last time she was here I warned her not to get attached. I was an idiot when I told her to keep her distance. She fits in so well with my friends, and I watch in fascination as she starts asking Kasey questions about the movie and giggling whenever Liam throws in one of his stupid jokes.

"Ahem."

I turn to find Derek settling in the seat next to mine, one eyebrow lifted so slightly that I almost don't notice it. "Hey," I say.

The eyebrow rises higher. "You never called me back."

Ah, right. I forgot how our conversation ended before I turned off the lights in the training room. "I was...busy." I wince at the clear guilt in my tone.

"Uh huh." Derek shifts back and leans one arm on the arm rest between us, dropping his chin into his hand. He's clean-shaven today, making me wonder if he started filming something new.

I shouldn't have to wonder. I used to know. Just how poor of a friend have I become?

"How's your homework coming?" he asks.

Don't look at Carissa. Do not *look at Carissa.*

"Nothing has changed since last night," I mutter. At least, nothing with the team. It's almost painful to keep my eyes on Derek when they want so badly to jump across the circle to the woman directly across from me. Why'd she have to choose that seat? "We'll see how practice is tomorrow, but I'm not feeling optimistic."

"Any word on Moxie?"

"No."

"It'll be okay, Cole."

"You don't know that." Against my will, my eyes lift to Carissa, and I'm surprised to find her frowning at me. Is that...worry...in her eyes? Something warm and solid settles in my chest at the thought that she might be worried about me, though I'm well aware she could be thinking about something other than me. She might even be thinking about Moxie, if she heard any of my conversation with Derek.

Derek clears his throat again. Chin still in his hand, he gives me a piercing look that makes me feel like I've done something wrong.

I swallow. "What?"

He drops his voice, though his expression doesn't shift an inch. "Curious that you would bring Carissa today. Last time she was here, you were convinced she was dangerous."

"She's still dangerous," I murmur.

"Hmm."

I narrow my eyes. "I don't like this look you're giving me, Riley. What are you insinuating?"

Again, Derek's expression doesn't change except for the slightest smile. I hate how much control he has over himself because it makes it impossible to get under his skin. I never know what he's thinking when he's like this. "I'm just curious," he says, eyes darting over to Carissa. "You've been different this week."

"You've barely seen me this week."

"Exactly."

"Well, I'm sorry I've—"

"It's a good thing, Cole." Derek sits up and smiles. "If someone—" his gaze jumps to Carissa again "—is taking up your time, I'm all for it."

For some reason, Derek's approval feels like all the permission I need to ignore the rules Carissa and I put into place and give a relationship a shot. Which is bad. We both individually need the team on our side, and that will never happen if we become a couple. And even if that wasn't the case, if things went wrong and Carissa decided she was better off without me, the guys would ostracize me more than they already have. I can't leave this team. I don't have high enough rugby stats for another SoCal team to want to take me, and I have no plans to leave California.

What would I do if I didn't play? Being an athlete is all I've ever known, and I don't know what it's like to have a normal job. A twenty-eight-year-old with no real work experience is a gamble not many would take, so who would hire me?

"Will you stop overthinking and start trusting yourself?" Derek says loudly, getting to his feet and clapping a hand on my shoulder. "I swear, you would think yourself into oblivion if you didn't have us to talk you out of things." He heads to the mini fridge sitting against the house and grabs a Coke like he isn't calling me out on my issues in front of everyone.

"What's your problem this time?" Liam asks.

You. I bite my tongue before the retort makes an escape. Liam would take the joke in stride and dish it right back, but I worry Carissa would think our bickering is real. It's not. Liam can get annoying, and his blissful relationship with Kasey has always felt like a slap to the face with everything that went down with Sage. But Liam is one of my best friends, and if I'm going to make a friendship with Carissa work, I need to show her that I can be a good friend.

So instead of poking at Liam, I opt for the truth. "Moxie got injured, and Coach put me in as captain to replace him even though the rest of the team doesn't like me."

Liam whistles low. "That'll be fun."

"They just don't know you," Bonnie says. "They'll warm up to you."

"It's been two years," Derek says. "I don't think the team is the problem."

I frown. He's saying *I'm* the problem. It's true, but I don't like that he's calling it out. "Thanks for that, Derek."

"I would offer to coach you on how to make friends," Liam says, "but I'm leaving on tour in less than a week." He pulls Kasey tighter against his body, both their expressions falling. I'm going to assume neither wants to be apart from the other.

Seriously, I know Liam has a ring. He just has to ask the question. It wouldn't solve the problem of being separated while he's on tour, but at least he would have a fiancée waiting for him when he got back.

"I could help," Bonnie says with a warm smile.

"You have reshoots this week," Hank tells her and kisses her hand.

While I appreciate her offer, Bonnie is similar to Carissa in that she is beautiful and kind. Essentially a magnet for men. The guys would be nice to me only when she was around or to get an in with her, despite the fact that she's in a surprisingly committed relationship for how short it's been.

"If only you knew someone friendly who could help you," Derek says with such a thick layer of sarcasm that I'm surprised he's not physically dripping with it.

I narrow my eyes at him. He glares right back in a clear challenge. "Do you have something to say, Riley?" I know he does, or he wouldn't have pulled the others into this conversation. Is this why he didn't give me a solution last night?

He leans against the mini fridge and shrugs. "If you knew someone with access to the Thunder who could help you connect with your teammates, maybe you would have more success."

I curse under my breath.

"Maybe I could help." Carissa sounds wary, but her expression carries more than a hint of excitement. And while a thrill rushes through me at the excuse to spend more time with her, she knows as well as I do that we shouldn't be finding excuses to be together when it's going to be hard enough to keep a friendly distance between us.

But the idea does have merit. Of course Carissa could help me connect with my teammates. They already love her. But if I spend time with her, it's going to get increasingly difficult to keep my hands to myself, and that would undo any progress I might make with her help.

"That's a great idea, Carissa," Derek says. "Though I warn you, Cole is stubborn and can be a difficult man to work with." With the way Derek is smirking at me, I know it won't do me any good to explain why I wouldn't want a reason to spend time with Carissa. Derek probably figured out within seconds of our arrival that I'm into her, and now he's trying to push us together because he thinks that's what I need.

I certainly don't need any help in that regard.

Carissa blushes a deep crimson as she smiles at Derek, sparking to life a nauseating jealousy in my gut that shouldn't be there because I know Derek would never put himself between me and someone I like. At the expense of his own happiness, he has a habit of looking out for everyone but himself.

Not that I think he has any interest in Carissa. But I still don't like the way he smiles right back at her.

"I think I have a pretty good idea of the man Cole is," Carissa says. "I can handle him."

Oh, she thinks she can handle me? She's mostly seen me at my weakest. It's a bad idea to give Derek more motivation to push us together, but I can't stop the playful glare I give Carissa as we gaze at each other across the patio.

Her eyes glitter as she returns my glare with her own, her lips twisting up in a smile she seems unable to fight. Dang, she's beautiful. I knew that from the beginning, but everything new I learn about her makes her all the more appealing. Her determined, feisty nature is especially attractive, in part because I know she'll never turn it into a weapon.

"Okay, whoa," Liam says, breaking the moment. He's glancing between us, his eyebrows high. "Are you two like—"

"No," Carissa and I say at the same time.

"We work together," Carissa says. "That's it."

Even I don't believe her.

"'Work together,'" Liam repeats, resting his chin on Kasey's shoulder. "Is that what the kids are calling it these days?"

Rolling my eyes, I stand and make my way to the mini fridge to give myself an excuse to look away from Carissa and cool down a bit. "Kasey," I say as I go, "will you kindly tell your boyfriend that he is way off the mark?"

"Is he?" Derek murmurs, stepping aside to give me access to the fridge. "Because I've never seen you look at anyone like that. Not even Sage."

I grab a bottle of water and drain it in one go. I'm delaying the inevitable, but I need a second to figure out what to say to Derek that won't give him too much hope but also won't be a lie. "We won't work," I mutter when I've swallowed the water.

Derek frowns. "Why not?"

Too many reasons to list them out. "Trust me. We've agreed it's better for us to be friends, so don't go making any schemes."

He scoffs, the sound overly dramatic. "Me? Make schemes? Never."

I point at him. "One of these days you're going to fall in love with someone who drives you crazy, and don't be surprised when all of us start meddling."

Calm as ever, Derek chuckles and glances back at Carissa, who is doing her best to pretend she's listening to Kasey and Liam rather than our conversation over by the fridge. Her eyes keep darting our way. "You're going to hate the question I'm about to ask."

I groan. "Why do you always do that? Just ask."

"You respond better with a warning, and you know it."

"Ask your question, Riley."

"Are you in love with Carissa?"

He's right. I hate that question. I hate it because I don't have a ready answer in either direction. Because my stomach churns with uncertainty. Because every time I look at Carissa, I feel more alive than I did mere seconds before looking her way.

And I'm terrified.

Derek puts a hand on my shoulder. "Whatever your reasons for pretending you don't feel something for her, I hope you're not letting fear get in your way of happiness, Cole."

My phone buzzes in my pocket, and I glance down to see a text from Freya.

Freya:

> Are you doing better than you were when we last talked? You were afraid of something, no matter how much you pretend to be well, and I worry for you.

"How does she do that?" I mumble, shaking my head at her timing. "Does Freya have your house bugged or something?"

Derek glances at the house behind him. "Not that I know of."

"That is not a very confident answer, Riley."

He shrugs. "That's because I'm not confident. I wouldn't put it past her."

Tempted to ask Freya if one of her bodyguards put up listening devices in all of our houses, I instead reply to her question honestly.

I chuckle, rolling my eyes at the way Freya refuses to use the nicknames of my teammates, but my amusement is short lived. Tomorrow, I'm going to have to face the team as their captain. I'm going to have to face *Moxie*. And I don't know if I can do that while also fighting my attraction to Carissa.

I'm only so strong.

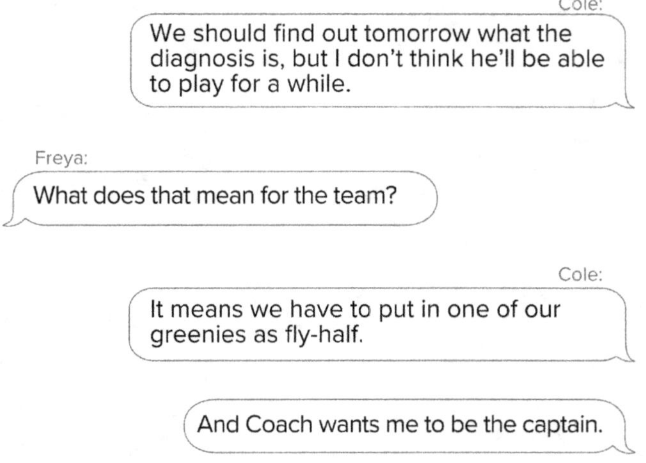

My phone lights up with a call from the princess, and I let out a heavy sigh. I shouldn't have said anything, but she would have found out at some point. "This is going to be a long conversation," I guess out loud and make my way into the house while Derek laughs. Sometimes I hate how attentive my friends are.

Chapter Twenty

CARISSA

THE NEXT WEEK IS one of the worst weeks of my life. Moxie's MRI results are even worse than I expected—he tore his ACL, MCL, *and* his meniscus, the holy trifecta of knee injuries. He's scheduled for surgery next week but comes to practice on Monday, looking perfectly normal as he carefully walks to the locker room with a knee brace. But every once in a while, one of his steps is wobbly and pain crosses his face. Mel, who apparently told him to stay home and isn't at all happy to see him, tells him that she will personally tackle him and tie him down if he tries to join in on practice, so he spends the day on the sidelines, directing drills and shouting encouragement.

Coach Galvin glares at him every time Moxie opens his mouth.

Cole and Moxie have a long conversation on Tuesday morning, and Moxie seems fine with Cole being captain by proxy. They fall into a sort of rhythm, where Moxie says things to Cole, who in turn says it to the team. It appeases Coach, who becomes increasingly less involved in practice as the week goes on, but the rest of the guys grumble every time Cole passes on Moxie's direction. At least they seem to understand *why* it's happening, and Cole almost always follows Moxie's lead when they're working on drills.

As the days go on, though, I can tell Cole is starting to get frustrated. Starting Tuesday morning, he heads to the stadium early and stays late in the weight room, so he orders rides rather than joining me, and his smiles have been painfully absent all week while he's out on the field. I don't know if he hates that he's forced into the captain spot or if he wants to lead his own way rather than Moxie's, and I can't ask which it is because Cole avoids me like the plague.

Apparently he took our boundaries to the extreme.

For my part, Mel and I have done a deep dive into preventing another injury like Moxie's. She's been drilling taping techniques into me, and I've been implementing more warmups into the daily routine, to the point where it feels like half of practice is spent stretching. That, plus extra time in the weight room, and hopefully no one else will end up with a non-contact injury like Moxie's. The work is a nice distraction from the fact that Cole and I have reverted back to strangers.

It's probably for the best, keeping our distance, but I already miss the flirting and the heated looks. I miss the way Cole was relaxed and happy.

On Friday, while I'm sitting on the field with tape in case anyone needs it while the team runs practice plays at the end of the night, Moxie comes to sit next to me, grunting as he stretches his leg out in front of him. Coach isn't here today, but Moxie seems perfectly content to let Cole and the assistant coaches run things. Or maybe he's done putting on a brave face now that Mel left early for the day to pick up her kid. He and Mel have been giving each other unreadable looks all week, though I'm not sure either of them realizes it.

I badly want to ask if something happened between them over the weekend, but I'm not brave enough for that.

"How's your knee feeling?" I ask.

Moxie grunts, eyes on his team. We haven't spoken much this week—Mel has been good about checking on him—but I've seen plenty of his frustration in his eyes. This injury must be driving him crazy. "It feels better now than it will next week," he says after a while.

I wince in sympathy. "Yeah, recovery isn't going to be fun. But you know you can't play with an injury like this."

"I know. Do you..." He ducks his head. "Has...has Cole said anything to you about the captain thing?"

He hasn't said anything to me at all. But I keep that frustration to myself and instead ask, "Like what?"

Moxie shrugs. "Something is holding him back. I told him that I'm fine with him stepping into that role, but he keeps deferring to me. Why? Coach gave him the captaincy, and it's not like I can be all that helpful. I know he has it in him, but he's..." He shakes his head. "He'll never be a good captain if he doesn't trust himself."

Moxie handed off the role? From what I've watched this week, I thought for sure Moxie wanted to do as much as he could to lead the team, with or without the title of captain. Hugging one of my legs, I watch the team run a play before I say anything. How much would Cole want me to share? I would know if he would talk to me.

"I think..." I swallow, hoping I'm making the right choice. "I don't think Cole is worried about himself. I think he's worried about how the other guys will respond."

Moxie falls onto his back and shuts his eyes. "He hasn't even tried!"

"Maybe, but you know how the team treats him." And I've been a terrible friend because I've done nothing to help him make connections with the other players. Not only have I failed Cole, but I've failed Derek and Freya and all the others who are expecting me to help Cole settle into his new role. "I want to help him," I say, letting the words wash over me. I do want that. I just have to make it happen instead of wallowing in my failing friendship. "Is there some sort of fairy godmother for connecting a guy to his teammates?"

Moxie looks over at me, a thoughtful look in his eyes. "*You* could convince them to give Cole a chance."

"Maybe," I agree. "But I should have done something earlier in the week. With no game tomorrow, I won't be able to do anything until Monday, and the guys will have a whole weekend to solidify their opinions of him after this nightmare of a week."

I watch as Cole says something to Wyatt, who completely ignores him as he walks past. Cole scowls, and it's clear this isn't the first time that has happened in recent minutes. Even if Cole wasn't the team captain, he's still the lead over the backs. No one bats an eye when Sharkie gives directions to the forwards.

"We can fix that," Moxie says, sitting up again. There's an eagerness in his expression that hasn't been there this week, and I'm glad to see some life in him again. "On bye weeks like this, the guys usually go out for drinks."

"I'm having a hard time picturing Cole out for drinks with the Thunder."

"That's because he never comes with us," Moxie says with a roll of his eyes. "But I'd bet you can convince him to change his tune tonight."

I don't know about that. Things have been strained between us all week, so there's no telling if he would actually listen to me. That's not to say I won't try. I am all for having an excuse to talk to him after going most of this week with barely a few words between us.

The team breaks up, heading toward us and the locker room behind us. None of the players look all that happy with the way practice has gone today, but none of them are as surly as Cole at the back.

"He's not in the best of moods today," Moxie says with some wariness. "But we can't keep going like this. The team's falling apart."

I told Derek that I can handle Cole. I guess it's time to find out if I was right. Hopping to my feet, I help Moxie stand as well and smile at the guys as they approach. "Hey," I say to Tink at the front. "I hear you guys are going out tonight. Can I come?"

Any of the single guys within hearing distance stop in their tracks, all of them with bright eyes and eager smiles. A few other guys stop as well, but most of the rest head for the locker rooms. Either they are planning to head home to their significant others, or they don't care whether I join in.

"You want to come with us?" Tink asks. He sounds completely shocked, and I have to do my best not to laugh.

"Is that okay?"

"Of course it's okay!" Wyatt says, scrambling to the front of the pack. We haven't interacted much since I turned him down, but the smile he gives me is warm. Either he still thinks he has a shot, or he's happy to just be my friend. I hope it's the latter because tonight I'm going to do my very best to convince him and Cole to get along. "You hear that, boys?" he says to the others, as if they aren't standing right there. "Rizzo's coming with us tonight!"

Cole, who was walking past the gathered men, stops dead. His eyes find mine for only a second before they zero in on the back of Wyatt's head.

Moxie chuckles at my side. "It might be easier to get him there than I thought," he mutters for only me to hear.

I agree, and I can't stop the smile that spreads across my face. "I've been wanting to hang out with you guys more, especially because I don't have many friends here."

Cole's eyes turn stormy as he looks at me again.

He can't blame me for saying something like that when he's spent the last week avoiding me, especially because I meant it. The few friends I've made have all been busy this week. Liam left for his tour, and Kasey went with him to San Francisco for the first concert and won't be back until tomorrow afternoon. Bonnie is doing reshoots while Hank settles into the house he's renting, and Derek is way too intimidating to hang out with one-on-one.

I look directly at Cole when I say, "I've been feeling pretty homesick this week, so hanging out with you guys will be nice."

"But maybe shower first," Moxie says, giving the boys a sharp look.

They all scramble for the locker room, leaving me alone with Moxie and Cole. Cole wastes no time stomping up to me and glaring as he asks, "What are you doing?"

I tilt my chin up in a challenge. "Exactly what I said. I need friends."

His jaw tightens. "You *have* friends."

"Not this week, I don't. They're all too busy for me."

A shadow passes over his features, and he folds his arms as he looks between Moxie and me. "You're planning something, aren't you?"

"I don't know what you're talking about," Moxie says calmly. "I told Carissa about drinks tonight, and she wanted to come."

Cole chews on his words for a moment. "Well, have fun with that." He takes a step toward the locker room but stops when I reply.

"I intend to. I don't know the team well enough, and it will be nice to get to know them away from work."

"I know what you're doing." He doesn't even look at me as he growls out the words. "But pretending to take an interest in the team won't get me to go out with them. You said yourself you don't want to give them the wrong impression, but this will—"

I scoff, shaking my head at him. "Geez, you really are the most stubborn man I've ever known."

He clenches his jaw, eyes locked on the turf beneath his feet.

"Cole, I'm allowed to have friends."

"They're not going to see you as a friend."

"You don't know that."

"I really do. Mox, tell her—"

"I'm not getting in the middle of whatever this is," Moxie says, holding his hands up. His eyebrows are high as he looks between us. "But I do think you should come out tonight or this week will look like a walk in the park compared to what's coming. I'm going to be down for the count after my surgery Monday, and I won't be flying out to Portland with you guys. You'll be on your own for the next game, Cole. You *need* to let them trust you."

When Cole turns his head to look at us, his irritation has made way for worry, and I desperately want to wrap him up in a hug. I hold myself back, knowing I need to make him come to me if I'm going to break him out of this funk.

"Stop fighting reality," Moxie begs. "It's not changing, no matter how much you want it to."

Without a word, Cole continues on his way to the locker room. He doesn't even look back.

An ache settles in my chest as I watch him go. "Do you think he'll come?"

"I don't know," Moxie admits. "But I'm going to guess there's more to you two than carpool buddies."

"There's not." If I sound miserable, it's because I am. Things were so easy on Sunday, but after Cole went inside to talk to Freya, something changed. *He* changed. I don't know what they talked about, but he was distant on the drive back from Derek's, and now...

Now I don't know what's going to happen between us.

Moxie puts a hand on my shoulder and offers a sympathetic smile. "Give him some time. And maybe flirt a bit with some of the guys tonight. Nothing crazy, just..." He shrugs. "You're right about Cole being stubborn, but he's a man of action when he wants to be. If you give him the right motivation, he'll realize that he has to change if he wants anything to get better." Is Moxie really telling me to make Cole *jealous*? I must be making a face of disgust because he laughs. "Okay, wow. Sorry. No flirting. It probably won't take that much, anyway. Just be your friendly self tonight, and I'll be there to keep the guys in line."

He leaves after that, and as I gather my stuff to bring back to the training room, I think about what I can do to help Cole get over whatever it is that has him in such a bad mood.

Being myself is by far my preferred method, but I don't know if that will be enough. I think I need to show Cole that I mean business. He tried things his own way this week, and it didn't work. Now it's my turn.

CHAPTER TWENTY-ONE

COLE

"I THOUGHT YOU WERE angry with me," Freya says through a yawn.

I narrow my eyes at her. I do feel a bit bad for waking her up, but I need some motivation here, and she's the only one who will get through to me right now. "I am angry with you. I'm angry because you're right."

She yawns again and shifts her phone. Half her face is buried in her pillow, and this might be the first time I've ever seen her without any trace of makeup. Even when she is "casual" and with us away from the public eye, she's always under scrutiny. She can't afford to get noticed by something like *Hollywood Hot Scoop* when she has a whole country that relies on her. Or soon will.

But tonight she looks like a regular human with bedhead and eye bags who just got woken by an early morning phone call. "What am I right about?" she asks. Before I can say anything, she adds, "A lot of things, yes, but what sparked this call?"

I sigh, checking around me to make sure no one is within hearing distance. A video call while standing outside a bar in Los Angeles is not my best idea, but here we are. "I'm scared."

Freya blinks. "And?"

"And I don't want to be. I did exactly what you told me not to do, and I'm worried I pushed things too far to fix them."

After taking a deep breath, she sits up and turns on a light, throwing her natural face into sharp relief. She looks so different from what I'm used to, like she's aged backward a few years. "What did you do?"

I bite the side of my tongue. "I ignored Carissa all week."

"Coleman!"

"I told you. I messed up." But it's Freya's fault. She told me she could tell something was different and rightly credited the change to Carissa. Then Freya guessed I was starting to let her into my heart in a way I didn't with Sage, and I panicked. I started imagining the horrible things that could happen to her if she loved me. Pictured her getting hurt—or worse. I can try to tell myself all I want that the Evanson curse isn't real, but that doesn't make it true.

"Cole," Freya says gently, "you look miserable."

"I am miserable. This week sucked."

"Then you should know what to do."

"But how? It was hard enough trying to do what Moxie does without adding in everything I'm starting to feel for Carissa."

"Why are you trying to do what someone else does? You are not him."

I am so aware of that. The team actually likes Moxie. They despise me.

"Cole." Freya's warning tone tells me she can read my thoughts clearly enough without me having to say them out loud. "I told you on Sunday. You cannot do the same as someone else because you are your own person. You must do things your own way."

"And what if I fail?"

"Then you fail. It happens to all of us, and your strength is measured by your ability to rise and try again. You cannot know your potential unless you give it space to spread its wings."

Rolling my eyes, I let her words sink in. It's four in the morning for her, and she still manages to say the right thing. "I hate how you always sound so inspirational."

"I am soon to be a queen, Cole. One would hope my ability to give a speech is greater than most."

"How humble of you."

"Humility is not the absence of confidence." She squints at the screen. "Where are you?"

I glance at the bar behind me. "I'm moments away from making things worse, probably, but you're going to tell me it's a great idea. Carissa went out for drinks with the team."

The sheer excitement on her face is almost enough to get me to turn around and start walking home. "Oh?"

"Don't look at me like that," I complain. "I'm just here to make sure they treat her right."

"Yes, I am certain that is your only reason."

"I know you think we're soulmates or whatever, but Carissa and I barely know each other."

"There is an easy fix for that."

I glare at my phone. "And what is that?"

"Stop talking to me and go inside. You cannot know her if you avoid her."

"That's less inspirational and more common sense."

"And yet I have to tell it to you."

I groan and drop my head against the wall behind me. Even knowing this was where the conversation would likely go, I don't like how simple

Freya makes it sound. It doesn't *feel* simple. "But what if I drove her away? She wasn't happy with me today."

"Nor am I, but I still care for you. If she is as special as you make her sound, she will forgive you for a few bad days. But you must give her the opportunity."

I want to do that. With my friends all busy—exactly as Carissa said—I was either at home by myself or with Dad and Gramps, who constantly asked when I would bring Carissa over next. Not talking to her has been the worst, but I hoped I could concentrate on settling into the role of captain. Not that I made any progress on that front, so this lonely week has been completely pointless.

All it has accomplished is stoking the fire of my interest.

"Cole," Freya says gently, "you need her in your life. You know you do. When will you allow yourself to be happy?"

When I feel like I deserve it.

A text notification drops from the top of the screen, and I glance at it. It's a picture from Moxie, but I can't tell what it is before the notification disappears. Unease settles in my stomach. Moxie's somewhere inside, and I can't imagine any reason he would send me a picture except to show me something I'm not going to like.

"I should go," I tell Freya.

"Yes, you should," she agrees, narrowing her eyes at me. "And do not be surprised when I call you in the middle of the night someday."

I roll my eyes. "You were going to be awake in an hour anyway, Peach."

"That is still an hour of lost sleep, and I have precious little time to sleep lately. So I *will* be returning the favor."

Her threat makes me smile, and I wish her a productive day despite her lack of sleep and hang up. I got lucky when Derek met Freya all those years ago, and I'm glad I called her tonight. Even if her constant nuggets of wisdom are hard to swallow.

With the call over, I pull up the photo Moxie sent and am instantly put on edge when I see Carissa tucked under Bean's arm as they sit at a table with a few other guys from the team. She's laughing, and Bean is looking at her in a way that makes my skin crawl. He's looking at her the way *I* do.

Swearing, I shove my phone into my pocket and head for the door, impatiently waiting for the bouncer to check my ID so I can get inside. As soon as I do, I follow the rowdy sounds of the Thunder congregated in the corner by the pool tables. I can't see Carissa anywhere, but I do find Moxie, who must have a view of her from where he's sitting.

"Where is she?" I ask, sliding into the booth across from him and scanning the bar.

"Hello to you too," Moxie says.

"*Mox.*"

He nods to his left. I see Bean first, sitting at a table just like in the photo, but it takes me longer than I'd like to find Carissa. She and Freddie, the new starting fly-half, are huddled together and giggling over something on Carissa's phone. She's holding the phone, but her hand is resting in Freddie's palm.

"Is the phone too heavy?" I grumble to myself, grabbing the drink in front of Moxie without looking away from Carissa. When I take a sip, expecting something bitter, I'm caught off guard by the ice water in the glass. I look at Moxie, raising an eyebrow.

He chuckles. "What, you think most of us actually come here to drink? Unlike you, a lot of us have jobs with early hours, and it's not worth the risk of a hangover."

I can't decide if I'm grateful for the lack of alcohol or annoyed that I can't distract myself from the way Carissa interacts so freely with my teammates. Mostly, I feel guilty realizing I have no idea what any of these guys do outside of rugby.

Returning Moxie's drink to him, I swallow my pride and ask, "What do you do?"

Chuckling again, he takes a long drink of water before he says, "I'm a vet. Finished school right before you joined the team."

I curse under my breath, trying to imagine going through veterinary school while playing a sport as rigorous as rugby. Moxie has been playing with the Thunder for three years, since the team was formed. "That's impressive," I tell him. "I barely managed two years of college."

"Not all of us can be champion NFL players with million-dollar paychecks right out of the gate."

I snort a laugh and relax in my seat. Mostly. Part of my focus is still on the way Carissa is now arm wrestling French Roast, who is easily twice her size. If I'm going to befriend my teammates, I need to start with the guy I know will talk to me. "I was third string my first two years," I tell Moxie. "Never saw a game."

"Ah, you're one of those underdog stories?"

"Hardly. I was good at what I did, but the other guys cost more so they got to play. If they hadn't gotten injured, I would have gotten my chance eventually. It just would have taken longer." I furrow my brow. "It's weird to have someone not know any of this. Sometimes it feels like the whole world knows my story."

Moxie's smile is half amusement, half sympathy. "I don't know how you do it, man. All those articles posted about you? That would drive me nuts."

I wonder if he's seen the ones with Carissa, though I'm too afraid to ask. We've been lucky that no other stories have dropped—probably because I've kept my distance—but speaking *Hot Scoop's* name out loud feels like tempting fate. "You get used to it," I say with a shrug.

Carissa's bright laugh rings out across the bar.

Tension fills my shoulders as I look over and watch her dance with Sharkie despite this being a crowded bar, not a club. She looks so...happy. Better than she's looked all week. Maybe she's better off without me.

"So," Moxie says, pulling my gaze back to him. "You came out tonight. Please tell me you didn't come just to talk to me."

"I came to make sure none of the guys bothered Carissa."

"Does she look bothered?"

No, and I hate it. She looks like her worries have melted away in a way I can't do for her because I come with tabloids and baggage and a curse that prevents me from really feeling for someone.

Sharkie spins Carissa right into Bean's arms as he steals the dance, and I feel like I'm watching something designed to poke at all my sore spots. These are good guys, and they're apparently not even drunk like I expected. They're just having a good time and enjoying the chance to experience Carissa's warmth up close.

I can't have any objections except my own selfish wants, and I don't deserve those wants in the first place because I spent a whole week ignoring her. But that doesn't make me want her any less.

Cursing under my breath, I push up to my feet and walk toward the guys before I can talk myself out of it.

Tink notices me first, and his jaw drops as soon as he realizes it's me. "What are *you* doing here?" His question comes during a break in the overhead music, which means everyone hears it and looks our way.

Instinct tells me to scowl at their shocked looks, but I force my expression to stay neutral. "I wanted to see what all the fuss was about," I say and nod at Bean, who stands stiff with Carissa still in his arms. "Where'd you learn to dance like that?"

Bean narrows his eyes. "What are you trying to—"

"He has four younger sisters!" Carissa says, cutting off the angry question. "Apparently they all use him to practice dancing before school dances."

Matching her smile is easy, even with my confused teammates staring at me. I talk to Bean, but I can't pull my eyes from Carissa and the way she looks overjoyed that I came tonight. "That's really cool of you, Bean. I always wanted a sister, but my dad never remarried after my mom died."

Whispers break out among the Thunder, and I do my best to ignore them. I don't know why I picked the guy who hates me more than most, but now that I've started, I need to keep pushing forward.

"Does your family live here in LA?" I ask.

Bean drops his arms from Carissa, like he's completely forgotten he was in the middle of a dance as he gapes at me. "Yeah," he says after a long time. "Yours?"

I nod. "It's just my dad and grandpa, though."

"His mom died when he was born," Carissa adds. Anyone else, and I might not have loved someone sharing that little tidbit, but there's something in the way she says it. Like that detail is crucial to understanding who I am.

Maybe it is.

"That sucks," Bean says.

I nod. "It does."

Carissa glances between us and reaches out for French Roast's hand. "Grayson, didn't you tell me your dad died a few years ago?"

He nods, meeting my gaze. I wonder if the rest of his family are all in New Zealand or if he's here on his own, but I'm too much a coward to ask. "I got to spend twenty years with my dad, though," he says. "You didn't get to know your mum."

"I don't know if it's harder to know and lose or to not know at all," I say.

"My oldest brother died when I was a kid," Tink says. *Noah*, I remind myself. His name is Noah. This isn't a conversation for nicknames. "My mom tells me all the time that I'm just like him, but I barely knew him so it feels like I'm just a copy and paste of someone else and not my own person because I only have memories to compare to."

My eyebrows rise, and a few of the other guys seem just as surprised as I am. That's not the kind of thing a guy willingly says out loud. "Hey," I mutter and touch his arm. "You get to be your own person. And sorry about your brother."

He gives me a grateful nod.

A silence settles over the group, heavy but not uncomfortable. I'm feeling a shift among us, not just between me and the team but with all of us. Like some of these guys have never connected this deeply with each other. Of all the ways tonight could have gone, I did not expect a somber conversation about lost loved ones in a noisy bar, but here we are.

"Death sucks," someone says. I don't know who, but murmurs of agreement follow his comment, along with a couple of chuckles.

Carissa, still holding Grayson's hand, looks at me in a way that makes me regret even more than I already did staying away from her. "Well," she says when no one has any other family deaths to add to the conversation, "in an effort to lighten the mood, anyone want to bet on if I can beat Evanson in an arm wrestle?"

The guys chuckle, but to my surprise they actually start placing bets, most of them *against* me. Either this is a fun way to tell me how they really feel about me, or I missed something from the earlier match with French Roast.

Frowning as they shuffle around to give us both space at the table, I try to read Carissa's expression. Obviously she could never win—her arms are tiny—but I'm happy to allow her the victory if she thinks it will help me break down more barriers between me and my team. I made some strides just now, but I've got a long way to go.

Carissa sets her elbow on the table, hand at the ready, and fixes me with a smug look. "You should know, Evanson, that I've beaten every other guy here so far. Grayson even tried for a rematch and lost, so battle at your own risk."

Is she serious? I glance at the guys, and their barely concealed laughter worries me. "What am I missing?"

"You can take the coward's way out," Wyatt says. "Or you can take the hit to your pride like the rest of us."

He's serious. They all are. Despite the amused looks they're giving each other, they all seem pretty convinced I'm going to lose.

I rest my elbow on the table and narrow my eyes at the woman across from me. "You're looking pretty smug for a woman who couldn't open a jar of pickles yesterday."

She gasps. "You saw that?"

"Saw Gator open it for you? Yes. Also, who eats pickles straight from the jar?"

"I do. Are we wrestling or not?"

Taking hold of her hand, I make sure I'm situated properly so I don't give Carissa any advantages. I still don't see how she could possibly beat me, but the guys all wait without breathing, like they're anticipating the match of the century.

"Ready?" Wyatt asks, standing beside us.

Carissa wiggles her fingers, adjusting her grip, but my focus is fully on the smirk on her lips. "Ready to lose, Rihanna?"

Oh, she did *not* just call me that. "In your dreams, Paxton."

"Go!" Wyatt says.

I start off easy, worried about hurting her. But when she withstands the pressure, I push harder. She doesn't budge. Worried now, I look down at our hands and realize she's curled her wrist inward, putting my own at an angle that makes it difficult to get the right leverage.

"Clever," I say, shocked when my voice comes out strained.

Carissa's sweet smile feels like a punch to the gut as it evokes memories of a week ago, before I took the idiot route. "You can give up now, if you'd like," she says.

I narrow my eyes. "No way."

"Fine." Next thing I know, she's leaping forward and pressing a kiss to my cheek. My arm goes slack, just enough for her to slam it down on the table. She whoops and high fives several of the guys as they cheer.

I stand stunned. Not only did the feel of her lips send an electric shock through me, but based on the reactions of my teammates, they all probably got the same treatment when they went up against her.

They all got kisses.

What does that mean for us?

Wyatt claps a hand on my shoulder, laughing like he just heard the world's best joke. "Guess you're not as heartless as we all thought."

Carissa scoffs before I can bite out an angry retort. "Are you kidding? You know that fancy car I've been driving?"

Grayson whistles low while Freddie says something about how nice it is. (I don't actually know Freddie's real name, which is something I should probably fix.)

"Cole lent it to me when he realized I don't have a car," Carissa says. She scoots around the table to stand at my side and press her palm against my chest, over my heart. I doubt the guys will like her closeness, but I can't bring myself to care. I've missed her, and it's taking everything in me not to place my hand over hers. "He and Moxie didn't like the idea of me taking the bus to the grocery store and things, so Cole took pity on me." Her eyes lift to meet mine, and heat spreads from where she touches until I'm overheating. "This man has always had a heart, but I don't think he has let any of you see it because his fame doesn't make it easy for him to trust. Not even the people closest to him."

I trust *her*.

I may not have shown it this week, but I've never trusted anyone the way I trust her. Even when she's talking about me like I'm not here, I want her to know every part of me. And that can't happen if I'm constantly running scared at every hint of trouble.

I look up at the guys, surprised to see more of them have gathered. It looks like half the team surrounds this table now. "I'm sorry," I say, hating how difficult this apology is before I've really started. "I'm sorry I haven't trusted any of you, that I've been distant, that I haven't come out with you in months. Sorry I've been a terrible teammate and friend."

Everyone is quiet for a long time, many of them shooting glances at each other, and it's Wyatt who breaks the silence. "We haven't exactly made it easy on you."

I snort. "No, you haven't."

Quiet laughter spreads through the team, and I meet Carissa's warm gaze just long enough for her to give me a look that says something along the lines of, "I told you so." I don't know how she did it. She's been here for two weeks and pulled down immovable barriers like they were tissue paper, and she has left me completely thunderstruck.

As the guys start chatting about cars, I pull out my phone and send a text.

I don't get a reply until several minutes later, when Carissa excuses herself to use the restroom. I've got a Coke in hand as I watch a few of the guys play a round of pool, but I'm content to lean against a wall and keep my focus on my phone for a minute or two.

Cole:
I'm sorry I avoided you this week.

Carissa:
Does this mean you'll start carpooling with me again?

Cole:
Only if you let me. I was a jerk.

Carissa:
You were, but I like to see the best in people.

Cole:
That's because you're the best.

Carissa:
I know.

Cole:
What's Freddie's real name?

Carissa:
You were right next to him all of practice this week and you don't know his name?

Cole:
We should be glad I've paid enough attention to know everyone's nicknames, all things considered. Cut me some slack.

Carissa:
Just this once. His name is actually Freddie.

Cole:
Huh. Why'd he get to skip the nickname plague?

Carissa:
I've been with the team less than two weeks. You've been here for TWO YEARS.

Cole:
Am I allowed to play the "got dumped" card?

Carissa:
That expires after three months.

Cole:
What about the "team grump" card?

Carissa:
I will admit you play the part well, but I don't think that's an excuse to not know your teammates. There are only 30 of you.

Cole:
How about "I didn't care about this team as much as I should have until you became a part of it"?

Carissa:
I'll allow that. But we should probably make a rule about no flirting over text, or it's going to be really hard to stick to the friend zone with you over there smiling like that.

I look up, finding her watching me from across the room with her bottom lip between her teeth. For the first time, I realize she's wearing an oversized navy Thunder t-shirt with our logo—a rugby ball with a lightning bolt in its center—plastered across the front. Her hair, curly as ever, spills over one shoulder, leaving the side of her neck bare. With her cutoff shorts and worn converse, she looks like she belongs here in California. Far more than she did the day she arrived.

The sight of her leaves an ache in my chest, and I turn back to my phone.

Cole:

> Nope. If I can't flirt with you face to face, I'm not giving up my only avenue.

Carissa:

> Are we sure it's better for us to stick to being friends?

No, I'm not sure. But something in my gut tells me to be careful. To take things slow.

With the way Carissa's looking at me, that's not going to be easy.

Hollywood Hot Scoop

Shame or Flame? A Relationship under Wraps

Spotted in North Hollywood: Cole Evanson and his latest fling, Thunder trainer Carissa Paxton. While it's no news that many of Los Angeles's favorite rugby players frequent Harry's Bar and Grill, tonight was the first time in months anyone has seen local legend Cole join his teammates out on the town. We all know Cole sightings are rare, but don't you worry your pretty little heads. We here at Hot Scoop are ready to share all the intel!

Cole and Carissa have been keeping their relationship quiet, to the point where not even Cole's teammates are aware of it! We spoke to several Thunder players last night, who all claimed they had no idea a romance was brewing under their noses. But anyone who looks at this photo would know that Cole has been captivated.

With Thunder captain Malcom Auxier injured, Cole has taken his place as the leader of the LA rugby team, and it looks like things are on the up and up for Cole as his ex's wedding looms right around the corner. One has to wonder if Cole is trying to sweeten the pot and get his old flame back in his arms by making himself more desirable. Could Auxier's injury have been planned? Is Carissa simply a pawn, or is she climbing a ladder too? We brought in a sports expert to analyze last week's home game, and what he found might shock you!

Stay tuned for the chilling truth behind Cole's rise to the top of yet another team, and let us know in the comments if you think the LA Thunder (and the team's cute new trainer) will be just another notch in the athlete's bedpost. XO

Chapter Twenty-Two

Carissa

I DON'T THINK IT'S normal to get nervous about a female friend coming to hang out, but I'm freaking out. Maybe it's because I never really had girlfriends after I hit puberty, so this feels like new territory to me. Like my sister, most of my friends in high school and college were guys. *Unlike* my sister, none of them were true friends. Once they realized I wasn't likely to let them out of the friend zone, they slinked away with their tails between their legs, leaving me alone in every sense of the word.

The solitude was nice while I was in PT school so I could focus on getting through all my training, but it did leave some things to be desired.

Like knowing what to do when a girl comes over.

Kasey shows up right when she said she would Saturday afternoon, a bag of junk food in her arms and a tote full of books hanging on her shoulder. Last week, when I was at Derek's, we talked about our shared love of reading, and Kasey asked if we could get together to talk books when she got back from San Francisco so she could have a distraction from Liam being away on his tour. Obviously I said yes—I need all the friends I can get—but now that our hangout is here…

"Hey!" I say, stepping back to let her into my apartment.

Dropping the junk food on the kitchen island, Kasey takes in the space with wide eyes. The kitchen and living room are lumped together in one open space—a lot like Cole's actual house—everything clean and bright and new. "You can afford all this working for Cole's team?"

I snort. "Not even a little bit. My brother-in-law is paying for it." And while I feel incredibly guilty for taking advantage of his generosity, I'd have to get two more part-time jobs to pay for something like this, and I wouldn't feel safe in anything less. The curse of not leaving home before now, probably.

"Rich people are the best. I pretty much moved in with Liam a week after I met him because his house was so much better than where I was living."

I raise an eyebrow. "I thought you stayed with him because of paparazzi stuff."

Her eyes practically sparkle as she grins at me. "That too, but Liam and his house were hard to resist."

This is my first time interacting with her without Liam's arms wrapped around her, and the longer I look at her, the more I realize how close in age we are. Plus, before Liam she didn't live in wealth like the rest of the group, and her shorts and tank top make me feel better about wearing leggings and an oversized t-shirt. She feels…normal.

After a new *Hot Scoop* article showed up this morning, I'm desperate for normal.

Kasey's eyebrows pull low. "Did I say something wrong?"

"Dang it," I mutter, as tears spill out of my eyes. "I promise there's a reason I'm crying, and it's not you. I mean, it's sort of you, but it's not…"

Grabbing my hand, she pulls me over to the couch and plops down, bringing me with her. "I could be way off base here, but I'm going to guess you're overwhelmed. I read the article they posted this morning."

I nod, amazed by how easily she locked on to the feelings that came out of nowhere. "I never wanted to be famous," I blubber. "And I'm not... Cole and I aren't even dating! And suddenly it feels like everyone knows who I am and they're talking about me and I don't know what to do." This feels like everything with Peter all over again, and my stomach is twisting itself into knots. "I don't know how to handle this again."

Kasey takes hold of my other hand and squeezes both. "Take it from someone who is still new to this world. It's okay to be overwhelmed, and it's okay to feel scared. But you also have a pretty great support system. What has Cole said about all this?"

I look at my phone, which I left on the kitchen counter as soon as I found the article. "I don't know. I've been comfort-watching *Bridgerton* all day, trying to keep my mind off of things."

"Hmm." Kasey pulls her phone out of her pocket and purses her lips as she reads something. "Now I understand why he asked if I was still hanging out with you today. He's clearly worried about you."

I know I shouldn't, but I shift her phone closer so I can read exactly what he said to her.

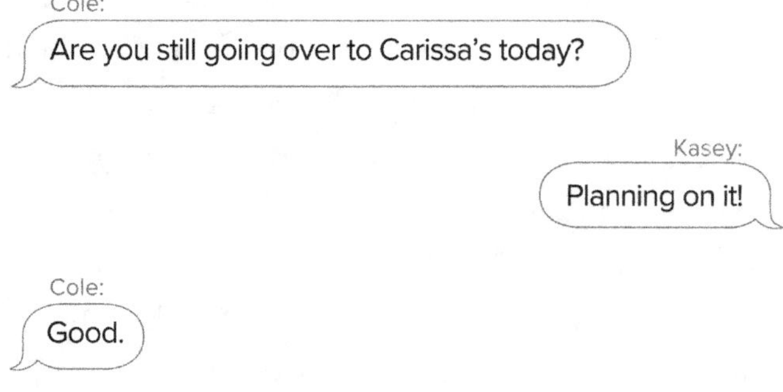

That's it? How did she get *worry* out of that?

Kasey chuckles and offers a soft smile. "Cole and I rarely have reasons to talk outside of the group chat, so the fact that he even asked is pretty damning."

"Damning?" I repeat.

"I just mean it's clear he didn't want you to be alone. Which is strange."

"Strange?" I repeat. I'm sounding like Liam's parakeet, Nelson, who is almost as famous as Liam himself.

Kasey nods. "I've only known Cole for a few months, and the first time I met him was the day after Sage broke up with him, so he was pretty miserable. The gang always says he hasn't been himself since, but I've had to take their word for it until now. He is stepping up to look out for you."

Warmth spreads through me, calming some of the fears and anxieties roiling in my gut.

"All that to say," Kasey continues, "Cole won't let *Hot Scoop* or anyone else hurt you. Neither will the rest of us. You can breathe."

I can breathe. Just having someone next to me who has been through something like this is making it easier to bear the potential backlash from the article, and I throw my arms around Kasey's shoulders to pull her into a tight hug. "Thank you," I whisper. I'm crying again, but these are tears of relief more than anything. "And I'm sorry that I'm not doing a very good job of distracting you."

She shrugs, cheeks turning pink as she tucks some hair behind her ear. "Oh, well, I'm doing better than I thought I would."

I gasp and grab her hand, staring at the glittering ring on her finger. "Did Liam *propose*?"

Her eyes go wide. "Yes?"

"Why did that sound like a question?" I ask with a laugh.

"I mean, he did propose. But then he...we..."

That's when I notice the second band pressed up against the first. The *wedding* band. "Kasey!" I shriek. "Did you guys...?"

She covers her face with her hands, but she can't hide the broad smile that stretches across her mouth. "We eloped. Yesterday. But you can't tell anyone! Liam wants to tell everyone in person, and he won't be back for *weeks*."

I squeal with excitement. "You got married!" And oh boy, how am I going to keep that secret? "Oh my gosh, everyone is going to be so mad when they find out!" Hopefully not from me...

"I know," Kasey says, still hiding behind her hands. "But we were talking about a wedding, and neither of us really wanted any pomp and circumstance. And after his first show, we decided we didn't want to wait and we just..." She shrugs, grinning again. "*I got married*. And my parents are going to kill me but I don't even care because I'm Liam Connolly's *wife*. If we didn't have to keep it a secret, I would let it slip to *Hot Scoop* to get the attention off of you for a bit, but..."

I hug her again. "Thanks, but you deserve privacy too. I've been through this before, so I just need to—"

"You have?" Eyebrows pulling low, Kasey stares at me like I just said something crazy.

Because I did. Grimacing, I nod and curl my legs up to my chest. "Back home, before I came here, I sort of got involved with a married man who was running for governor, and someone found out." It's way easier to say than I would have thought, but maybe that's because Kasey shared her secret with me first. "I didn't know he was married. And he was my client too, so it was all..."

"Messy?" Kasey guesses. When I nod, she squeezes my hand. "My boyfriend in college stole my script and sold it to a producer, who got it turned into a movie, and I didn't get any of the credit."

My jaw drops. "Seriously? Okay, why do men suck?"

Snickering, she hops off the couch, grabbing the food and her books. "Not all men. I ended up with one of the good ones, and I couldn't be happier with the way the dumb things in life led me to him." She pulls out a bag of gummy worms and, to my amusement, a copy of the first *Bridgerton* book. "Anyway, if you can get through something like that with your ex, you can handle anything that *Hot Scoop* might dish out. And for the record?" She takes my hand and smiles. "Cole Evanson is not the type of guy who has bedpost notches. And I'm pretty sure he likes you."

I *know* he likes me, which is part of the problem. But I keep that to myself, grateful for a friend who seems perfectly content to get lost in a fantasy world with me for an afternoon and pretend everyone can get a happily ever after. Kasey is right. She got one, even if her new husband is in a different state right now, and if she can be happy in a world of tabloids and gossip, maybe I can be too.

When the timing is right.

CHAPTER TWENTY-THREE

COLE

I THINK I'VE OFFICIALLY stepped into stalker territory. I pace back and forth down the hallway outside Carissa's apartment, telling myself that it's perfectly normal for me, her friend, to be here. Unannounced. Uninvited. Unwanted.

Hopefully not that last one.

The worst part is I had to get Carissa's apartment number from *Bean*, who definitely didn't buy my story about needing to get my car for something but was gracious enough to tell me anyway.

Wyatt, I remind myself. I should call him Wyatt. Our team nicknames are a way the Thunder has bonded as a team since its formation, but for me, I'm going to need to show some genuine connection. Some effort. I made progress last night at the bar, but I still have a lot of work to do.

I should probably be focused on finding my own style as a captain, rather than pacing a hallway and psyching myself up to knock on Carissa's door, but Carissa hasn't answered any of my texts all day. After our text flirting last night, as well as a nonstop conversation on the drive home, I'm desperate to talk to her again.

I don't think I can go very long without talking to her, which is a bad sign. I'm falling for her, and I shouldn't be, but I need to know she's okay after that last *Hot Scoop* article.

I'm just about to suck it up and knock when Carissa's door opens and Kasey steps out, eyes going wide when she sees me standing there. "Cole!" She tucks her hands behind her back and turns progressively redder the longer we stand here. "What are you doing here?"

I try to see through the crack in the open door behind her, but all I've got is a view of a white wall. "How is she?"

Snickering, Kasey glances behind her. "She's stronger than you seem to think."

"Not possible," I mumble. Carissa has proven time and time again that I should never underestimate her, so I'm convinced she's the strongest person in the world. In every way. "Are you leaving?"

Still pink-cheeked, Kasey nods. "Liam is playing in Vancouver in an hour, and his manager set up a livestream for me."

"Are you ever not attached at the hip?" I grumble. I shouldn't be irritated by their connection, but I'm blaming my grumpiness on the fact that I haven't heard from Carissa all day and the only thing standing between me and her is a door. And a woman who is every bit as loving and loyal as my friend deserves. Swallowing, I duck my head. "Sorry. You and Liam are great together."

Kasey snickers. "I sure hope so, 'cause now he's stuck with me."

I frown. "What—"

"You can go inside. Carissa's pretty deep into the book she's reading, so you might have to get her attention. But she'll be glad to see you. Bye, Cole!"

As Kasey scurries toward the elevator, I feel like I'm missing something, but I don't care because the door is open and Carissa is inside. I'm hoping she won't be angry about me interrupting, but Kasey doesn't seem worried.

As I step inside, my phone buzzes in my pocket. I'm tempted to ignore the text, but when I see that it's Freya, I open it because it's literally in the middle of the night for her.

Freya:

> If you see Carissa tonight, tell her that she cannot give any power to that ghastly website. She has not answered my text, so she may not have gotten it, but you will see her, yes?

Okay, now I'm wondering if Freya has bugged our *phones*, not our houses. Though I can hear Carissa munching on chips at the other end of the hallway, I stay where I am and type out a reply.

Cole:

> Do you ever sleep?

Freya:

> Sometimes. Are you with Carissa?

I debate how to answer that one and settle on the truth.

Cole:

> Not yet. And I haven't talked to her today, so I might not get a chance to pass on your wisdom.

Freya:

> You will.

I'm glad she feels so confident. I certainly don't.

Pocketing my phone, I slowly make my way forward and poke my head around the corner. Carissa is sprawled on a gray couch, one hand holding a colorful paperback and the other deep in a bag of Funyuns. Other assorted junk foods lay scattered around her, and she looks...okay. Like the article didn't bother her too much. I hope that's true, but I know there's still a high chance *Hot Scoop* is going to mention her affair with the politician.

Ethan found the story on a Philadelphia site earlier today, so there's no doubt other people have found it too.

As I stand and watch her, Carissa is so absorbed in whatever she's reading that I don't think she has any idea that I'm here.

I cough.

Carissa screams.

The book flies at my face as Funyuns fly over Carissa's head. I catch the book, but she's not so lucky with the chips, many of which land in her messy bun.

"Sorry," I say, wincing as I look down at the cover of the book in my hand. A cartoon hockey player in skates stands at the edge of a rink, smirking at a woman in street clothes. It looks like one Sage has read, but honestly they all look the same to me.

Curious, I flip to a page in the middle and lift an eyebrow as my eyes trace a scene that definitely falls under 'spice.' "I thought you didn't read these ones," I mutter, my stomach twisting. It was one of the many reasons I like Carissa.

She isn't like Sage.

Blushing, she pulls onion rings out of her hair and says, "I don't, usually. But Kasey likes that one, and the story is really compelling and well written. I mostly skimmed the...uh..." She turns an even brighter red and shrugs.

I grunt. Maybe it was a bad idea for me to show up here.

"You okay?"

I look up, surprised to see concern in her eyes. "Hmm?"

"You're back to looking glowery."

I gently toss the book back to her and tuck my hands into my pockets to hide the way they tremble. This isn't about hockey, or even about the book, but there's no good way for me to explain the knot in my gut to Carissa when I'm barely starting to understand it myself. "You can read whatever you want."

She tilts her head. "But?"

But Sage expected me to be aggressive and domineering like some of the men in her books, and I didn't realize how much I struggled with that until right now. I know I should speak those words out loud. I haven't been to therapy in a few years, but I still remember the way my old therapist told me I shouldn't avoid letting myself feel, that I should own what I'm experiencing instead of burying it.

But how am I supposed to tell someone as kind and innocent as Carissa that my ex had a habit of using intimacy to manipulate the nature of our relationship? I didn't realize it at the time, but the further I get from the situation and the longer I'm around Carissa, the easier it is to see that Sage never truly wanted to be with *me*. She wanted the man she thought she could turn me into if she made enough promises.

I was only twenty-four when we met after my first winning game as a starting quarterback. Sage was only a couple of years older, but I think she knew, even then, that I would do anything to please her. She made me feel so valued at first, like she needed me in her life, but the deeper our relationship became, the more she pushed me into things I didn't want. I told myself that I wanted to make Sage happy, that giving in to her fantasies was a part of making our relationship work.

Looking back, I hate how easily I put aside the things I wanted and ignored the way I felt whenever I was with her.

"Cole?"

There's a measure of hurt in Carissa's expression that's pulling at my heart in a way I don't like. Especially because I'm the one who put it there by withholding my thoughts. It's probably better if I step back again. Keep my distance. Follow the rules.

"Hey." Carissa slithers out from her junk food blanket and pads over to me, looking so vulnerable as she gazes up at me with those gold-flecked eyes. "I know you said Sage liked to read these kinds of books. I don't usually—"

"Don't worry about it," I say, my voice rough. "You really can read about whoever you want. That has nothing to do with me."

"I think it does, though." She runs her hand down my arm, fingers light against my skin, and she pulls my hand from my pocket so she can lace our fingers together. "I don't judge people who read that stuff, but most of the time it's not for me. If that kind of thing bothers you, I'm fine to avoid it entirely. Especially if it reminds you of...you know."

I frown, looking down at our hands. "Are *you* not bothered?" I ask, almost desperate for her answer. "I tell you I'm interested in you, and then I go and compare you to a woman I shouldn't be thinking about anymore. I'm as bad as Peter."

To my shock, Carissa laughs, and the sound brightens the room. Warms me from the inside out. "First of all, if you were anything like Peter, you wouldn't care that something reminding you of your ex—a woman you dated for *four years*—might bother your friend that you're definitely not dating. Second of all..." She reaches up and brushes her fingers through my hair, sending a shiver through me. "The man cheated on his wife with his physical therapist, who had no idea he had a family."

Maybe I'm not a cheater, but that doesn't mean I'm good for her. "But I'll never be..." I shake my head. "I'm never going to be like the men in these books you read."

She leans up on her toes, though we're still nowhere close to the same height. She presses a hand to my chest to hold herself steady, and I am completely riveted on her words. "I'll always like you better than the men in these books because you're *real*. And far more interesting."

Leaning down, I'm desperate to give that declaration a proper response in the form of a kiss, but a stray piece of Funyun in her hair distracts me and holds me back. It's for the best, though I don't think I'll look at the snack the same way as I pluck the piece from her hair. They'll always make me think of her.

"Dangerous," I murmur, amazed by how effortlessly she puts me at ease. "You are incredibly dangerous."

"And you smell amazing," she replies, unashamedly taking a deep breath. "I think I've gotten too used to your post-practice smell. Or maybe the smell of the other guys temporarily killed my scent sensors."

I groan and step back. "Nice mood killer."

"I do my best." She tilts her head again, studying me. "Is there a reason you broke into my apartment tonight? One that wasn't getting me to confess how much I like you?"

"That was the main reason." But I smile and shake my head, returning my hands to my pockets before I get any ideas about pulling her back into my personal space. "Or I wanted to make sure you're okay after that article."

Shrugging, she looks into the kitchen, where her phone is sitting on the counter. "I'm good now."

"Now?"

"Kasey talked me down, and the article really wasn't that bad. But it triggered some memories."

"Theme of the day," I mutter, rolling my eyes. I'd be a lot happier if memories of Sage didn't ruin things for me. "If you're okay, I'll get out of your hair. Like the Funyuns."

Her intoxicating laugh fills the room once more, and I soak it up before turning to let myself out. "Wait," she says. "You can stay. If you want."

I clench my jaw. I do want, but... "That's a bad idea."

"Probably." Carissa smirks and points to an armchair that's just as gray and lifeless as the couch. While the apartment is nice, it doesn't have any verve, and I can't imagine Carissa living here long term. She doesn't fit this place. "You can keep to the chair if you decide to stay. I'll stay on the couch."

I raise an eyebrow. "And what am I supposed to do while sitting in the chair?" It's not like I'm going to argue with her plan, whatever it is. This goes against our rules, but I'm happy to take any time with Carissa that I can get. Wherever she does belong, I hope it's close to me.

She looks around thoughtfully, then digs into a canvas tote and pulls out another book with a cartoon cover. I wrinkle my nose as she hands it to me, and she laughs. "This one is really good, I promise. It doesn't have any spicy scenes, and the main characters are both personal trainers who pretend they're not totally into each other. They get pulled into a fake relationship because of social media."

I roll the book over in my hand. "Sounds familiar."

Carissa's voice turns mischievous. "And the guy is scared to love because everyone leaves him."

I look up, eyebrows lifting high. "Maybe too familiar."

Snickering, she settles back on the couch and picks up a different book from the hockey one. I appreciate that more than I can say. "*And* he has anxiety," she adds before opening the new book and diving in.

I settle in the armchair, curious what kind of book Carissa usually reads. I'm more intrigued by the character's similarities to me than I care to admit, and if Carissa likes this book, I want to at least give it a try.

There are a lot of things I'd like to do for Carissa.

And the best part? She never asks for anything, which makes me all the more inclined to give her the world.

Chapter Twenty-Four

CARISSA

"I've said it before, and I'll say it again. I will take down that website once and for all."

I raise an eyebrow at Wyatt. "When have you ever said that?" Before he can answer, I run my hands along his calf muscle and grin when he lets out a squeal and nearly kicks me with the foot that's resting on my shoulder as I loosen a knot in his leg. "And what happened to stretching before practice, Mr. 'I promise to stretch'?"

Lying on his belly, Wyatt presses his face into his arms and moans. "I *was* stretching! Just not—" he hisses as I dig my fingers into his muscle again "—today. Geez, Rizzo, are you trying to make me lame?"

"You do that all on your own, Bean." I work through the knot in his calf a few more times, then step back, letting his leg fall. "I'm pretty sure you need more potassium in your diet or something, because that was ridiculous." At the rate these men are needing my services, I'm going to have to get certified as a massage therapist before long.

Wyatt gingerly stands, testing his legs by bouncing on the balls of his feet. "Thanks," he says humbly. "I promise I was doing better, but this morning French Roast found that article, so we've all been kind of tense."

After a weekend spent eating junk food and reading non-spicy books with Cole, I was determined to get back to the practice field and try to focus on work again, but all evening the guys have been acting like the *Hot Scoop* article has condemned me to death.

"It's really not that bad," I say for the umpteenth time. "But I appreciate you looking out for me."

"I swear, that website is getting worse and worse," Wyatt says, running a hand through his hair. "Of course none of us know you and Cole are dating. It's because you're not dating!"

"Yep," I confirm right as Cole steps into the doorway of the training room, sending my heart skittering at the sight of him. "Not dating."

Unfortunately.

Over the weekend, he finished two of the books I gave him and started a third, apparently eager to read the whole series when the first one was better than he expected. And there is nothing sexier than a man reading romance.

Except maybe that man wearing a form-fitting white t-shirt and leaning against a door frame with folded arms. Does he have any idea how many boxes he's checking just by standing like that?

"Still talking about that stupid article?" Cole asks with a roll of his eyes.

Wyatt snorts a laugh. "As if Rizzo would date a guy like you, Evanson."

No one has called him Rihanna all day, which is an improvement after last week. They also haven't used his first name, but I don't think Cole minds. Most of the team actually listened to him when he suggested today's drills, so I think something shifted at the bar on Friday.

"As if," Cole repeats, winking at me when Wyatt bends to pick up his shoes.

My face heating, I glare back at him. While he dutifully kept to his chair over the weekend, he spent a decent amount of time sending me flirty texts instead of reading, and I have a feeling he's going to push any lines he can find as we wait for the timing to be better.

I don't know how long I'll actually be able to wait.

"By the way," Cole says, sounding so casual, "I had an idea for a play that will only work with a strong wing."

Wyatt lets out a sound somewhere between a scoff and a laugh as he heads for the door. "Great."

Cole grabs his arm. "Want to try it out tomorrow? I don't think anyone could pull it off except you."

Wyatt's eyebrows shoot up, and he glances at me as if trying to figure out if I heard the same thing he did. "Oh. Really? Yeah, okay." But then he deflates. "But if Coach shows up, he'll—"

"Let me deal with Coach." Cole's eyes dance as he smiles. "The guy put me in as captain, and I kind of want to make him regret it."

"How?" I ask, and I'm pretty sure Wyatt is wondering the same thing.

Cole grins at me, hitting me with the full force of his magnificent smile, but he says his reply to Wyatt. "Coach wants me to take charge. I want to give the team a chance to be what *they* want to be. I'm not the smartest guy here, not by a longshot, and I think Coach has spent too long underestimating his team."

Though Wyatt doesn't say anything, he gives Cole an examining look and a smile before heading to the locker room.

Cole doesn't leave his spot in the doorway, which is a good thing because his gaze heats as soon as we're alone. "Any word from Mel?" he asks, eyes trailing over me in a slow movement.

It's not easy, but I try to ignore the fire that runs through me under his gaze. "She said Moxie is out of surgery and everything went well. She'll be here tomorrow."

"Great."

"That was good of you." I nod toward the corridor behind him. "I think Wyatt is too used to being underestimated." I feel like I'm baking beneath Cole's stare, so I start cleaning up the room and pretending I can't still feel his eyes on me. "Are you worried what Coach will do if he finds out you're empowering the guys?"

Cole huffs a laugh. "One, that can only make the team better. And two, the coach happens to think I'm something special because I used to be a pro quarterback, and I don't think he would risk the publicity of turning against me. I don't know if you know this, but I happen to be pretty famous."

He sounds so smug, but when I look up at him, his smile is nothing but playful and amused.

"You're famous?" I ask in mock surprise. "Do I know who you are? Are you that fancy movie star that everyone likes to hang posters of on their walls?"

That breaks Cole's smile, replacing it with fear that almost looks real. "Please don't tell me you have a Derek Riley poster on your wall."

I laugh. "No, I've never had Derek on my wall. Liam, on the other hand..."

After a quick glance into the hallway behind him, Cole rushes forward, grabbing me and lifting me onto the table so he can pin me on my back with his giant arms, leaving me breathless. "You take that back," he growls, a spark flickering in his eyes as he fights a smile.

I try to look innocent as I start singing Liam's most popular love song under my breath. I'm tempted to tell him that while I don't have a Liam poster on my wall back home, I do own records of all three of Liam's albums, including the newest one. I even spent the extra money to get a signed copy. But maybe I should take it easy on the poor guy, so I finish the chorus and grin up at him.

Cole growls again and steps back, setting me free. "You're really a fan, huh?"

I laugh and sit up. "How could I not be? His music is amazing."

"So I shouldn't tell you that he's playing in Portland the night after we play the Pathfinders and he sent me two VIP tickets to his show?"

I scream, clapping a hand over my mouth after it's too late to hold it in. "Are you serious?" I whisper right as a few sets of footsteps pound down the hall.

Sharkie, Tink, and French Roast stumble through the door with ready fists, but all three of them look extra confused when they see me sitting on the table with Cole standing several feet away.

"Uh." French Roast—Grayson—furrows his brow. "Everything okay, Rizzo?"

I grin. "Cole saw a spider and got spooked."

"That..." Tink—Noah—cocks his head at Cole. "That was you who screamed?"

Cole's jaw is so tight that it looks like he might snap a muscle. He'll obviously deny my claim, but it's fun to see him squirm. But then, to my utter shock, he says, "Yep. Hate the things."

The guys snicker, muttering to each other, and then Sharkie—Loren—says, "Anything we can do for you, Miss Carissa?"

Goodness, I thought they were attentive *before* I caught *Hot Scoop's* attention. I smile and shake my head. "No, but thank you, boys. Actually, Cole and Wyatt were just talking about new plays, and Cole was wondering if anyone else had any ideas to try out in practice this week before we slaughter the Pathfinders."

That seems to catch them off guard, but it only takes a second for Grayson to perk up and say something about how to fix their lineout issue. That's when they throw the ball from the sideline and catch it high in the air—I'm learning—but I never would have guessed they had an issue.

Cole listens attentively as Grayson offers his ideas, suggesting they try it out at practice tomorrow. The other guys apparently have ideas too, and as the four of them start talking strategies, Cole looks over at me and offers the warmest smile I've ever seen. It practically melts me from the inside out, leaving me a puddle of goo on the table as I watch this man *finally* find his place on his team.

And hopefully he can find a place with me too. I know we're waiting on the right timing, but...

I've never been known for my patience.

Chapter Twenty-Five

Cole

After a week of grueling practice full of new plays, more time spent in the weight room, and convincing Coach that I have a whole strategy for winning Saturday's game, I am so ready to crush Portland and spend a well-earned day with Carissa before we fly back home.

Our previous two games were at home with our own crowd, which usually amps up the energy of the team more than when we're on the road, but our last game was when Moxie got injured. As we make our way into the hotel Friday night, the guys seem to be buzzing with something new. I don't know if it's the new strategies we've been trying or if it's because we're determined to prove ourselves after that doozy of a game, but we're clearly here to win.

The guys are loud as they pair off to go up to their rooms, though it sounds like many of them plan to head to the pool to wind down before hitting an early bedtime. A couple of them ask if I'm joining as they pass me, which is a miracle unto itself. While I'd much rather decompress in my room, I probably need to keep up the momentum of this whole bonding thing. Freya hasn't said anything about my homework, but I'm sure she will.

Sage's wedding is on Sunday. Here in Portland. Something in me wonders if Sage planned it that way, knowing I would be here for a game, though I can't imagine what she hopes to accomplish. *She* broke up with *me*. And I'm over her.

"Doing the whole solo room thing still?" Wyatt asks, stopping next to me on his way to the elevator. I figured I would let the rest of the team get settled before I get my key, so I'm standing off to the side and trying not to think about my ex when Carissa is upstairs in her shared room with Mel.

I chuckle. "I'd rather pay for my own room than have to share with one of you."

"I don't blame you. I'd do the same if I could afford it, but no." Wyatt wrinkles his nose and watches Wilson, one of the locks on the team, fumble with his bag and lose half his clothes across the lobby floor. "I get to bunk with that."

"Hey, Wilson is our best tackle," I argue.

"Oh, he's great on a pitch. Not so much in a hotel room. The man's the messiest person I've ever met." He sighs and starts heading over to help Wilson, talking to me as he goes. "If you're ever feeling extra generous, Evanson, feel free to book me a single room like yours next time."

"Don't count on it!"

Truth be told, I've thought about paying for rooms for the whole team more than once, but it has always felt like trying to buy my way into their good graces, and that would have backfired. I don't think my money alone can do me any good, but I wish it could.

When the rest of the team has checked in and headed upstairs, I make my way to the desk right as my phone rings. *Freya*. I give my name to the desk attendant, then answer the phone.

"I'm not going."

Freya laughs. "Am I that predictable?"

I roll my eyes, tugging the hood of my sweatshirt over my head as if that might hide me from this conversation. "The wedding is in two days, and you haven't said anything about it in almost a week."

"Yes, well, I have been busy. But now I must know if I need to alert our pilot of my intention to come to Oregon or if Carissa will be your date."

"I'm not going," I repeat, nodding a thank you to the concierge and taking my key. The sooner I get upstairs, the better.

"You have made friends?"

"Does Carissa count?"

"No."

I hit the button for the elevator and let out a deep sigh. "I figured. Moxie?"

"He was your friend before I made my edict; therefore, he does not qualify. Cole, I thought you had a plan. Derek said—"

"From my understanding of your terms," I interrupt, "I simply had to try. I've done that." But I don't think I can say any of the guys would consider me a friend. A teammate? Sure. Captain? Getting there. But friend? I'm not sure that will ever happen.

"Coleman, if you had tried, truly, you would have succeeded."

The elevator opens, and I slip inside, grateful that there's no one else in the lobby wanting to go up with me. This isn't a conversation I want people overhearing. "Freya, do I need to remind you that friendship is a two-way thing? Whatever has changed on my end, it doesn't say anything about how the guys see me. I'm not paying the consequences of their choices."

Freya lets out a heavy sigh. "You are complicating this," she says as the door slides open on the third floor.

"And you think I'm more likable than I...am." My words trail off when I realize Carissa is standing in front of me in a striped blue-and-white swimsuit that shows off...everything. "Gotta go," I say into the phone and hang up, stepping back to let Carissa inside.

Carissa presses her lips together as she joins me right before the doors close again. Though she has a white hotel towel slung over her shoulder, I still have a full view of the bikini that exposes most of her fair skin. "Are you going down?" she asks, her cheeks glowing pink.

My mouth has gone dry, so I nod.

Carissa's eyes jump to my bag. "You sure about that?"

"I'm exactly where I want to be."

She bites her lip, but her smile tugs the pink flesh from between her teeth as she meets my gaze.

"That's against the rules, Paxton," I growl, dropping my bag and stepping forward. I back her into the corner of the elevator without taking my eyes off her. I've been good all week, enduring the fifteen-minute drive to and from practice without touching her. I've done my best not to watch her whenever she's on the field with us, bossing the guys around. I've resisted showing up at her apartment every night just to be around her.

But this? Seeing how strong she is despite her small size, catching hints of the warmth of her skin in the space between us, watching the stray curl that falls from her bun? That's asking too much of me.

I press my hands against the silver wall of the elevator on either side of her head, noting the way her breaths come in short bursts as she stares up at me, pink-cheeked and beautiful. "I didn't ask the last time," I whisper, leaning down until our noses touch. "But I'm asking now."

She nods, pushing my hood off my head. "Kiss me."

Right as our lips brush, the elevator shudders to life around us and moves upward. I drop my head with a groan, resting it on Carissa's shoulder. I could still go for it, but I'd rather not be interrupted.

I step back to the other corner of the small space right as we come to a stop and the door opens for half a dozen of the team, all of them in swim trunks and shirtless. I don't miss the way Carissa's eyes go wide as they shuffle in, and I think back to the day she went into the locker room to get my bag for me. I still don't know how much she saw, but she clearly likes the show today.

"You're coming swimming with us, Miss Carissa?" Freddie asks happily.

She beams. "Of course!"

The guys are all admiring her as much as she admires them, and unease settles in my stomach. Maybe I *should* keep to my room tonight. Jealousy isn't going to help me keep my distance from the woman when she's surrounded by half-naked athletes. Not just athletes. *Rugby players.* They put most of my football buddies to shame.

"You joining us, Captain?" Carissa asks, pulling my eyes back to her.

The guys all look at me.

I swallow and shrug. "Sure. Once I get settled."

"Which floor?" Grayson asks.

"Three."

"Hey!" Carissa says. "Me too!"

Oh good. Even more temptation. Grayson hits the button for my floor and the one for the lobby, and it's with great reluctance that I step out when it's my stop. I'm leaving an incredibly alluring woman with a team full of guys who have not been shy about their interest. Put them in a pool, and...

I swallow thickly and meet Carissa's eyes as the door slides closed, and I'm pretty sure she's laughing at me. She's going to enjoy tonight.

I'm going to completely hate it.

chapter Twenty-six

CARISSA

A GIRL CAN ONLY play so many rounds of chicken before she feels like she has violated one too many sets of pectorals. There is no classy way to play the game, and all of the guys want me as their partner, which means I've spent at least the last half an hour sitting on a man's shoulders while shoving another man's wet chest, trying to knock him over.

Don't get me wrong. I'm enjoying all these muscles, and under different circumstances I'd probably be in heaven surrounded by so many abs.

But Cole isn't here.

After winning yet another round—the guys are absolutely letting me win—I slide from Grayson's shoulders and swim to the edge of the indoor pool so I can hang on to the side while Grayson trash talks Noah and Jeff. I didn't realize how deep the water was until I was no longer sitting atop a six foot three fullback. I'm exhausted, and if Cole doesn't show up soon, I might as well just go to bed so I can be ready for tomorrow's game.

"Wanna give it a go?" Loren asks, swimming up beside me. He looks right at home in the water, which might be what earned him the nickname Sharkie.

I smile at him, knowing he's about to be very disappointed. "I think I'm all chickened out."

"Oh, but you haven't gone up against me yet," a familiar voice says above my head.

I look up, way more excited to see Cole than I should be. "That's big talk from a guy still fully dressed," I say.

Cole looks down. While he did change into swim trunks and flip flops, he's still wearing a shirt. And I am way more disappointed by that than I should be. I haven't seen him shirtless, and while I know he's strong, I wouldn't mind seeing exactly what's under there.

"That's because I just got here, Paxton," he says. "Now, don't tell me you're too scared to fight me." He nods at Gator in the pool. "Think you and I could take Sharkie and Rizzo?"

Gator grins. "Yeah."

"Great." Then he pulls off his shirt.

That's not a good way to describe his movement. Pulling off a shirt is basic. Instinctual. What Cole does is...*intentional*. His arms flex as he reaches back and grabs the collar of his shirt, pulling it over his head with slow deliberation and revealing his torso inch by agonizing inch. His abdominal muscles tense and strain as they come into view, and it's all I can do to hold on to the edge to keep from sinking to the bottom.

Tossing his shirt aside, he lifts both arms overhead, a smirk on his lips as he twists and stretches. After a few more flexes, he dives over top of me and into the water. When he surfaces and does that little head shake thing to get his dark hair out of his eyes, I nearly whimper, and then he climbs onto Gator's shoulders and is lifted into the air, water running over his tanned skin as he runs a hand through his hair and sends a grin my way.

"You up for this, Paxton?" he asks, his voice low and rumbling.

He knows exactly what he's doing.

I'm shaking as I get onto Loren's shoulders, and I know before we've even started that Cole won't let me win like the other guys did. There is an undeniable challenge in his eyes. The rest of the team surrounds us like this is going to be the match of the century, but they'll probably be disappointed. All of these guys are insanely strong and fit, but there's something about Cole's ridged torso and rippling arms that makes him look unbreakable. Like nothing in the world can touch him. Like silly tabloids could say whatever they want about him and he'd keep living his life how he wants. Combine that stability with his flirty smile, and I'm a goner.

Loren's hands wrap around my shins, and he tilts his head back to look up at me. "Ready?"

Cole cocks his head and lifts one eyebrow, silently asking me the same thing.

Oh boy. I'm so not ready.

"Ready," I squeak.

As the rest of the guys start cheering, Loren and Gator both surge forward, and instinctively I raise my hands, grabbing Cole's fingers before he can push my shoulders back and knock me from my perch. He locks our fingers together and shoves, but I throw my elbows back so the force of his push simply brings him closer. That was a bad idea. He's so close that I see the caramel tint to his brown eyes and the flash of his tongue between his lips.

Lips that almost captured mine in that elevator.

Cole pushes again, aided by Gator's powerful stance, and I squeak as I fall backward. But Loren keeps us upright and moves a few steps back, giving me some space to sit up even though I'm still gripping Cole's big hands. I've been through this enough times tonight that my core muscles are on fire, but I'm determined to give this my all.

"Forward!" I command, and Loren obeys, surging through the water like it's nothing. I pull our arms in so they're between Cole and me, hoping Loren's power is enough to push the other two back and off balance.

But Cole easily spreads my arms out again, and the sudden loss of resistance sends my face careening right into his broad chest. By some miracle he keeps me from breaking my nose on his collar bone by leaning back, but my relief lasts only a moment. Still gripping my hands, he tucks my arms behind me and lets go so he can wrap his arms around my back as he tugs us both to the side, tearing me free from Loren's shoulders and dunking me in the water.

The cheers overhead muffle as we sink deeper, locked together, and I don't care that my lungs are burning because I am pressed against the most beautiful man I've ever met and have never felt safer.

I feel him kick against the bottom, pushing us upward, and I gulp a lungful of air as soon as we break the surface. Cole immediately pushes my hair out of my face, still holding on to me with his other arm, and I don't need to kick my legs because he's keeping us afloat even though I don't think he can touch the bottom right here.

"You good?" he asks, eyes locked on me as he shifts a few inches to the side to where he can stand.

I narrow my eyes, still taking deep breaths as I try to recover from that whirlwind few seconds. "You were supposed to let me win."

"Where's the fun in that?"

"We all know you're bigger and stronger and perfect," I argue. "How about you show a girl some gallantry?"

His hand brushes over my hair again, even though he's already cleared my face. I think he just wants the excuse to touch me. (For the record, I don't blame him. My own hands are splayed across his chest, admiring the muscle on this man.) "I'm always gallant," he says with a smirk, and his fingers tighten against my waist, drawing a gasp from me. We're pressed together, skin to skin and our faces only inches apart, and I can see his thoughts racing behind his eyes as he studies my face.

His voice drops to a gruff whisper. "But I'm also losing patience."

"Me too," I whisper back.

"You guys good?" Wyatt says loudly.

We break apart, and my head slips beneath the water before I grab Cole's shoulder to pull myself up again. Does my other hand happen to press against his abs while I do? Maybe.

Not only is Wyatt staring at us as he sits on the edge of the pool, but the rest of the guys are doing the same. I hadn't realized how quiet the pool had gotten after Cole's win.

Cole clears his throat. "I was making sure she was okay after that tackle," he says to no one in particular.

"Sure," Wyatt says.

"Maybe that article isn't as phony as we thought," Grayson adds, folding his arms as his eyes jump between Cole and me. I can't tell if he's angry or simply curious. Either way, it's dangerous.

Stomach clenching, I slip away from Cole and swim to where Wyatt is sitting. I hold out my hand, which he grabs, and I plant my feet high on the wall so he can pull me up and out. I grab my towel, wrapping it around my torso, and smile at the guys, who are all watching me.

"Cole and I are not dating," I say as confidently as I can. "I don't date my patients."

"Why not?" Loren asks, frowning up at me.

"It's none of our business," Cole says. He hasn't moved from his spot in the pool, and neither has he done anything to curb the longing in his expression. That's not exactly going to help things, but I also don't want him to stop looking at me like that. "She doesn't have to tell us anything."

I can't stop my smile as his defense warms me from the inside out. "It's because," I say, though I'm probably going to regret being honest, "I can't trust my ability to make decisions lately. And I like working with you guys, so I don't want to ruin that."

A few murmurs spread through the guys as they look at each other. Wyatt speaks first. "Say we think you shouldn't let us hold you back from something you want," he says slowly. "Would you date one of us then?"

My eyes flit to Cole, whose eyes have somehow gotten darker in the last few seconds. "Maybe."

"But it would be me, yeah?" Grayson says, giving me a wide grin.

Loren punches him in the arm. "It would obviously be me."

"You're the only one who made her lose at chicken fighting," Grayson argues.

Loren jumps on him, dunking him under the water, and suddenly the guys still in the pool are all joining in a sort of brawl that makes me glad I'm on solid ground.

Regrettably, Cole lifts himself out of the pool on the other side, drying off with a towel without looking my way, but before I can head his direction, Wyatt touches my arm.

"You can be with him, you know."

I blink, tearing my eyes away from the corded muscle in Cole's back to look at Wyatt. "What?"

Though he smiles, the expression looks almost defeated. "Cole. I think we all knew he had your attention from the beginning, though none of us wanted to admit it."

Maybe I shouldn't be surprised that our glances and stolen moments haven't gone unnoticed, but I hoped we had avoided making things awkward with everyone else. I frown, shaking my head and tucking my towel tighter around me. Now that I'm out of the water and away from the warm bodies of the team, I'm starting to get cold in the air conditioning.

"Cole and me, it's a bad idea," I mutter. Movement pulls my eyes back to Cole, who pushes through the door to the hotel without looking back. I already miss him, but I need the distance before I start letting myself think I can have him.

"Why is it a bad idea?" Wyatt asks, folding his arms. "He's clearly into you."

"Him and everyone else," I mumble, wincing as soon as the words leave my mouth. How vain can I be? "I didn't mean—"

"Hey, you'll hear no arguments from me." Wyatt chuckles, shaking his head as if he can't understand anything I'm telling him. "We all like you for a reason, Carissa. If Rihanna is the one who gets your heart going, then none of us are going to stand in your way. Believe it or not, we're tough guys. We can handle a little rejection now and then."

I'm not sure I believe him, but before I can call his bluff, he jumps into the pool with a shout and joins the brawl.

Shivering, I stand there for another minute, trying to figure out what to do now. If Wyatt is right, the team won't go back to hating Cole if I start dating him. That's one obstacle down, even if it doesn't lessen my fears of something going wrong and costing me a job I'm really starting to like. But why am I so afraid? It's not like Cole is harboring a secret family, and I know he would never deliberately hurt me. My reasons for staying away from him don't stand up on their own anymore.

Cole has his own reasons, but again... If the team is okay with us dating...

Unsure what this means for us, I grab my flip flops and Cole's abandoned shirt, slipping the warm fabric on before I head around the pool to the same door Cole used. He's probably halfway to his room by now, and I am desperate for a shower to warm up, but as I pad down the hallway in my bare feet, shoes and towel in hand, I'm thinking I might text him as soon as I'm rinsed off so we can talk about this whole timing thing. What if the right time is now?

Oh, but what if he doesn't agree? That might be worse than waiting. After the way he nearly kissed me in the elevator, it feels silly to worry, but if he still thinks we need to keep our distance, then I don't—

A hand grips my arm, tugging me into a vending machine alcove right before the lobby. I only get a moment to study the intense determination in Cole's eyes before his mouth is on mine. Hungry. Needy. *Perfect.*

Dropping everything, I melt into him, wrapping my arms around his neck and pulling myself closer. He groans as my fingers find his wet hair, and his warm hands slide beneath my thighs to lift me up and better match his height. He leans me up against a wall and coaxes the kiss deeper until all sense of reason leaves me and there is nothing but this man and his mouth and this kiss.

Cole kisses like something inside him needs to be set free, his bare shoulders taut beneath my fingers as he expertly moves his lips against mine and keeps me suspended against the wall with the weight of his body, my legs locked around his waist. One of his hands is in my hair, the other pressed against my waist, and every place we touch burns with electricity. For all the enthusiasm in his efforts, I *feel* his restraint and the way it seems to slip more and more every few seconds, like whatever control he has will soon be hanging by a thread. I'm all for it, doing my best to match his every action because I have been desperate to experience this for so long.

He pulls away first, mouth lingering against mine as he breathes heavily and presses his hand to my cheek. "Carissa," he whispers, my name on his breath like a balm against my swollen lips.

It's a terrible reaction to the world's best kiss, but I laugh. It feels like the only thing I can do when I'm unraveling from the inside out. Everything about that kiss exceeded my wildest imaginings, and I will forever be changed after tonight. Reality won't be the same. "Where did that come from?" I breathe.

Opening his eyes, Cole studies me for a beat and then covers my ears with his hands just long enough for him to whisper something I can't hear. I can't read lips either, so I have no idea what he just said to me.

It wasn't "I love you." I know that much. But it was something that feels important, and as his hands fall from my ears to my neck, I try to read his thoughts in his dark eyes. Whatever he's thinking, it's making him anything but happy.

"I told you," Cole says after a moment, slowly lowering me back to my feet, which probably means I'm not getting another kiss like that tonight. "No more patience."

I can barely stand upright because my body is still reacting to that kiss, so I lean against the wall and wish he was wearing his shirt so I could grab hold of it and keep him from leaving. Grabbing his bare waist feels too desperate, even for me.

Cole seems to realize what I'm wearing at the same moment I'm thinking this, his eyes tracing the way his gray shirt hangs at my mid-thigh, and his muscles contract as he takes a step back, making him look even stronger than a moment ago. "Can I add something to the rules?" he asks, voice strained.

My heart sinks. "I thought we were done with rules."

Shaking his head, he runs a hand through his damp hair and takes another step away from me. "Carissa, we can't—"

"The guys are okay with it. With us." But even as I say it, I know that's not Cole's only hangup. "And you're not cursed."

"But what if I am?" He swallows thickly. "What if you get hurt because of me?"

"I won't!"

"What. If." His eyes glisten with moisture, the first time I've seen any kind of emotion like that with him. His pain settles deep inside me, an ache that I already know won't go away until I can heal him first. "Carissa, you're too special to risk."

"So you would rather lose me now?" I fold my arms, anger surging in my belly. "You can't kiss me like that and then say you don't want to be with me. I know you do, and *I* want to be with *you*. Why are we still fighting this?"

He growls. "Because—"

I don't let him finish. Rising to my toes, I grab his neck and pull myself up to kiss him again. He responds immediately, hands gripping the shirt at my waist and tugging me closer as he explores my mouth with a desperation that matches mine. We're two souls pulled together by a force stronger than anything I've ever felt, and I never want to stop kissing him.

But I do, slipping from his hold and grabbing my towel and shoes with shaky fingers.

"We have a game to focus on tomorrow," I murmur, keeping my eyes on my toes. "So I'm going to go up to my room and try to sleep. But after you win?" I peek up at him, my face heating when I see the burning desire in his gaze. "We're going to talk about this. I'm not letting you go that easily, Coleman Evanson."

He doesn't call me back or say anything to argue as I slip from the alcove and head to the elevator. I can't decide if that's good or bad, and I get back to my room quickly.

Mel's already asleep, though her phone is lying on the bed next to her, in the middle of a call. I smile when I see that it's Moxie on the other end. Moxie's surgery went well, but Mel has been worried about him all week, leaving practice early most days to stop by and check on him on her way home. Thankfully she finally found a reliable daycare that she can afford, which has given her the chance to keep an eye on Moxie and spend more time with him.

Something tells me it's not just about helping his recovery.

Carefully reaching across the bed and ending the call—from the silence on the other end, I'm guessing Moxie is asleep too—I quickly hop in the shower. I don't need to warm up anymore thanks to Cole, but I'm eager to wash away the day and let my heart rate calm despite my racing thoughts.

I get that Cole is scared. History has set convincing precedence to believe in a family curse. But if he's going to let that fear keep us from being more than friends, I need to know now. I value his friendship too much to lose him, but I'm done giving my heart away to men who won't give me theirs in return.

This is exactly why I avoided Cole in the first place.

By the time I get out of the shower and climb into bed, I'm ready to sleep as long as I possibly can, but my phone buzzes on the end table. I frown—it's late—but grab it to see who texted me.

My stomach dips when I see Cole's name on the screen.

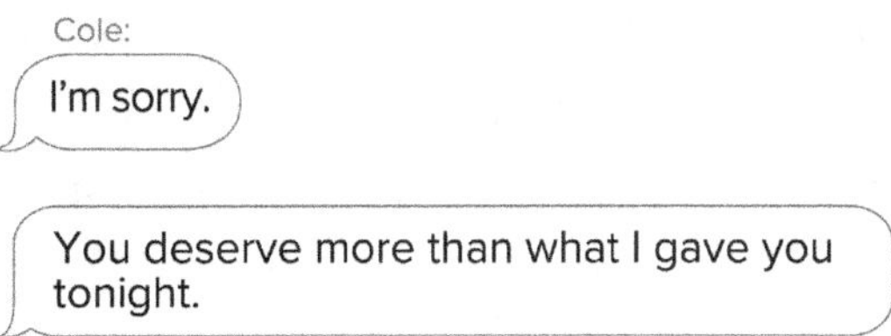

Frowning, I think through the many possible meanings of his words. Is he saying I deserve more than a man who's too scared to try? More conversation? More kissing?

He texts again before I can wonder for too long.

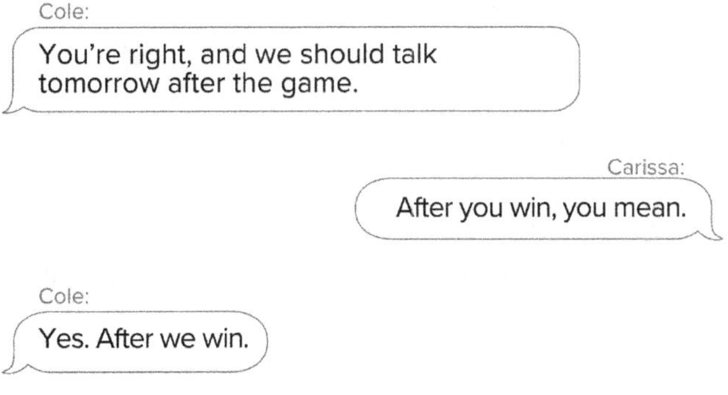

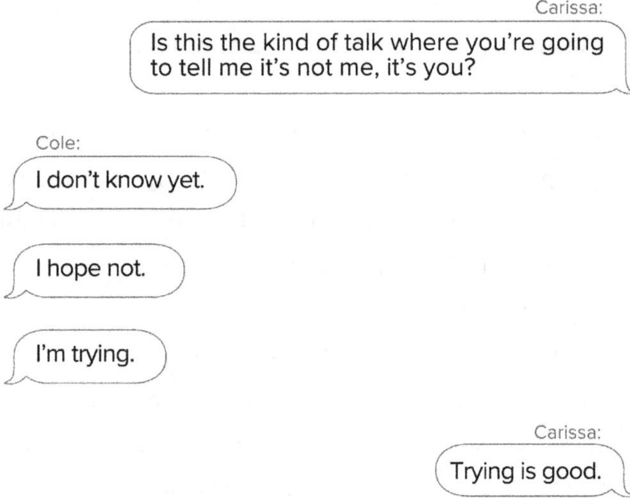

I pause with my fingers over the screen, wondering how much I should say in a text. I would rather say it all in person, but I'm worried about giving him too much room to think over the next twenty-four hours. Biting my lip, I type out another text and hit send before I can overthink things.

I grin, feeling his praise down to my toes. Maybe I don't have to be too worried just yet. He's willing to talk tomorrow, which is a step in the right direction.

Cole:
As a fair warning, I'm going to avoid you tomorrow.

Carissa:
That's a terrible idea.

Cole:
Like you said, I need to focus on winning tomorrow's game, and if I get too close to you, I'm going to want to remind you about what happened downstairs.

Carissa:
What happened downstairs? I've already forgotten. I think I need ALL the reminders.

Cole:
You are dangerous.

Carissa:
That's my middle name.

Cole:
Your middle name is Lynn.

I gasp. How in the world does he know that?

Cole:
I'm avoiding you tomorrow. Just know that I don't want to.

I appreciate the clarification, though I still don't like it. Nor do I like the idea of ending this conversation.

Carissa:
What's your middle name?

Maybe that was too bold of me because Cole doesn't reply. I settle myself beneath the covers, wondering how tomorrow is going to go. This is my first away game, and I think the guys badly need a win after what happened to Moxie. Part of me wishes Cole had waited until after the game to kiss me so we wouldn't have a distraction, but the bigger part of me keeps reliving the kiss as I close my eyes and try to sleep.

Another text comes in right before I fall asleep, and I look at it with bleary eyes.

My heart skips a beat, and I roll my eyes as I type the website into my search bar. Surely he knows me better than—oh. My stomach twists into knot after knot as I quickly read the article. Yeah, maybe I should have listened.

Hollywood Hot Scoop

Carissa Paxton—Carouser, Cavorter, and Completely No Good for Cole

Scoopers, someone needs to help Cole find a good woman to love because this guy is oh for two now. Either the man has terrible taste, or he's way too trusting, but after the heartache he endured at the hands of soon-to-be Badger bride, Sage Morrow, Cole has found himself attached to yet another heartbreaker.

I mean, this picture alone is bad enough. Carissa Paxton, new rehab specialist for the Los Angeles Thunder rugby team, was seen at an airport bar earlier today making eyes at a whole slew of strangers and flirting her way to free libations, leaving Cole miserable and broody on his own while waiting to board. Clearly she's not as invested in this relationship as our favorite scrum-half.

But wait, Scoopers, it gets so much worse!

Only six weeks ago, Paxton was intimately involved with Pennsylvania governor candidate Peter Huntsman, a married man with two children. And if you think that's bad, Huntsman was a physical therapy patient at the clinic where Paxton worked as an intern, and she clearly abused her connections to try to create a scandal and sabotage Huntsman's political career. There's no word on whether Paxton used extortion to get Huntsman to agree to an affair, but it's clear she's up to no good.

Cole, if you're reading this, I hope you stay far away from this woman. We may not know what her goals are, but considering she arrived in California at the side of notorious sports journalist Tamlin Park, chances are good Paxton is out for blood. Yours, specifically.

Be safe out there, Scoopers! You never really know who you can trust, but you can always trust *Hollywood Hot Scoop* for all your celebrity news. XO

Chapter Twenty-Seven

Cole

We're halfway through the game. Portland is up by ten. I'm completely exhausted. But it feels like the only way to fix anything right now is to win this game, and I'm staring down thirty men who all look like they've been knocked to the ground one too many times and are ready to give up.

Coach didn't bother coming into the locker room after the first half ended, which means the only thing between us and total failure is...me.

I really don't like that. After a morning spent on the phone with Ethan, Derek, and Freya, I'm no closer to finding a way to fix things for Carissa. She hasn't talked to anyone except Mel, who told me partway through the game that Carissa is barely holding it together. I want so badly to pull her into my arms and never let go, but that won't solve anything, and my team needs me too.

I hate this. I hate that the reason the whole country thinks she's a horrible human is because of me and my fame. I hate that people forget that there are real people on the other side of screens. People with tender hearts and vulnerable souls. I hate that whoever created *Hollywood Hot Scoop* doesn't care what they say as long as it gets them views.

Cursing loudly, I resist the urge to punch my fist into a wall as I make my way to the front of the locker room. We only have a few minutes left before we have to go back onto the pitch and pretend our hearts are in the game instead of with the woman who stole all our hearts the moment she arrived.

"This sucks," I say to the team. Half of them don't even look at me. "And it's been a long time since I had to give any sort of pep talk, so you're not going to get any motivational speeches from me." I shake my head. "I wish Moxie were here. He would know what to say right now. He'd say something stupid to get you to laugh, and then he'd throw out some piece of wisdom that would somehow resonate with each and every one of you. And then we would go out there and change that score and come out victorious because Moxie knew how to captain a winning team. I don't."

My voice breaks on those last two words, and I don't care and my anger and frustration are in full force. They're the only thing I have right now. "You all deserve better than me, and you deserve a win because you've all put in the work."

"We don't care about the game," Wyatt says, lifting his head to glare at me. A few men murmur in agreement. "We care about Carissa and the fact that you're the reason she looks like she's about to fall apart."

Clenching my jaw, I search the faces of the rest of the guys, realizing they're all in agreement. "This is exactly why I kept my distance from her," I argue.

"Distance?" Noah says with a laugh. "You've been carpooling with her every day."

"You went to her apartment," Wyatt says.

"I saw you making out by the vending machines last night," Freddie adds, turning a deep crimson when I shift my glare to him.

I grunt, trying not to get lost in memories of that kiss. It was so much better than I could have imagined, and I still don't know how I got myself to stop. Kissing Carissa unlocked something in me. Made me think, if only for a moment, I could have my own love story. Made me think I wasn't broken.

I shake my head. "Okay, so that all might be true, but—"

"How are you going to fix this, Cole?" Wyatt asks. "Because we've all come up blank, and it's killing us seeing her miserable."

As much as I wish I had an answer, I don't, and I run a hand down my face in frustration. "I don't know. And as much as it's killing you, it's killing me more. I lo..." I stop myself halfway through the word. That's not a thing I can admit out loud. Not right now. Not to them.

"Love her," Grayson grunts. "Got it. So what are you going to do?"

"*I don't know,*" I growl again, as panicked by the fact that I can't argue his claim as I am by my inability to help her. "There's enough truth in the story that I can't disprove anything."

"You're saying she extorted a politician?" Wyatt asks, raising an eyebrow.

I groan. "No. I'm saying she had no idea the guy was married, but she *did* date him. *And* she was his physical therapist. I can't explain the airport thing, but that picture was—"

"That one might have been my fault," Jeff says, ducking his head. "I said something about how they looked like they were having a rough morning, so she went over to talk to them." Several guys throw towels at him, and he looks properly ashamed of himself when he emerges from the onslaught. "How was I supposed to know there would be someone taking pictures of her?"

"Because she's Carissa," I grumble as the guys continue to shout angry remarks at Jeff. "It's safe to assume she is noticed pretty much everywhere she goes." As someone who is constantly watched, I know the feeling, though it's not Carissa's fault that she's beautiful and approachable. She brings light wherever she goes, and I can't figure out why *Hot Scoop* would be so determined to tear her down. A week ago they were completely indifferent to her and annoying at best when it came to me, but now it's like they decided to switch gears and push me higher up the social ladder and knock Carissa to the ground.

There has to be a way to show the world who she really is, but I can't focus on that because I still have forty minutes of game play to deal with. It's not like we can shout our love and appreciation for Carissa while we're in the middle of a ruck and she's on the sidelines. The only way we can interact with her is if we get injured.

"Wait," I say as an idea sparks to life in my head. No one's paying attention to me, so I stuff my fingers into my mouth and let out a shrill whistle that cuts through the grumbling. "Hey! I have an idea that probably won't work."

"Tell us," Wyatt says immediately.

I manage a smile as I nod at him. His support means more than he'll ever know. "Here's what we'll do..."

CHAPTER TWENTY-EIGHT

CARISSA

"Carissa, honey, are you sure you want to be here right now?" Mel rubs her hand along my back as we make our way out onto the field after all the Thunder players leave the locker room. "I promise I can handle everything on my own. I was doing it before you came along, and one more game won't hurt me."

She has no idea how tempted I am to say yes to her offer. When I read the article last night, I did my best to brush it off, and I mostly succeeded. Only half of what they said about me was true, and I'm smart enough to know that someone's opinion of me doesn't matter more than my opinion of myself. At least, I know that in theory.

After a morning of watching whatever romcoms I could find on the hotel TV channels, and an afternoon of fielding Darcy's calls and apology texts by telling her I'm totally fine, I thought I was doing okay.

But that was before all the staring.

Apparently many of the Portland Pathfinder fans are also *Hot Scoop* readers.

I can't hear anything they say from the stands, but I can see them pointing and looking at their phones. Even now, as Portland kicks off to start the second half, people are clearly talking about me, none of them with smiles or warmth.

Don't they have better things to worry about?

The first forty minutes of this game were brutal, and it didn't help that I spent the whole time trying to distract myself from the crowd by watching Cole, who has looked weighed down by the stress of trying to captain his team while the coach shouts useless insults from the sidelines. Cole has had a permanent crease in his forehead all night, and I worry about what will happen to his spirit if the Thunder lose their first game with him as captain.

Summed up, this game is awful all around.

During the first play of the second half, Noah gets knocked down and stays down, and memories of Moxie's injury grip my heart in a vise. But when Mel rushes over, neither of them look too concerned as they talk. After a few seconds, Mel looks over at me, nods, and jogs back to the sideline, leaving Noah sitting in the middle of the field.

"He wants you to help," she says before I can ask.

I frown. "But—"

"Better hurry. Don't want to waste too much time."

While I'd much prefer to stay where I am, I grip the straps of my medic backpack and hurry out onto the field, ignoring the whispers that fill the arena like wind. "Where does it hurt?" I ask, crouching in front of Noah.

He grins at me. "Hamstring."

I cock my head as I reach to feel how tight the muscle is. "I don't see how that's a smiling matter, Tinkerbell."

His smile only grows. "Tape me up?"

More confused than anything, I wrap tape around his thigh and below his knee. "Better?"

"I hope so," he replies and hops up, holding out his hand to help me stand. "Thanks, Rizzo!" He hurries off to rejoin the rest of the team, and I wander back to Mel with my brow drawn low.

"That was weird," I mutter.

"I think the boys like you," Mel replies.

Only a couple of minutes later, Wyatt apparently does something to his arm and rushes over to me, begging me to add some tape to his shoulder even though the ball is still in play. I do what he asks as quickly as I can, and he kisses my cheek before darting back into play just in time to catch the ball Cole throws to him. He skirts around a defender with a spin move and bolts, leaving the other players in the dust as he reaches the try line and sets the ball down dead center field.

The Thunder fans who came up to Portland erupt into cheers, and the guys all congratulate each other while Cole sets up his conversion kick and gets us two more points so we're only down by three.

After the next scrum, Grayson claims to have pulled a muscle in his calf, though he tells me so with a smile on his face, just like Noah. Not two minutes later, Freddie needs a bandage for a cut I can't see.

As the game continues, player after player finds himself injured and needing my services, all the while Cole keeps the ball moving forward while we have possession and away from the try zone when we don't. Every time I make my way onto the field to take care of what I'm starting to expect are fake injuries, Cole sends me a warm, reassuring smile, no matter how far he is from me.

I don't know what his play is, but he planned this. Whatever this is.

Freddie kicks the ball forward, and Wyatt speeds ahead to catch it and score another try. When Cole takes the ball to kick the conversion, he finds me on the sideline and points at me before putting his hand over his heart.

My own heart stumbles in my chest as the crowd quiets for the first time all night, like they can't believe Cole would acknowledge me after that *Hot Scoop* article.

The rest of the guys, lined up behind Cole, all look over at me in unison, their smiles wide and stances relaxed. After a tense first half, it's like they've suddenly stopped caring about what happens with the game. And I feel their support in every bit of me.

Tears prick my eyes as Cole sets up his kick and sends the ball flying straight down the middle of the posts. Even the Portland announcer remarks on the perfect trajectory, his tone clearly impressed. Cole walks back to the team, his eyes on me the whole time, and smiles when I blink away my welling tears to meet his gaze.

"You okay?" he asks, too far for me to hear, but I can read the question on his lips.

I nod, and I actually mean it. He and the guys have every reason to keep their distance from me after *Hot Scoop's* scathing assessment of my character, but as the game comes to a close a few minutes later, the Thunder ahead by four, the entire team swarms around me, pulling me in to join their celebration while the announcer says something about me being a good luck charm.

My tears break loose for the first time all day as the guys jump and whoop around me, clapping each other on the backs and throwing out hugs like candy at a parade. Many of them pat my shoulder or squeeze my hand, like I was actually part of helping them win the game. And when a familiar pair of arms wrap around me from behind in a supportive embrace, I feel like I might fall apart if not for his hold.

"What was that?" I whisper, gripping Cole's arms and praying he never lets go. I doubt he heard my question through the hullabaloo, but I don't care.

He tucks his chin over my shoulder and speaks into my ear, his voice a gentle purr. "That was us showing you that we know the real Carissa and don't care what someone else might say. We love you exactly as you are, past and all, and we wanted everyone else to know it too."

Love. Okay, so he said *we* love you and not *I* love you, but it was still him saying the word, and I'm desperate to believe his comment is a precursor to our impending conversation tonight. I don't expect him to be in love with me after only a few weeks of knowing me, but I want him to be willing to give us a chance. See where we might go.

"Thank you," I say, pressing my cheek against his.

"It was the guys," he replies, arms pulling me tighter against his chest. He may be sweaty, but he's warm and comfortable and safe, and I never want to leave his hold.

I shake my head. "That plan had you all over it."

"What makes you so sure?"

"Because I know you better than you seem to think." I twist in his arms so I'm looking up into his face and can see the concern etched into his brow. I thought for sure he was worried about the game all night, but now I'm starting to think he was worried about *me*. "You risked losing the game to cheer me up."

His lips pull up in a crooked smile. "Trust me, we definitely would have lost if we *hadn't* cheered you up. These guys care about you more than I think you realize."

"You're basically our mascot now, Rizzo," someone says, though I'm not about to turn around to see who.

Mostly because I'm realizing that Cole is holding me close in the midst of his team and looking at me like I'm the most important thing in the world. And he doesn't seem to care about being seen. Reaching up, I press my palm to his cheek and smile when he leans into my touch. I hope this means good things for us.

"We'll talk later," he murmurs, as if reading my thoughts. "But maybe not tonight." Before my heart has a chance to sink, he leans forward and presses his lips to mine in a gentle kiss. "I am too tired to trust myself to act rationally right now, and you deserve my full and present attention. I'm not willing to make any mistakes when it comes to you." He kisses me again, then lets his arms drop as he steps back and tells the team to head to the locker room.

Cole is the last to go into the tunnel, and he pauses and looks back at me. "Don't worry, Paxton," he says, letting loose a full and real smile. "I'm not letting you go just yet."

Just yet. As Mel and I start gathering up our supplies and bringing it all to the bus that will take us back to the hotel, those two words keep running through my head. There's not a lot of confidence in those words, even if the rest of what he said was exactly what I wanted to hear.

It'll take a while for the guys to shower and change, so once we have everything loaded and Mel goes in search of a quiet corner of the stadium to make a phone call, I sit on the bus with my own phone in hand and make one of the most terrifying phone calls I've ever made. I almost hope he doesn't answer, but I think if anyone can help me figure out my best options here, he can.

The line connects, making my heart skip a beat. "Derek Riley's phone."

Hearing the unfamiliar female voice on the line, I frown down at my phone. "Um. Who is this?"

"Janie. Who is *this*?"

"Carissa."

"Cole's Carissa?"

Before I can respond, there's a shuffling sound and then Derek's deep voice says, "Hey, Carissa. Sorry about that."

"Derek. Hi. Um, do you have a second?" It's after ten on a Saturday night, and I can't imagine what sort of thing might keep Derek Riley busy on a weekend. But he's also one of the most well-known people I've ever known. He could be filming a movie right now. Or at a fancy party. Or on a date. *What if he's on a date?*

"For you, I have all the seconds," Derek says. Goodness, how does anyone talk to this man without swooning? I can't see him, but his deep and velvety voice feels like slipping into a perfect temperature lavender bubble bath. He says something I can't make out, the same female voice responds, and there's a few seconds of silence and a sound like a closing door before Derek says, "Sorry about my assistant. I didn't realize she had my phone. How did the game go?"

Assistant. At least he's not on a date, though I still feel like I interrupted something so my reply comes out squeaky. "Good! We won, so that's good."

"Great! And how are you doing?"

Derek Riley is asking after my wellbeing. "Good," I chirp. And since that sounds dumb, I tell him about what the guys did with their made-up injuries. The longer I talk, the easier it gets, and I almost sound normal by the end. "They totally made my night."

He hums. He was quiet while I recounted the second half of the game, and it still takes him a while to say anything. "I think," he says slowly, "Cole had the right idea. From what I'm seeing online, a lot of people are questioning that last *Hot Scoop* article."

Relief rushes through me. "Really?"

"Don't freak out, but there are a whole bunch of pictures of you circulating around."

"Please tell me they're good pictures."

"It's you with the Thunder, and all of the guys are looking at you like you're their best friend."

That's good, right? That sounds good. "Okay, but what if it's the same situation as that airport photo? I swear I barely talked to any of those guys, but everyone thinks I was—"

"All the commentary is looking pretty good, Carissa. You can relax." Derek's words are warm and comforting, for which I am grateful. "I wouldn't be surprised if there's another *Hot Scoop* article tomorrow, but they'd be stupid to keep trying to tear you down when you have a whole team behind you. Ah."

I frown at that last surprised word, gripping my phone tighter. "What?"

"Janie just sent me another picture of you, and now I'm thinking you didn't call me to talk about you. Or *Hot Scoop* for that matter."

What sort of picture could tell him all that? He's right, but still... "What picture?"

"I just texted it to you."

I look down as the text comes in, a smile cracking through my nerves when I see a photo of me held in Cole's arms. Our heads are pressed together and my eyes are closed, my lips up in a smile. But it's Cole's expression that has me riveted. He looks entirely at peace wrapped around me, smiling gently and completely relaxed.

"That's a man I've never seen before," Derek says. "You've obviously done something to him."

"Is that good or bad?"

"Why did you call me?"

I take a deep breath, hoping this conversation was a good idea. "Because I think he's willing to try a relationship, but something is still holding him back from committing. And I'm terrified he's going to break my heart if I give it to him." Is this the kind of conversation I should be having with a guy's best friend? I don't know. But I'm pretty sure Cole doesn't trust anyone as much as he trusts Derek, except maybe his dad and Gramps, and I am so scared that this little life I'm building for myself is going to fall apart and leave me drifting again.

"He told you about his family curse, right?" Derek asks.

"Yeah. Do you think it's real?"

"Logically, no. But I believe Cole believes in it, and a conviction like his is enough to give something power. Curse or not, if he's worried he's going to lose you, then he will."

"That's what I'm afraid of," I breathe, sinking lower in my seat. "Are we doomed?"

"Not according to that picture I sent you."

Sighing, I lift my feet up onto the seat in front of me, scrunching myself up. "So I know you're all famous and stuff and I have no right to ask you anything, but will you tell me what to do? You seem like the kind of guy who knows what to do in every situation."

He laughs, and once again I wonder how the whole world isn't in love with this man. Well, they probably are, now that I think about it. I've never seen a tabloid say anything bad about Derek Riley, like he has some kind of superpower of likability. "I'm glad you have a high opinion of me, Carissa, but I'm sure Cole will be the first one to tell you that I'm not that smart. Though..."

I roll my eyes at his thoughtful tone. "Do you know what to do in this situation?" I ask in a deadpan.

"Maybe. I think we need to get Cole to go to Sage's wedding."

Of all the things I thought he might say, it wasn't that. "Just to clarify, I'm asking you to convince Cole to date *me*. In a permanent sort of way."

He laughs again. "I'm aware. And the more I know you, Carissa, the more I think you're perfect for Cole."

"Oh. Well, thanks? But do you really think his ex's wedding is a good place to—"

"He needs to confront his demons."

I think about that for a second. "Are you telling me that Cole is still hung up on Sage?" I hate that idea.

"No, he's too smart to think his life is better with her in it. But Cole is..." He sighs. "He put so much of himself into that relationship, and I'm pretty sure when it ended, he came to the conclusion that he wasn't good enough. That he doesn't deserve that kind of happiness."

Tears prick my eyes at the thought of someone as amazing as Cole feeling so contrary to reality. He deserves all the happiness in the world. "How is the wedding supposed to fix that?"

"I don't think Cole knows what he wants anymore, which is why he isn't willing to commit to the best thing to ever happen to him. That's you, by the way."

My grin is huge, and I'm glad no one is around right now to see me. "Thanks."

"Seeing what might have been should, in theory, help him see clearly and realize what he actually wants in life. Slapping him in the face with Sage marrying Javi might be the only thing to snap him out of all of this."

At this point, I'm willing to try anything, though I still don't know how it will do me any good. I may not know Derek very well, but I trust him. "That feels like a lot of pressure to put on this event he doesn't want to go to. How are we supposed to get Cole to that wedding?"

"Luckily for us, Freya already took care of that for us. But we'll probably want to put in some fail-safes, just in case. Plan for all contingencies."

"I can't decide if you sound like a spy because you played one in a movie or because you're actually a spy."

He groans. "Have you been talking to Liam?"

"Does he think you're a spy too?"

"I'm not a spy."

"That's exactly what a spy would say," I whisper.

"Please don't start—" He cuts himself off and growls. "Carissa, I'm an actor, not a spy. Let's stay on track here. We're helping Cole."

Right. Cole. The man I'm quickly falling in love with. *Focus, Carissa.* "What do we need to do for fail-safes?" I still don't know how Freya could manage to get Cole to go to that wedding, but at this point it's probably better if I just take my orders and do what I can.

"We're going to need the team to help. Think you can talk to them?"

I snort a laugh. "They just spent half a game pretending to be hurt so they could make me feel better. Yeah, I can talk to them."

"Great. And it's important that we keep Cole completely in the dark, or this will never work."

That might be harder, but I'm sure I can manage it. "What do I tell them?"

I can practically hear the smile in his voice. "Tell them they need to go back to hating Cole."

CHAPTER TWENTY-NINE

COLE

THE LAST PERSON I want to talk to right now is Coach Galvin, but he corners me as I leave the locker room, and the wild look in his eyes tells me I should probably give him at least a few minutes of my attention.

"That was quite a win, son!"

I clench my jaw before I tell him not to call me that. "We have a good team, and we owe those last two tries to—"

"See, I knew making you captain was a great idea." He puts his arm around my shoulders. "Didn't I tell you that? And then you go and beat Portland!"

I step away from his touch and fold my arms. "You sound surprised that we won."

"Yes, well, practices weren't looking so—"

"What practices? You were hardly there for them." I bite my tongue as soon as the words leave my mouth. But like I told Carissa, I'm too tired tonight to be rational, and after Coach spent ten minutes lauding his coaching skills as we were changing, my patience level is at an all-time low.

He chuckles but narrows his eyes. "Is something bothering you, Evanson?"

Everything about this man bothers me. Even when he does show up to practice, it's not like he does anything to benefit the team. I've had a hellish day and I want to go to bed so it can be tomorrow and I can talk to Carissa and figure out a way to stop being so afraid to let her into my life.

"Nothing at all, sir," I say instead of the truth. "I'm sure the team would like to get some sleep, so we should probably—"

"After your stellar performance today, I'm beginning to think you and I could do great things together on the back end. Turn this team into something more...lucrative."

Cold dread washes over me, leaving me chilled to the bone as I stare at the familiar glint of greed in his eyes. My last coach said almost exactly the same thing to me two years ago. I had had my suspicions for a while, when some of my guys fumbled plays they knew by heart and weren't bothered by the mistakes, but when the Badgers' coach asked if I was interested in making some extra cash by tweaking the outcomes of games, I knew for sure. The team was corrupt, driven by rich men hoping to get richer.

And the worst part is I almost agreed. Sage had been pestering me to try to get more recognition and a better contract once mine was up at the end of the season, as if my salary of millions wasn't enough. I *was* working on a contract, but when Sage learned about the corruption, she tried to convince me it was an opportunity too good to pass up. Anyone in the inner circle of the betting ring was making far more than their regular paychecks could ever get them, and I was in a unique position to affect entire games, not just single plays.

Swallowing, I grip the strap of my bag and do my best to keep my expression neutral. "All we have to do is win more games."

"Sure, sure," Coach says, rubbing his hands together, "but I'm talking about lucrative for you specifically. I know you know what I mean, coming from the Badgers and their...special strategies. It would be like a bonus for—"

"Sir, I'm here to play rugby. I don't want more than that. And I'll only be your captain until Auxier is healed and back to full strength."

Coach scoffs, looking down his nose at me now. "Auxier may never see a game again."

"Is that a threat?" The question slips out of me before I can stop it, even though it would probably be better to pretend I have no clue what he means.

He laughs, shaking his head. "It's business, Evanson. Something you clearly don't understand. I'll admit I'm disappointed, but I should have expected as much from a gutless quitter." He steps past me, shoulder bumping into mine, but stops a few feet away and looks back. "How long do you think you'll last in this sport before you move on to something new? Another year? Less?" Grinning wickedly, he turns on his heel and disappears down the tunnel.

My bag slips from my shoulder, landing with a thump at my feet as the last few minutes replay in my head. Coach Galvin is just as bad as the Badgers. Maybe worse. Moxie's career with the Thunder might be in jeopardy. *My* career might be under threat. And what happens if Coach convinces some of the guys to team up with him? There's not enough money in rugby to cause any real problems, but... But what if that changes? Coach clearly knows what's going down with my old team and seems to have plans to start his own scheme.

Cursing under my breath, I dig into my bag for my phone and ignore the two texts Carissa has sent me to ask where I am. Instead I dial my dad's number and hope he hasn't gone to bed yet.

I need advice. Desperately.

He answers after two rings. "Hey, Lemon! Congrats on the—"

"The Badgers were corrupt. Rigging games and stats to boost certain bets."

He's quiet for a long beat before he clears his throat. "Uh, Gramps is here too."

I curse, switching the phone to my other ear as I start to pace. I barely wanted to tell my dad the truth, and I worry Gramps will try to do something to fix the problem and get himself into trouble.

"Watch that language," Gramps chides. "You're not with that girl-friend of yours, are you?"

"She's not my..." She's not my what? I'm in love with the woman, and she clearly wants to be with me. But I don't know if it's a good idea to date her, especially now, so what am I supposed to call Carissa?

"How long has this corruption been happening?" Dad asks, thankfully steering the conversation back to the important matter.

"I don't know," I say as I pace. "Since before I left."

"Were you—"

"No." I'm so glad that I can tell him that truth, even if the rest of this conversation sucks. "It's why I got out when my initial contract was up. I didn't want to be a part of anything like that."

"Why haven't we heard about this?" Gramps asks. "That would be a big story."

"It would be if I had ever told anyone about it," I agree. "But there are good guys on that team, and if this got out, it would ruin their careers."

Dad hums thoughtfully. "I always knew I raised you right, Cole."

"Only because I raised *you* right, Aug," Gramps throws in. "Why tell us now?"

I take a deep breath. "Because Galvin just asked me to do something similar, and I don't know what to do. I don't know how to protect my team. He's not happy that I turned him down, and I'm worried—"

"That coach of yours is a real piece of work," Gramps says gruffly. "And who's betting on MLR games anyway? No one."

"No one except you," Dad says.

"Exactly, so my odds are always good."

"But your returns are not."

"Maybe not now, but—"

"Stop betting on my games, Gramps," I say, shaking my head. "I'm stressed enough as it is."

"Mm, we can discuss that later," Gramps says. "Right now we need to know if that pretend coach of yours is going to do something he'll regret."

My phone buzzes with a text, and I glance at it to see Carissa asking where I am again. The team is probably waiting on me, but I have no idea how long this conversation might go.

"I don't care if he does something to me," I mutter, typing out a reply text and telling Carissa to leave without me. I'll get myself a ride back to the hotel. "But the rest of the guys? If Galvin is serious about trying to build up some kind of betting ring within Major League Rugby, that money is going to tempt a lot of players. No one makes enough in this sport to live off of."

Another text pops up.

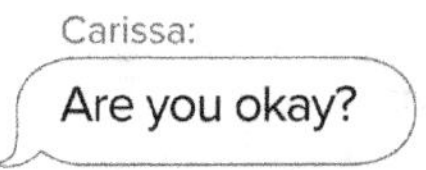

"What does Carissa think you should do?" Dad asks, like he knows I'm staring at her name right now.

I sigh. "I haven't told her any of this."

"Why the heck not?"

"You know why. My feelings for her are dangerous enough as it is, and I don't want—"

"Cole, are you telling me you're letting a stupid family curse keep you from opening your heart to that woman?" Dad actually sounds angry. "We saw the way you looked at her tonight, and I know that little injury stunt was your idea."

"You're so eager to protect everyone around you," Gramps says, "but you forget you're not the only one with strength. If you're busy holding up the world, you can't do anything more fun with your hands."

"Gramps!" I say in shock, laughing despite the seriousness of the conversation. Already I'm remembering how it felt to hold Carissa in the pool. By the vending machines. After the game. I shake my head, forcing myself to concentrate. "It's bad enough that I'm telling the two of you about all of this. I'm not risking Carissa's career or worse by bringing her into this mess."

"You love her," Dad says. Not a question.

I grip my phone tighter. "I think I do."

"I'm glad you didn't buy into any of that hooey *Hot Scoop* said about her," Gramps says. "I only spoke to her for five minutes, and even I know it's all nonsense. That girl is special."

My phone buzzes.

Carissa:

> If I don't hear from you in thirty seconds, I'm coming to find you.

I sigh and quickly type out a response.

Cole:

> I'm fine. Or I will be. Get back to the hotel safe, and I'll see you in the morning for breakfast. I promise.

"I know she's special," I murmur, gazing at the heart emoji she sends back. "That's why I'm not going to be the reason she gets hurt. I need to fix this without bringing her into it."

"I hate to say it, Lemon," Dad says, "but I don't think this is something you can fix on your own."

"I won't—"

"You can keep Carissa out of it if you think you need to. But she's not the only person on your team. Gramps and I will try to think of a solution for you, but I think you should tell Derek."

I groan, but I should have expected that. "I know you think Derek Riley is some all-knowing, all-powerful being, but he's not."

"No," Dad agrees, "but he has a knack for solving problems, and you know it. If you tell him about the corruption—on both teams—he won't stop looking for a solution until it's all fixed. Besides, he's your best friend. Don't you think he deserves to know what's been weighing you down all this time?"

I sink against the wall, letting those words soak in. I know it has bothered Derek to be kept in the dark about my reasons for leaving football, but I've never let myself really think about what it's like for him. How would I feel if he suddenly stopped acting and refused to tell me why? If he told me that it was for my protection, I would tell him that I can take care of myself. Anything he's up against is something I would gladly go up against too.

Derek would do the same for me, and I've been a jerk by not letting him support me as a friend. I've been a jerk to all my friends.

"Ah, I think you've gotten through to him, August," Gramps says in a mock whisper.

"Shut up, old man," I grumble. "I'm sorry I've wanted to protect my friends."

"It's one thing to protect them," Gramps replies. "It's another to trust them enough to let them protect *you*. In case it isn't clear, I'm not just talking about Derek. Again, if you're always taking care of the people around you, that leaves no room for things like kissing."

I hum as the memory of Carissa's mouth on mine leaves my lips tingling. Her kiss was electric. Explosive. *Exquisite.* "There's still time for that," I murmur.

"There's my boy," Dad says with a chuckle. "Now, stop talking to a couple of geezers and get Riley's big brain working. The sooner you get help solving your problem, the sooner you can stop letting guilt hold you back from love."

I frown as I consider that. I thought it was the curse keeping me from opening my heart to Carissa. The fear that she'll get hurt or worse. But I trust my dad, and he knows me better than anyone. Could my problem be so simple?.

"Cole?" Dad says.

"Hmm?"

"I know you feel responsible for anything you touch—you're not. People make choices, and that's on them. And I know you're scared to lose someone you love. No one will fault you for that. But take it from me. No matter how little time I got with your mom, having her in my life was worth all the heartache that came from losing her. I pray Carissa has a long life ahead of her, but if fate decides that she doesn't, nothing you do or don't do will change that. Wouldn't you rather soak up the time you can get? Enjoy the moments you can share with her?"

Of course I would rather have her in my life. There's no question of that. "But what if—"

"Stop living scared," Gramps snaps. "Don't make me come up there and knock some sense into you!"

I chuckle. "You think you can take me in a fight?"

"With ease. One of these days you have to stop underestimating people, Coleman."

Maybe he's right, and as I start heading out of the stadium to finally make my way back to the hotel, I think back to the night Carissa challenged me to an arm wrestle. She comes across as delicate and fragile, but she's anything but. Maybe I've been underestimating her determination when it comes to tempting fate. She doesn't live life scared. Even when she came to the Thunder and knew it was a bad idea to go against her rules, she almost always went with her heart rather than her head.

If she hadn't, I never would have gotten the chance to know her. To kiss her. *To love her.*

"I should go," I tell my family. "Thanks for listening tonight. I'm going to talk to Derek, but if you come up with any brilliant plans for saving my team, let me know."

"We'll figure this out," Dad replies. "We've got your back, Cole. And just so you know, if you aren't willing to admit that you're head over heels for Carissa when you get back home, we're going to have another talk. None of this 'I *think* I love her' nonsense."

I'm not going to grace that comment with a response. "See you when I get back."

I order myself a rideshare—the closest car is several minutes away—and then I dial Derek's number, silently telling myself that filling him in on the corruption is a good thing. That it won't threaten the life I'm building in Los Angeles or the friends who mean so much to me.

Derek answers at the last second, which is unusual for him. He either answers immediately or his phone goes straight to voicemail; there is no in between. "What's up?"

I frown and glance at the phone. "Why do you sound suspicious?"

"I don't sound suspicious." And he doesn't. *Now.* But I swear his greeting came with a healthy measure of anticipation, like he was waiting for something. Now it sounds like he has slipped on his actor mask, which means I'll have no idea what he's thinking about anything.

Much as I hate that, I press forward after glancing around to make sure no one is around me. This isn't exactly something I want anyone to overhear. "I'm going to tell you why I left football, but I need you to promise to keep it to yourself."

"Of course," he answers without hesitation. At least I can count on Derek to hold to that; he doesn't make promises lightly.

Though I have to psych myself up, I tell him everything about the game manipulation and under-the-table bribes, giving him as much detail as I can before he starts asking questions. My body is tense the whole time I talk, but something inside me feels like it's shifting. Coming loose.

Much like when I kissed Carissa last night, it feels like I'm setting down a boulder that has weighed me down for a long time.

"When Javi got involved, I knew I had to get out," I finish, exhaling all at once, like I'm finally letting go of a breath I've been holding for years. "He would have never stopped trying to get me in on the scheme, and there was no way I could renew my contract without being part of the problem once I knew about it. And now it feels like all that crap has followed me to the Thunder, and I don't know what to do. Tell me what to do."

For some reason, Derek laughs, though I have no idea how any of this can amuse him. "You all have a lot more faith in me than you should."

"C'mon, man. Don't make me regret calling you."

"I'm glad you called. And I'm glad you told me about the corruption. That sucks."

I sigh. "It does suck. And I don't know how to fix it, which is why I'm coming to you and your resources."

He chuckles again, and I can picture him shaking his head at me like I'm being ridiculous. "I like how you pretend you're a perfectly average person when we both know you're not."

"What's the point of having fame and fortune when it can't do anything to solve my problems?" I groan. All of this would be so much easier if I *wasn't* famous. I've never craved an average life more than I do right now. "I haven't told you the worst part."

Once I've explained Coach Galvin's offer, Derek whistles low. "Sounds like your 'coach' isn't fond of his paycheck." His irritation comes out clear when he mentions Galvin, making me smile.

As a car pulls up, I quickly verify that it's my driver and climb into the backseat, dropping my voice to try to keep my phone conversation private as the driver heads for the hotel. "He's making more than he deserves, whatever it is."

"You're probably right." Derek sounds thoughtful now, which is a good sign. He's likely already halfway to a brilliant plan that will solve all my problems. "Before I say anything, I need to know what it is you want here, Cole. Let's start with the Badgers. What's your goal?"

I could probably leave that part of my life behind me and be fine, but as we start moving through the streets of Portland, memories of my old life start to surface. I was too focused on Carissa today to really think about the years I spent here, but now that she is in a better place emotionally, my thoughts begin to stray to the city around me.

I liked it here, with the river and the rain. I liked playing in front of sold-out crowds and working as a team and doing something I loved with guys I admired and respected.

"There are still good guys on that team," I say, frowning at the city as it passes by. "At some point, they're all going to get recruited or they'll be shut out, and not all of them will have the same luck of finding something new if they don't give in to the pressure. I wish there was a way to expose the bad agents and protect the good."

Derek hums thoughtfully. "Have you talked to Carissa's sister? Darcy?"

I frown. "Why?"

I can practically hear him roll his eyes. "Because if anyone can expose something like this without hurting the innocent players, Tamlin Park can."

I feel like I just got punched in the jaw. "How did you know she—you know what? Never mind." I know better than to question Derek and his limitless knowledge. "If I tell her what's happening, they'll know I'm the one who let the cat out of the bag when it all goes south."

"How?" Derek argues. "Darcy has sources all over the country and it could have come from anywhere. You haven't been with the team in two years. You're going to be at Javi's wedding and showing everyone that you have no hard feelings toward any of the Badgers."

I pull my phone from my ear, staring at my screen as if I might be able to see Derek through it. "You're joking, right?"

"Nope. I told you there would be consequences if you didn't do your homework."

I curse loudly, startling my driver, and speak as forcefully as I can. "There is no way in hell I'm going to that wedding."

Derek chuckles. "Are you sure about that? Because you of all people know it's a bad idea to bet against Princess Freya Alverra."

CHAPTER THIRTY

COLE

"Freya, I'm done having this argument."

"You can say that all you wish, but I will have my way."

I groan, all too aware of Carissa's eyes on me on the other side of the room. After a long night of back-and-forth texts with Freya and fruitlessly trying to get some sleep, I almost didn't come down to the hotel dining area to meet Carissa for breakfast. It was only the thought of disappointing her that pulled me out of my room and down to the bottom floor. She hasn't texted me at all since last night, and her expression is pretty impossible to read right now as she waits for me to *actually* join her.

I will as soon as the princess stops talking.

"Freya," I say with a heavy sigh. Even some of the guys are watching me now as I pace in an empty corner, probably looking like a mangy raccoon who has been cornered.

Not exactly the kind of mood I should be in after a win like we had last night.

"Cole," Freya replies, her voice clipped. I'm pretty sure she skipped a meeting for this phone call, and that is not something she often chooses to do. Freya is nothing if not driven by duty. "Unless I have proof that you have friends on your team, you are going to that wedding."

She keeps saying that, and I keep telling her that I didn't have enough time to meet her terms. Granted, I didn't start trying until a week ago, but my efforts should count for something.

"I can't get you proof," I grumble. "But I swear I did everything I could."

"That is not true, and you know it."

Carissa meets my gaze again and offers a smile that doesn't reach her eyes. I hate that smile. I hate more watching Wyatt and Grayson slide in on either side of her with plates of food like they're all the best of friends, Carissa's smile turning brighter at their arrival.

Growling, I grip my phone and stalk across the dining area, slipping into the chair across the table from Carissa before anyone else can. This is going to be a disaster, but I'm out of arguments. "Wyatt, would you consider us friends?"

All three of them—Wyatt, Carissa, Grayson—stare at me like I've grown a second head. I don't blame them, considering I cut Carissa off mid-sentence to ask a ridiculous question and am still holding my phone to my ear.

Wyatt coughs and picks up his fork, spearing some scrambled eggs. "Friends? Evanson, you're lucky I *tolerate* you."

About what I expected. I look at Grayson. "You?"

He lifts an eyebrow. "I don't know, Cole. You've been a decent captain this week, but that doesn't mean I'm keen to go to the farmer's market with you or anything."

"Everything okay, Cole?" Carissa asks.

Gator is chowing down on a breakfast burrito one table over, and I point a finger at him. "Hey, Finau, are we friends?"

He chuckles and shakes his head.

I could keep going, but now the rest of the team is looking at me like I've gone crazy, so I can probably guess at their answers. Turning my attention back to my phone, I shake my head as if Freya can see me. "It was never going to happen, and you know it, Peach."

"Perhaps you are right."

"Why are you so determined that I go to the wedding of my ex and my best friend?"

A couple of the guys wince and offer sympathetic sounds of pain, but they turn their focus to their plates when I glare at them.

"Because you either needed closure, Coleman, or you needed to make friends," Freya says. "I thought it would be enough of a motivator to get one or the other. You are going to that wedding."

"I'm not going."

"If you do not go to the reception at the very least, then I will not allow you entrance to my coronation in the fall." She hangs up with a finality that leaves my ears ringing. *She wouldn't...* Except, Freya never makes empty threats and absolutely would put me on a blacklist, and if I had to miss the most important day of her life...

I curse under my breath, setting my phone onto the table with a slow exhale as a sharp pain enters my ribs. If Freya is willing to go to such extremes, she must believe this wedding is going to do something for me. There is no world in which I would miss Freya's coronation, but Sage's wedding? Even the reception sounds like torture.

"I don't know what to do," I whisper to myself because that truth is too heavy to keep inside. I *hate* feeling helpless, but there is no choice here where I can win. I look up, meeting Carissa's gaze, and she gives me a sympathetic smile. There's only so much context she could have gotten from my end of the conversation, but she seems to understand my predicament. "Freya just gave me an ultimatum, and..."

Carissa tilts her head to one side, glancing at Wyatt and Grayson next to her, who both quickly look at their phones and pretend they're not intently listening. "Would going to the wedding really be all that bad?"

"Yes."

"Why?"

Because it's Sage. I may not say that out loud, but Carissa has to understand, right? She's been at the forefront of all my issues the last few weeks. "It feels like a backwards step," I admit. "And no good can come from going."

"What about your old teammates? Wouldn't it be nice to see some of them again?"

Some of them, yes. And it would be nice to get a sense of how many of them have caved to the corruption. But I still don't know if it's a good idea to tell Carissa about that stuff, and I'm definitely not going to say anything when we're surrounded by the Thunder. They're all in danger too right now.

"I...could go with you," Carissa says, though her voice sounds thin. I doubt she really wants to go to something like that, though I feel the weight of her offer in my gut. I don't deserve her.

I shake my head. "You're going to Liam's show. I know you would hate to miss that."

"I could always go another time," she argues. "It's not like I don't know the headliner and his wi—girlfriend." Red splashes across her cheeks, and she drops her gaze to the mostly untouched food in front of her.

Narrowing my eyes, I stare at her for a second. "What did you almost say?"

She doesn't look at me. "I really think you should go to the wedding, Cole."

Yeah, I'm not doing that. I'm more interested in her slip of tongue. "Did you almost say *wife*?" Liam wouldn't do that, would he? I huff out a laugh, shaking my head. He would. And if he did... "Carissa, what do you know?"

"I know your old teammates would love to see you."

"That's not what I mean, Paxton, and you know it."

She looks up and fixes a surprisingly powerful glare on me. "Coleman Evanson, why are you so afraid of this wedding? I wouldn't have guessed you were a coward."

Her comment feels like a slap in the face, even if she immediately flinches as soon as the words are out of her mouth. Wyatt and Grayson both choke on their food, glancing from me to Carissa before grabbing their plates and slipping away. We're still surrounded by the team and their obnoxious staring, but at least Carissa and I are alone at our table now.

I grit my teeth, though I can't decide if I'm more bothered by her thinking me a coward or by whatever secret she's keeping from me about Liam.

"You're not a coward," Carissa says, though her expression remains firm. "I know you're not. So why won't you let yourself get a little closure?"

"Because..." I can't find a way to finish that sentence. Derek, Freya, even Carissa. For some reason, they all think I need this, and if I can't trust them... I let out a heavy sigh. "Fine. We'll go to the reception." No way am I sitting through that ceremony, and I'm going to need something to wash away the discomfort that's going to be all over me while I'm there. "But we're also going to Liam's show so I can figure out whatever it is you know that I don't."

Blushing brighter than before, Carissa lifts her chin, looking defiant and beautiful and completely irresistible. "Great."

"Great." I clench my jaw, studying the way her eyes light up with a sense of triumph. She clearly think she's gained the upper hand. And she's right. "You think you're so clever, don't you?"

Her lips twist up in a smile, pulling me closer. "Clever? No. I'm just right."

"This could get messy."

"I can handle messy."

I curse under my breath as a wave of desire rolls over me. This is neither the time nor place, but I can only resist this woman for so long. "I'm going to kiss you now." I lean over the table and capture her mouth with mine, all too aware of my team watching us. Carissa doesn't seem to mind, melting into me the same way she did after the game last night.

The small taste I get of her is not nearly enough, but she pulls away and looks at me, her soft hand pressing against my cheek as her thumb brushes the dark circle beneath my eye. "What else is bothering you?" she asks. "And don't even think about pretending it's nothing. What happened last night?"

Something I can't tell her with the whole team trying to listen in. I sigh. "Did you get enough to eat?"

She glances down at the giant waffle on her plate, of which she's only taken a couple of bites. "Yeah, I'm not really hungry."

I accept her claim only because I'll be with her the rest of the day and can make sure she eats at some point. The team is flying back to Cali in a couple of hours, but I booked us an extra night in our rooms so we can go to Liam's show. Which means I get her all to myself until that stupid reception. As soon as the team's out of the way, I'm going to take advantage of this time while I've got it.

"Can I take you somewhere?" I ask.

Carissa's eyes light up, her excitement settling deep inside me. "Where?"

Anywhere. "Somewhere special."

Nodding, Carissa reaches for her plate, but Sharkie grabs it first. "You kids go," he says, his tone light and friendly, though the look he gives me is anything but.

My body tenses when I realize he's not the only one looking at me like that. It's like the whole team is suddenly giving me silent threats that I read loud and clear. If I do anything that might hurt Carissa, they'll be out for my blood.

I did the same thing to Hank when he started dating Bonnie, so I know better than to underestimate their warnings. They mean business.

"Thanks, Loren," Carissa says to Sharkie at the same time he shifts his expression to a smile. "Cole, I just need to run up to my room for a sec. Meet you back down here in twenty minutes?"

I don't especially want her to leave my side, but based on the way a few of the guys stand and give me sharp looks, I have a feeling they don't want their threats to remain silent. Swallowing, I nod and take Carissa's hand to give it a squeeze. "Take all the time you need."

As soon as she's gone, I'm surrounded by Thunder.

CHAPTER THIRTY-ONE

CARISSA

Based on my experiences with him so far, I had a decent idea of what a date with Cole Evanson would look like. The man has already cooked for me and spent a weekend reading romance novels, something he clearly had a distaste for before that night he came to my apartment. He's a cut above most men I've dated already.

But he just set the bar so high, I don't think anyone will ever be able to top it.

Okay, maybe that's not true. It's not like he hired a horse-drawn carriage or flew me to Paris on a private jet. Those would be pretty cool. But he did bring me to the Portland Japanese Gardens, which are absolutely *gorgeous*, and as we walked he told me all about what it was like growing up with his dad and Gramps. He told me about his first football game when he was eight and how he fell in love with the sport almost immediately. He told me about how he went to tryouts for the Thunder on a whim and something about the game clicked the moment he touched a rugby ball.

He asked a stranger to take a picture of us standing on a beautiful bridge in the middle of the gardens. He held me so close, like he never wanted to let go. I didn't want him to let go either.

Then he brought me to his favorite restaurant in Portland and ordered dessert first, continuing his nonstop talking as I ate my weight in pizookies and pasta.

And now? He took me to a place called Pittock Mansion, which apparently is an interesting hundred-year-old building, but Cole took me around the back instead of going inside. And I've been staring with my mouth open for I don't know how long.

From up here, we can see all of downtown Portland, with its many trees and buildings bathed in late afternoon light. In the distance, a true mountain peak looms by itself like some dormant volcano, which is probably exactly what it is. It doesn't look real, though that could be because I've never seen a real mountain before. Not like that one.

"I can't believe you lived here," I whisper, still taking in the view with a pounding heart.

Chuckling, Cole tucks me up against his firm chest and wraps his arms around me. I appreciate his sturdiness as the day starts catching up to me. The whole *weekend*. Everything about this trip has been overwhelming, in so many different ways. "I don't think I ever would have picked Oregon if the Badgers hadn't picked me, but I liked it here. And..." His arms tighten around me. "And I want to tell you why I left."

My breath catches in my throat. This is exactly the thing Darcy wanted to know about Cole from the beginning. "Wait," I say, tucking my hands around his arms. "I've already proven I'm not great at keeping secrets, and if you don't want me to—"

"Hey." He presses a kiss to my cheek, calming my nerves almost instantly. "I'm already planning to talk to your sister tomorrow. I think this is something she can fix."

"Fix?" I repeat, twisting around to look at him. "What do you mean?"

Eyebrows pulling low, he sighs and sits down on one of the picnic benches that litter the overlook. He settles me onto his lap, taking a slow breath. "I mean the Badgers are a mess, and I'm lucky I was able to leave when I did. The coach is part of a betting ring of sorts and pays players to manipulate their stats wherever they can. Purposefully drop passes, make certain tackles, even lose whole games if that's where the money is. They tried to pull me into it, but I was at the end of my current contract, so I passed on the chance to play another five years with the team and moved back to California to put some distance between me and all of that."

Pain laces his voice as much as it shows on his face, and I press my palms to his scruffy cheeks. He looks so tired, like the last few years have suddenly caught up to him now that he has admitted the truth to me. "Oh, Cole, that's awful. You never actually wanted to leave football, did you?"

He shakes his head. "But even if I'd tried to sign with another team, I knew too much. My coach wouldn't have let me go quietly."

"Why did you never tell anyone?"

"Because I don't want the whole team to go down because of a few bad apples. And..." He clenches his jaw, his gaze shifting to the view beyond our spot. "I think that's why Coach Galvin brought me on to the team. Or if not at first, it's why he kept me. He must know something about what's happening with the Badgers, and last night he..."

I can guess what he doesn't say. "The same thing is happening again, isn't it?" When he nods, I wrap my arms around his waist and hold him tight. "No wonder you look terrible."

That gets a laugh out of him. "I look terrible?"

I sit up again to examine his face and the dark circles beneath his eyes. The tension in his shoulders. The weariness he can't hide. "You look tired. The scruff is a nice look for you, but yeah. I can't imagine how heavy this burden has been."

He responds with a gentle kiss. "Thank you for listening. And for not asking if I was part of the corruption."

Even though he's clearly hurting, I can't fight the smile that spreads across my face. "You may be a bit of a grump sometimes, Cole, but I don't think you could ever be corrupt. You're too good of a man. You didn't like me when we first met, and you still worried about my safety despite your opinion of me. You paid for half of the daycare costs for Mel's kid."

Cole's jaw drops. "How did you—"

"And," I say, ignoring his unfinished question, "deep down you're just a big softy who will always do the right thing even when it does nothing to benefit you. So no, I didn't need to ask if you were a part of it all because I already knew the answer."

Closing his eyes, he nuzzles his nose against mine. "Do you think your sister can keep the good players safe? Because I'm kind of banking on her being able to do something."

I'm still new to the idea that Darcy is one of the most notorious sports reporters of the last decade, but from the few articles of hers I looked up, she has a knack for saying exactly the right thing to expose the athletes who aren't playing the game fair, no matter which sport. She's like the opposite of *Hollywood Hot Scoop.* "I don't know," I say honestly, "but I'd bet she can answer that question for you. You might not believe me, but my sister is one of the good ones."

"If she's half the woman you are, then she's a saint," Cole mutters and kisses me again, momentarily making me forget where and when and who I am as he pulls me close and explores my mouth.

It could be minutes later or it could be hours, but eventually I remember that we can't sit here all day and make out. Breaking the kiss, I fight to breathe again and say, "We have a reception to get to." Granted, I agree with Cole when he groans and drops his head onto my shoulder. Derek said Cole needs to get closure from his last relationship before he can commit to a new one, but today's adventures have felt pretty committed. Especially here at the mansion. Cole confiding in me about the Badgers feels like he's fully trusting me.

But I think Derek is right. I don't think everything is solved quite yet.

"We don't have to stay for long," I tell Cole, running my hands through his dark hair. "But I would hate for you to miss Freya's coronation."

He looks up, narrowing his eyes. "She told you?"

I fail to fight my grin. "I'm on texting terms with a princess. How cool is that?"

"Not cool at all," he grumbles, lifting me off his lap and to my feet like I weigh nothing. "I love her, but she's a pain in my—"

"Wedding first, curse the princess later."

Taking my hand, he leads me back to the parking lot and the car that he asked to wait for us. We climb into the back seat, and Cole hands the woman a chunk of money that looks like more than I've ever held in my life.

I can't help myself. "Just how much money did you make in the NFL, anyway?"

Cole flushes red and is a little too deliberate in fastening his seatbelt, but he's smart enough to know he can't avoid the question forever. He clears his throat. "When I started, I was third string, so my paycheck was small compared to—"

"How much?"

"Twenty-two million." He practically whispers the number, wincing as he does. My jaw drops, and he shrugs as he adds, "Per year."

For some reason, my reaction to that is to punch him, which brings a tentative smile to his face. "Are you serious?" I whisper back.

His smile grows. "I was negotiating a new contract before the whole...you know...thing went down, and it was going to be thirty-eight."

"And you *gave that up*? That's like a bazillion candy bars and enough to buy a yacht and now I get why you have two houses and why you fit right in with Derek and Liam and a freaking *princess*." I know I'm rambling, but I can't comprehend having that much money. Technically I have *negative* money because at some point I need to pay my parents back for paying for my schooling, no matter how many times they tell me I don't need to. And I thought Houston was rich! And okay, yes, he is. The guy made something like twenty-five million every year he pitched for the Sun City Red-tails, and he was on the team for something like a decade. But still. "What does someone even do with that kind of money?" I ask breathlessly.

Something shifts in Cole's expression, taking his amusement and pulling it in a completely different direction so he looks...surprised? That's not right. Alarmed? No, he looks like a lightbulb turned on in his head.

"What?" I ask.

He scrambles to grab his phone from his pocket and starts typing furiously, pausing only long enough to say, "They buy a rugby team."

CHAPTER THIRTY-TWO

COLE

Princess or not, Freya deserves a good kick in the pants for making me come to this thing. Sure, I'm not complaining about the flowy blue dress Carissa is wearing or the fact that she's clinging to my arm for dear life as we enter the venue. But there are so many better things I could be doing right now, like sitting in an ice bath or figuring out how to buy the Thunder from the current owners or kissing Carissa until I can't breathe. Especially that last one.

I pause just inside the doors of the massive event center Sage and Javi booked, clenching my jaw. "What if we just tell Freya that we came?" I hold up my phone, camera already on to take a selfie of us and the wedding behind us. "See? We came. Now we can leave."

Snickering, Carissa pinches my side, somehow hitting the one spot I've always been ticklish. I nearly drop my phone as I yelp and twist away, and her eyes go wide. "You're ticklish?" she whispers, like it's the greatest discovery she's ever made.

"Nope." I tug her deeper into the room. We missed dinner as well as the ceremony, which is fine by me, and if I'm going to endure this reception, I'm going to make it happen quickly.

"Evanson?" a deep voice says, pulling me to a stop.

My mouth stretches into a wide grin as soon as I turn around. "Burley!" Slipping away from Carissa, I grab the wide receiver and pull him into a tight hug. He hugs me back, each of us trying to squeeze harder than the other. "It's good to see you, man!"

Once he's free of my hold, he lifts an eyebrow as he studies me, grinning wide. "Did you get bigger or did you just buy a tighter suit?"

I laugh and shrug. "Rugby."

The word sobers him immediately, as if he just now remembered who I am and how long it's been. "Right." He glances to the right, where Sage and Javi are mingling with a group of people. "What are you doing here, Evanson?"

It's a valid question, and one I'm not sure how to answer until a soft hand slips into mine. I look down at Carissa, offering her a smile, and then I say, "Sage invited me," like it's a perfectly normal thing for me to be here. Before Burley can reply, I pull Carissa closer and say, "Carissa, this is Chuck Burley, one of the best receivers in the country. Burley, this is Carissa."

Though Burley waves my praise away, he takes an interest in Carissa, studying her with keen eyes. "Ballsy move," he tells me, "bringing a date like her. You," he says to Carissa, taking her hand and bowing over it, "are exquisite."

"And you are a bit too bold," I growl back.

But Carissa laughs as Burley kisses the back of her hand. "Was Cole this much of a grump when he played with you?" she asks.

"Worse," Burley says, standing straight again. He grins and shakes his head. "Nah, Evanson's always been an easy guy. He just doesn't like when someone plays with his stuff." His eyes dart over to Javi again before fixing on me. "Does he know you're here?"

I shake my head. "I doubt he knows she invited me."

"Probably not," Burley agrees, folding his arms and pressing his lips together. He's clearly expecting some sort of drama to go down, and I'm right there with him. I haven't talked to Javi since the day I quit, and after Sage's whole spiel a few weeks ago about how we weren't good for each other, I can only assume she gave me the invitation for one of two reasons. Either she wanted to deal a wound deeper than she already had, or she hoped I would come and stir up some trouble because she thrives on conflict.

Another thing I didn't realize until I was looking at our relationship in the rearview... Or maybe I realized it because of Carissa, who is anything but confrontational. She's honest and open, and I never wonder what she's thinking. Even now, as she meets my gaze in the soft lighting of the venue, I can practically hear her telling me that she's here to support me however I need.

Burley chuckles, glancing between Carissa and me. "This could be fun. Do me a favor and talk to the bride and groom *after* they serve the cake."

"Hey." I grab his arm before he can leave. Burley's a good guy and has always been more committed to the game than making money, but I still need to be careful. "How are...things?"

His eyes jump to Javi again before resting on me. "Depends on who you ask," he grunts. "I, for one, miss the good old days when we had guys like you. Take care of yourself, Evanson." He wanders off, pointing a couple of guys in my direction as he goes.

There are so many layers to what he said—and didn't say—and guilt settles heavy in my chest. "It must be worse than I thought," I mutter, clasping Carissa's hand tighter.

"What are you going to do?"

If I hang around and try to get a better sense of how many guys are involved in the bets, my chances of having to talk to Sage and Javi will only get higher. I don't see any of that ending well, but I already abandoned this team once. I don't know if I can do it again now that I'm here.

"I'll be with you the whole time," Carissa says, leaning up on her toes to kiss my cheek.

Her support gives me the courage to step forward and greet another teammate.

I learn some important things while mingling with the Badgers. One, I am clearly not incapable of friendships outside of Derek and his gang because I fall right into step with some of my favorite players like no time has passed at all. Two, the guys I know are into the betting mess do their best to avoid me at all costs, and I am perfectly fine with that. Three, there aren't as many of my former teammates here as I expected, and the ones who don't avoid me look almost relieved to see me, which only reaffirms my resolve to fix things if I can.

It's not easy to bring up the corruption in casual conversation without coming right out and asking, but I do my best, and I've come to a solid conclusion: the good guys all know exactly what's going on and are only playing for Portland because of contracts, and they badly need a rescue. I'm more determined than ever to talk to Darcy and find a way to bring the team back to playing honestly. There are enough players who aren't in on the scheme that the team could survive if there was a way to prove only certain players are rotten.

The other thing I learn, though it's more of a reminder than anything, is Carissa is *great* at making friends. She and Liam have that in common, and I swear she becomes the most popular person in the whole place in a matter of minutes. In Liam, the trait is maddening because it gets him into trouble, but I can't help but admire the way Carissa so easily connects with people. It gets Carissa into trouble too, but at least she has me to keep an eye on her.

I guess Liam has Kasey now, which reminds me that my night is far from over and I have one more mystery to solve.

When conversation ends between Carissa and the wife of one of the defensive linemen, leaving us relatively alone at the side of the room, I press my hand to Carissa's back and lean in close to speak in her ear. "Are you ready to tell me about your slipup when talking about Liam earlier?"

As I expected, Carissa's face blossoms with pink. "I don't know what you're talking about," she says, but her voice wavers.

I press a lingering kiss to her jaw, loving the way her skin pebbles with goosebumps as I begin trailing kisses down her neck and along her collarbone. "Are you sure?"

"Mmm..." She shivers and grabs my arm, like she's trying to steady herself, so I slide my hand around her waist to offer support and continue brushing kisses along her skin. These explorations of mine are new, but Carissa seems to like them, and I'm thoroughly enjoying myself. Forget Liam. Maybe we can go back to the hotel instead. Spend some time in the hot tub. Watch a movie on the couch in my suite, snuggled up together. Kiss until the sun rises.

"Cole?" The last voice I want to hear cuts through my fantasies, chilling the air around me.

I could ignore her. She would deserve it. But I was forced to come to this wedding for a reason, and it wasn't to kiss the woman in my arms where everyone can see. I don't actually know what the reason is, but I'm probably about to find out.

Lifting my head, I keep Carissa close to my side as I make eye contact with Sage for the first time in weeks. She looks beautiful, her dark hair pulled up in an elegant twist, with a silky white dress hugging her curves and fanning out behind her. It is low cut but elegant at the same time, and she's glowing. The perfect bride. Javier stands beside her wearing a tailored burgundy suit and a clenched jaw, not nearly as flawless as his wife.

"I wasn't sure you would come," Sage says as her eyes drift to Carissa. I can't tell what she thinks of my date, but I also don't care.

Javi turns to look at his bride. "You invited him?" He's a lot easier to read, and he's clearly not happy I'm here.

Sage ignores the question. "Who did you bring with you?"

Before I can say anything, Carissa steps forward and offers her hand. "I'm Carissa. I'm on the Thunder's sports medicine team."

I frown. Of all the ways to introduce herself, why did she choose that? With everyone else, she introduced herself as my friend. I didn't love that label either, but it was better than "coworker."

"Oh, you work with Cole? What is that like?" Sage takes Carissa's hand, but barely. And she does it with her left hand rather than her right so she can show off the ridiculous diamond sitting on her finger.

My mind jumps to the ring still hidden in a drawer in my dresser. I easily could have afforded something just as flashy as the ring Javi bought, considering my salary as quarterback was five times his, but I have always wanted the woman I marry to wear my mom's ring. It doesn't catch the light and sparkle as much as Sage's, but it means so much more.

I wonder if Sage would have even worn it.

"How's your little rugby team?" Javi asks as Carissa tells an indifferent Sage about working with Mel. I don't miss the ice in his tone, but I won't let it bother me.

I simply smile. "They're great. Probably not making the championships this year, but we'll get there."

"I hear you're in charge now, so maybe don't count on it."

Wow. He's clearly not going to pull his punches, and my smile grows as I think about the friends waiting back home. I don't think I've ever heard any of them speak a bad word about anyone and mean it. Liam likes to make his jokes, particularly about me, but he's still one of the best friends I've ever had. And way better than Javi ever was.

I slip my hand into Carissa's, happier than ever that she's just as kind-hearted as my friends. "Well, luckily for me, my team is pretty good at what they do, so they don't need a good captain at their helm. They'll be fine, even stuck with me."

"Hey!" Carissa says, smacking my arm. "You're a great captain! Grayson even said so this morning, and I happen to agree with him."

Huh. I guess he did. Huffing a laugh, I bend down and kiss her temple. "Thanks, Riz."

Javi's eyes jump from Carissa to me, and he grabs Sage by the waist and pulls her against his side, nearly tugging her off her feet. Anger flashes across her face but disappears quickly as she smiles at the two of us, her eyes lingering on our clasped hands.

"I noticed you're extra friendly with everyone you meet, Carissa," she says sweetly. Too sweetly. She's practically dripping with sweetness. "Seems the Thunder couldn't keep away from you during the game last night, so is Cole your flavor of the day?"

"You watched his game?" Javi asks at the same time I step forward and growl, "Watch what you say, Sage."

Carissa puts her hand on my arm and smiles. "It's okay, Cole," she says, even though it's definitely not. "Not everyone knows better than to believe websites like *Hollywood Hot Scoop.*"

Sage scoffs. "I wasn't talking about a stupid tabloid site. I watched—"

"Why were you watching his game the night before our wedding?" Javi asks again.

For the first time, I notice something lurking in Sage's eyes as she looks at me. A disappointment of sorts, or maybe even regret. "Because you were passed out drunk," she mutters under her breath, dropping her gaze to the floor. "What else was I supposed to do?"

Javi scoffs, shaking his head and wandering to the bar on the other side of the room, clapping fellow players on the back as he goes.

Carissa reaches out and takes hold of Sage's hand, connected to both of us now. "You look so beautiful, Sage," she says, and *her* sweetness is genuine. "I'm sorry we missed the ceremony, but I'm sure it was lovely."

Tears well up in Sage's eyes, but she blinks them away and lifts her head high. "Thank you. It was."

I feel like I should say something, but what am I supposed to say? "He won't drink during the season." *That was the best you've got?* Grimacing, I look at Carissa and hope she has something better.

But it's Sage who speaks next. "You're more than coworkers, aren't you?"

Meeting Carissa's gaze, I wonder how she might answer that question. But it's clear she's waiting for me, which makes sense. She's been up front about what she wants, and I'm the one who can't find the courage to admit what *I* want.

I know what I *don't* want. I don't want to be at my wedding reception, wondering if I made a mistake because Carissa is there with someone who makes her smile and brings out the best in her. I don't want my bride wandering away to talk to her friends rather than sticking by my side. I don't want to be forty years down the road wondering "what if" when I have a chance to find out instead.

Swallowing, I keep my eyes on Carissa as I say, "We are so much more than coworkers. More than friends. And I hope that it keeps turning into more."

Carissa beams and squeezes my hand, and if Sage wasn't standing right in front of us, I would pull Carissa into a kiss and prove that I mean what I said. No curse can keep me from doing everything I can to live my life to its fullest, and I want to live it with Carissa. I can't imagine life could ever be better than it would be with her.

"Huh." Sage pulls her hand free from Carissa's, looking at me like she's never seen me before. "So that's what it looks like when you're really in love."

My stomach twists into a knot as she wraps an arm around herself and takes a step back, looking smaller than I've ever seen her. "Sage."

She holds up a hand and smiles. "No. Don't say anything. We weren't good together, and you were never going to try to stop my wedding, so I shouldn't have..." Pursing her lips, she turns without another word and follows Javi to the bar.

Part of me wants to follow her and make sure she's okay, but the larger part of me is frozen, trying to understand why she would ever think I would do something like that. I didn't stop her from breaking up with me, which I realize now is probably why she came back to tell me about her wedding, hoping I would beg her to take me back.

What if I had begged?

Since the breakup, there has always been a part of me that hated how easily I gave up on us, but as I stand in the middle of a gaudy wedding that could have been mine, I feel nothing but relief. I wasn't meant for this life. I wasn't meant for Sage.

"I hope she'll be okay," Carissa says, her eyes still on Sage and full of concern.

Letting out a single laugh, I pull her into my side—gently—and kiss the top of her head. "You are spectacular, Carissa Paxton."

"Maybe we should—"

"We should leave. Sage can look after herself; she always has."

Thankfully, Carissa doesn't argue even though I can tell she still worries about leaving. But if I know Sage like I think I do, odds are high she's going to be filing for divorce within the year and taking Javi for everything he's worth. She'll be fine.

Hand in hand, we pass by the table with the cake and steal a couple of plates to go, and I snag the first car we can get so we can head to the Moda Center where Liam's opening act is probably in the middle of her set right now. We eat our cake as we ride through downtown Portland, and I'm not sure I've ever been happier.

CHAPTER THIRTY-THREE

CARISSA

THIS ISN'T THE FIRST time I've been to a Liam Connolly concert, but this is definitely the first time I've had a VIP pass, and I don't know if I'll ever be able to go back to being a regular concert-goer because I have officially been spoiled. We have our own sectioned-off area near the front of the stage so we don't get mauled by the mosh pit of screaming women, and we can order whatever drinks and snacks we want without paying for them. I even got a free signed Liam t-shirt, though I gave that to a girl in the main crowd who burst into tears as soon as I handed it to her.

Cole rewarded my generosity with a kiss, which made me curious to see what else I could give away, but then the show started.

Liam Connolly is, in a word, phenomenal. I've loved his music since he first got his big break, but there's something about a live performance that makes the music so much more real. Liam isn't just talented; he's passionate, and he connects with his fans the instant he strikes the first chord on his guitar. I sing along to his songs with everyone else while Cole hangs back and grins at me like he's never had more fun than watching me dance and scream with the crowd behind us.

Two songs in, Liam grabs his mic and makes his way down the walkway that leads deeper into the crowd, close to where we're standing, though I don't think he's seen us yet. He likely knows we're here, but he's focused on his fans.

"What's up, Portland?" he shouts into the mic, holding it up to catch the cheers and applause from the audience. "Man, it's good to be out playing again. I've missed you guys!"

Cole's hand is suddenly on my back as he comes up to where I'm standing, but his focus is fully on Liam, his eyes narrowed. What is he looking at?

"Let's give it up for Layla Knight!" Liam continues, talking about his opening act. "Wasn't she awesome? I wish I could play the piano as well as she does. That was brilliant!"

"He didn't," Cole mutters incredulously. As Liam starts talking about his latest album and how he came up with the next song he's going to sing, Cole turns wide eyes to me. "You *were* about to say wife!"

My stomach drops. I hoped he'd forgotten about that after all the drama with Sage and Javier. "What? Nnnnnn..." I can't lie to him. Not after what he said to Sage about wanting us to be more. "Maybe," I amend. "But how—"

Cole sticks his thumb and middle finger into his mouth and whistles so shrilly that the whole arena goes quiet for half a second.

Liam looks over, catches sight of Cole's glare, and says some sort of curse in another language into the mic before remembering to drop it. Though he looks properly spooked, he recovers quickly and flashes a bright smile at the crowd. "Wow, this crowd sure is expressive tonight! Sounds like you want more music. Yeah?" He turns to head back to the main stage where a roadie waits with his guitar ready for him, but he pauses just long enough to look down at us.

"You and Kasey *got married*?" Cole growls. Thankfully, we're close enough that Liam seems to be able to hear us over the cheers of the crowd.

Clenching his jaw, Liam adjusts his earpiece and glances around to make sure no one else heard Cole. "How did you figure it out?"

Cole rolls his eyes. "Dude. You have a ring tattooed on your finger that wasn't there a week ago."

Liam glances down at his left hand, where sure enough a dark band with a Celtic design loops around his ring finger. He curses again and heads to grab his guitar with the look of someone who knows he messed up.

"We're not done talking about this," Cole warns before he gets very far.

Liam pauses, glances back with a thoughtful expression, and smiles. "Wanna bet?" He takes his guitar and slings it over his shoulder before counting off to his band.

"I'm going to kill him." As a keyboardist starts off the song, Cole grabs his phone and is about to start a text to Derek when I grab his hand to stop him.

"Don't," I say.

Cole furrows his brow. "But he didn't tell—"

"Let Liam be the one to tell everyone. You know that's why he hasn't said anything yet, right? He wants to tell you in person, and I wouldn't be surprised if he was planning on breaking the news to you tonight after the show."

Groaning, Cole runs a hand through his hair, leaving it a deliciously mussed up mess because it's insanely warm and humid in this arena. "How long have you known?"

I bite my lip. "Kasey told me the night you came by my apartment."

"And you didn't tell me?"

"Hey, I can keep *some* secrets." Except, I'm pretty sure I technically gave this one away this morning, even if I didn't finish the word 'wife.' But I almost kept the secret!

Cole can't sit still during the song and starts pacing in the small space. He looks like a cat. Like, a big cat. A jaguar who has too much energy and nowhere to put it. I have a few ideas of where he can use that energy, but Liam finishes his song and says a few things to his band before he's back on the microphone as they shift to different instruments.

"I don't know how many of you have been lucky enough to fall in love," he says, eyes landing on Cole on that last word. He moves to a gorgeous grand piano and leans against the body of it like he's having a casual conversation with the crowd rather than putting on a show. "But it's kind of the best, and there just aren't enough words to describe how it feels, you know? I had to write a whole album to express even a fraction of what I feel for my Kasey, and it will never be enough." He has to pause when the crowd goes crazy, and his grin is wide and genuine.

"Recently my friend Bonnie met a great guy who's head over heels for her." Another pause for cheers because the world *loves* Hank. "The guy's a freaking novelist, and he still can't find the words to say, which isn't a great sign for the rest of us, you know?" He looks at Cole again, and something in his expression turns mischievous. "I was going to play a different song next, but something tells me one of you out there is having a hard time finding the words, so we're going to change it up a bit and sing one of my favorites."

Several people shout guesses of which song, but Liam's smile turns downright devious as he sits in front of the piano and puts his microphone in the stand. "Nah, this is one you haven't heard yet."

I gasp along with everyone else. "A new song?"

Only a few measures into the intro, Cole swears under his breath and turns pale. "Don't you dare," he breathes, his eyes on Liam.

Liam meets his gaze as he plays the opening notes, and there is a clear challenge in his eyes.

"I have no idea what's going on," I say right as Liam starts singing.

You got that look in your eyes,
One you can't seem to hide,
And you try to keep it quiet
But I think that you should try it.

Don't matter 'bout the past
Or if you think that it might last
'Cuz the more that you deny it,
Well, the less anyone buys it.

Cole looks at me like he's about to tell me I got a failing grade on my last final. Or maybe like he's about to be sick. "What's your take on public displays of affection?"

I'm more interested in the chorus Liam is about to sing, and I cock my head, trying to figure out why Cole's fingers are shaking. "What?" But my attention turns back to the song.

Say it loud, say it proud,
Let your heart do all the talking
When your head is full of fear and doubt
All you gotta do is—

"Shout," Cole moans, finishing the lyric as Liam grabs his mic and repeats the chorus while he makes his way down the walkway again, heading right for us as the energy of the song rises. His eyes are locked on Cole, who definitely looks like he might throw up but has a determined glint in his eyes. "Carissa," Cole says, "whatever happens in the next two minutes, don't think less of me."

I don't have time to wonder what he means because Cole reaches for Liam's hand and climbs up onto the stage. For a moment the two men stare at each other while the band holds a note, like they're waiting for something to happen.

"Make or break time, big guy," Liam says with a smirk. "Give them something else to talk about."

Cole rips the microphone out of Liam's hand, and in the next moment he's singing. *Cole is singing at Liam's show* for the whole arena to hear.

And he's dang good at it.

I don't have words. I simply gape at the man who sings about being in love and being too afraid to admit it out loud. *Love.* My heart is stuck in my throat as Liam grabs another mic and joins in, and the song was clearly meant as a duet because it's basically a conversation between the two of them.

Where Liam's voice is clear and strong, Cole's has a rougher quality to it that I can practically feel rumbling through my chest. Their voices shouldn't mix as well as they do, but the two of them combined are magical. I swear the audience is losing their minds just like I am, though I doubt half of them realize who Cole is. They will soon; they're clearly fans now.

Back off, ladies. He's mine.

Cole is *mine.* I feel that from my head to my toes, like my whole being has tied itself to this beautiful, sweet, *wonderful* man in a way that may never be undone. I've known for so long that he's special, but watching him drop all of his shields in front of a crowd of I don't know how many thousands, I realize I have severely underestimated just how amazing Cole is.

When the song hits the final chorus, the band drops out and Liam rushes back to the piano to accompany Cole as he sings the final words.

Sings them right to me.

Cole crouches directly in front of me, looking amazing in his button-down and slacks and dark eyes fixed on me as he sings an altered version of the chorus.

I'll say it loud, I'll say it proud,
I'll let my heart do all the talking
'Cause with you I've got no fear or doubt
And all I gotta do is shout...

"I love you," he says into the mic. The crowd goes nuts, chanting for more, but Cole's eyes never leave mine. A staff member takes the mic from him, and he jumps back into our box and pulls me into a kiss to end all kisses.

The rest of the concert is a blur.

"I still can't believe you actually did it." Liam looks exhausted, but he also looks like he had the best night of his life as he lies stretched out on a couch in the green room after the show. He hasn't stopped smiling since playing the final notes of Cole's song.

Which, apparently, is called "Cole's Song." *Really original, Liam.*

"And risk being the first to back down? No way." Cole, reclined on a second couch, pulls me closer even though I'm literally on top of him, my back pressed into his chest and his arms tucked around me. I can't possibly get any closer.

"I was worried you never learned the words," Liam says.

Cole chuckles. "I know you better than to be unprepared."

I could fall asleep right here if given the chance, but I have too many questions. "I need to know everything," I say, which hopefully sums up most of my confusion.

Cole and Liam both laugh. "It's always a bad idea to leave the two of us alone for very long," Liam says. "We have a habit of making bets and stupid challenges."

"Okay?" I would twist to look at Cole if I wasn't so darn comfy. "Keep explaining."

"We made a bet like a year ago," Cole says. "Liam thought I was too chicken to propose to Sage."

"I was right," Liam adds.

"And he said I was going to take so long that he would be married before I ever popped the question, even though at the time Liam was pretty against the whole idea of marriage and relationships."

Liam grins, running a hand through his blond hair. "So I said that if I ended up married before he struck up the nerve to propose, he had to come to one of my shows and sing that song to do the deed."

I do twist around now so I can catch sight of Cole's face. "But you didn't propose," I point out.

Blushing, Cole kisses the tip of my nose. "I've known you less than a month, Carissa. I think even Liam can accept that it would be kind of crazy to ask you to marry me tonight. Bet or no bet, I couldn't do that."

"I'll count it," Liam agrees as I settle back into my spot against Cole, kind of disappointed.

And then, almost so quietly that I don't hear it, Cole adds the word, "Yet."

I nearly squeal with pleasure but rein myself in despite a swarm of excited butterflies flooding my belly. "Okay, but since you did your part, does that mean Liam owes you something?"

Liam's eyebrows dip low. "I don't know about—"

"That only seems fair," Cole says, and I can hear the mischief in his voice. "But what would we have him do?"

"There is no 'we' in this bargain," Liam complains. "And that was never part of the challenge."

"We'll think of something," I say and cuddle up close to Cole again. I probably shouldn't get too comfy, so to keep myself awake, I ask something that has bothered me for two days now. "Hey, Cole?"

"Hmm?"

"What did you say to me at the vending machines?"

Cole's hand splays across my stomach, fingers digging in slightly like he's revisiting that night in his mind just like I've done a million times. He buries his nose into my hair and speaks softly, but his words wash over me like a tidal wave. "I said 'I wish I could keep you.'"

My heart does a somersault in my chest. "Really?"

"Really. I meant it then, but now I'm going to do everything I can to make it happen. No more passively letting life pass me by."

If this is how love feels, I was so wrong when it came to Peter and every guy before that. Nothing I felt for any of them comes close to the way I feel about Cole. It's like we were made for each other. "I want to keep you too," I whisper.

Cole squeezes me and kisses my temple. "Ready to go to bed?"

"Yeah." I really could fall asleep right here, but I'm sure the venue will be kicking Liam out eventually, so I reluctantly get to my feet. As soon as Liam is standing as well, I attack him with a hug that nearly knocks him over.

"Whoa! What's this for?"

"I'm really happy for you and Kasey."

Liam's not a scrawny guy—he nearly caused a wave of swoons when he used the hem of his t-shirt to wipe the sweat from his forehead, showing off an impressive set of abs—but hugging him isn't nearly as satisfying as hugging Cole. I don't last long before I'm slipping back to Cole's side and tucking myself under his arm.

Liam laughs and grabs a bottle of water before following his bodyguard out to where his limo is waiting. "Thanks. It wasn't a planned thing, but after I proposed to Kase, I had this vision of never getting the chance to call her my wife because of something going wrong while I was on tour, and I panicked."

"Great reason to get married," Cole grumbles.

"I don't regret anything. And I *was* going to tell you."

Cole sighs. "I know." He releases me long enough to give Liam a hug, and then he's back at my side. "Congrats. Even if I'm mad you didn't let any of us be there with you to celebrate."

"We can celebrate when I get back."

"After you get a proper honeymoon," I throw in.

Liam snorts, a wistful look entering his eyes. "Yeah, after that. Come on," he says, nodding toward the car. "Let us give you a ride."

By the time we get to the hotel, I'm dead on my feet and so ready to crash, and Cole is the only reason I make it to the elevator upright. He pushes the button for the third floor, and I push the number five.

"I thought you were on the same floor as me," he says, frowning at the button like it offended him.

"I was, but there was a mix-up with the second night when Mel was checking out, so I had to switch rooms this morning. It's fine."

The elevator stops at the third floor, and Cole reluctantly steps out, looking back at me with an expression I can't quite read.

I smile. "I'll see you in the morning for breakfast."

The door slides closed, and I slump against the handrail as the last of my energy slips away. This weekend was a wild ride, but like Liam, I don't regret anything. Except maybe the fact that I didn't kiss Cole goodnight. That was stupid of me.

The elevator slows on the fourth floor and comes to a stop, and when the door slides open, I shift to make room. Only, it's Cole who stumbles inside, gasping for air, and I stand up straight in surprise as he boxes me into the corner.

"Did you just run up the stairs?" I ask in alarm.

He nods, still heaving, and then his mouth is on mine, hungrily claiming that goodnight kiss I was too tired to remember until it was too late. We reach the fifth floor, but neither of us moves to exit. I'm too busy memorizing the feel of his mouth because I'll have to go a whole night without him.

"No," he says against my lips, like he's reading my mind. "Stay with me tonight."

I stiffen. That's a big step. "Cole..."

He shakes his head, eyebrows pulled low and his caramel chocolate eyes fixed on mine. "I just want you near me. Please. Two floors is too far."

As the elevator door slides closed again, leaving us alone in a silver box, I smile and press my hand over his heart. "I couldn't agree more."

We kiss until someone triggers the elevator down to the lobby, and then we head back up to the third floor where I fall asleep in Cole's arms, dreaming of this and everything else for many nights to come.

Hollywood Hot Scoop

Rugby Rockstar—Cole's Secret Talent

Look out, Liam Lovers, because we may have found a reason for you to pick a new favorite of the Glam Gang! In a shocking reveal, rugby legend and former Portland Badger Cole Evanson took to the stage at Liam Connolly's Oregon show and blew the crowd away with the dulcet sounds of a voice made for the stage.

That's right! Cole can *sing*.

And it gets even better, Scoopers, because Cole sang straight to his sweetheart, Carissa Paxton. Carissa, who has been lauded as the best addition to the team in recent years by many of the LA Thunder, was in tears over the emotional display of Cole's affection at the show, and something tells me these two aren't going to take long to follow their fellow Glam Gang members in settling down with their soulmates.

(Did you miss our story on Liam's proposal to Kasey Graham or our top five picks of paint colors for Hank McAllister's front door on his new LA residence? Check them out here, and be sure to subscribe so you don't miss anything in the future!)

And never fear, my Scoopers. Of course we have a video of Cole's debut performance! What do you think? Will we be seeing an album in the scrum-half's future? Only time will tell, but we here at *Hot Scoop* will be the first to let you know! XO

Chapter Thirty-Four

Cole

The world looks different now that Carissa is officially a part of it with me. I can't quite explain what has caused the change other than the feeling of stability in my chest that keeps me grounded, but everything is brighter. Bolder. Full of colors I've never seen before. And though I've been to Derek's house more times than I can count, I feel like this is the first time I set foot on the stone patio overlooking the ocean.

I need to be at practice in an hour, but this conversation is important too.

Derek leans on the wall surrounding the patio, his gaze on the horizon and a far-off look in the eyes, like he's not really here. He gets this way sometimes when he has a quiet moment, something that has been happening less and less often lately, and I'm tempted to wait instead of interrupting. He probably needs to cherish whatever downtime he can get.

Unfortunately, he's not as alone as I thought he was, and Freya's voice breaks the silence through the phone in Derek's hand. "Cole! You are back from Oregon!"

As Derek glances back at me, snapping back to the present moment with a couple of blinks, I move closer and smile at the princess on the screen. I wonder how long she's been sitting in silence. "Hey, Peach. You're lucky I survived long enough to make it back, after what you put me through."

"You were fine," Derek says.

"Only because I had Carissa with me," I argue.

"That was the point," Freya says. "Derek never would have let you go without her."

I glance at him, and when he lifts an eyebrow, I groan. "There was a whole scheme happening yesterday, wasn't there?"

"You must know there is always a scheme when Derek Riley is involved," Freya says, a bit of a grumble in her tone.

"What's he doing to you?" I ask.

"Nothing," Derek says at the same time Freya says, "Derek is so determined to send me an American soldier to be my bodyguard that he has already spoken with my mother, which means the matter is settled despite my reservations."

Derek rolls his eyes, and I'm guessing this is a conversation that has been going on for most of the afternoon. "He's not just a soldier, Peach. He's a master sergeant in the Special Forces and has probably completed more missions than any of your past bodyguards combined."

"How do you know a soldier in the Special Forces?" I ask. Am I really surprised? No. This is Derek we're talking about.

Sure enough, Derek shrugs and mutters something along the lines of, "I know a lot of people."

One of these days he's going to say something about how he's actually related to the King of England and only a few spots away from the throne, and I would believe him. "What's wrong with an American?" I ask Freya with mock offense.

She heaves a huge sigh, practically pouting as she gazes at us through the phone. "Nothing. But an American *soldier*? That is a different story."

"If it helps, he's leaving the Army," Derek offers.

Freya narrows her eyes. "Why?"

"To come look after you, obviously."

That was a hedge if ever I saw one, but I'm not about to get in between Derek and Freya. They're both far too strong-headed and tend to turn into dogs fighting over a fresh steak if they have differing opinions, which happens about as often as you would expect between an altruistic European princess and an American actor with a tendency to play god.

"Sorry, Peach," I say before she can keep pressing for information, "but I'm going to have to steal Derek. I've got to get to practice soon, and he's not done helping me fix a problem."

"I'm not?" Derek asks with genuine surprise.

I chuckle. "Are you ever? Believe it or not, you're not as perfect as you look."

"Ah, it is nice to have you back, Cole," Freya says. "You were getting far too serious for my liking. Goodnight, boys." She blows a kiss to the camera and ends the call.

Sighing, Derek slips his phone into his pocket and returns to leaning on the wall. "*She* is getting too serious. The closer she gets to that election, the more she's convinced she's going to lose."

Despite being the heir to her mother's throne, Freya still has to be elected by her people. So far, no one is running against her, but there's still time. In a country as small as Candora, a lot could happen in three months.

"How about we focus on my problems instead of ones you can't fix?" I say, clapping Derek on the back. "I need to figure out how to buy a rugby team. As soon as possible."

It's not often I can break through Derek's uncrackable exterior, but for a moment he looks completely dumbstruck. Then his eyes light up. "Cole, that's genius."

"Contrary to popular belief, I can sometimes have good ideas."

"Literally no one thinks you're not smart." He grabs his phone and opens up his contacts, poised to call the perfect person to help me take the steps I need to acquire the Thunder. But he pauses.

I furrow my brow. "What's wrong?"

When he looks up at me, his blue eyes pierce through me. "Are you sure this is what you want? I'm assuming you've talked to Darcy."

I nod. I spent the last couple of hours we had at the hotel this morning giving Darcy as much information as I could, and she was confident she could get the right facts to save the team from itself. She also threatened me when it came to treating Carissa right, so it was quite the conversation. "Yeah. Why?"

"You know Oregon would take you back." Derek narrows his eyes as he studies me. "You could go back to the game you love and get another chance at a Super Bowl, and you could win."

"It would take a few years to rebuild the team," I counter, but my words come out hesitant. I hadn't considered...

"You still have a solid decade in you, if not more," Derek says. "Give Tom Brady a run for his money."

I chuckle. "Brady only wishes he was as good as me."

Derek purses his lips as he pockets his phone, like he thinks he's convinced me to change my plan. "You can still try to save the Thunder, Cole, but you don't have to put all your money into something that isn't your passion. You're..." He bites his tongue, like he isn't sure if he should keep talking.

I nudge his shoulder. "Say it."

"You were happier in Oregon."

Shaking my head, I look out along the Malibu coast as it glitters in the sun. "I may have been happy in Oregon, but I'm happier *here*. This is where I grew up. This is where my family is."

"And your friends," Derek adds, raising an eyebrow.

"I said what I said. *Family*. And Carissa is here."

"You really like her, don't you?"

That gets a laugh out of me, mostly because I don't remember a time when Derek wasn't the first to be in the know about celebrity gossip. I swear he has a whole team of people who keep him updated on anything of note, particularly when it relates to one of us, so he has either been talking to Freya for too long to have been informed about my adventures last night, or he has been avoiding things entirely. I don't know what's up with him today, but I have a way to cheer him up. At the very least, I can distract him from whatever he's probably overthinking.

"Maybe you should see what's trending on *Hot Scoop* today," I say. "I think you might find it interesting. But first, give me the number of whoever can help me spend a whole lot of money on a so-so rugby team."

Curiosity burns in Derek's eyes, and of course he pulls up the tabloid first and finds the latest article right off the bat, his eyes reading quickly before he pulls up the video.

It might be the first time Derek Riley is left truly, completely dumb-founded.

The guys are on fire at practice. They're riding high after their win against Portland, but Coach Galvin is nowhere in sight and Moxie shows up halfway through on crutches, so it's good things all around. Mel and Carissa both get after Moxie for not taking it easy, but it's clear they're both happy to see him. Especially Mel.

It takes a lot of concentration to keep my focus on practice rather than the woman with blonde curls who laughs and jokes with the team as they get taped or discuss certain stretches or workouts to help with whatever trouble spots they have. Carissa looks like she's in her element now. Like she belongs here.

And when I say I keep my focus on practice, I really don't manage it at all, which is how a laugh from Carissa pulls my eyes to the sideline where she sits with Moxie, right as Loren slams into me and knocks me flat on my back in an impressive tackle.

I shove him off of me as he laughs. "Thanks," I grunt, sitting up with a good deal of struggle.

"You've got it bad, Stitch."

"Yeah." My eyes flit to him. "What did you just call me?"

"He called you Stitch," Wyatt says and holds out a hand to help me to my feet.

"Why?"

Both men chuckle and move back to run the play again.

"No," I growl, holding my hands up instead of taking the ball from Freddie. "No, you can't just give me a new nickname and not tell me why."

"Would you relax?" Wyatt says. "It's a good thing. It means you're one of us."

Gaping, I look around to the other backs to make sure I heard him right. "What?"

Some of the forwards must have noticed my bewilderment because they come over from the other side of the practice field and gather around us. Grayson puts an arm around Wyatt and grins at me. "Did we break him?"

"Apparently he doesn't like his new nickname," Wyatt replies, rolling his eyes.

I groan, folding my arms as if that might intimidate them into explaining. Now that the forwards have joined in, I am all too aware that I am nowhere near the biggest guy here. "I never said I didn't like it," I grumble. "I just don't understand why—"

"Don't overthink it or we'll go back to calling you Rihanna." Wyatt steps forward, shaking his head at me. "Dude, just accept that you are part of the team now before we change our minds."

"But you don't like me."

The group erupts into laughter.

"Maybe not a week ago," Grayson says, "but you've made yourself weirdly likable."

Weirdly likable? I can't tell if that's a compliment. "You said we aren't friends," I argue, though I know those two things don't have to go together.

Grayson and Wyatt look at each other, shrug, and Wyatt says, "You'll have to take that one up with Carissa, Stitch. We were just following orders."

"Ord..." I turn to Carissa, who likely has no idea what we're talking about out on the pitch but meets my gaze and immediately flushes pink. "Everyone run some laps," I growl, as if that might get rid of the guys surrounding me.

To my surprise, they all pick up a jog and head in the opposite direction of Carissa.

Taking the opportunity they give me, I stalk across the pitch, never taking my eyes off of Carissa even though she says something to Mel and Moxie and looks ready to bolt.

"You look angry," she says to me when I'm within earshot.

"Want me to beat him up for you, Carissa?" Moxie asks, shifting his weight on his crutches so he's somewhat in front of her.

I ignore him and continue my path directly for Carissa. My steps don't slow, even when I'm right in front of her, so she scrambles backward until I have her pressed against the concrete wall behind her. I place one hand on either side of her head, boxing her in.

"Did you tell the guys to pretend they don't see me as a friend so I would be forced into going to Sage's wedding?" I ask, my voice gruff.

She bites her lip, pulling my gaze to her mouth. "Um."

"Why?"

"Because Derek thought—"

"Of course he did." Sighing, I move in closer until my face is only inches from hers. While technically I've already spent most of the day with her, offering her seatmate on the plane a hundred bucks to switch seats with me, I haven't had a chance to get this close to her for several hours. I don't like that, though I'll need to learn to survive time away from her if this relationship of ours is going to be healthy. At least she'll come to away games with me, or I might be less reluctant to stay with the team as a player and not just as an owner as soon as that goes through.

Though I'm distracted by her pink lips, I should probably tell Carissa how close I am to buying the team. The current owners, a business duo from Long Beach, were more than interested in my proposal, considering the Thunder isn't good enough yet to bring in much of a return on their investment. They pushed my original offer to six million, but I think I can talk them down to five and a half. If not, I'll pay whatever it takes.

I want this team to succeed, as much for the players' sake as for a way to keep Carissa here with me. I intend to keep her for as long as I possibly can.

"You're really thinking hard about something there, Stitch."

My eyes jump to hers. "You too?"

Grinning, she shifts her hands so they're pressed against my chest. "I think it's a great nickname for you."

"Please tell me it didn't come from the fuzzy blue alien guy." Now that she's touching me, I can't resist moving my hands from the wall to her waist. She's wearing that tank top again, the pink one with the unicorn, and it's such a contrast from my navy blue kit that I can't help but smile. Everything about us is a contrast, but I think that's what makes us work.

"There might have been some Disney influence," Carissa says, closing her eyes as I pull her closer to my body and brush her nose with mine. "The whole concept of family and all that. But I think it goes deeper than that. I think..." She takes a sharp breath when my lips find her jaw. "I think you can't kiss me like that if you want me to explain."

I groan and pull away. "Fine. We may want to come up with some rules for while we're at practice so I don't end up blowing off the team to hang out with you."

"There is nothing close to the concept of 'hanging out' running through your head right now, Evanson." Narrowing her eyes, she gives me a gentle push so I take a step back and allow her some space to breathe. "And whatever you're thinking, you'll have to save that for later. Here, we're at work. And we are going to stay professional."

I fold my arms. "What if I can't?"

"Then you need to work through some things and learn self-control." Her response comes with a teasing smile, but I know she's serious. And I seriously love how intentional she wants to be with this job.

Lifting my hands in the air, I take several steps back and bump into Moxie, who thankfully keeps himself upright. "Sorry," I mutter to him before turning back to Carissa. "Better?"

Moxie laughs as he looks between us. "I didn't think anyone would have that kind of control over you," he tells me. "Who knew all it would take is you falling in love?"

"Shut up. You." I point at Carissa, who tilts her head. "Keep talking. Why Stitch?"

"Because things would have fallen apart without you," she says, tucking her hands into the pockets of her shorts. "With Moxie in recovery, they need someone to hold them together because we all know it won't be Coach Galvin."

Okay. Well. That nickname is better than I could have hoped for. A pressure builds in my chest, not unwelcome but not comfortable either because it forces me to be vulnerable. *Acceptance*. It's an emotion I don't feel often outside of my friends—the Glam Gang, according to *Hot Scoop*—and I never expected to feel it here.

"Really?" I'm not sure I can actually believe it after the season I've had so far.

"Really," Moxie says as Mel nods next to him, which is confirmation enough for me. "I wish I didn't have to blow my knee to get you there, but you are the best thing to happen to this team. I'm glad you've finally accepted it."

I frown, my eyes jumping down to the wrapped up mass that is his leg. He shouldn't be standing here making me feel better about myself when he's only a week off his surgery. "You'll be captain again soon."

"Not if Galvin has anything to say about it," Mel grumbles.

I clear my throat. "About that..."

Moxie's eyebrows shoot up. "I'm almost afraid to ask."

"Cole is buying the Thunder," Carissa says before I can. She joins me at my side, slipping her hand into mine even though that's probably going to end up on our list of rules.

"You're *what*?" Moxie's shout makes a couple of the guys stumble as they run past, curiosity clear in their eyes. Thankfully, Moxie drops his voice. "How in the world could you possibly afford that? An MLR franchise is at least four million, and that doesn't say anything about an already established team."

Apparently he's done his research. Scratching my jaw, I pretend to consider what he's saying to me before I say, "Well, outside of buying my house, I haven't spent all that much since moving back to California."

"Did you miss the part where I said the word 'million'?" Moxie says, rolling his eyes. "You could be the best paid player in the league, and you still wouldn't—"

"I made twenty-two in the NFL. Million," I add when he doesn't react. "Every year. And I happen to be good at investing, so my net worth has been steadily growing over the last couple of years."

Still staring at me, Moxie seems to have lost all function until he finally lets out a short laugh and a muttered curse. "How much are we talking here, Evanson?"

"I want to know this too," Carissa says with a smirk.

This conversation was a terrible idea. I should have waited until I actually owned the team before I said anything. "Does it really matter?" I ask Moxie. "I'm buying the team. And I'll tell you later," I say to Carissa, "as long as you promise you don't love me for my money."

"I fell in love with you before I knew you were rich," she replies brightly.

Suddenly it feels like I swallowed a bowling ball, and I gape at her. She didn't say...did she?

Eyes going wide, Carissa claps a hand over her mouth. "No! I was going to say that for the first time in a way more romantic way!"

"I don't care about romance," I breathe and cover her mouth with mine, hardly caring about rules or professionalism or anything except the fact that she loves me. She could have told me that in the middle of the security line at the airport, and I still would have loved hearing her say the words.

I know Carissa cares about romance, so I fully intend to find ways to surprise her and brighten up her day, no matter how bright she already makes the world. This life of ours may not be a hockey romance, but it is a rugby romance, and as I kiss the woman I love on the side of a pitch, I make a vow to ensure Carissa's life exceeds her every expectation.

I have a feeling our reality is going to be so much better than any book.

I'll make sure it is.

EPILOGUE

CARISSA

Three months later

I EXPECTED CANDORA TO look different. I can probably blame my expectations on the fact that most of what I've seen of this country has been over video chats with Freya, who almost never leaves her castle when she's at home. Everything inside the royal residence is antique or designed to look timeless, and Freya is always so poised and proper that I sort of expected to be walking into *Downton Abbey*.

Sure, there are sheep on the side of most roads and people riding horses down the highway, but other than that, Invem, the capital city of Candora, looks like any other modern city. If that city is crazy clean and teeming with trees, of course.

"I might move here," I say, tilting my head back and soaking up the sun as we sit outside a cute little café in the middle of the city. Invem is just as full of people as Los Angeles, but there aren't nearly as many cars. Everyone is either on bikes or horses if they're not walking, which means the air is impossibly fresh. But that could also be because of the rain this morning. I didn't realize how much I love rain until I moved to a place where it has only rained like four times in four months, if that. "The only drawback is the fact that it's freezing."

Cole laughs and stretches out his legs, looking for all the world like he has never been more relaxed. "That's the only drawback? Not the fact that I live in California?"

I peek at him, still trying to get as much sun as I can. "You could move here too."

"But my team is in Los Angeles."

"They have rugby in Candora."

"What about Dad and Gramps?"

That makes me pause. I think August would murder me if I convinced Cole to move to a different country. Gramps, on the other hand... "Gramps would totally move here with us. He's still secretly hoping he has a shot with Freya."

Cole rolls his eyes. "Right now, I don't think *anyone* has a shot with Freya. I've never seen her this stressed."

"Can you blame her?" I think back to this morning when we arrived at the castle and Freya practically kicked us out as soon as we walked through the doors. I know she's happy to see us, but today's election will decide if she actually gets to be queen. Apparently it's not as much of a done deal as she would like.

With a yawn—neither of us has slept in almost twenty-four hours—Cole checks the time on his phone and gathers up his jacket from the back of the chair next to his. "We should probably head back up. Derek has probably landed by now, and someone needs to wake Liam up."

"Not it!" I say, putting my finger on my nose just in case. We'll probably make Derek do it regardless, but I need to cover my bases. "The last time I tried to wake Liam up, he wrote an angry song about me."

I actually kind of love that song, and Liam has become a de facto big brother to me over the last few months. He says he likes my energy and the fact that I managed to keep his and Kasey's elopement a secret until he got back from his tour and broke the news to Bonnie and Derek.

It helps that I was a bit distracted by my new boss.

Taking my hand, Cole helps me to my feet and presses a kiss to my knuckles. Since we landed in Candora this morning, he has become quite the romantic. I don't know if it's the setting or something else, but I'm not mad about it. That's not to say he's *not* romantic most of the time, but there's something different today.

Giggling at his gesture, I curl myself up against him and soak up the warmth he offers. It's like fifty degrees today, which is way colder than what I've gotten used to in Los Angeles. And maybe I just like cuddling with him. "I kind of wish we could keep exploring Invem together."

"I kind of wish I'd followed Liam and Kasey's example and taken a nap." But he kisses the top of my head and wraps me up in a proper hug. "We can explore tomorrow, and the next day, and the next..."

We have a whole week in Candora before Cole needs to be back to introduce the Thunder to the new head coach he hired, and I fully plan to take advantage of this time we have together. Once training starts up, we're both going to be incredibly busy. Next year is the year we're going to win the championship; I can feel it.

Even if we don't, I'm going to be right there at Cole's side, where I plan to be for the rest of forever.

By the time we get back to the castle and shower and change after our morning adventure through Invem, everyone has gathered in the antechamber off the press room, where Freya is pacing and running her hands through her blonde hair. Her hair was in an intricate updo earlier, but now it runs down her back in thick waves and gives me serious hair envy. I thought my hair was thick, but Freya is reaching Rapunzel levels.

"Oh boy," Cole says as soon as he sees the princess's wild look. "Peach! You need to calm down."

"Already tried that," Derek mutters. He's standing next to Freya's most recent bodyguard, Elliot, and watching Freya with a grimace. I wonder how long he's been trying to talk her down. Leaning to the bodyguard, he mutters something that makes Elliot chuckle.

"I'm not going anywhere near that," Elliot says, nodding toward Freya.

Freya throws him a glare. "You are on thin ice, Mr. Reid."

"Good thing I know how to float," he replies lightly and raises his glass in a toast.

Freya groans and keeps up her pacing vigil.

It seems Derek was right about the American soldier, and Elliot has managed to keep his position for almost a month now, which apparently is a good sign compared to some of her other bodyguards. Despite that, Elliot drives her crazy. Cole is shocked Freya has kept Elliot around this long, based on some of the things she's said to us, and Cole has been nothing but barely civil to Elliot since we got here. He doesn't like how easily Elliot gets under Freya's skin, and Cole is clearly pulling out the protective brother moves on this trip.

"You should probably stop glaring," I whisper to him.

He grunts. "Not until he proves he deserves otherwise."

"How much longer?" Hank asks. He and Bonnie are sitting with Liam and Kasey, the four of them barely awake from the looks of it. They got in yesterday and are struggling with the jet lag that hasn't hit me yet. I can feel exhaustion lurking in the corners of my eyes, but I'm too excited to let myself be tired. Besides, Derek recommended that we stay awake as long as we can so we can reset our body clocks, and I am determined to follow his advice.

Mostly because Derek looks wide awake and refreshed even though he arrived just a few hours ago.

"Any minute now," Derek says.

"Coleman!" Freya says, suddenly altering her trajectory and coming over to where we're standing. "I need a distraction. Tell me about the Badgers. *Someone*—" she throws another glare to Elliot, who smirks "—won't let me on the internet, but I have heard that that sports reporter released a story about your corrupted teammates."

Cole narrows his eyes. "Did you just say *won't*? Like, an actual contraction?"

"Distraction!" Freya growls, pointing at him. Then she softens, looking wearier than I've ever seen her. "Please."

Smiling, he puts a hand on her arm. "Tamlin Park managed to dig up proof on everyone involved, and the FBI is launching an investigation into the entire league. All signs are looking good that there will be a purge before the season officially starts. It's going to shake things up, but I think in the end it will be a good thing for football."

Freya's eyebrows rise high. "You think there are other teams doing the same thing?"

"I don't know, but Tamlin wanted to be sure."

I'm so proud of my big sister. Darcy didn't mention the corruption to anyone until she was absolutely positive she wouldn't get innocent players into trouble, and this is likely the biggest story she's ever run. I am so glad she uses her alias as Tamlin instead of her real name and face because otherwise I would be terrified for her safety. Then again, she has a loyal and loving husband who would never let anything happen to her.

"Your Highness?" Elliot suddenly stands at attention, looking more like a bodyguard than he did a moment ago. "It's almost time."

Freya hunches her shoulders and clutches her hair like it might protect her. "Do I have to?"

"No," Derek says, "but I doubt the people will be very happy if you're not on camera when you find out you won the election."

"Camera!" She squeaks and looks down at the hair in her fingers.

Bonnie and I both rush forward, quickly working together to wrangle her hair into a braided crown like it was before. It doesn't help my hair envy, but I'm glad I can be somewhat useful. Other than this, I'm basically just along for the ride.

As soon as she's presentable, Freya stands in front of the doors and takes several deep breaths. "You can do this," she tells herself shakily, and I've never seen her act *less* like a princess. "You...you can..."

Derek and Cole both step forward, but it's Elliot who reaches the princess first. Instead of words of encouragement, like I expect, he says, "If you don't go out there, I will *make* you go out there. I'm not letting you miss out on your future just because you're scared." He ducks down, almost like he's going to pick her up.

Freya flinches, but other than that she stands up tall and lifts her chin. "That will not be necessary at the moment, Mr. Reid." Something changes in her expression as she looks at him, a quick flash of something I can't name, and then she pushes through the doors and leads the way into the press room and its flashing cameras.

I step forward to take up the rear, but Cole grabs my arm. I turn to frown at him. "What are you— Cole, *are you doing what I think you're doing?*"

He sinks to one knee, his eyebrows pulled together and a look of such worry that it instantly brings tears to my eyes. This precious man... "I need you to know that I had a whole plan in the gardens with candlelight and chocolate," he says.

A squeak slips out of me. "Then why—"

"I can't let myself take away from celebrating Freya tonight because we know she's going to win. And I also can't wait until tomorrow. So you're getting me here and now. No spectacle. No grand gesture. Just me." He slips his hand into his jacket pocket and pulls out the most beautiful ring. The stone is a gorgeous square-cut morganite, circled about by smaller stones of the same pinkish color, all of which sits on a rose gold band. I recognize it immediately from pictures I've seen in Cole's house.

His mother's ring.

"Carissa Lynn Paxton, I knew from the first moment I met you that you were special, and sometimes I hate myself for thinking I could be better off without you in my life. Your light and goodness have completely changed me and the way I see the world. I can't promise you a long life, but I *can* promise I will always fight to keep you, no matter what happens. I love you with everything in me, and I want to spend the rest of my life with you. I want to protect you and bring you joy and raise a family with you because you are the best person I know and make me want to be more."

I hiccup. It's a ridiculous sound that makes me laugh even as tears stream down my face, and even Cole cracks a smile. "Oh, this is ridiculous," I say, dabbing at my eyes with my fingertips. "You picked a terrible time to do this, Coleman Evanson! I can't go out there looking like this!"

Cole swallows. "You can't go out there at all if you don't answer the question."

"You didn't ask one!" I complain.

Chuckling, he settles on both knees and sits back on his heels, looking up at me with his warm, dark eyes. *Just him* is pretty spectacular. "Will you risk the curse and marry me, Carissa?"

I shake my head, and his shoulders fall. "No," I say through my tears and put my hands on his shoulders. "No, because there is no curse so there is no risk. I'll marry you with the intention of living exactly as long as you do."

Face full of anguish but with a hint of hope, he cocks his head. "So...that's a yes?"

"Of course that's a yes!" I throw my arms around him and fall into his embrace, hardly caring that he holds me so tight that I can barely breathe. "Goodness, I don't think I could ever say no to you, Cole. You're everything I've ever dreamed of. No, you're *more* than the man of my dreams."

He takes a shuddering breath, like those words have settled deep inside him. "I don't deserve you."

"Sure you do." Pulling back, I press my palms to his cheeks and smile. I'm sure I'm a mess, but as long as we don't leave this room, that's perfectly fine. "I'm more concerned about the fact that *I* don't deserve *you*."

He furrows his brow. "Are we going to argue about this for the rest of our lives?"

"Probably."

"Great." He kisses me, and it feels like a promise. One neither of us intends to break, no matter what the universe has in store for us.

The End

ALSO BY Dana LeCHeMinant

Starstruck Love Stories
Moonstruck
Lovestruck
Dumbstruck
Thunderstruck
Awestruck
Wonderstruck

Love in Sun City
Kiss Me if You Can
She Likes It, Hey Micah
The Chad Next Door
Crossing the Brooklyn Briggs
Houston, We Have a Problem

Standalone Romances
For Butter or For Worse
The Fear of Falling

The Wonder Boys
Love on Camera
Love in Writing
Love on Display
Love in Disguise

Simple Love Stories (Sweet Love Stories)
Simplicity
Growing Young
Bittersweet Brews
In Front of Me
As Long as You Love Me
Dear Dalia
Let Go

Terms of Inheritance (Sweet Romance)
Forever You and Me
Holding On to Everything
A World without You
Love, Strictly Speaking

Historical Romances
The Thief and the Noble
A Twist of Christmas (part of The Holly and the Ivy anthology)
What Dreams May Come
This above All
Never Doubt I Love

ABOUT THE AUTHOR

Dana LeCheminant has been telling stories since she was old enough to know what stories were. After spending most of her childhood reading everything she could get her hands on, she eventually realized she could write her own books too, and since then she always has plots brewing and characters clamoring to be next to have their stories told. A lover of all things outdoors, she finds inspiration while hiking the remote Utah backcountry and cruising down rivers. Until her endless imagination runs dry, she will always have another story to tell.

Dana loves connecting with her readers!
You can find her on social media (**@authordanalecheminant**) and on her website, **lecheminantbooks.com**.